MOLLY KNOX OSTERTAG

THE HIDDEN WITCH

graphix

AN IMPRINT OF

SC

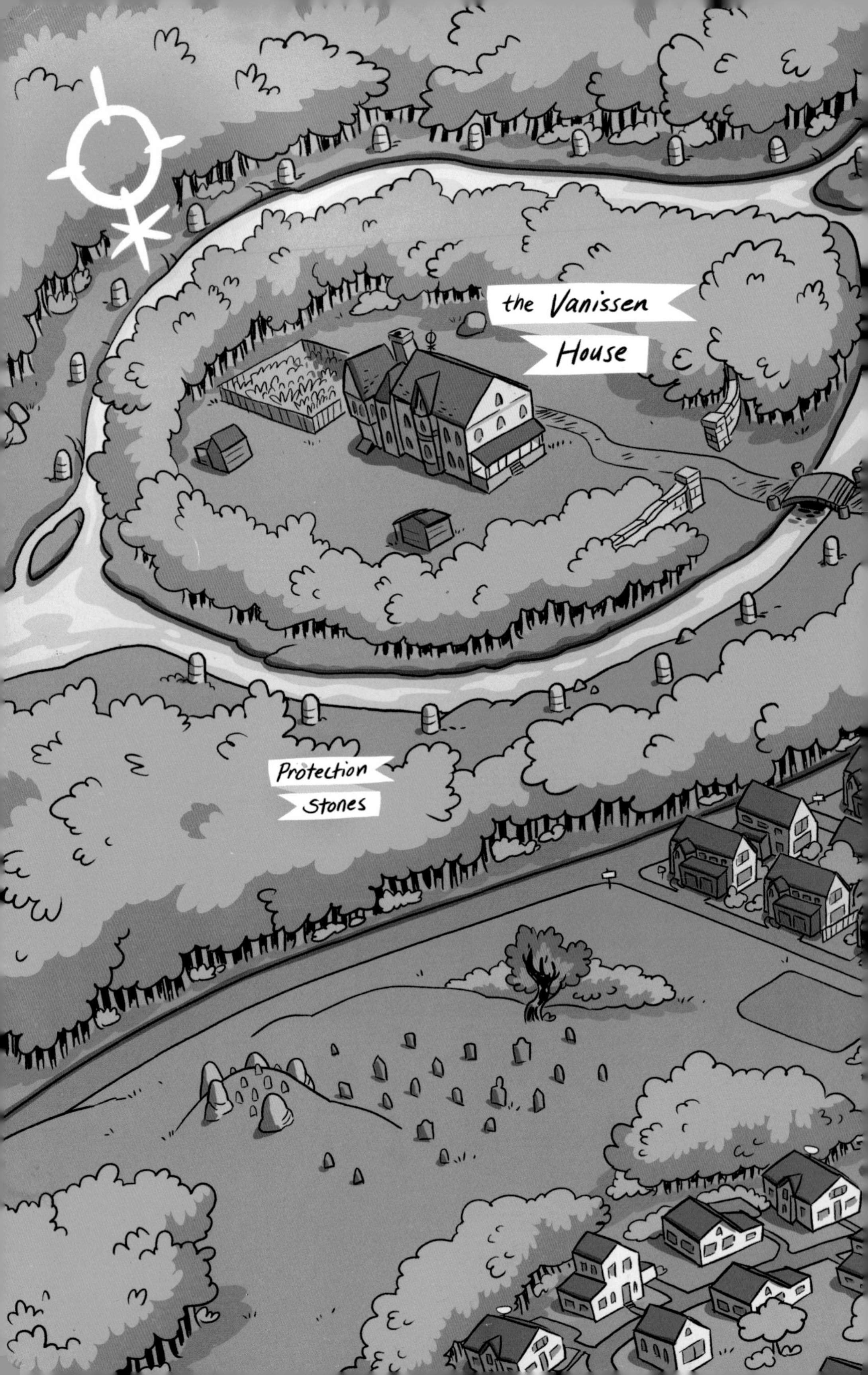
the Vanissen
House
Protection
Stones

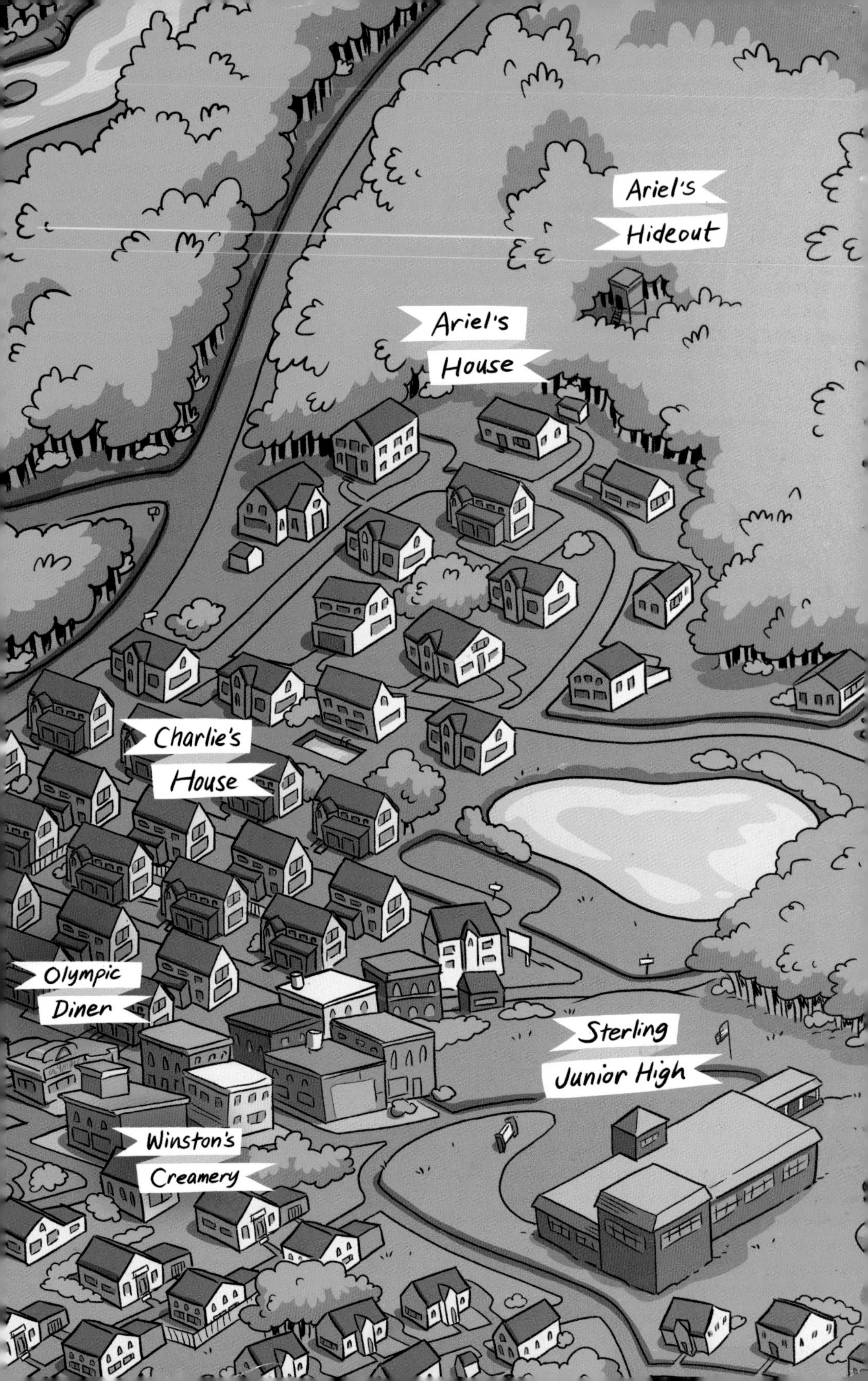
Ariel's Hideout
Ariel's House
Charlie's House
Olympic Diner
Sterling Junior High
Winston's Creamery

This book is dedicated to Noelle,
who is my very favorite witch.

Library of Congress Control Number Available

ISBN 978-1-338-25376-4 (hardcover)
ISBN 978-1-338-25375-7 (paperback)

10 9 8 7 6 5 4 3 2 1   18 19 20 21 22

Printed in China   38
First edition, November 2018
Edited by Amanda Maciel
Lettering and Color by Molly Knox Ostertag
Additional color by Niki Smith
Author photo © Leslie Ranne
Book design by Molly Knox Ostertag and Phil Falco
Creative Director: David Saylor

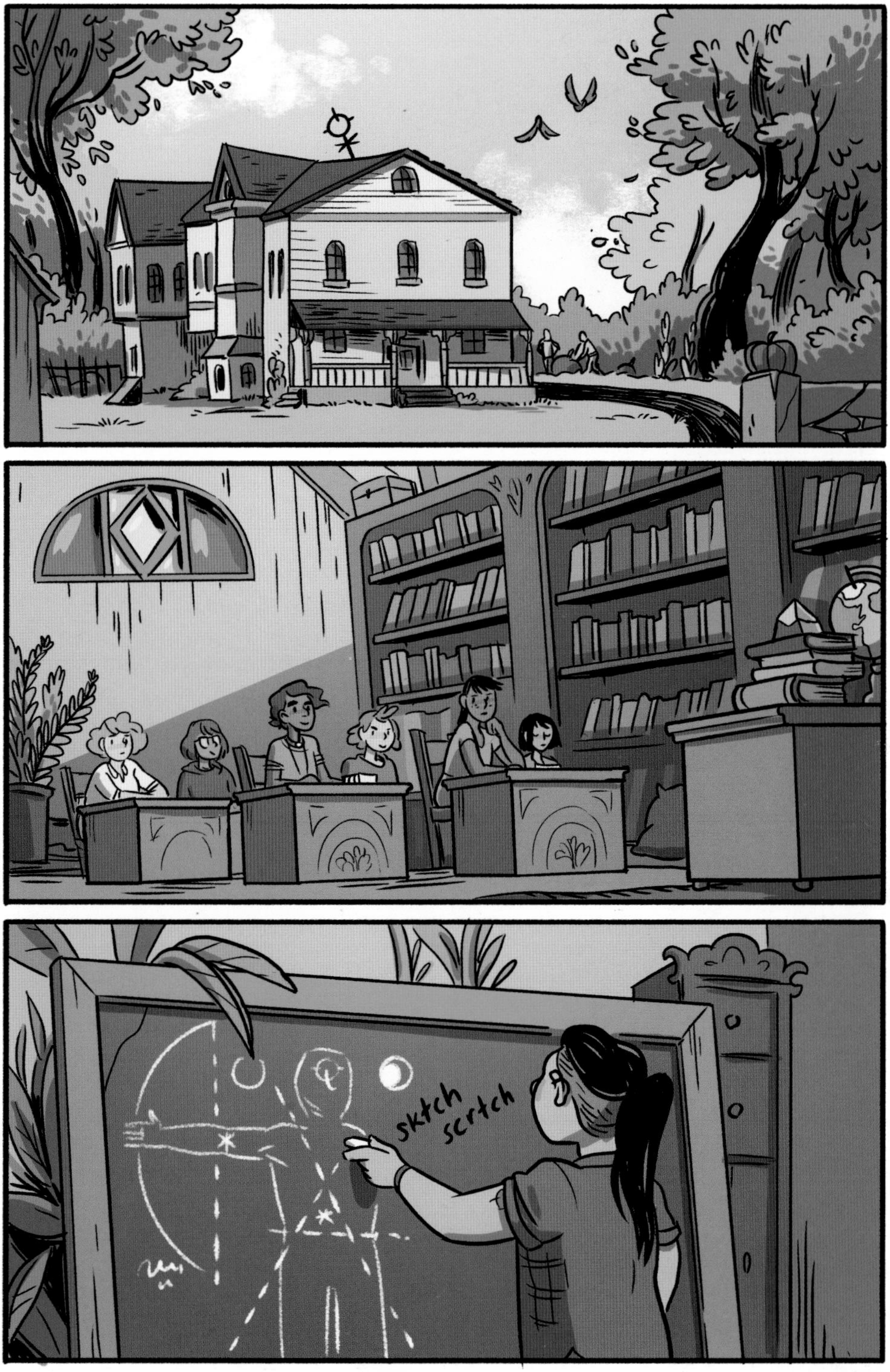
sktch scrtch

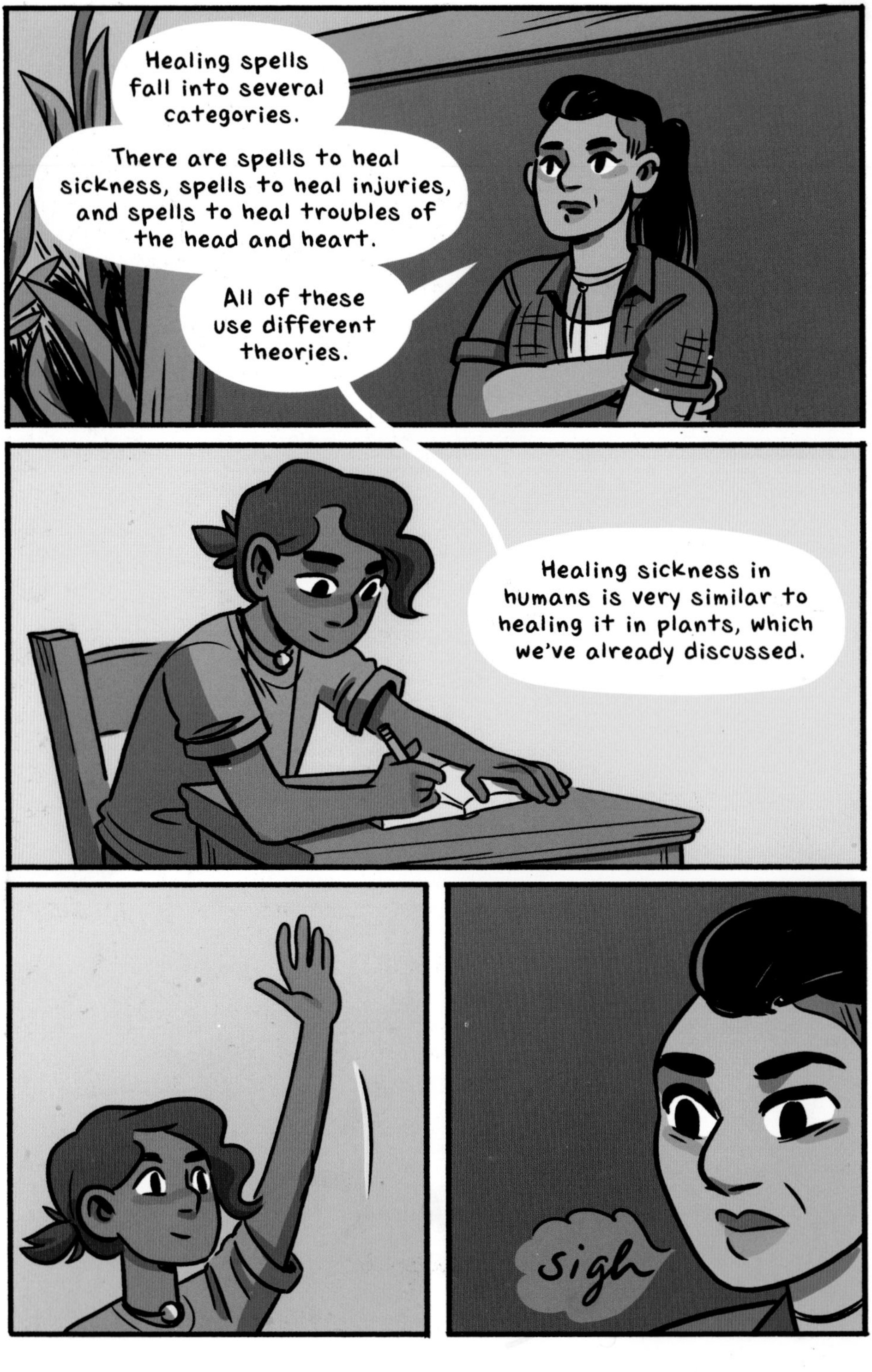
Healing spells fall into several categories.
There are spells to heal sickness, spells to heal injuries, and spells to heal troubles of the head and heart.
All of these use different theories.
Healing sickness in humans is very similar to healing it in plants, which we've already discussed.
sigh

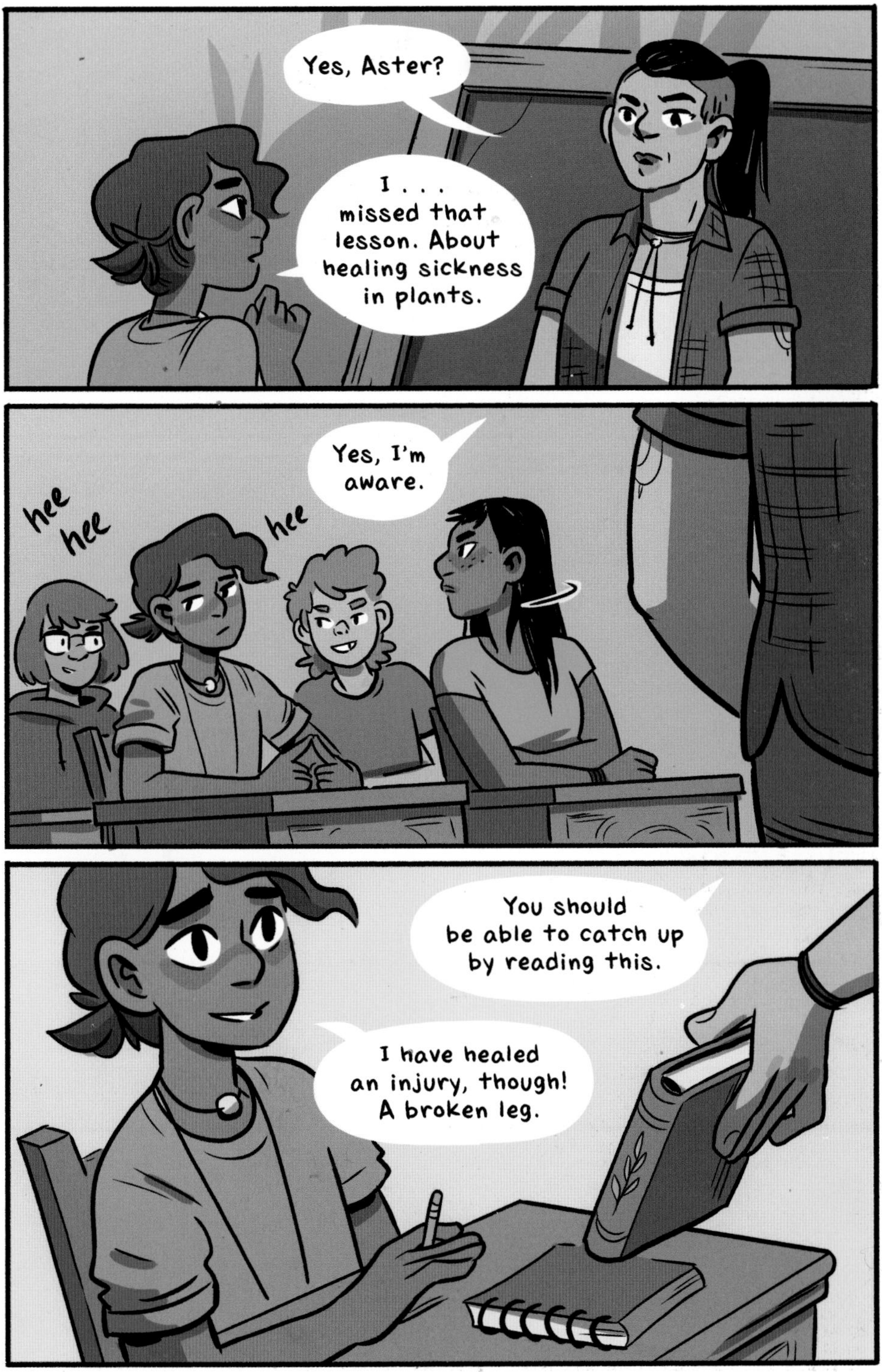
Yes, Aster?
I . . . missed that lesson. About healing sickness in plants.
Yes, I'm aware.
hee hee
hee
You should be able to catch up by reading this.
I have healed an injury, though! A broken leg.

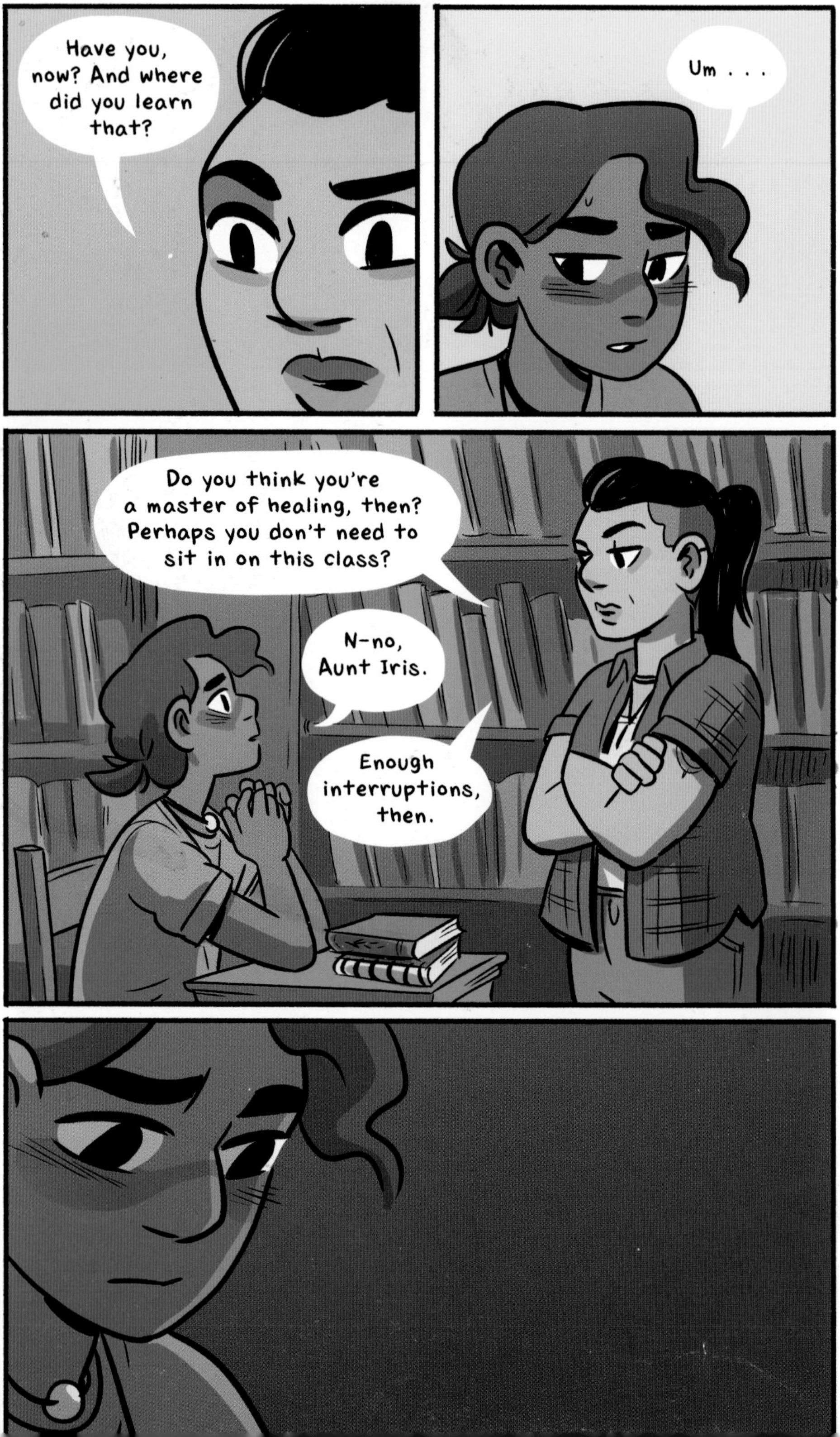

Have you, now? And where did you learn that?
Um . . .
Do you think you're a master of healing, then? Perhaps you don't need to sit in on this class?
N-no, Aunt Iris.
Enough interruptions, then.

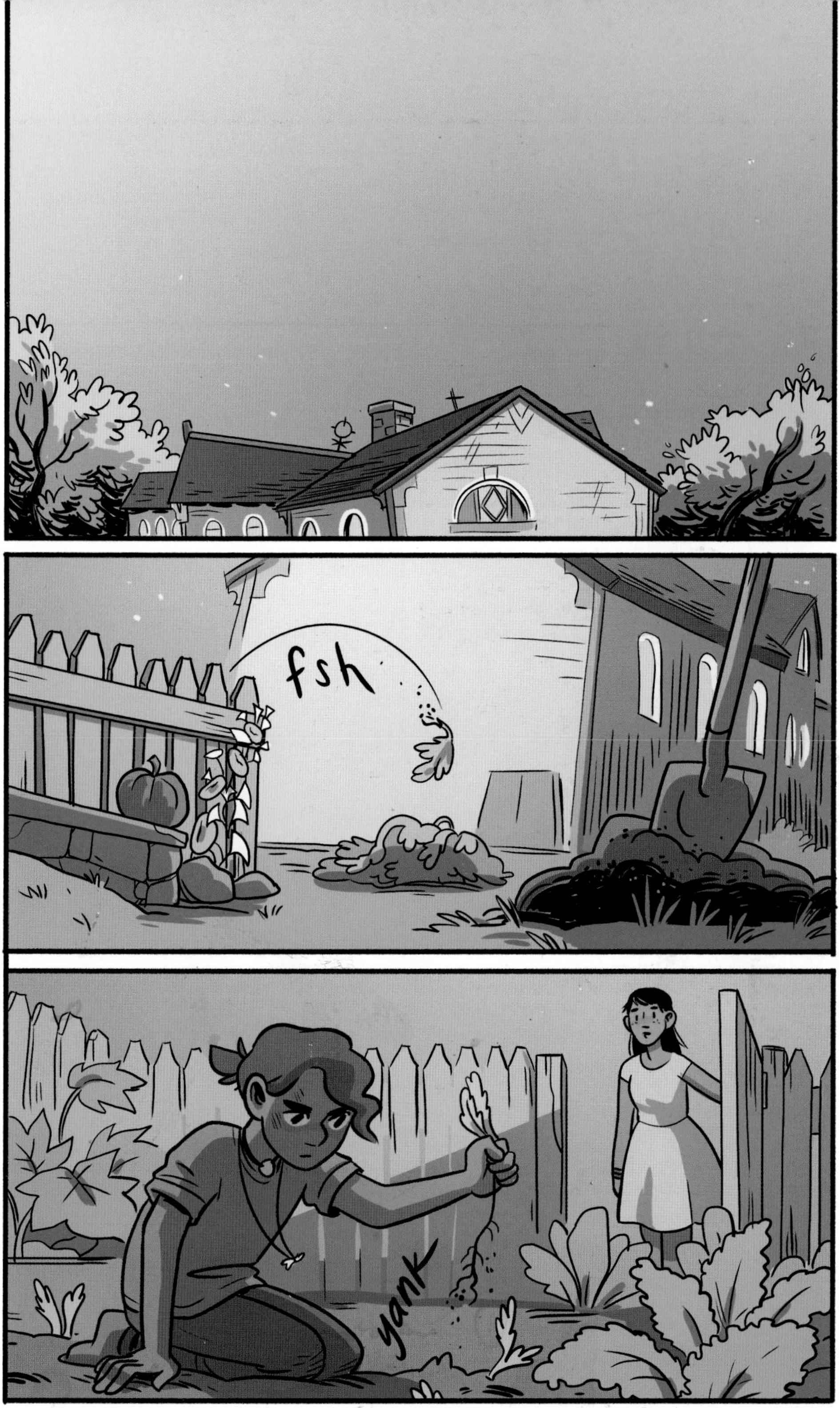
fsh
yank

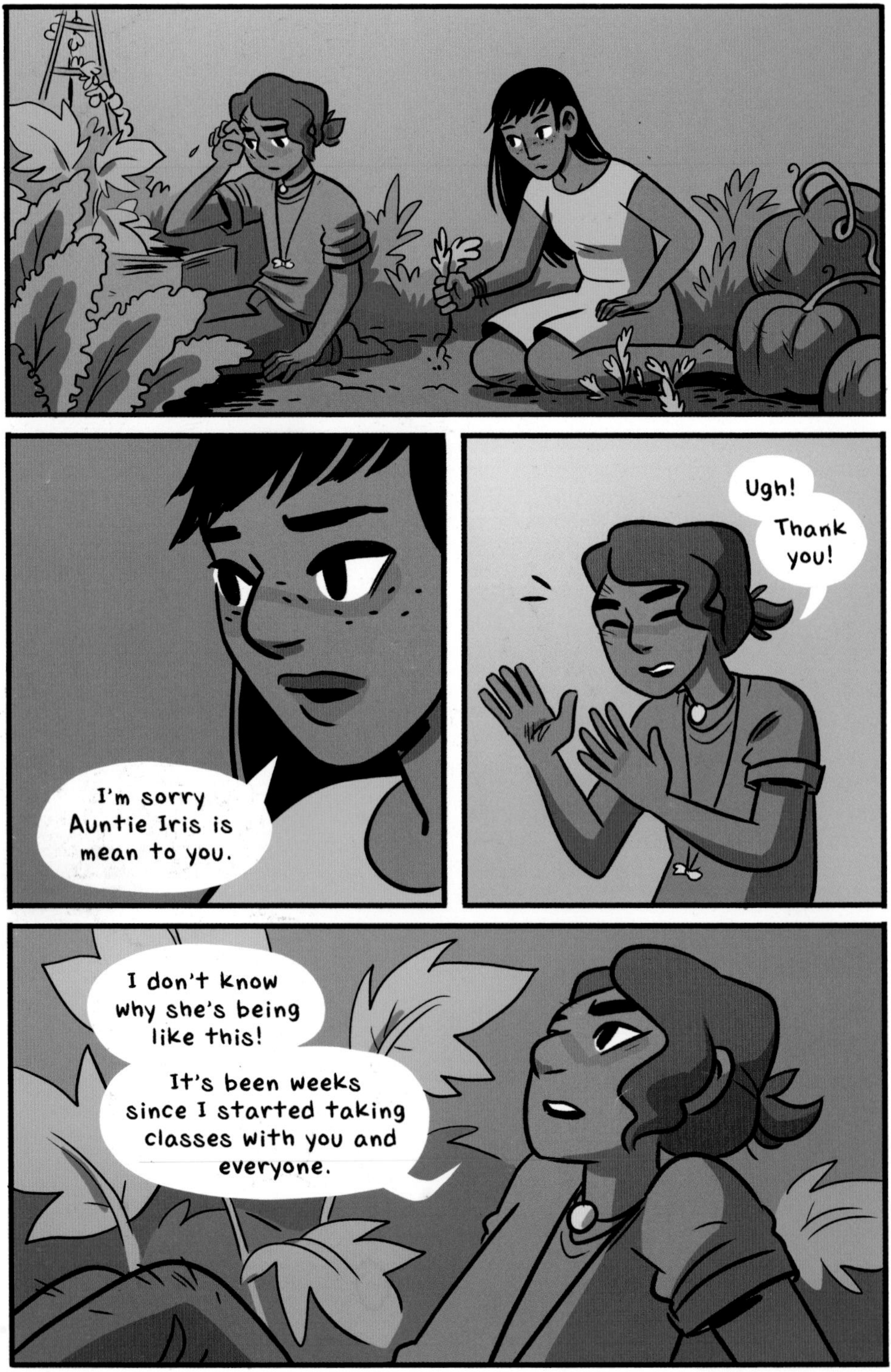
Ugh!
Thank you!
I'm sorry Auntie Iris is mean to you.
I don't know why she's being like this!
It's been weeks since I started taking classes with you and everyone.

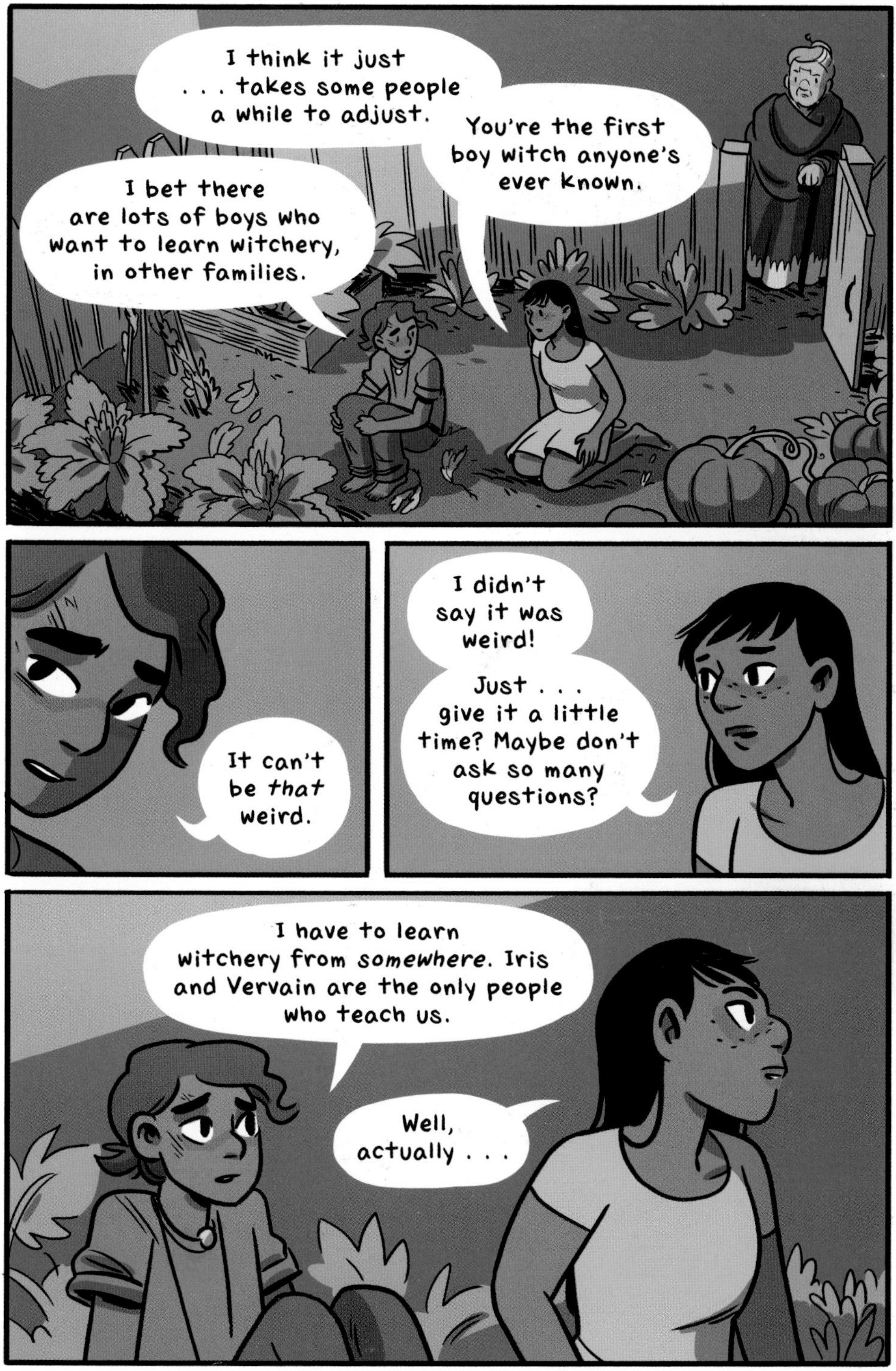
I think it just . . . takes some people a while to adjust.
You're the first boy witch anyone's ever known.
I bet there are lots of boys who want to learn witchery, in other families.
It can't be *that* weird.
I didn't say it was weird!
Just . . . give it a little time? Maybe don't ask so many questions?
I have to learn witchery from *somewhere*. Iris and Vervain are the only people who teach us.
Well, actually . . .

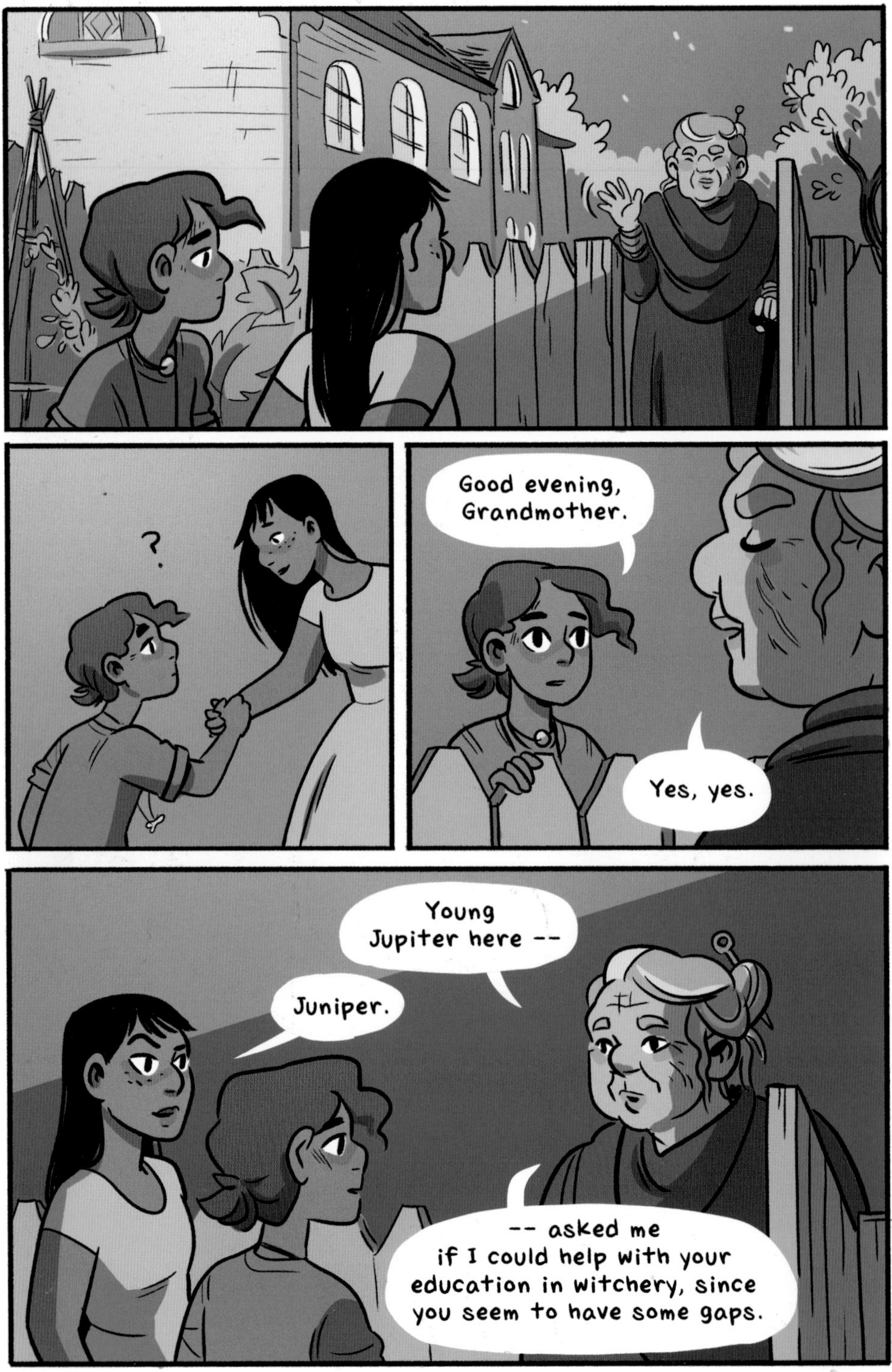
?
Good evening, Grandmother.
Yes, yes.
Young Jupiter here --
Juniper.
-- asked me if I could help with your education in witchery, since you seem to have some gaps.

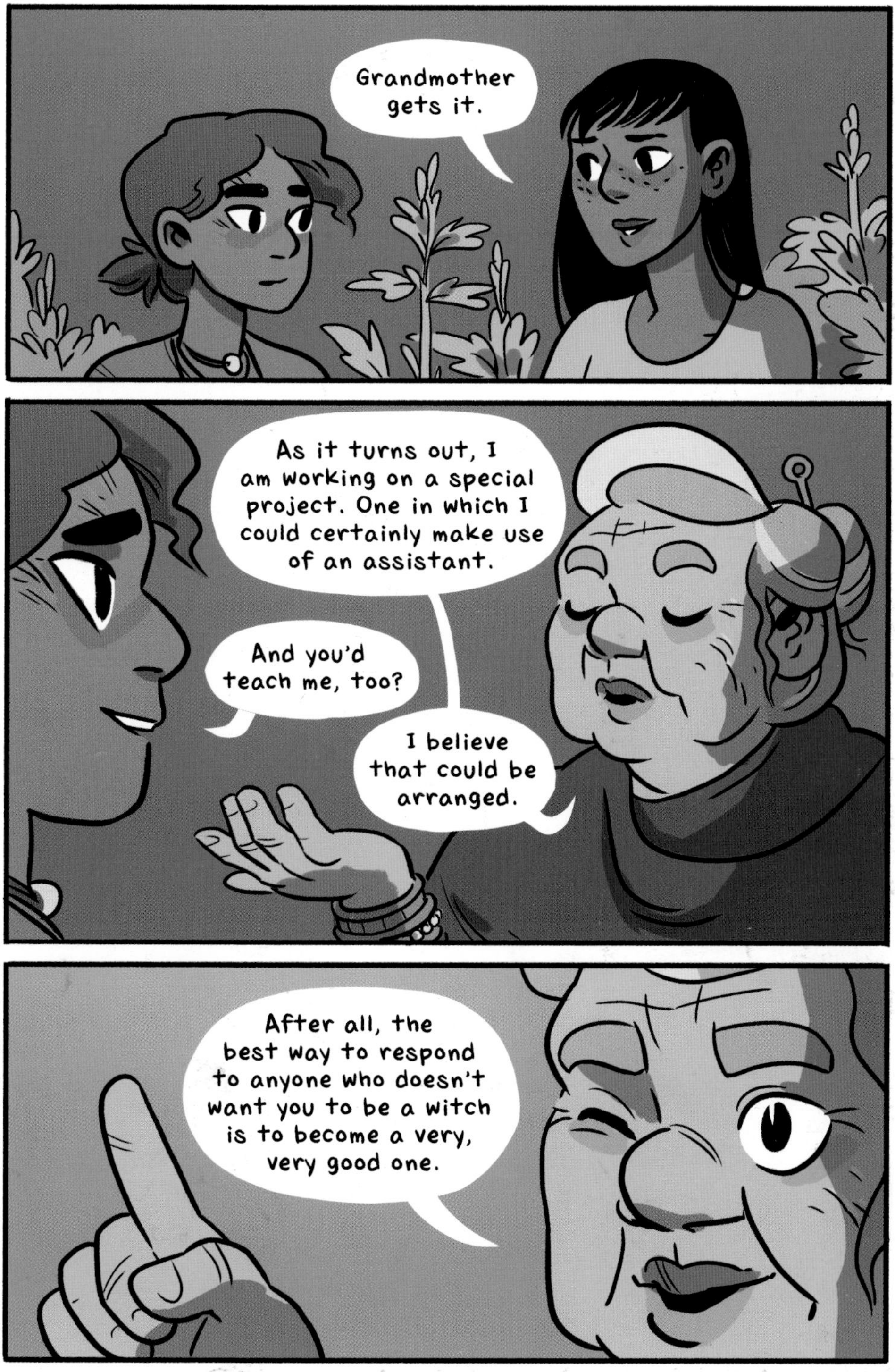
Grandmother gets it.
As it turns out, I am working on a special project. One in which I could certainly make use of an assistant.
And you'd teach me, too?
I believe that could be arranged.
After all, the best way to respond to anyone who doesn't want you to be a witch is to become a very, very good one.

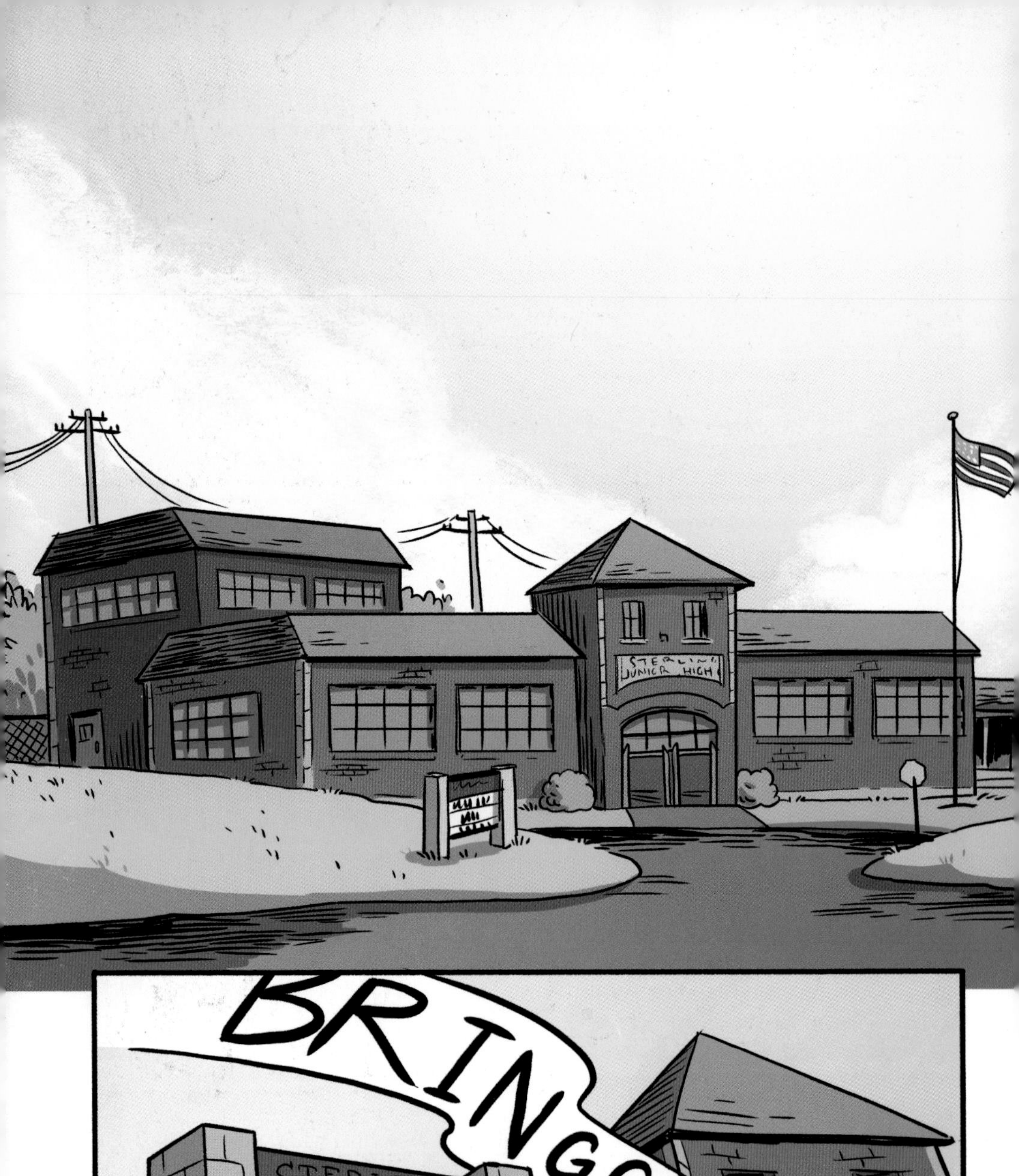
STERLING JUNIOR HIGH

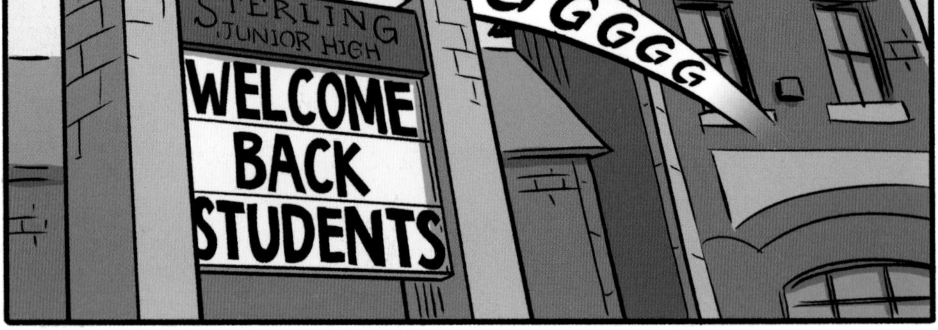
BRINGGGGGG
STERLING JUNIOR HIGH
WELCOME BACK STUDENTS

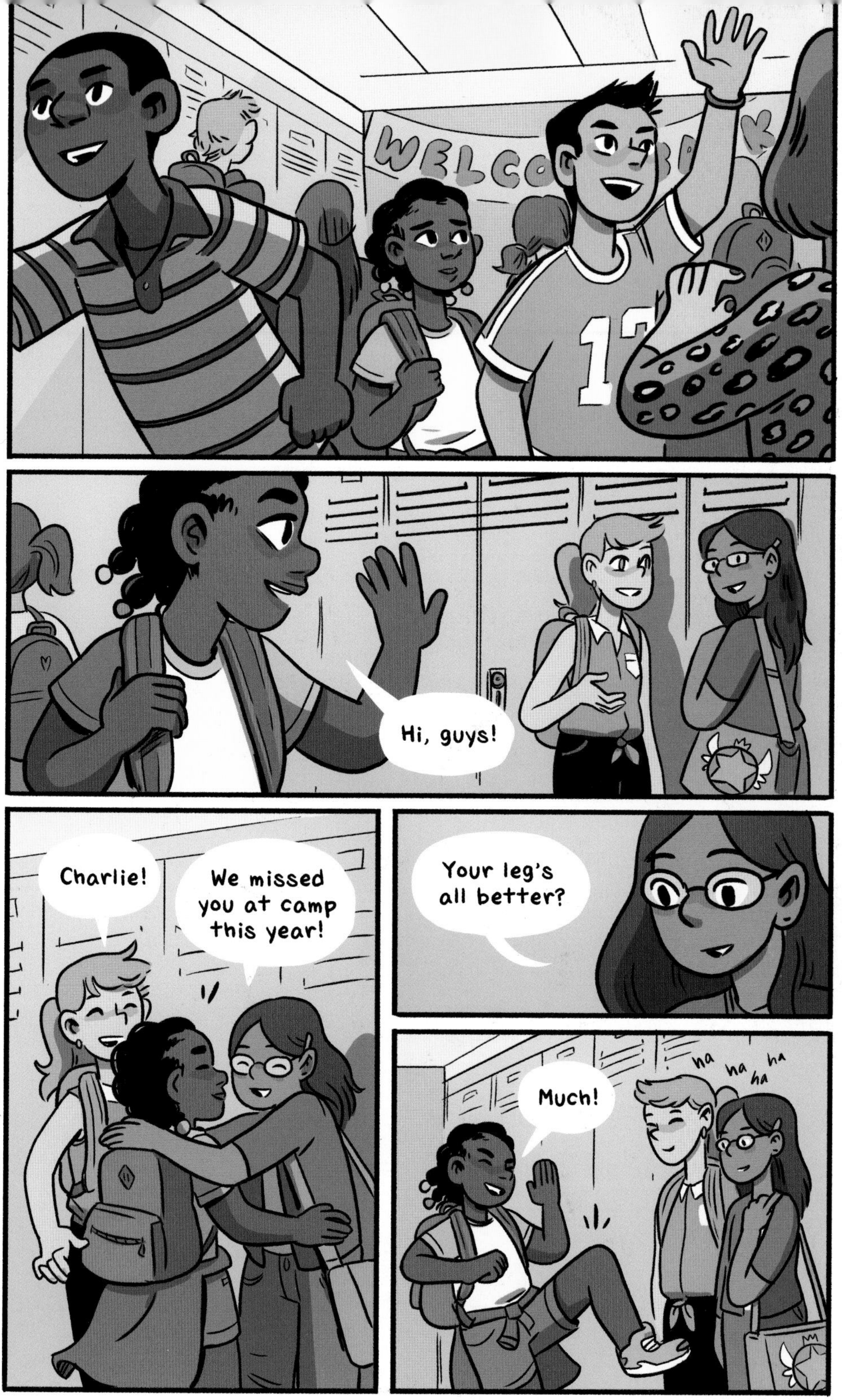
WELCO
Hi, guys!
Charlie!
We missed you at camp this year!
Your leg's all better?
Much!
ha ha ha ha

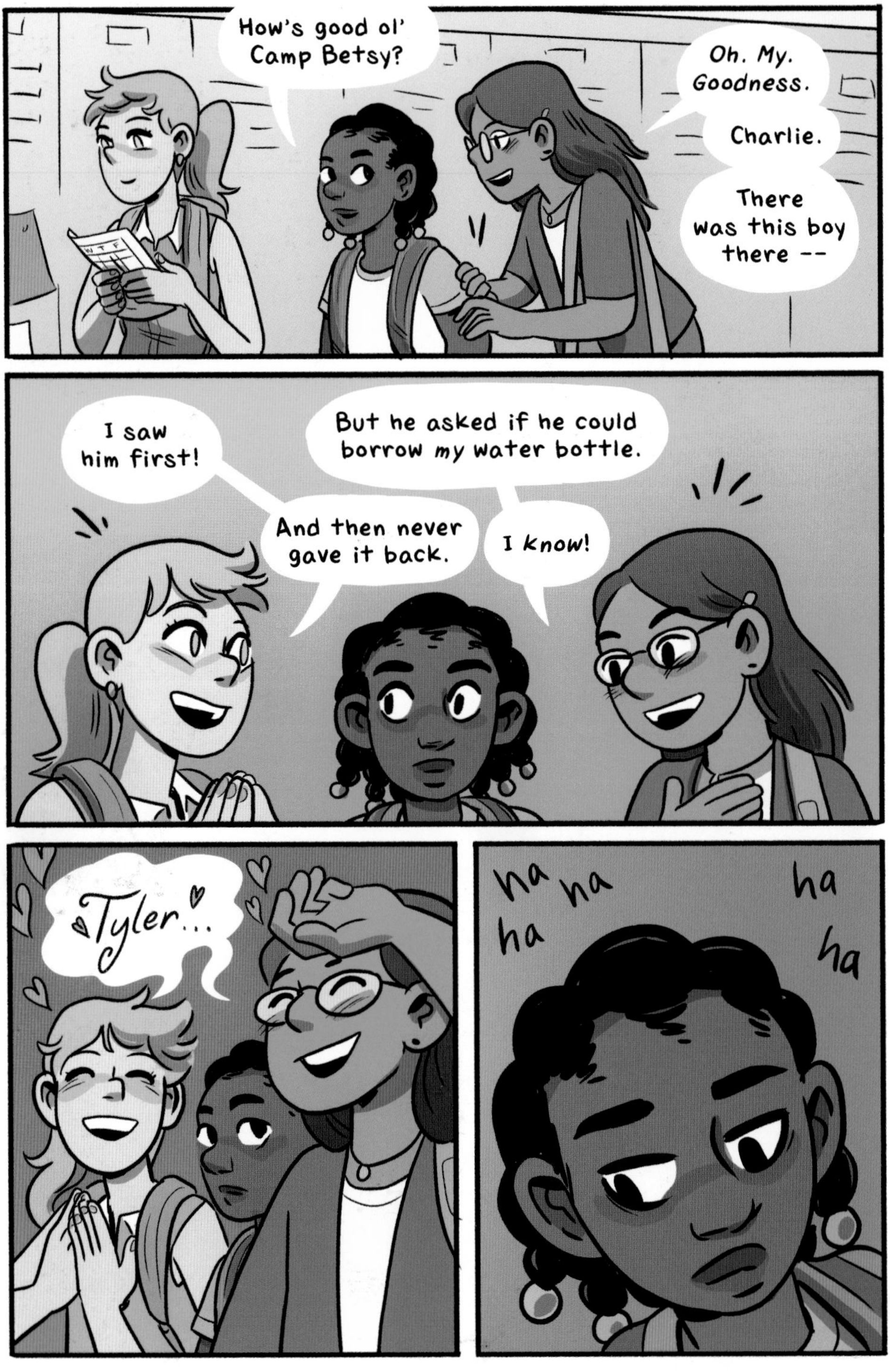
How's good ol' Camp Betsy?
Oh. My. Goodness.
Charlie.
There was this boy there --
I saw him first!
But he asked if he could borrow *my* water bottle.
And then never gave it back.
I know!
Tyler...
ha ha ha
ha ha

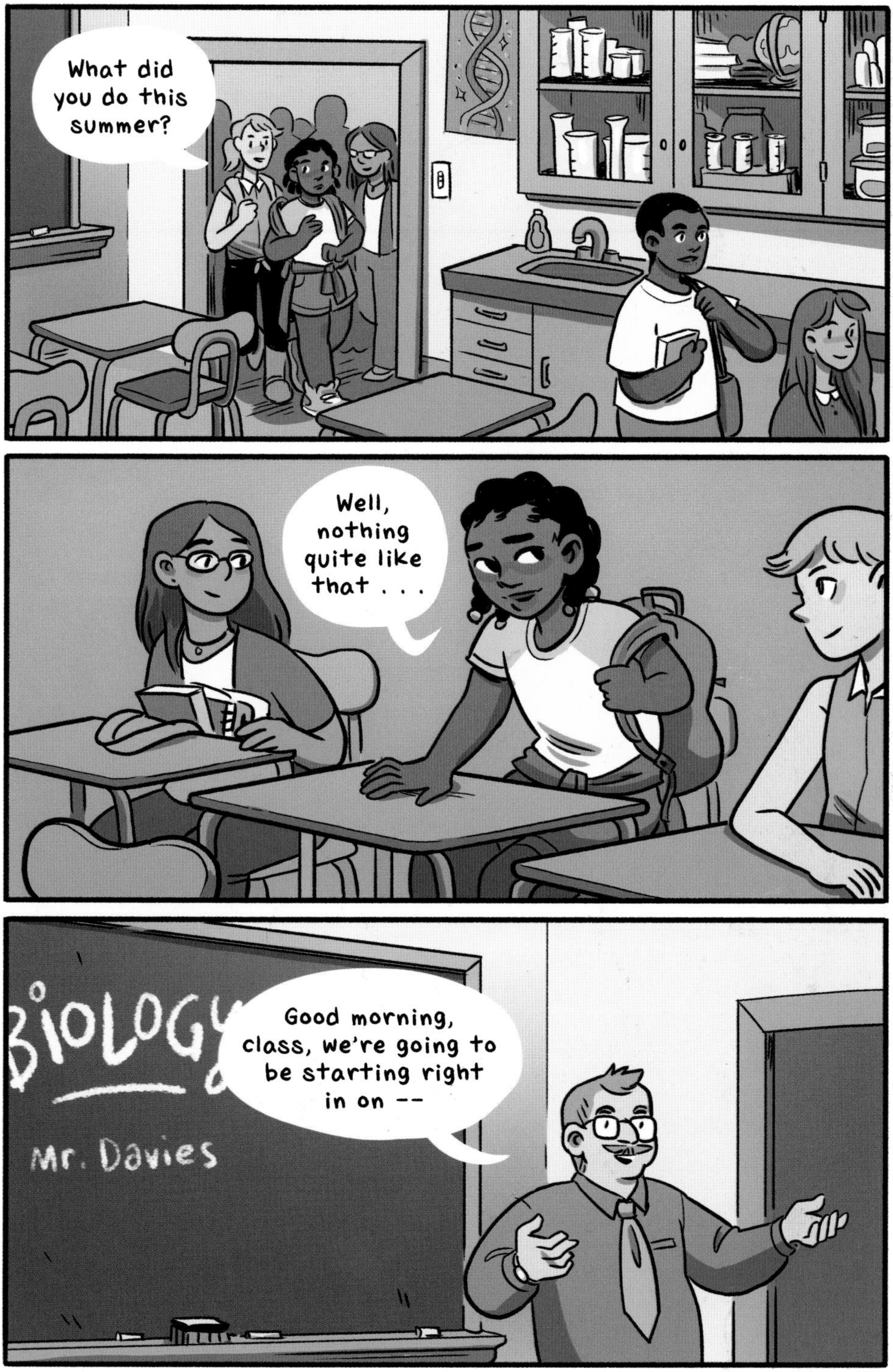
What did you do this summer?
Well, nothing quite like that . . .
BIOLOGY
Good morning, class, we're going to be starting right in on --
Mr. Davies

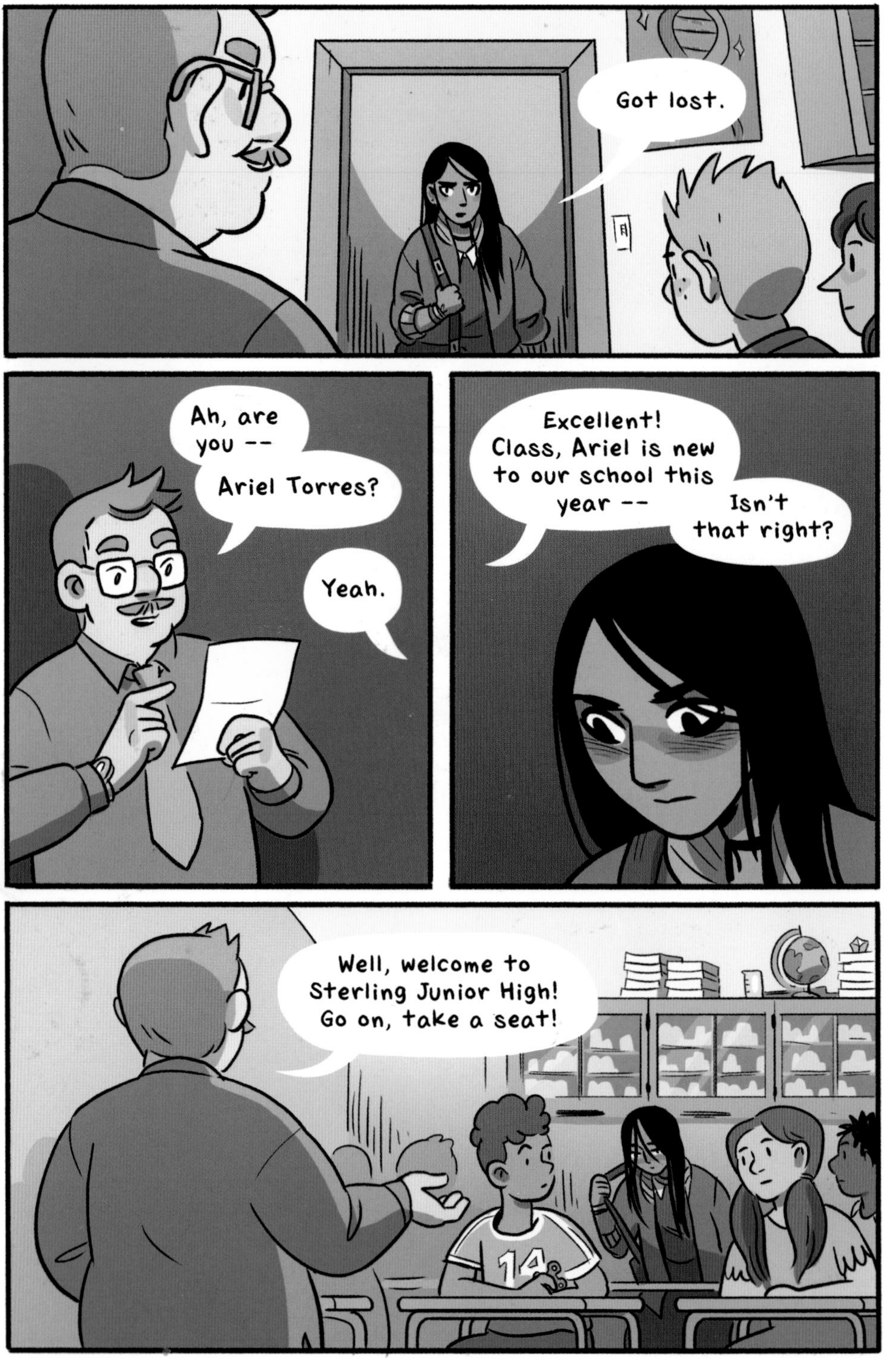
Got lost.
Ah, are you --
Ariel Torres?
Yeah.
Excellent! Class, Ariel is new to our school this year --
Isn't that right?
Well, welcome to Sterling Junior High! Go on, take a seat!

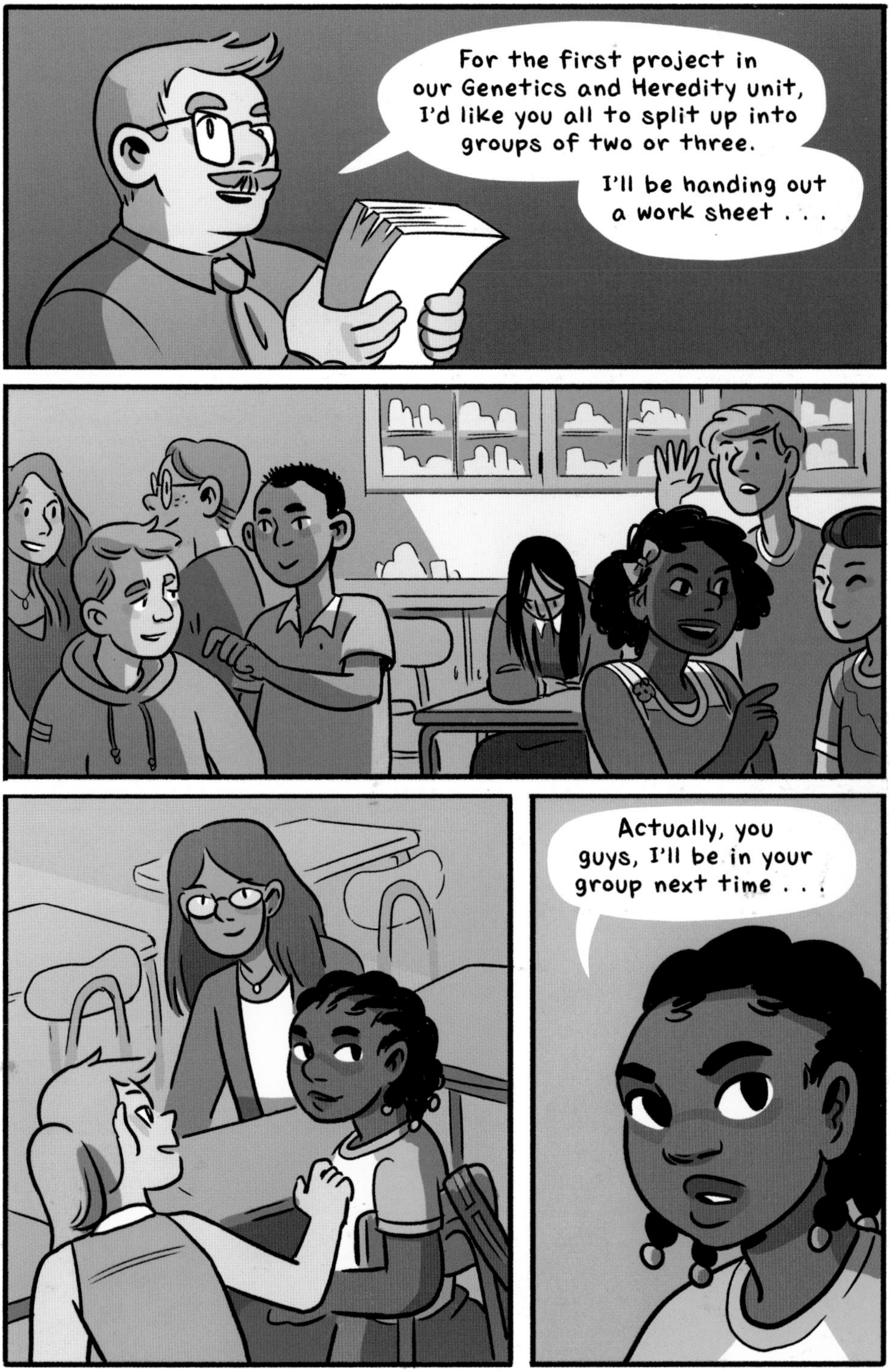
For the first project in our Genetics and Heredity unit, I'd like you all to split up into groups of two or three.
I'll be handing out a work sheet . . .
Actually, you guys, I'll be in your group next time . . .

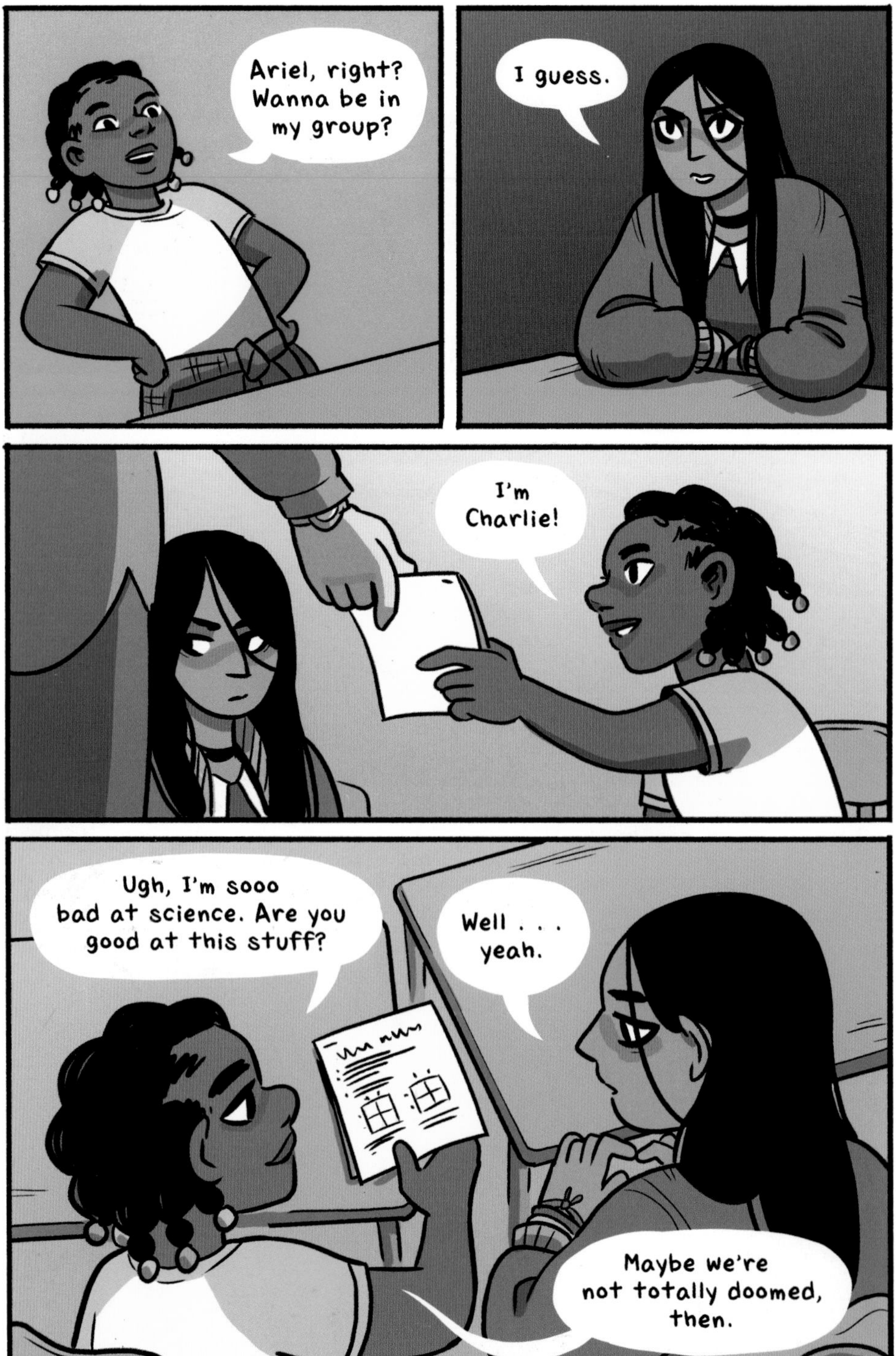
Ariel, right? Wanna be in my group?
I guess.
I'm Charlie!
Ugh, I'm sooo bad at science. Are you good at this stuff?
Well . . . yeah.
Maybe we're not totally doomed, then.

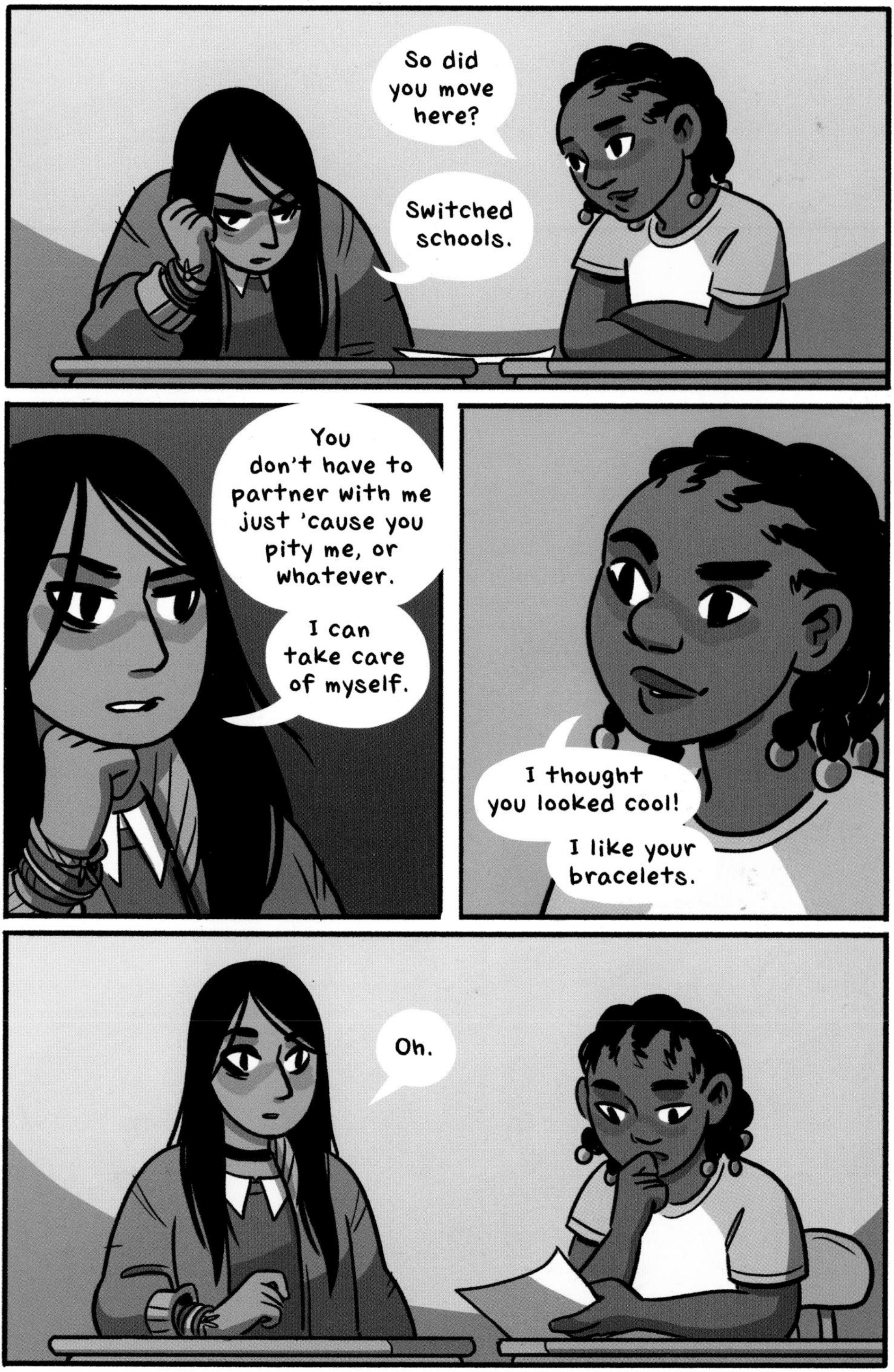
So did you move here?
Switched schools.
You don't have to partner with me just 'cause you pity me, or whatever.
I can take care of myself.
I thought you looked cool!
I like your bracelets.
Oh.

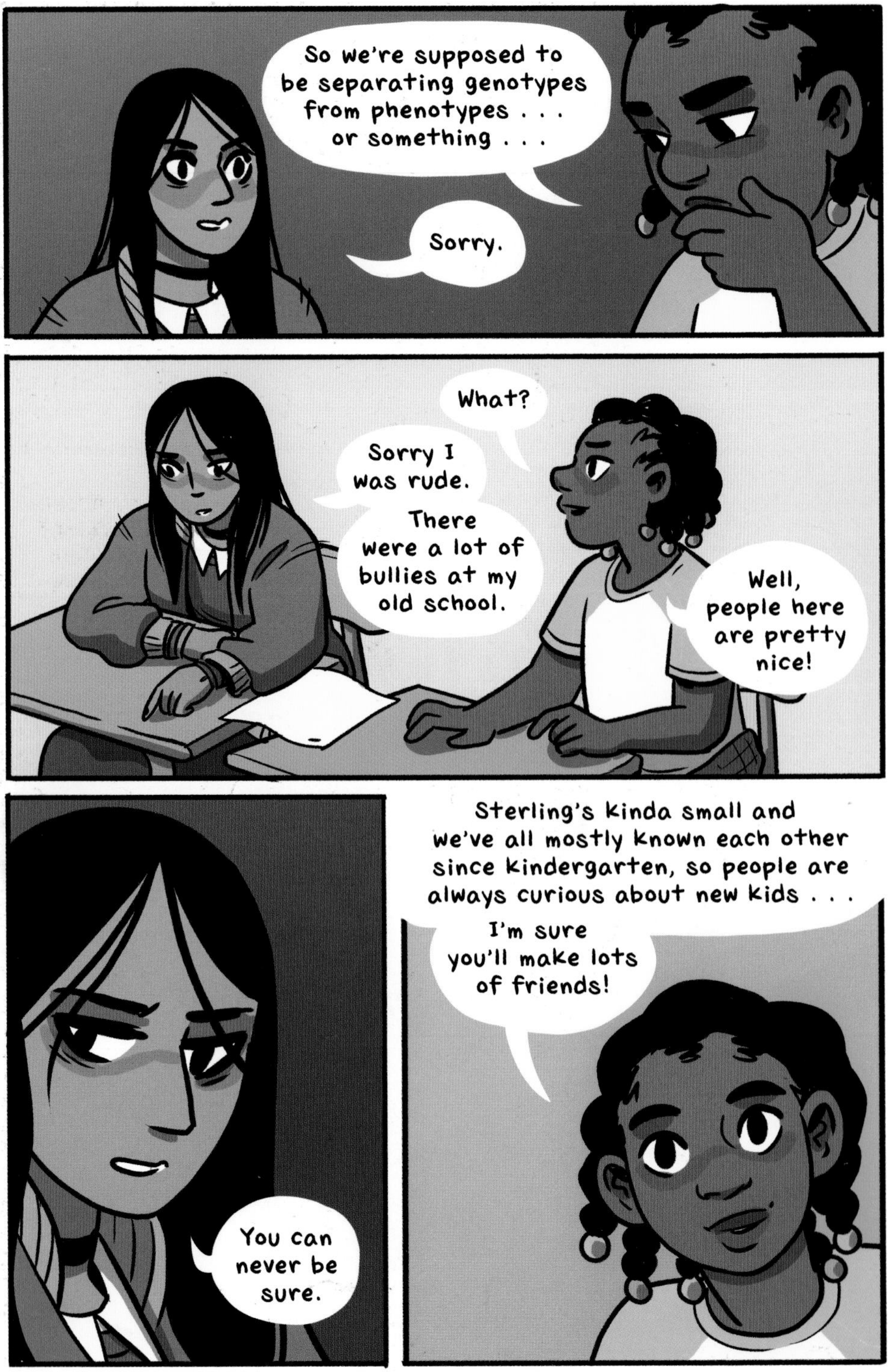
So we're supposed to be separating genotypes from phenotypes . . . or something . . .
Sorry.
What?
Sorry I was rude.
There were a lot of bullies at my old school.
Well, people here are pretty nice!
Sterling's kinda small and we've all mostly known each other since kindergarten, so people are always curious about new kids . . .
I'm sure you'll make lots of friends!
You can never be sure.

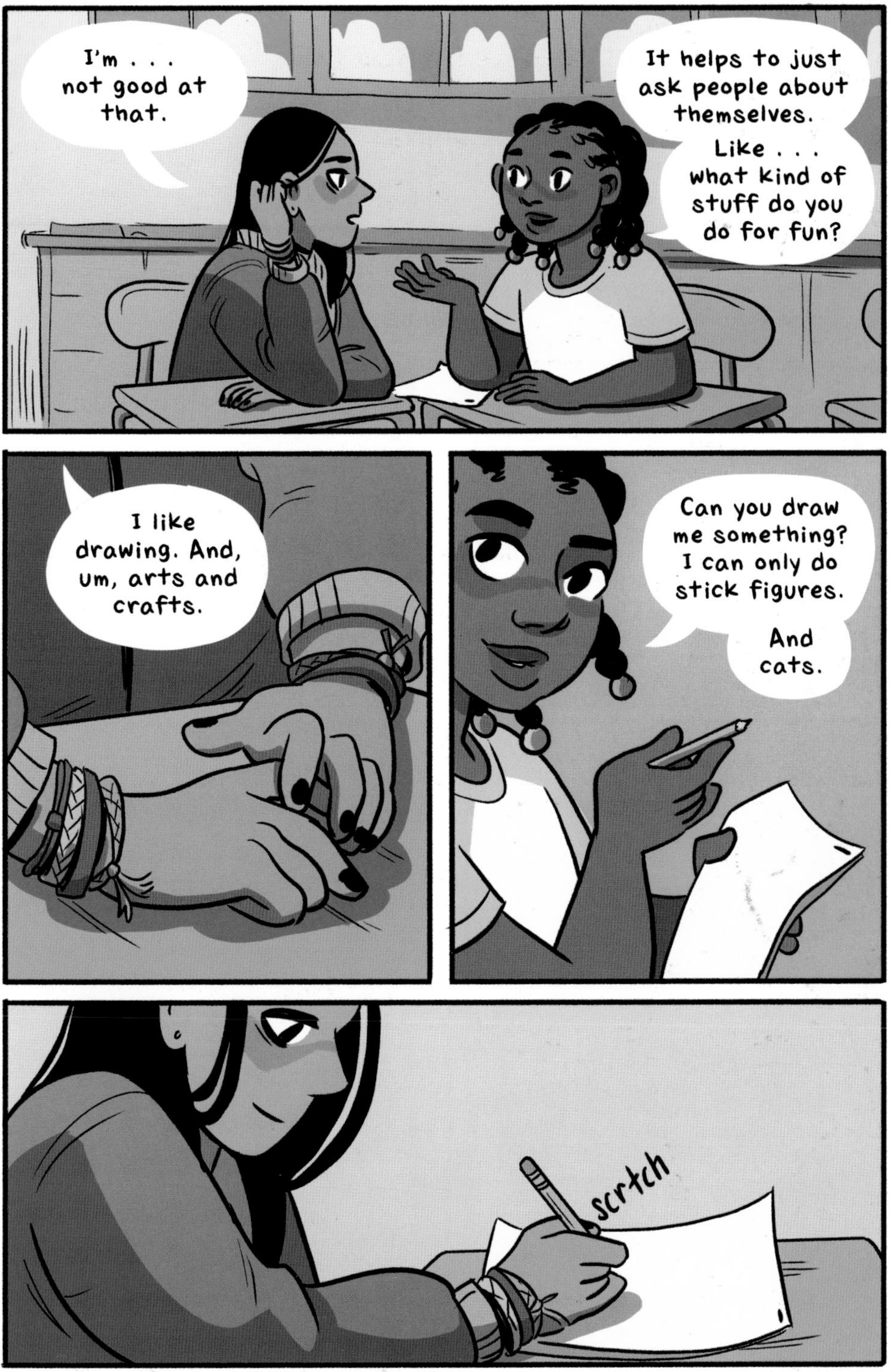
I'm . . .
not good at
that.
It helps to just
ask people about
themselves.
Like . . .
what kind of
stuff do you
do for fun?
I like
drawing. And,
um, arts and
crafts.
Can you draw
me something?
I can only do
stick figures.
And
cats.
scrtch

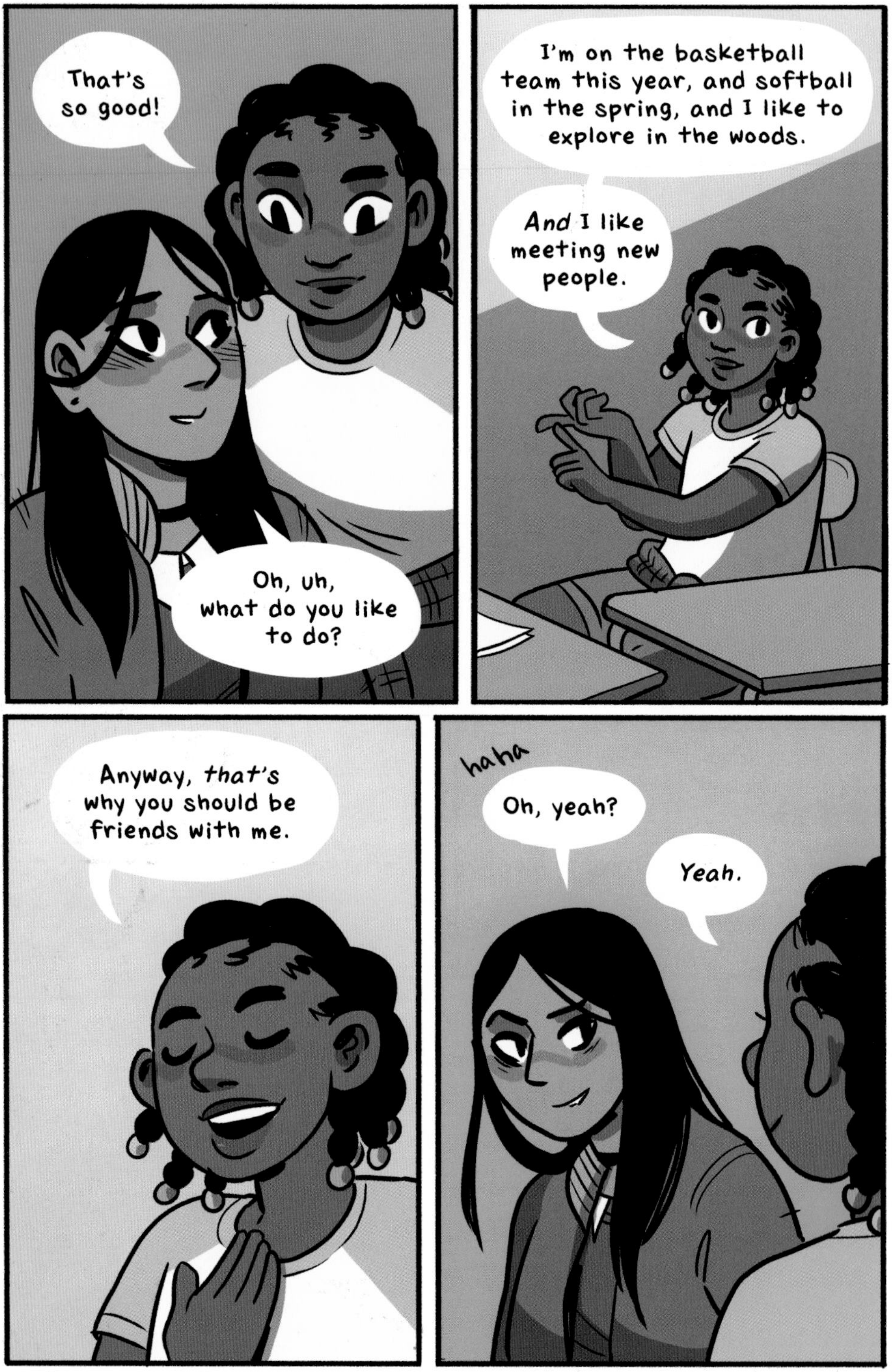
That's so good!
Oh, uh, what do you like to do?
I'm on the basketball team this year, and softball in the spring, and I like to explore in the woods.
And I like meeting new people.
Anyway, *that's* why you should be friends with me.
haha
Oh, yeah?
Yeah.

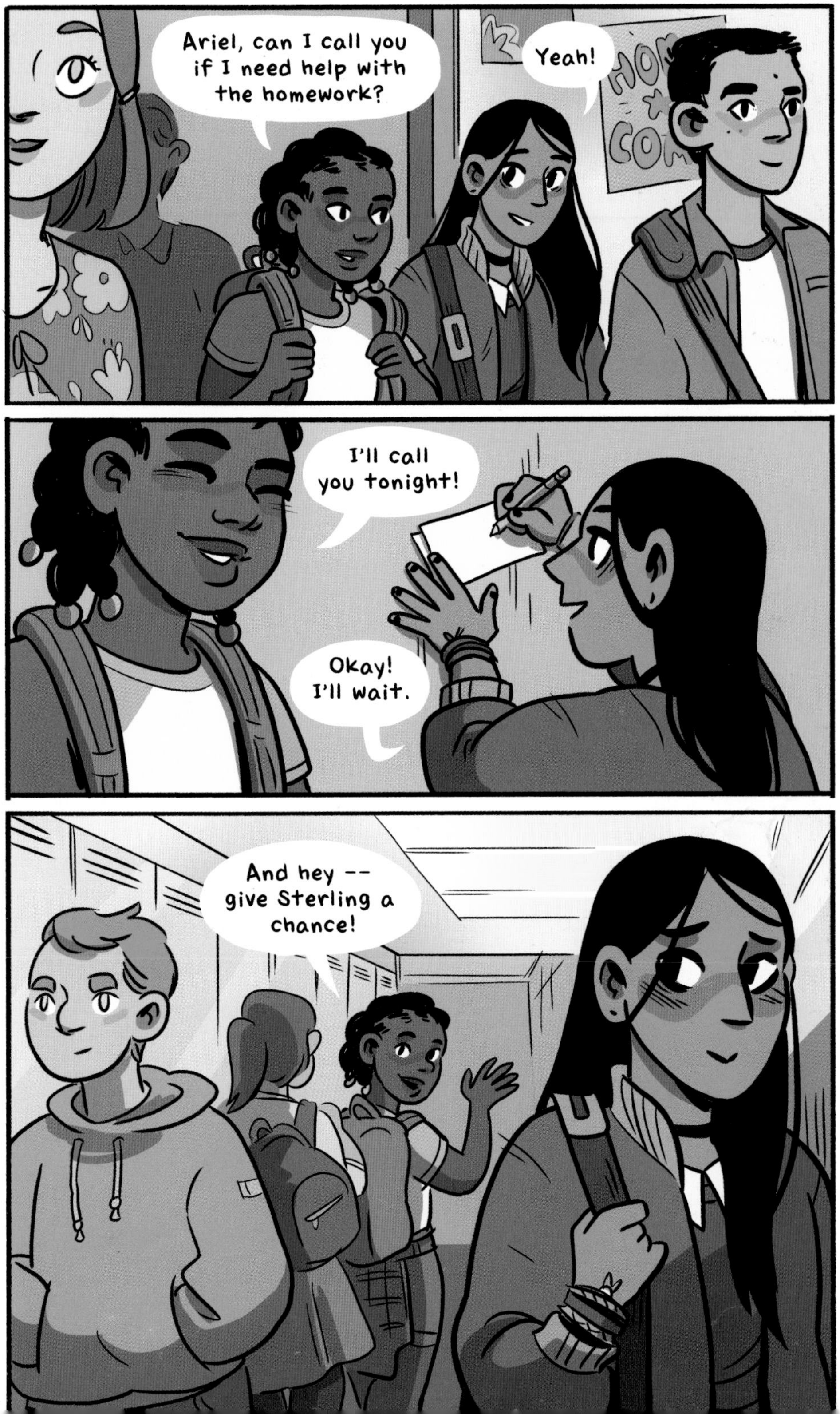
Ariel, can I call you if I need help with the homework?
Yeah!
I'll call you tonight!
Okay! I'll wait.
And hey -- give Sterling a chance!

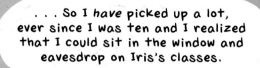

. . . So I *have* picked up a lot, ever since I was ten and I realized that I could sit in the window and eavesdrop on Iris's classes.

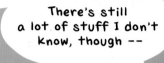

There's still a lot of stuff I don't know, though --

Yes, you've missed a good deal of the *theory* of witchery. Also known as the boring parts.

Pass me that green glass bottle.

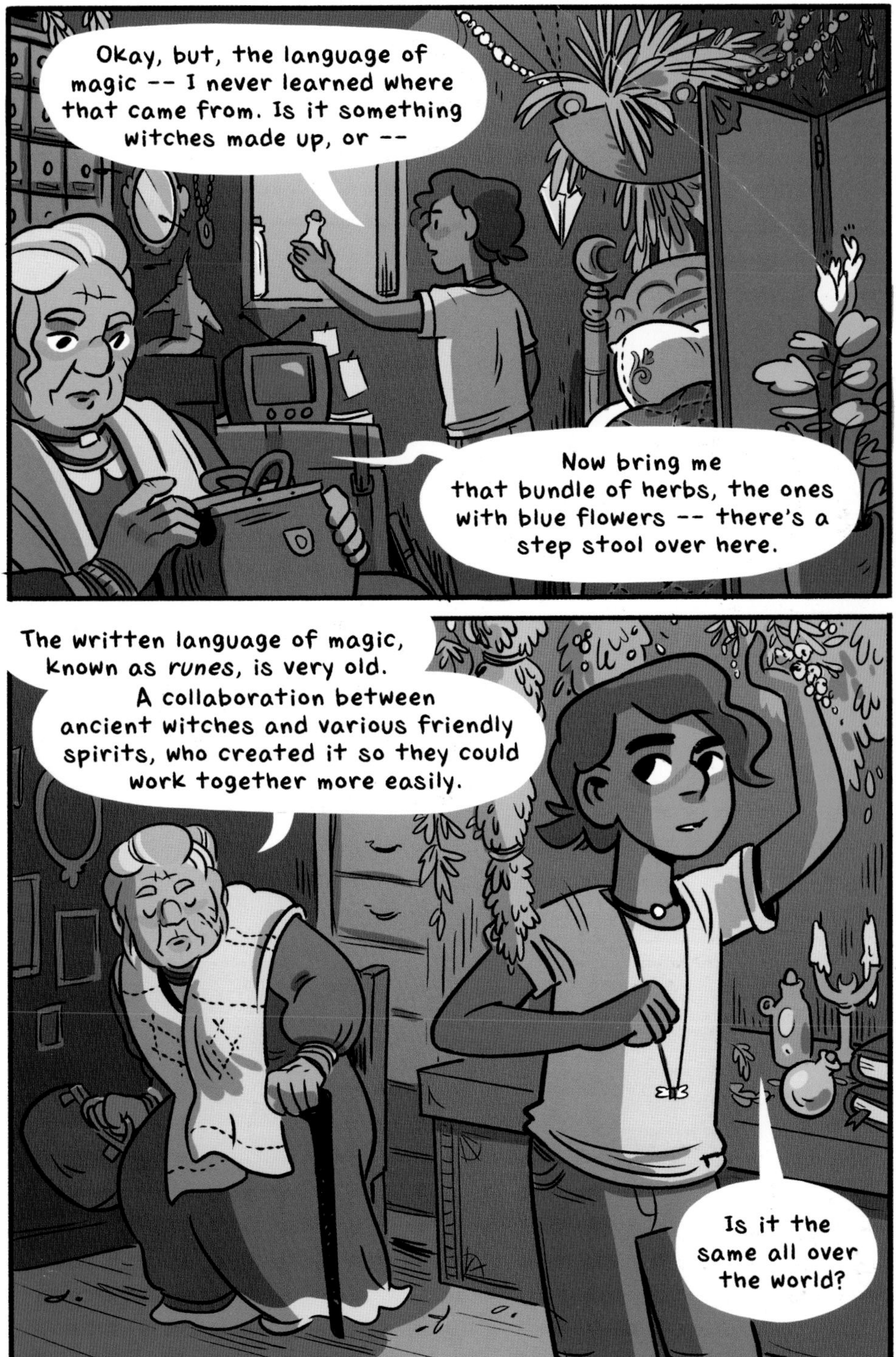
Okay, but, the language of magic -- I never learned where that came from. Is it something witches made up, or --
Now bring me that bundle of herbs, the ones with blue flowers -- there's a step stool over here.
The written language of magic, known as *runes*, is very old.
A collaboration between ancient witches and various friendly spirits, who created it so they could work together more easily.
Is it the same all over the world?

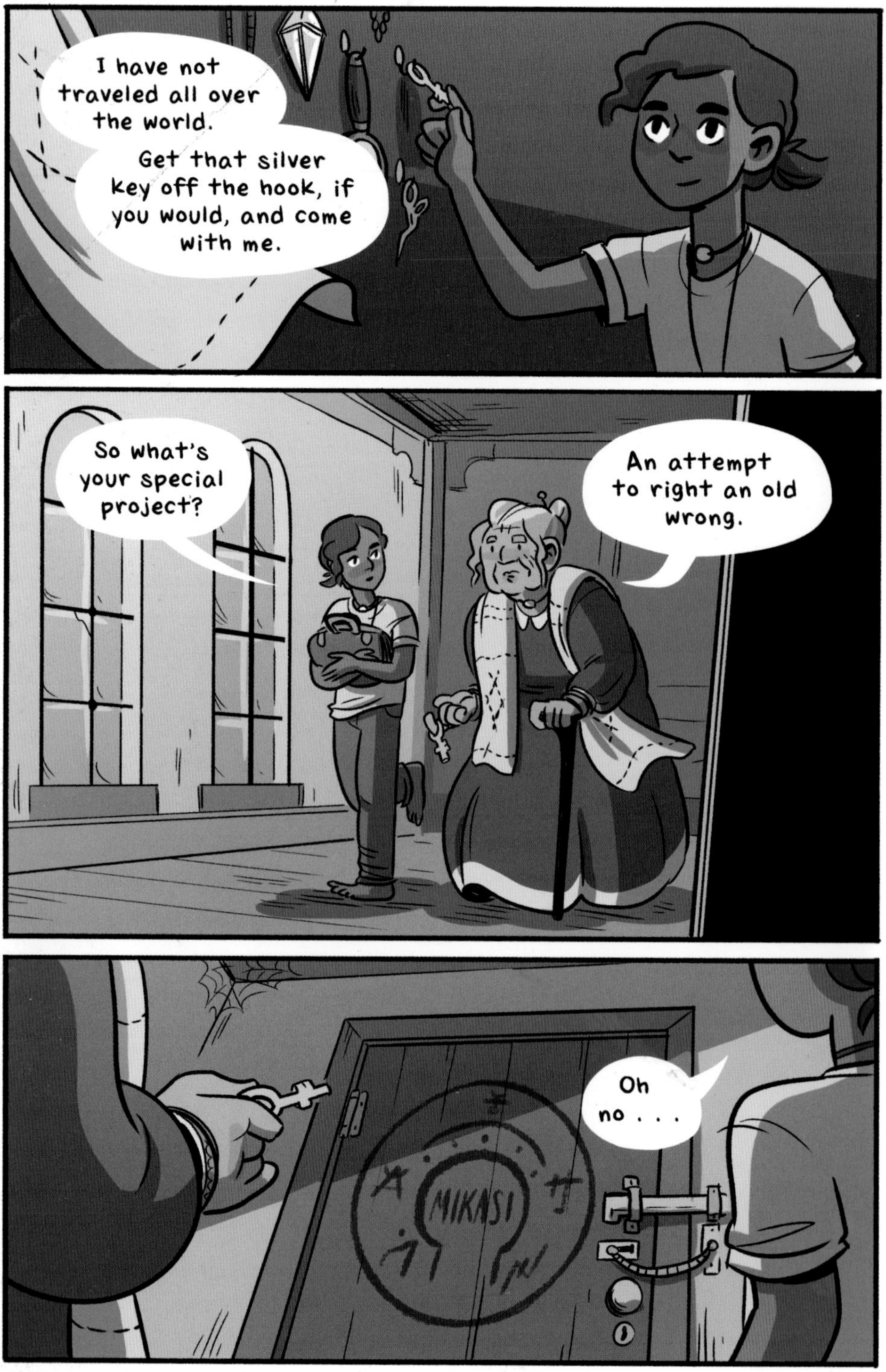
I have not traveled all over the world.
Get that silver key off the hook, if you would, and come with me.
So what's your special project?
An attempt to right an old wrong.
MIKASI
Oh no . . .

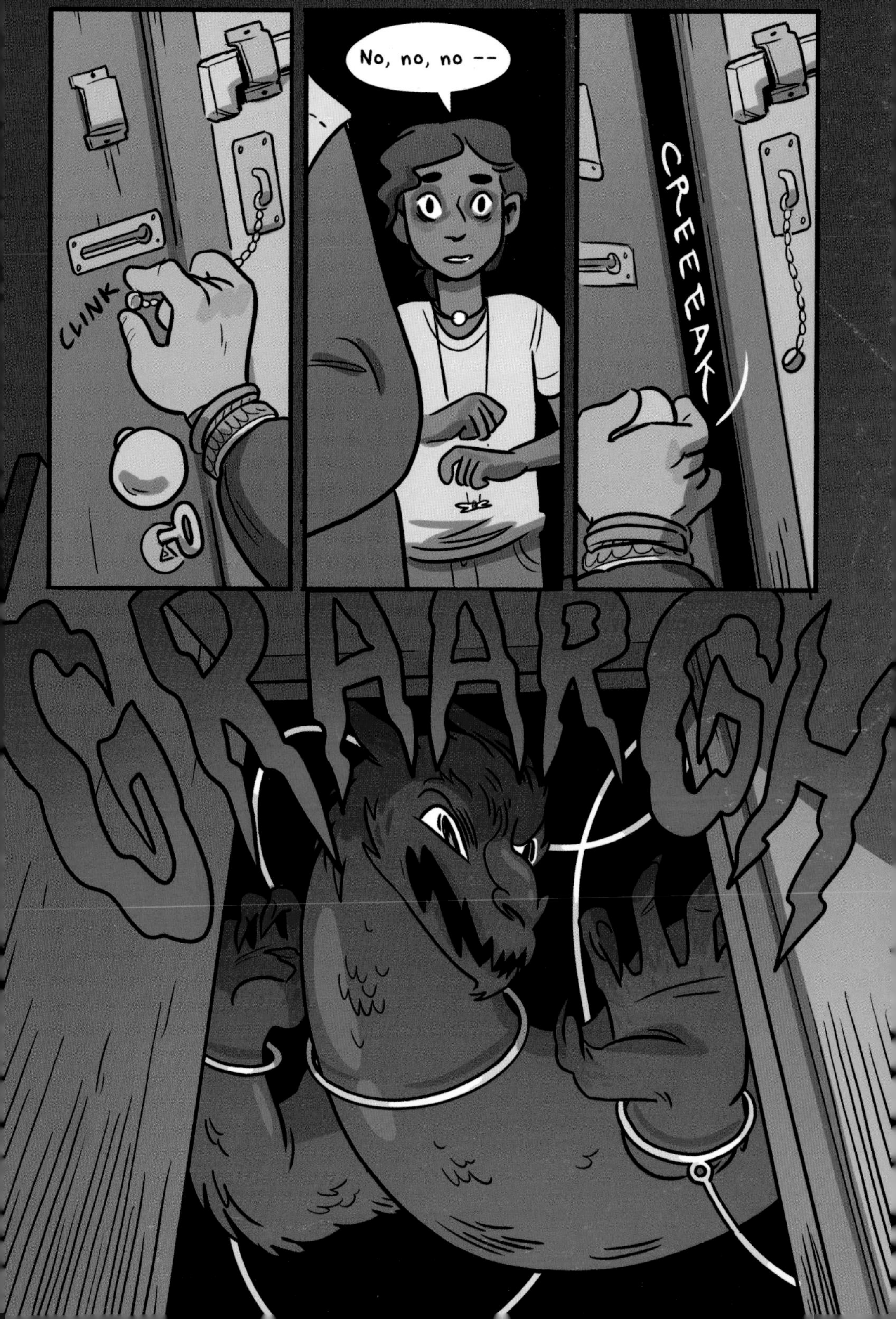
CLINK
No, no, no --
CREEEAK
GRAARGK

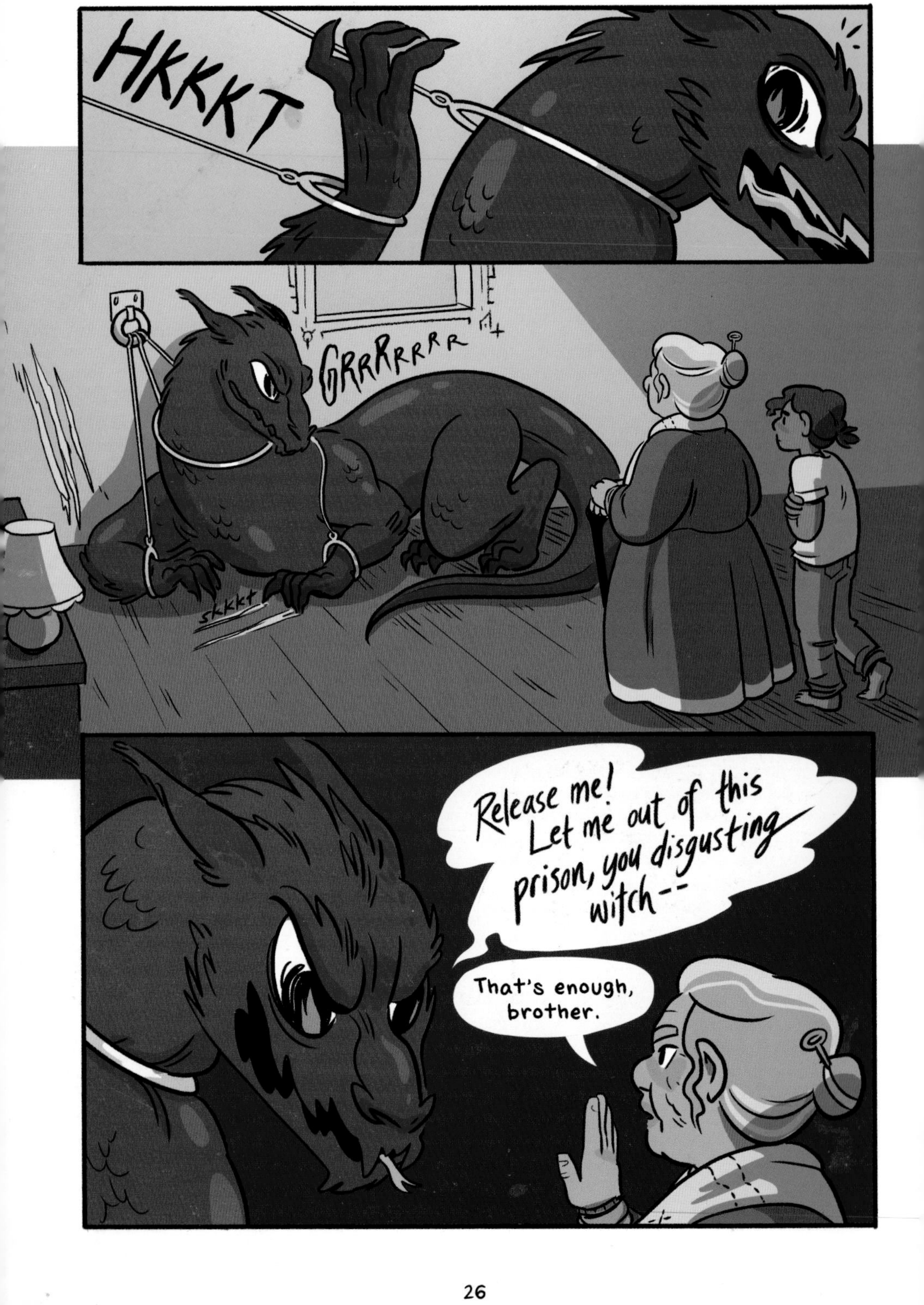
HKKKT
GRRRRRRR
skkkt
Release me! Let me out of this prison, you disgusting witch--
That's enough, brother.

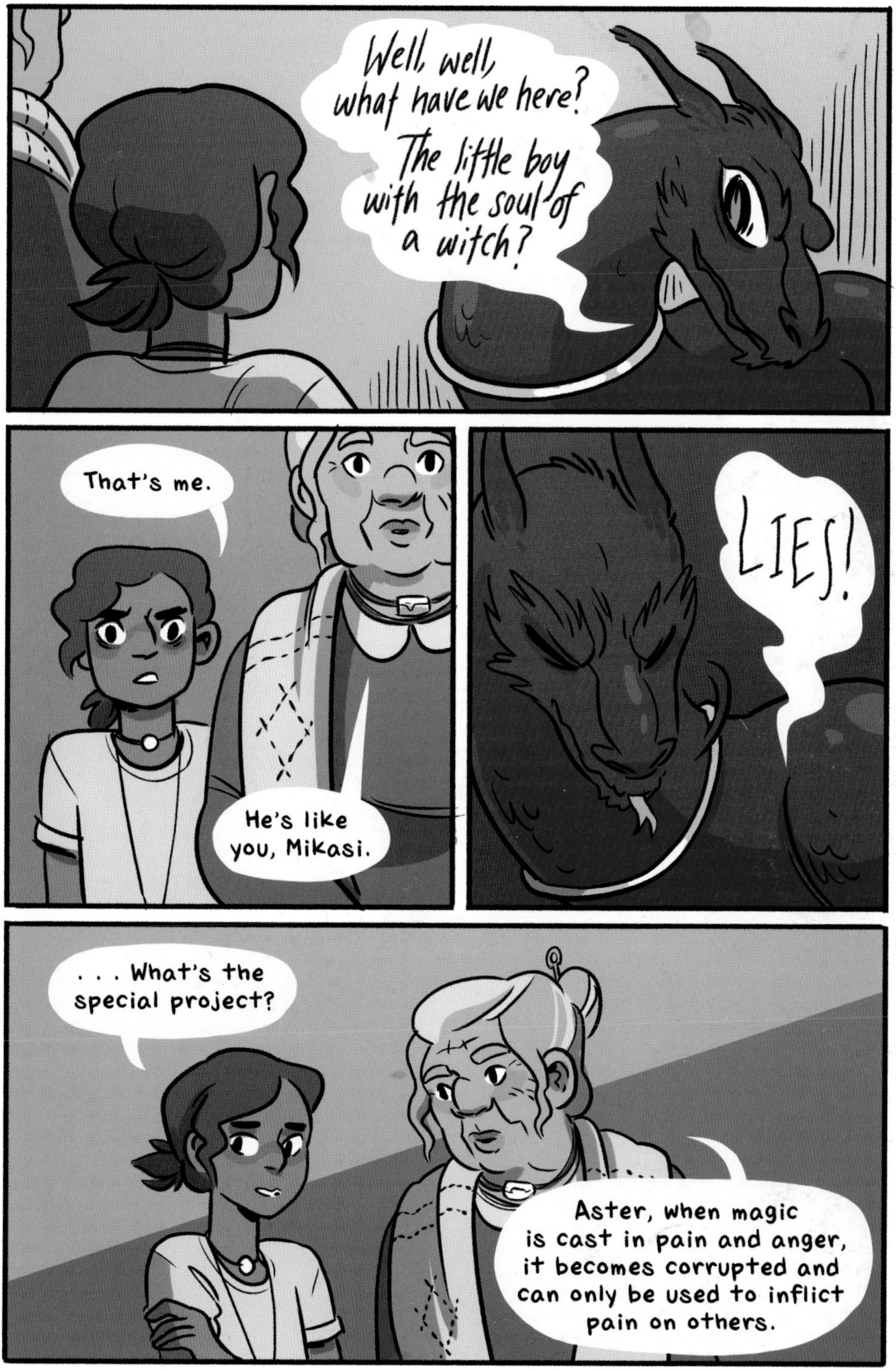
Well, well, what have we here? The little boy with the soul of a witch?
That's me.
He's like you, Mikasi.
LIES!
. . . What's the special project?
Aster, when magic is cast in pain and anger, it becomes corrupted and can only be used to inflict pain on others.

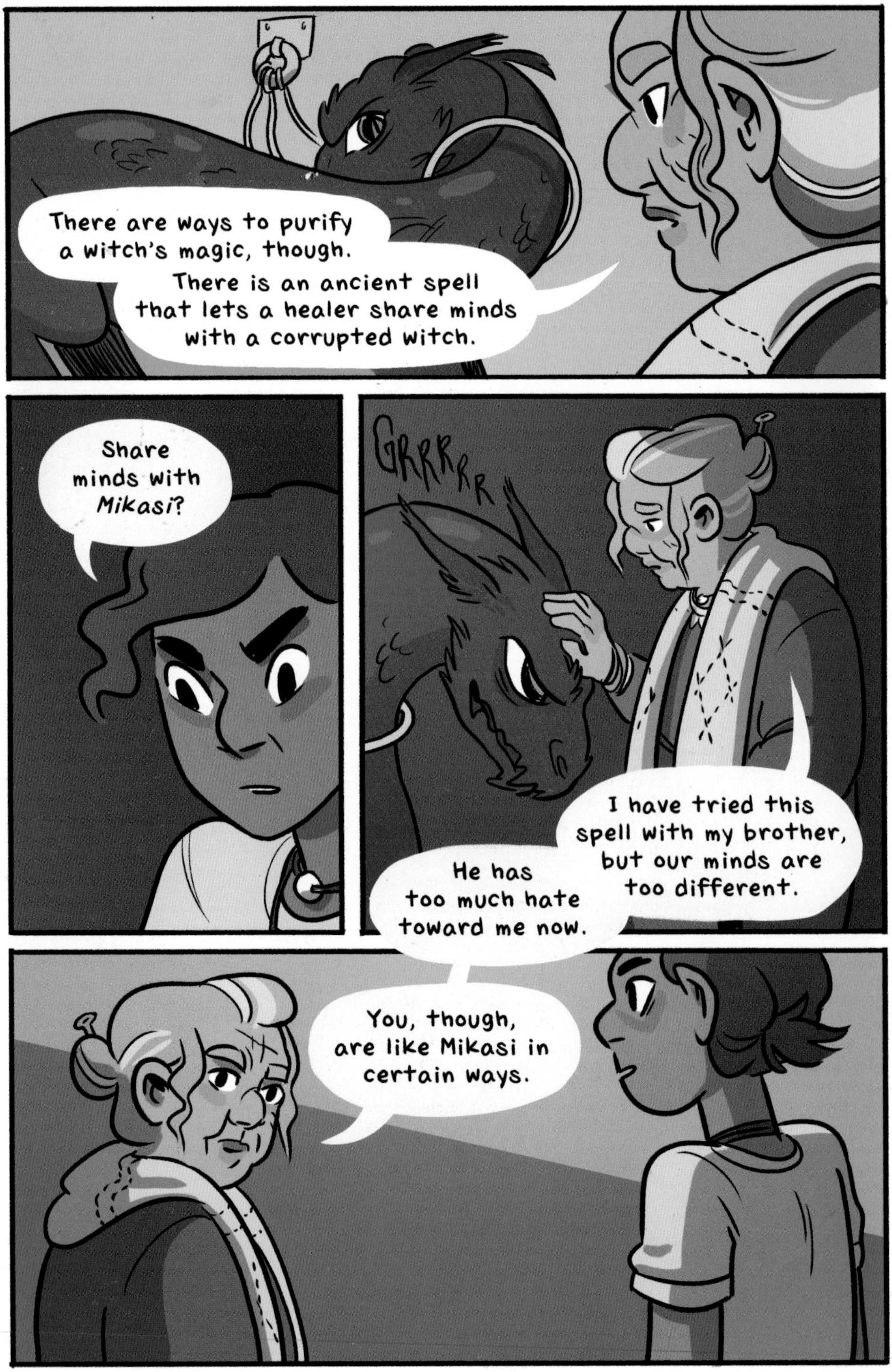
There are ways to purify a witch's magic, though.
There is an ancient spell that lets a healer share minds with a corrupted witch.
Share minds with *Mikasi*?
GRRRRR
I have tried this spell with my brother, but our minds are too different.
He has too much hate toward me now.
You, though, are like Mikasi in certain ways.

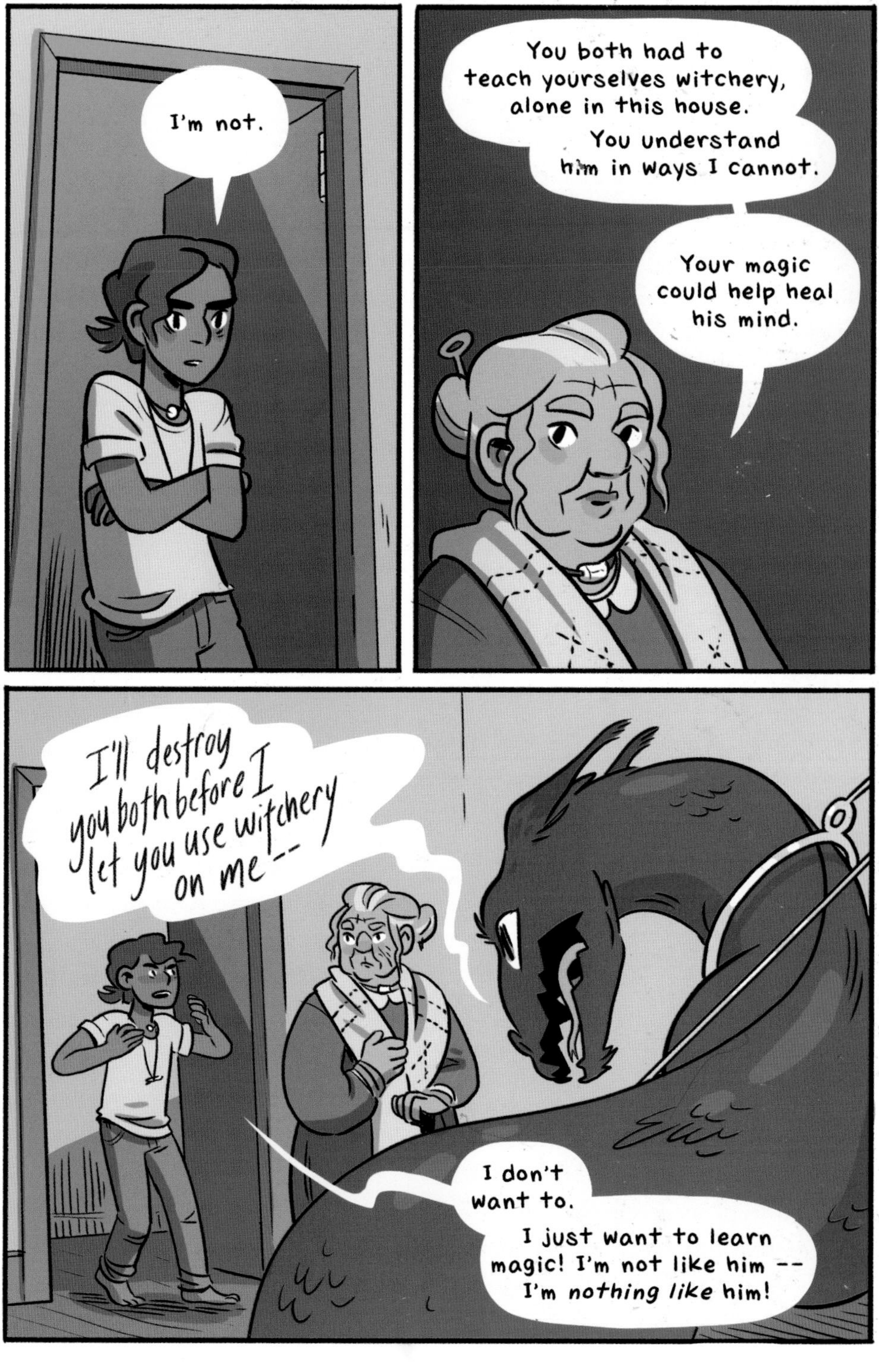
I'm not.
You both had to teach yourselves witchery, alone in this house.
You understand him in ways I cannot.
Your magic could help heal his mind.
I'll destroy you both before I let you use witchery on me--
I don't want to.
I just want to learn magic! I'm not like him -- I'm *nothing like* him!

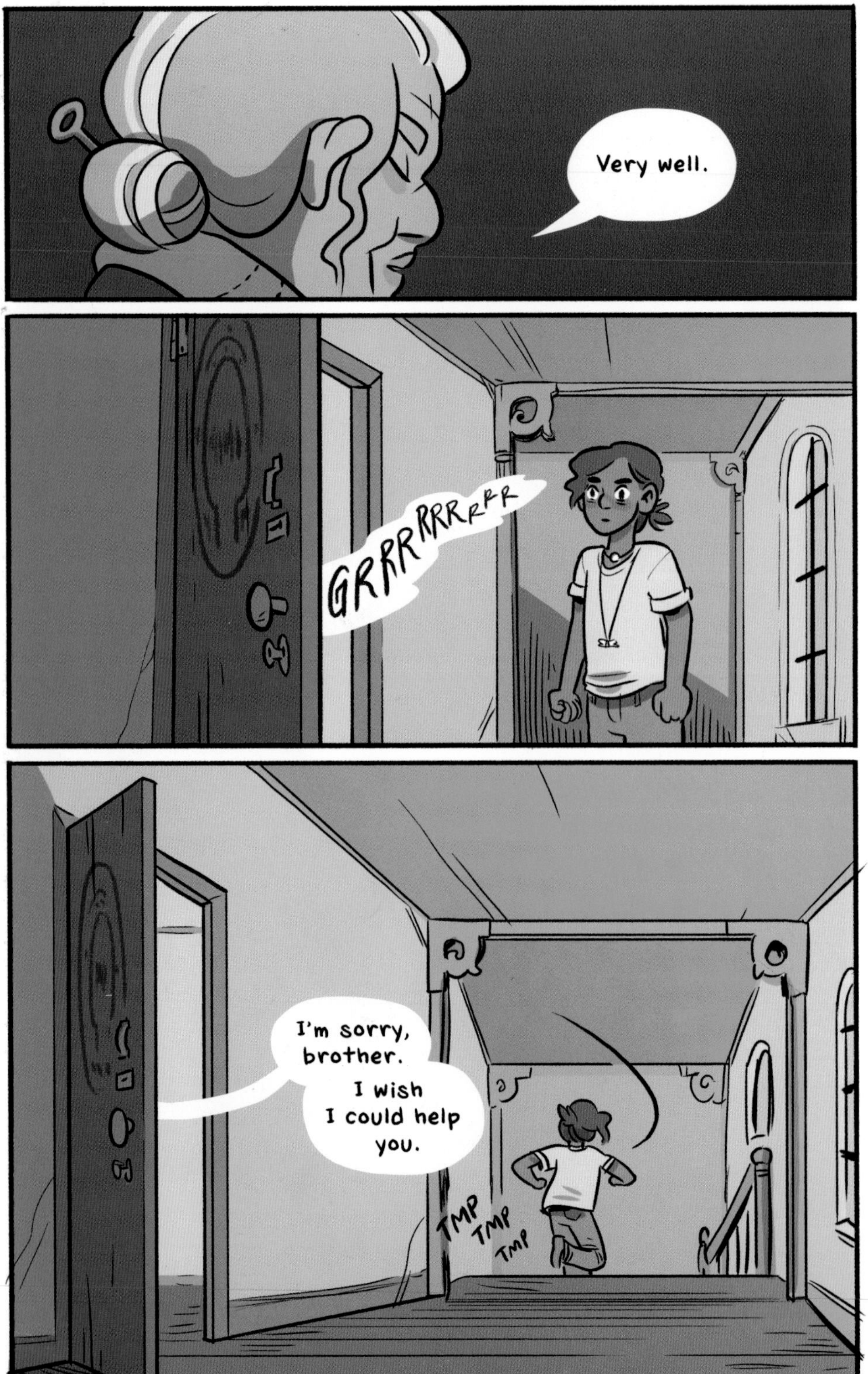
Very well.
GRRRRRRRRR
I'm sorry, brother.
I wish I could help you.
TMP TMP TMP

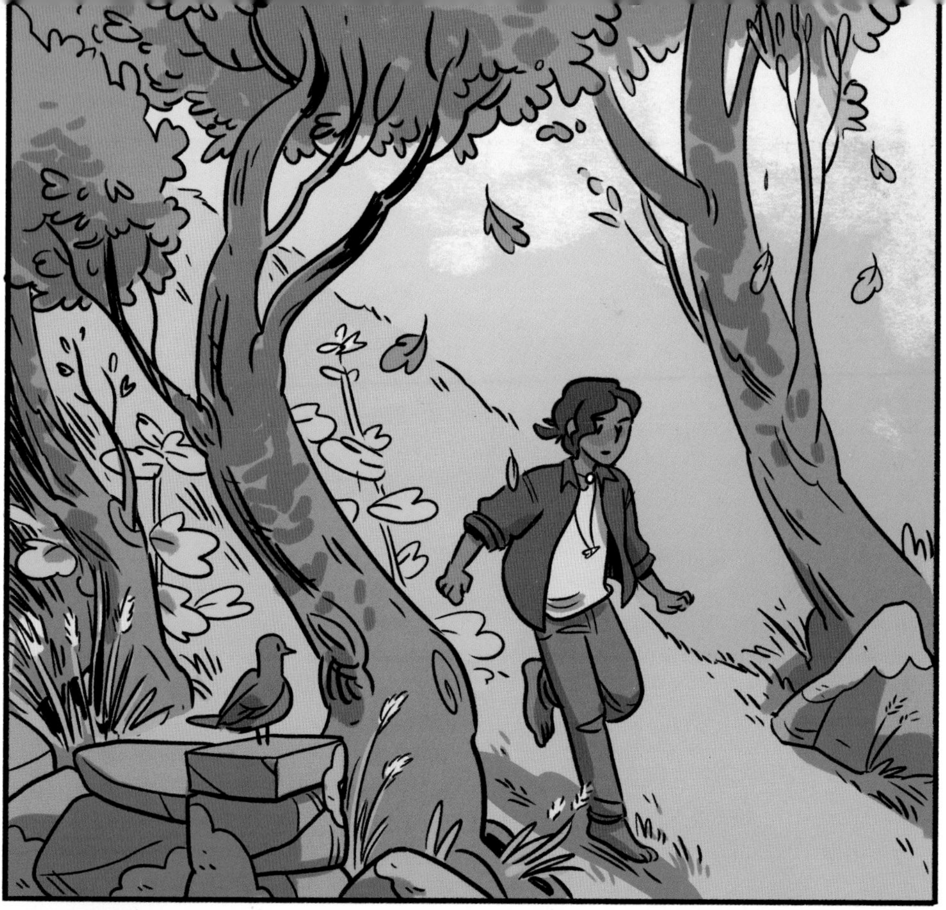

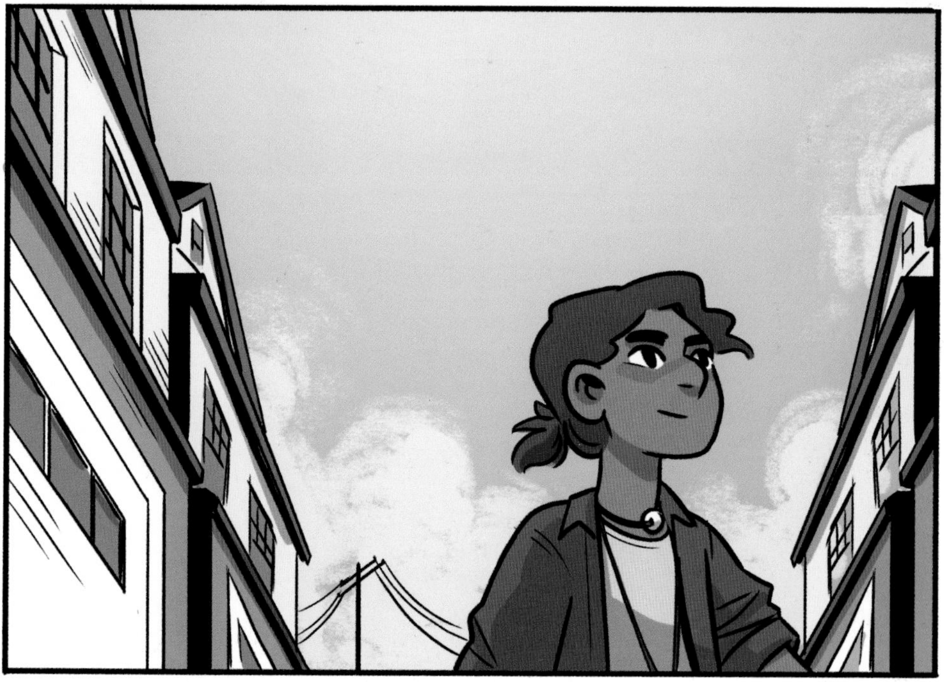

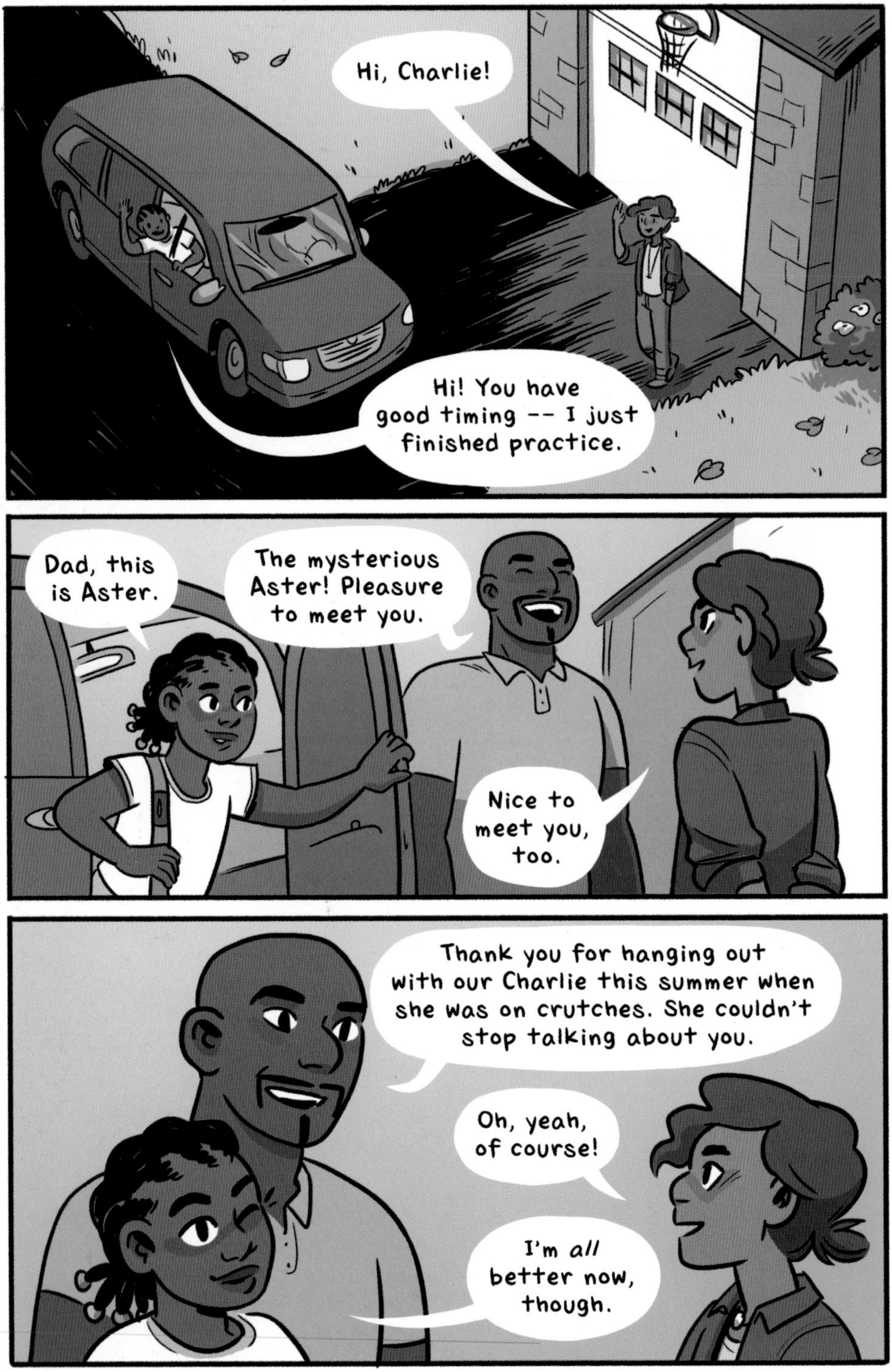
Hi, Charlie!
Hi! You have good timing -- I just finished practice.
Dad, this is Aster.
The mysterious Aster! Pleasure to meet you.
Nice to meet you, too.
Thank you for hanging out with our Charlie this summer when she was on crutches. She couldn't stop talking about you.
Oh, yeah, of course!
I'm *all* better now, though.

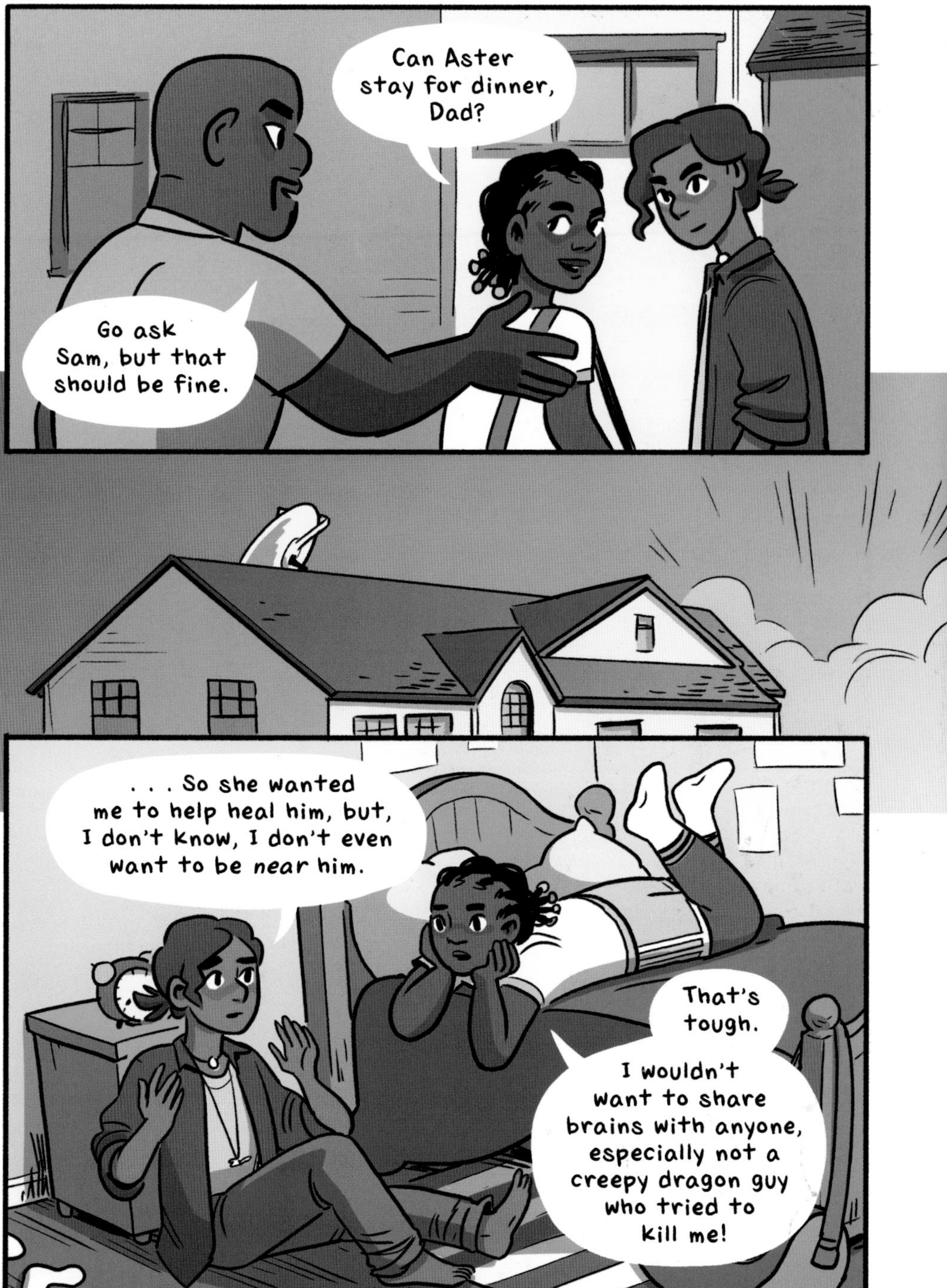
Can Aster stay for dinner, Dad?
Go ask Sam, but that should be fine.
. . . So she wanted me to help heal him, but, I don't know, I don't even want to be *near* him.
That's tough.
I wouldn't want to share brains with anyone, especially not a creepy dragon guy who tried to kill me!

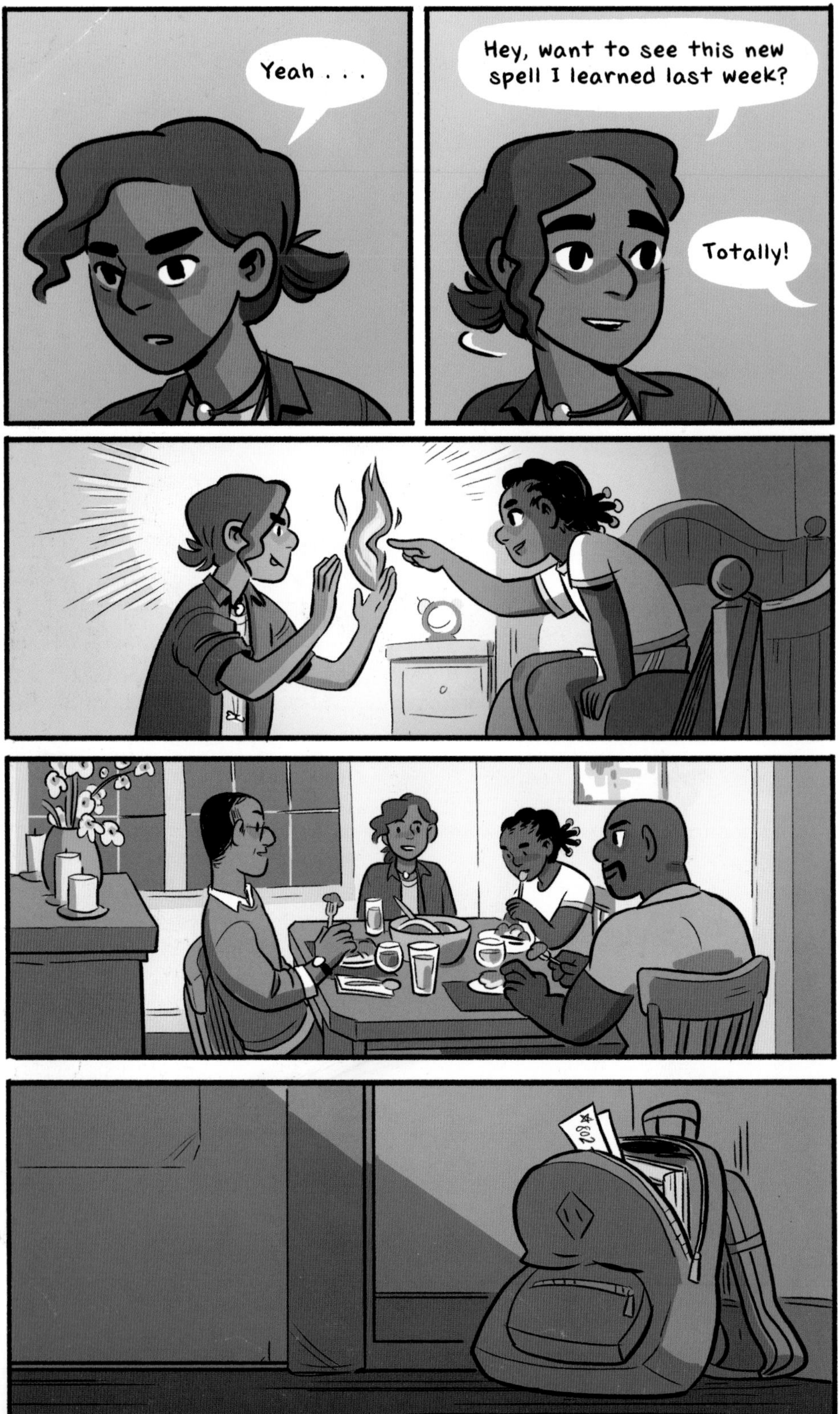
Yeah . . .
Hey, want to see this new spell I learned last week?
Totally!

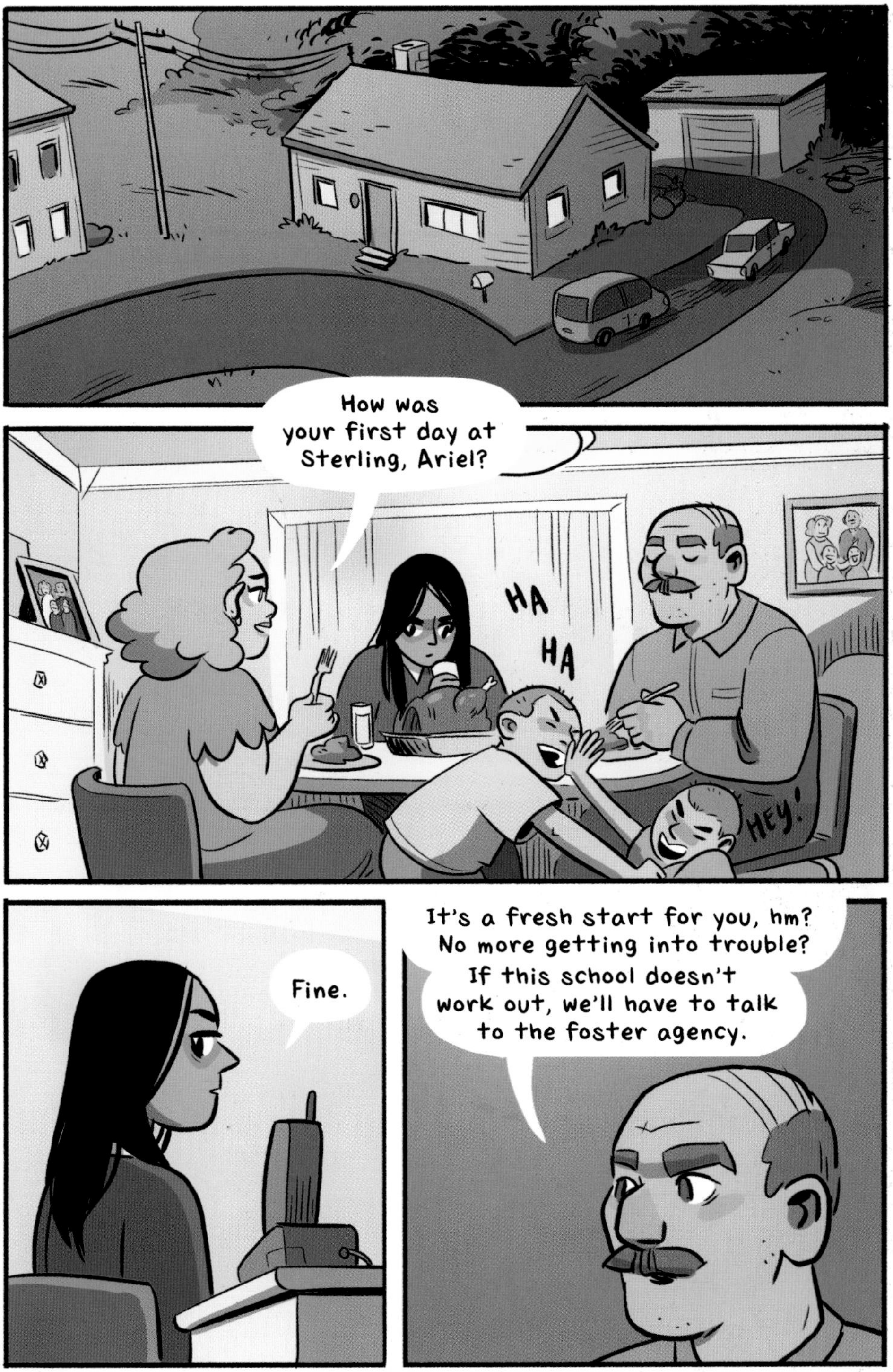
How was your first day at Sterling, Ariel?
HA HA
HEY!
Fine.
It's a fresh start for you, hm? No more getting into trouble? If this school doesn't work out, we'll have to talk to the foster agency.

I don't get into trouble. Trouble finds me.
Those boys *were* bullies, Hector.
Yeah, it wasn't my fault.
I didn't do anything to them.
Hm.
You think you might make a few friends at this school?
Maybe . . .

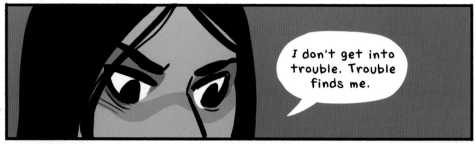

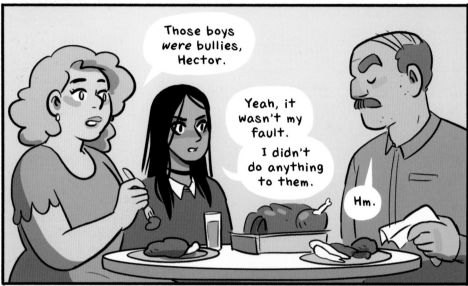

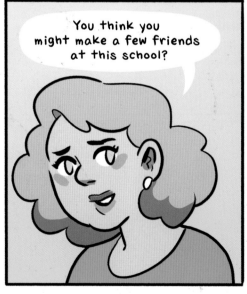

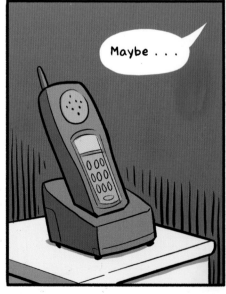

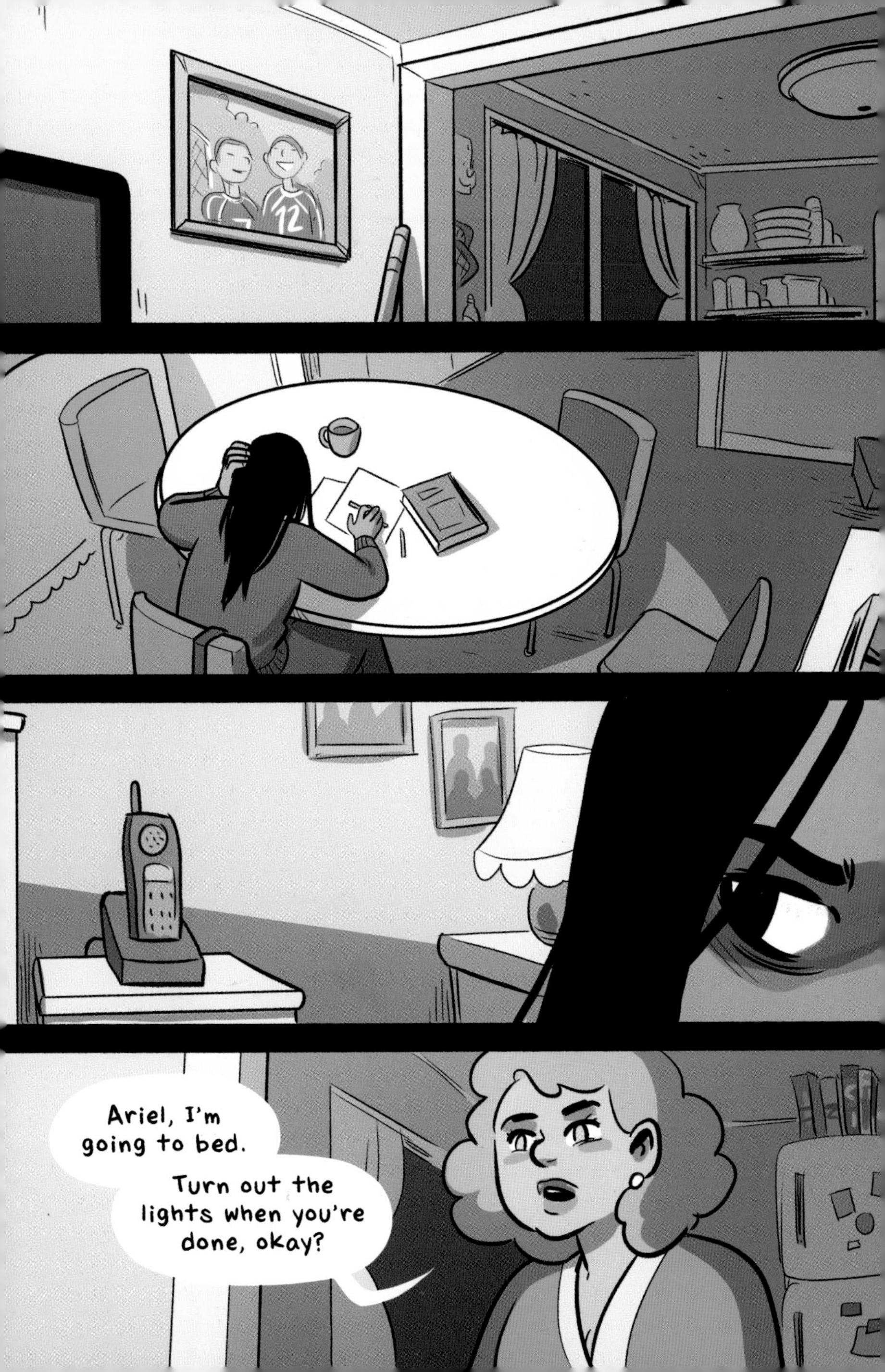
12
Ariel, I'm going to bed.
Turn out the lights when you're done, okay?

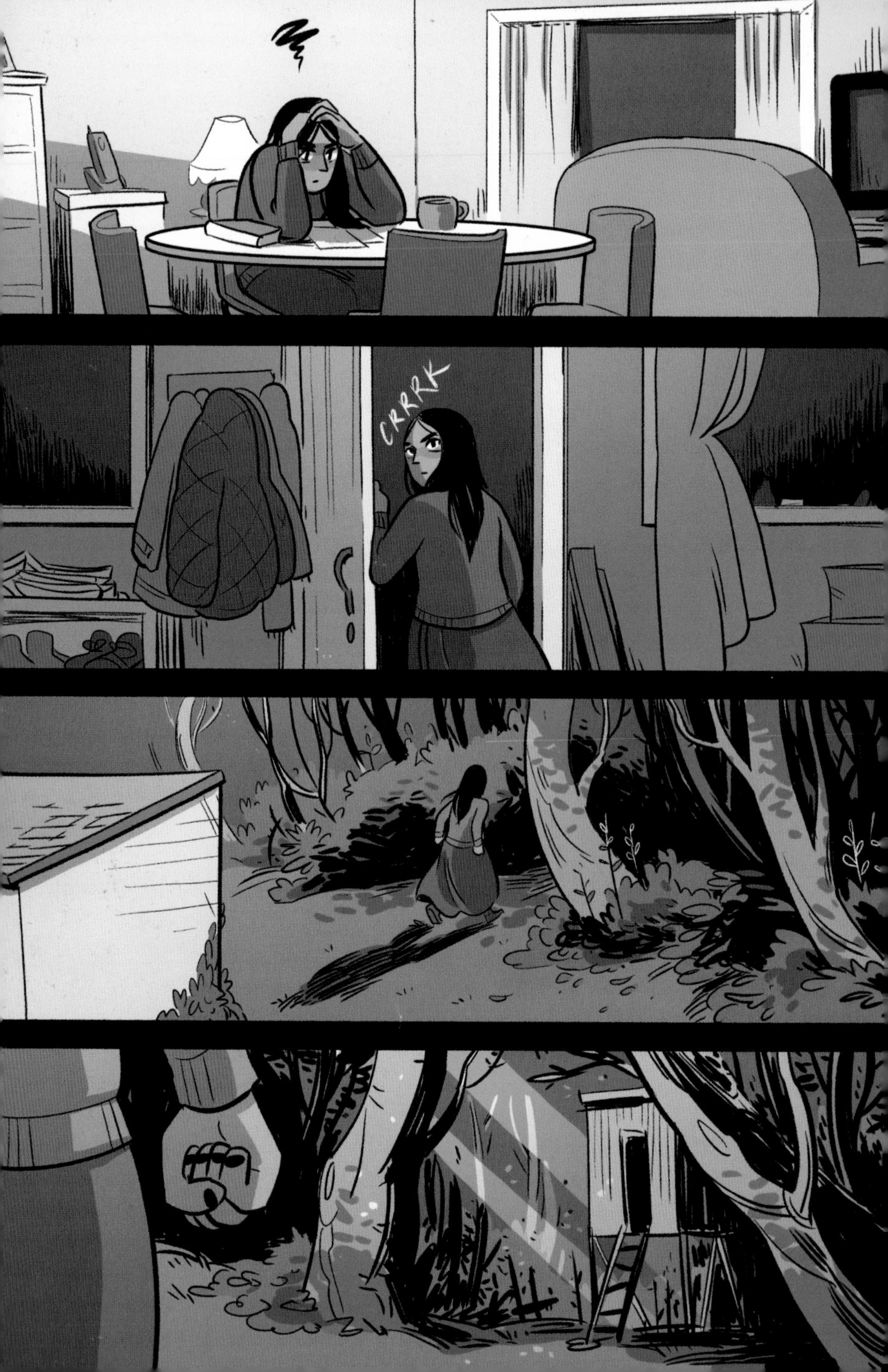
CRRRK

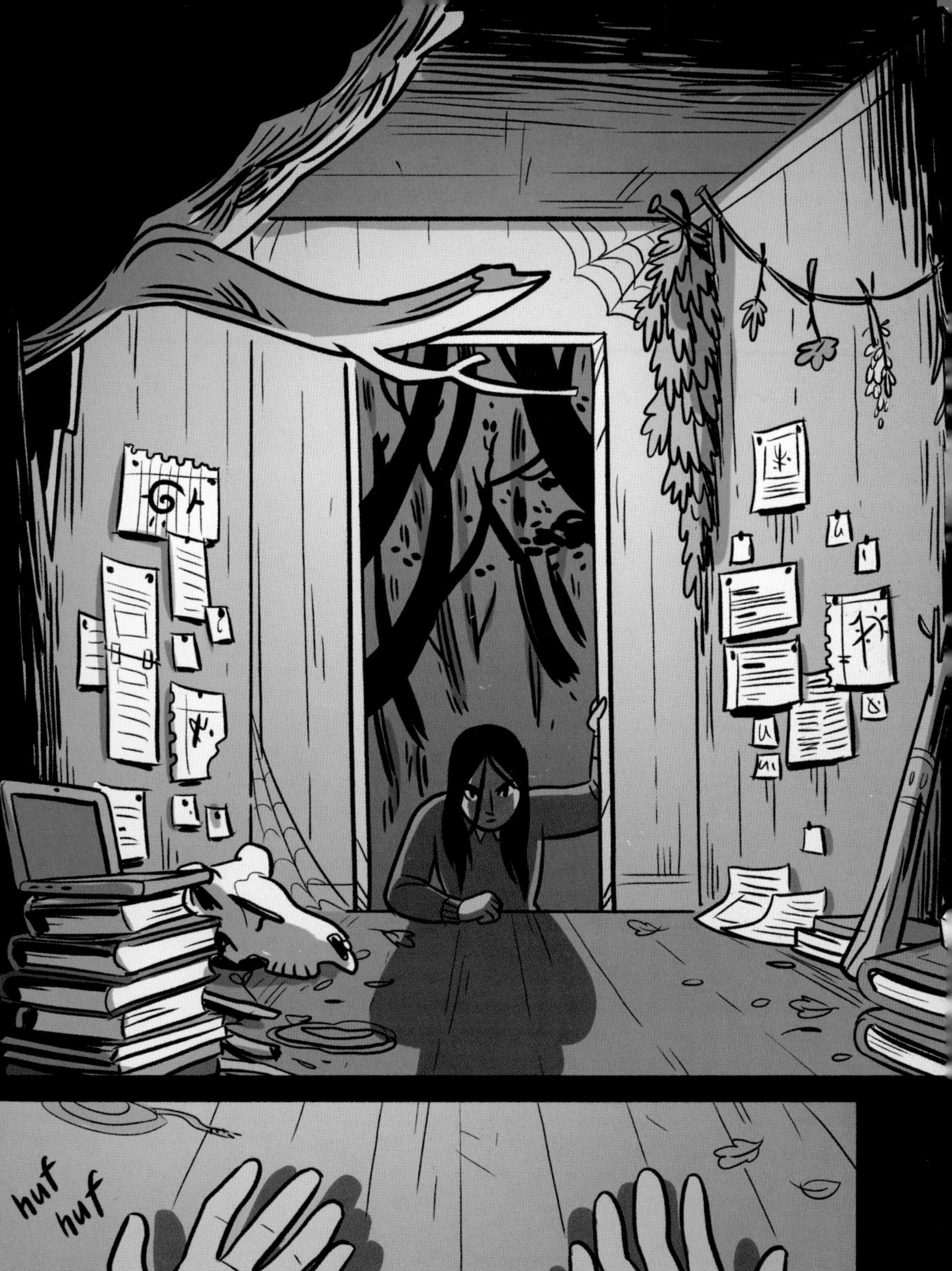

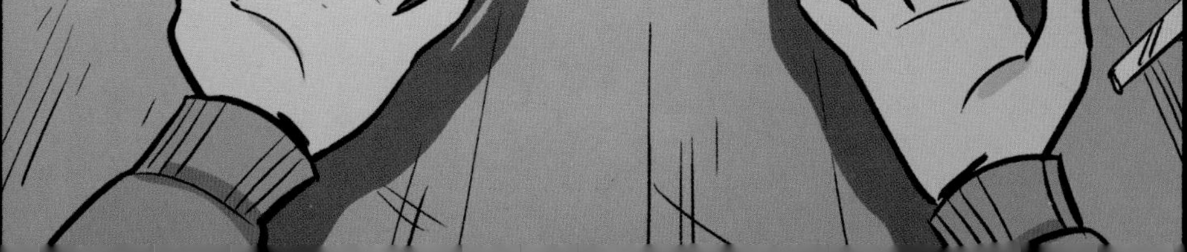
huf
huf

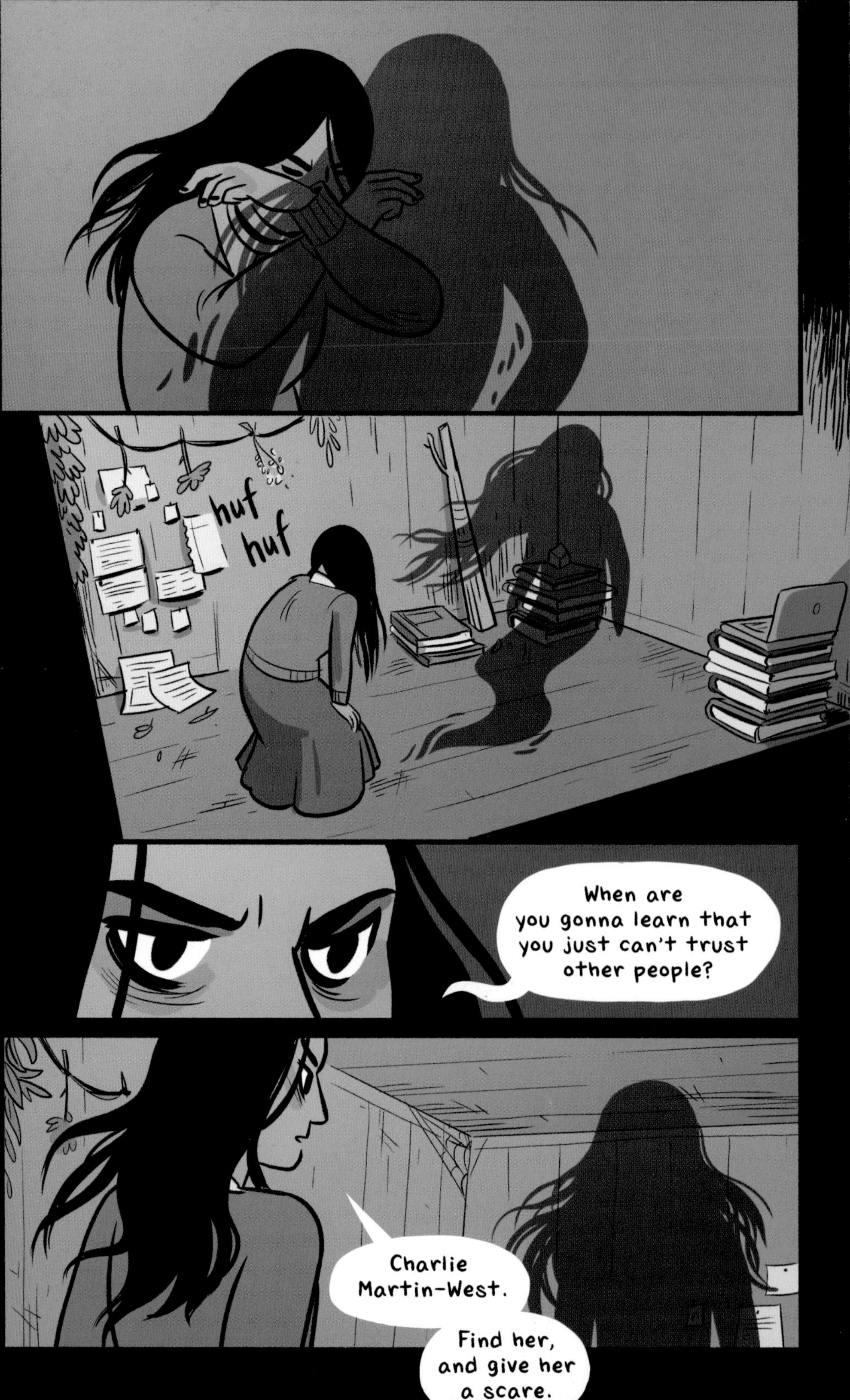
huf
huf
When are you gonna learn that you just can't trust other people?
Charlie Martin-West.
Find her, and give her a scare.

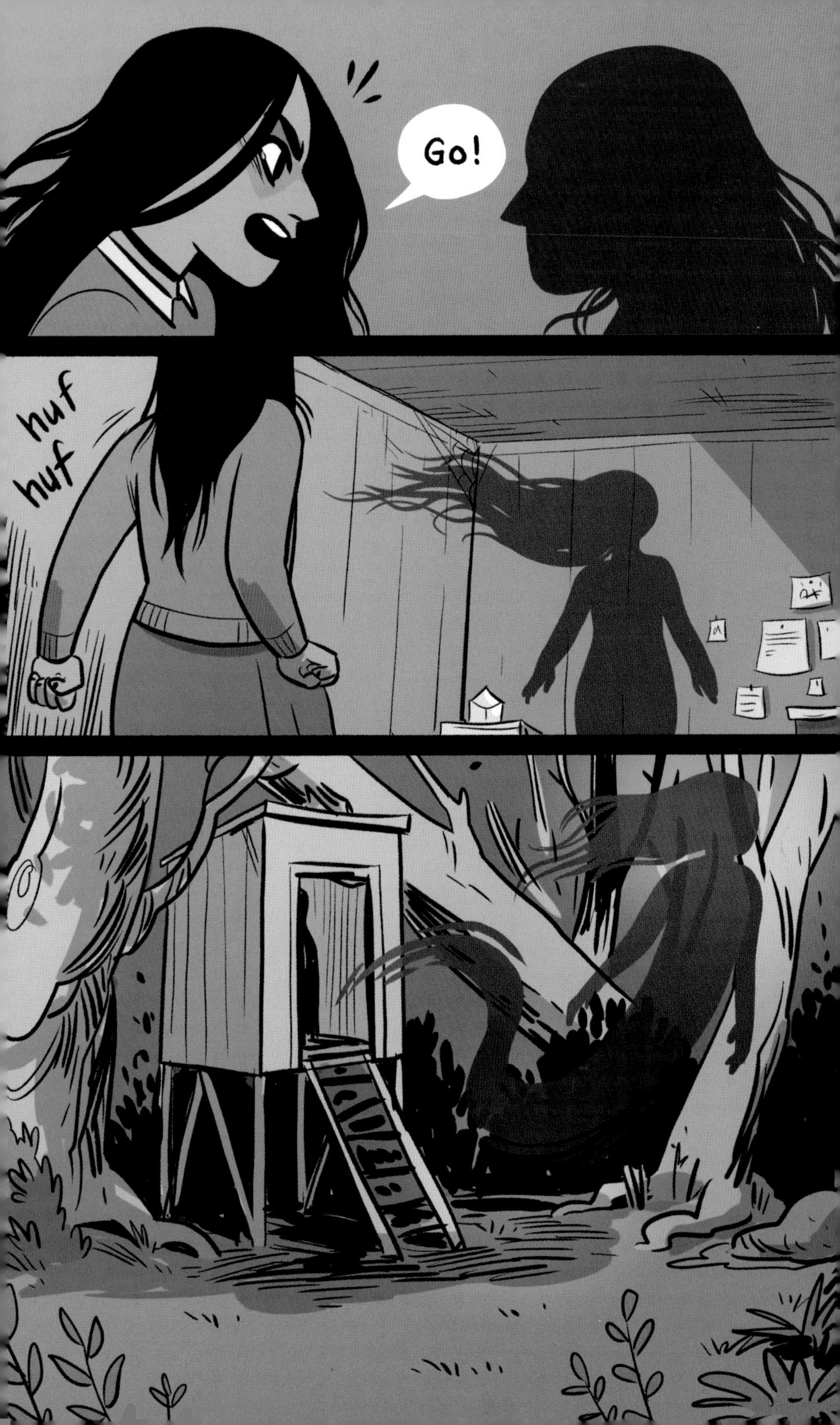
Go!
huf
huf

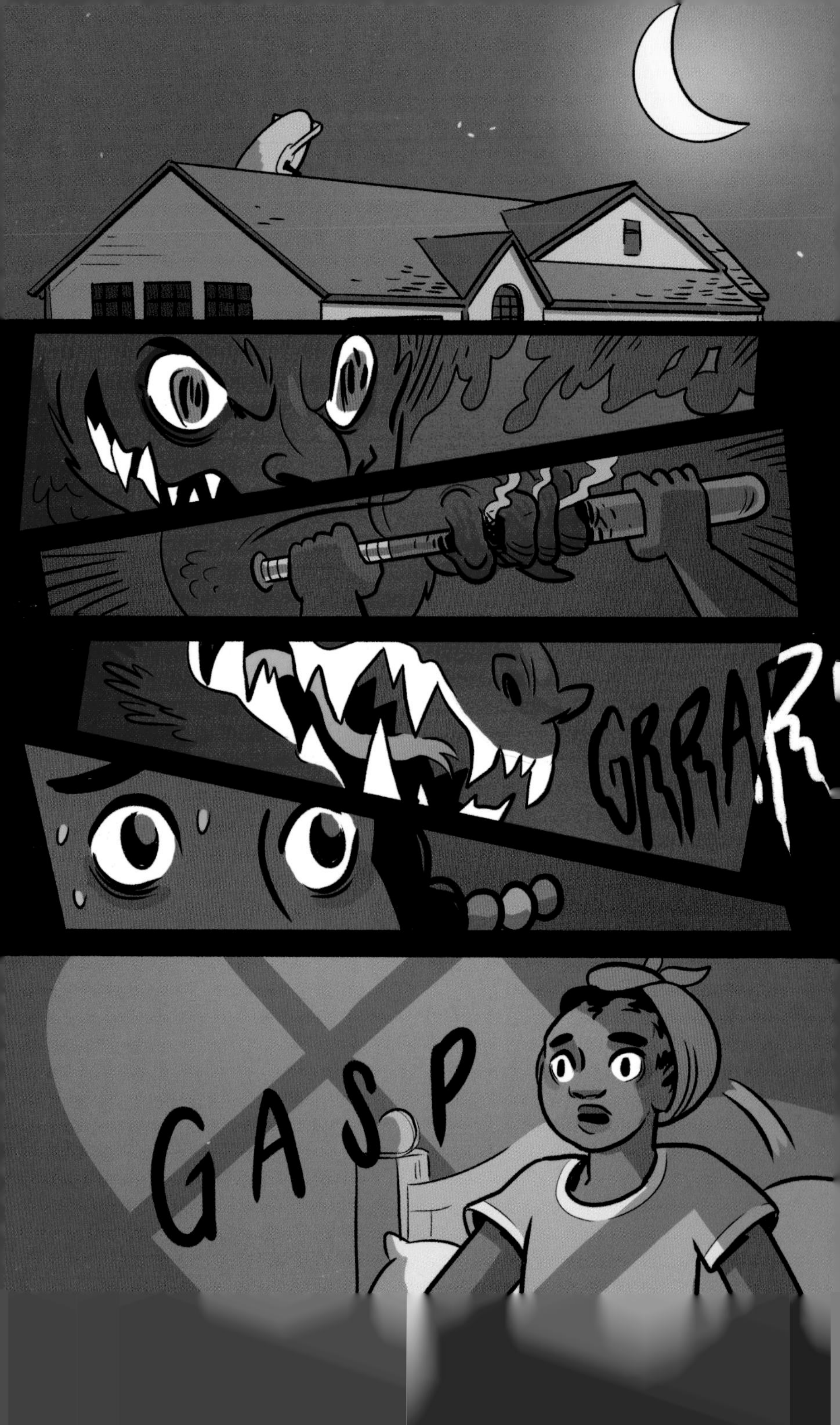
GRRAR!
GASP

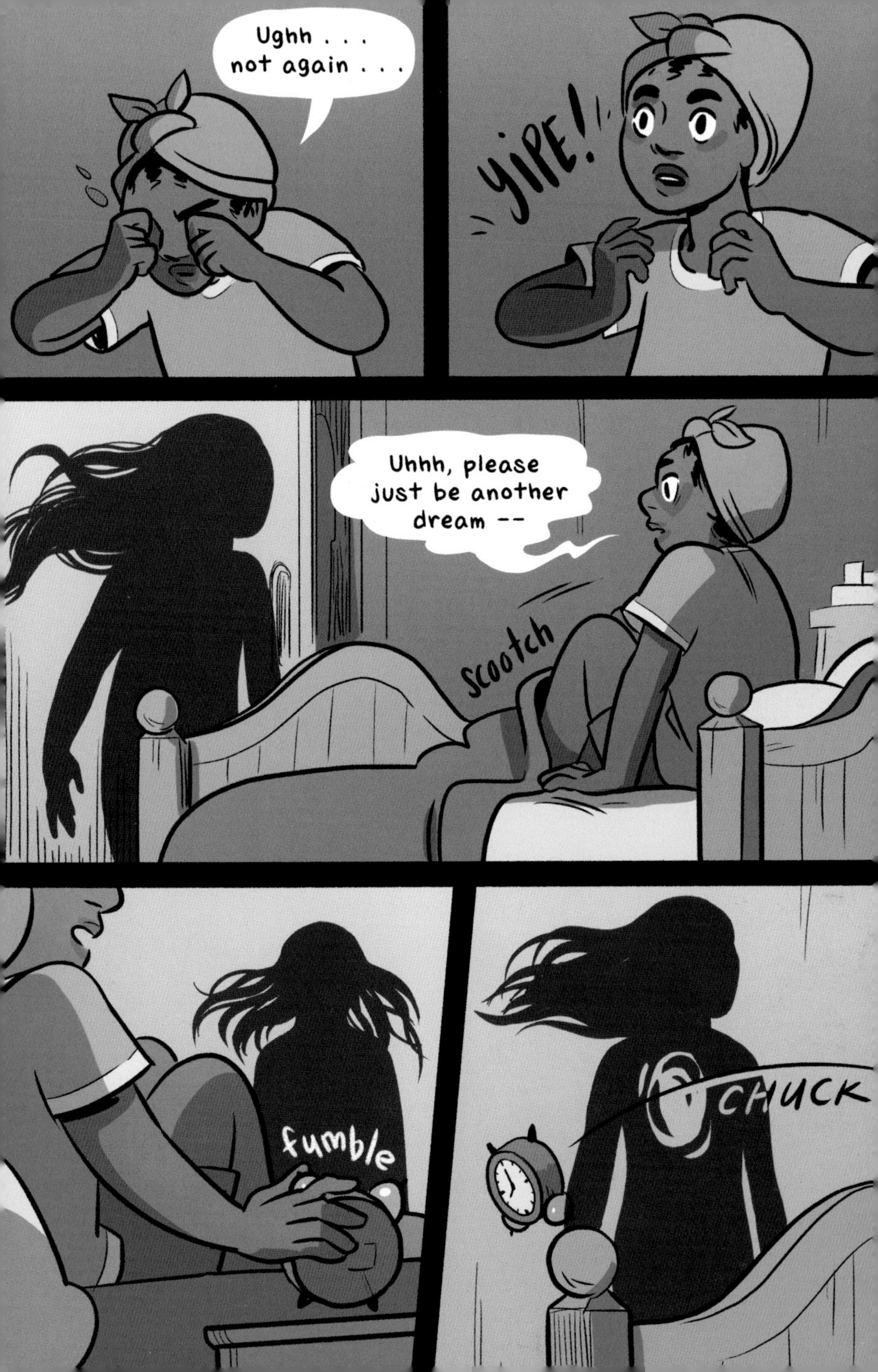
Ughh . . .
not again . . .
YIPE!
Uhhh, please
just be another
dream --
scootch
fumble
CHUCK

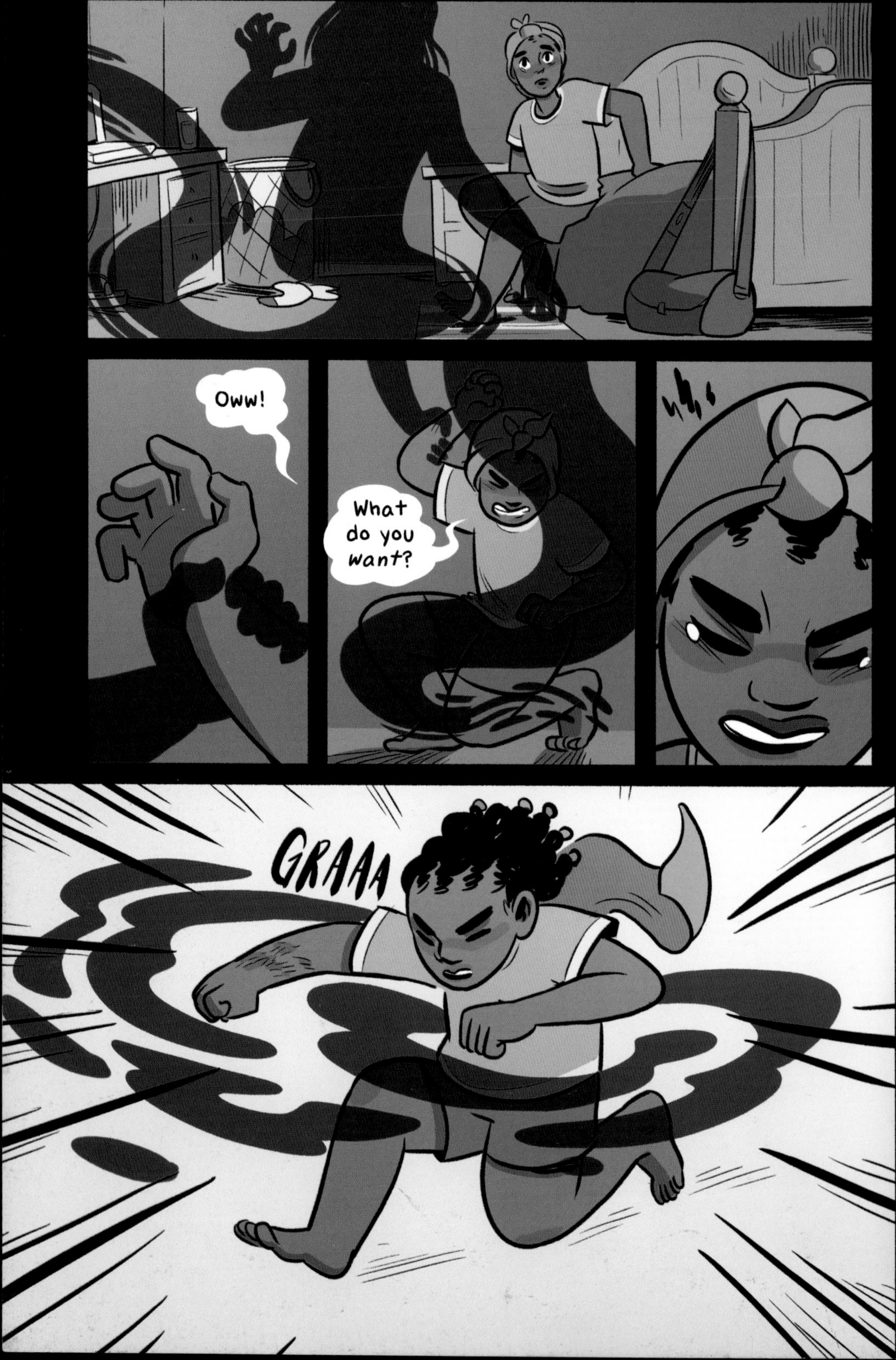
Oww!
What do you want?
GRAAA

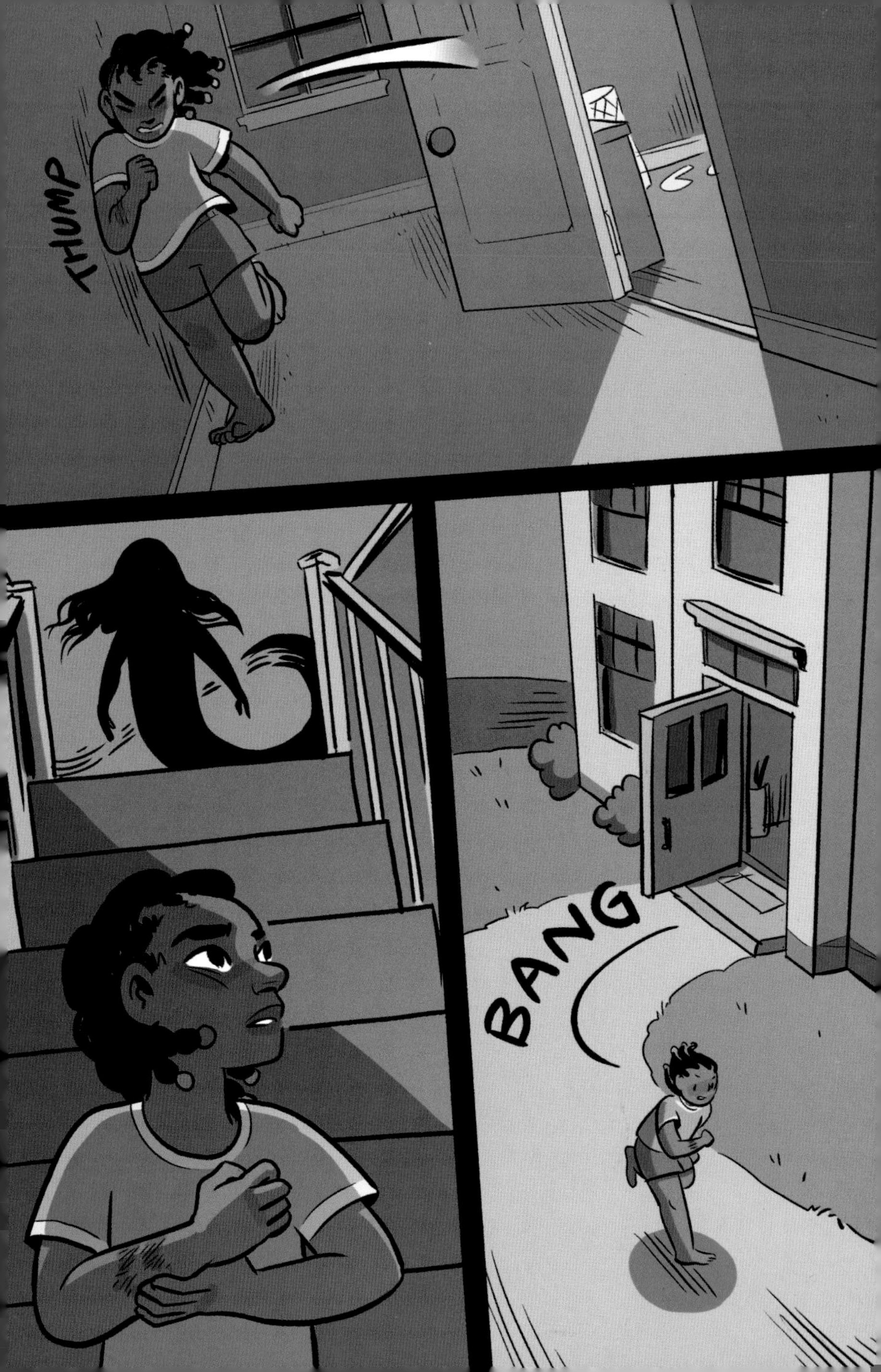
THUMP
BANG

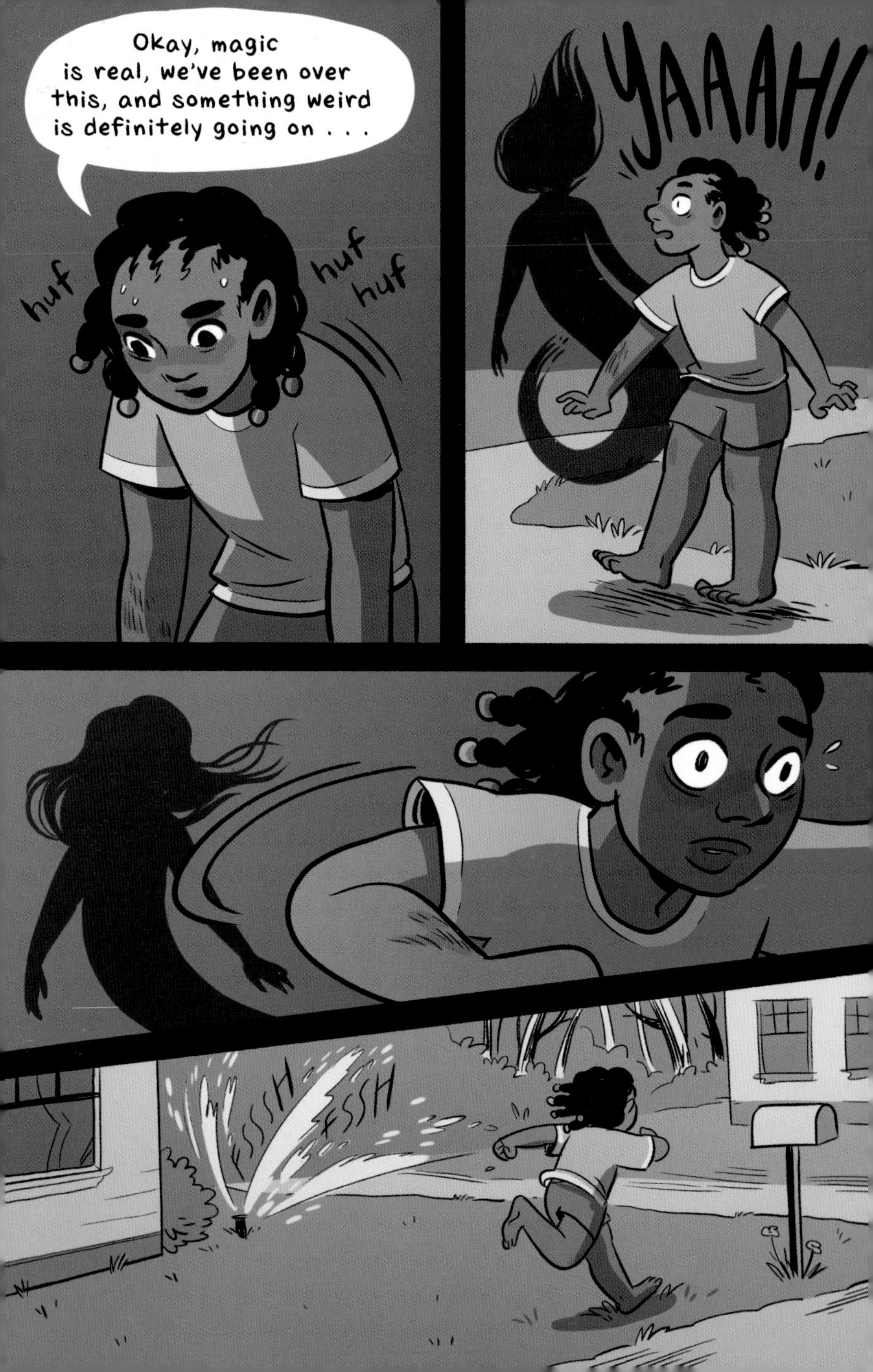
Okay, magic is real, we've been over this, and something weird is definitely going on . . .
huf
huf
huf
YAAAH!
FSSSH
FSSH

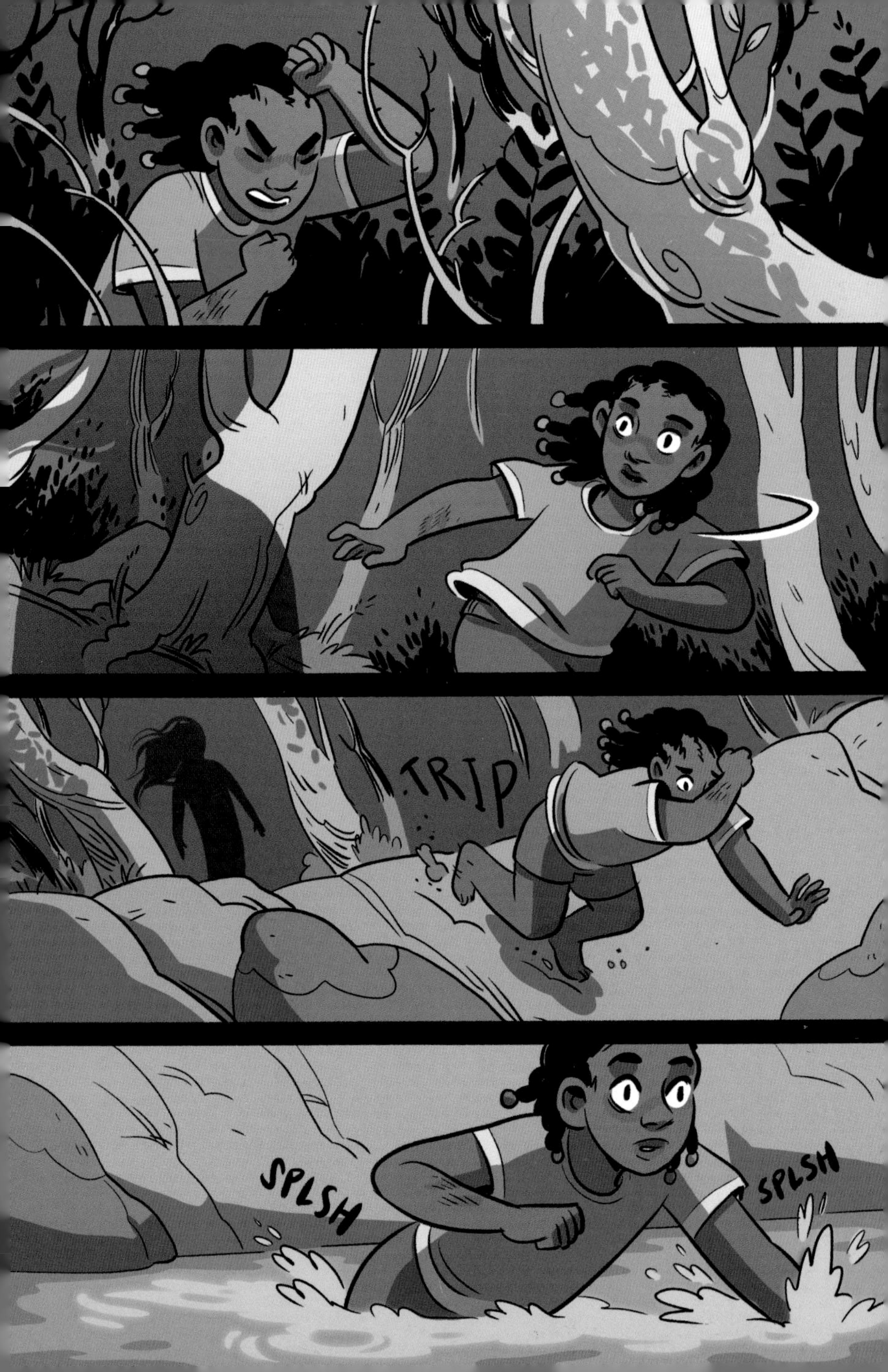
TRIP
SPLSH
SPLSH

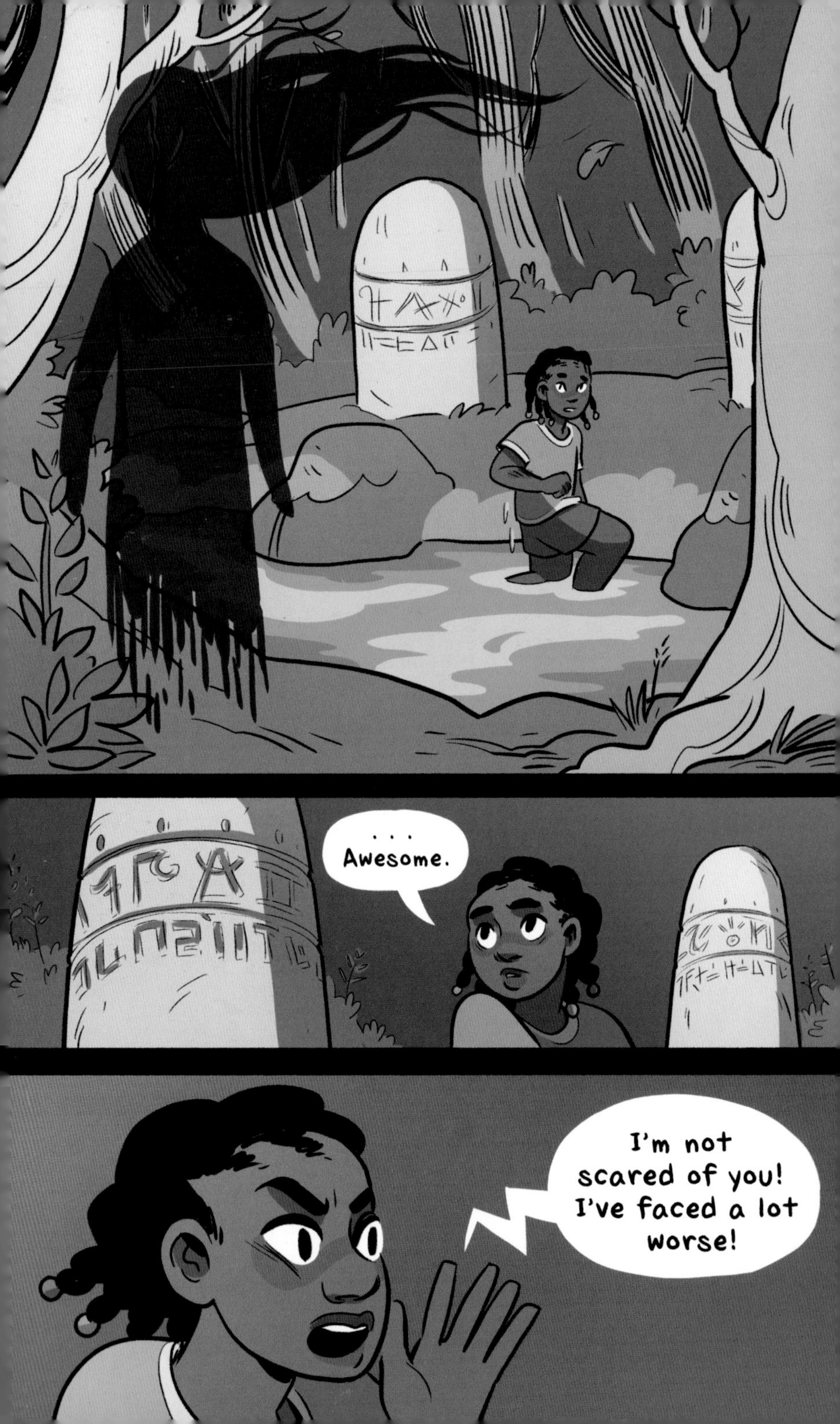
. . . Awesome.
I'm not scared of you! I've faced a lot worse!

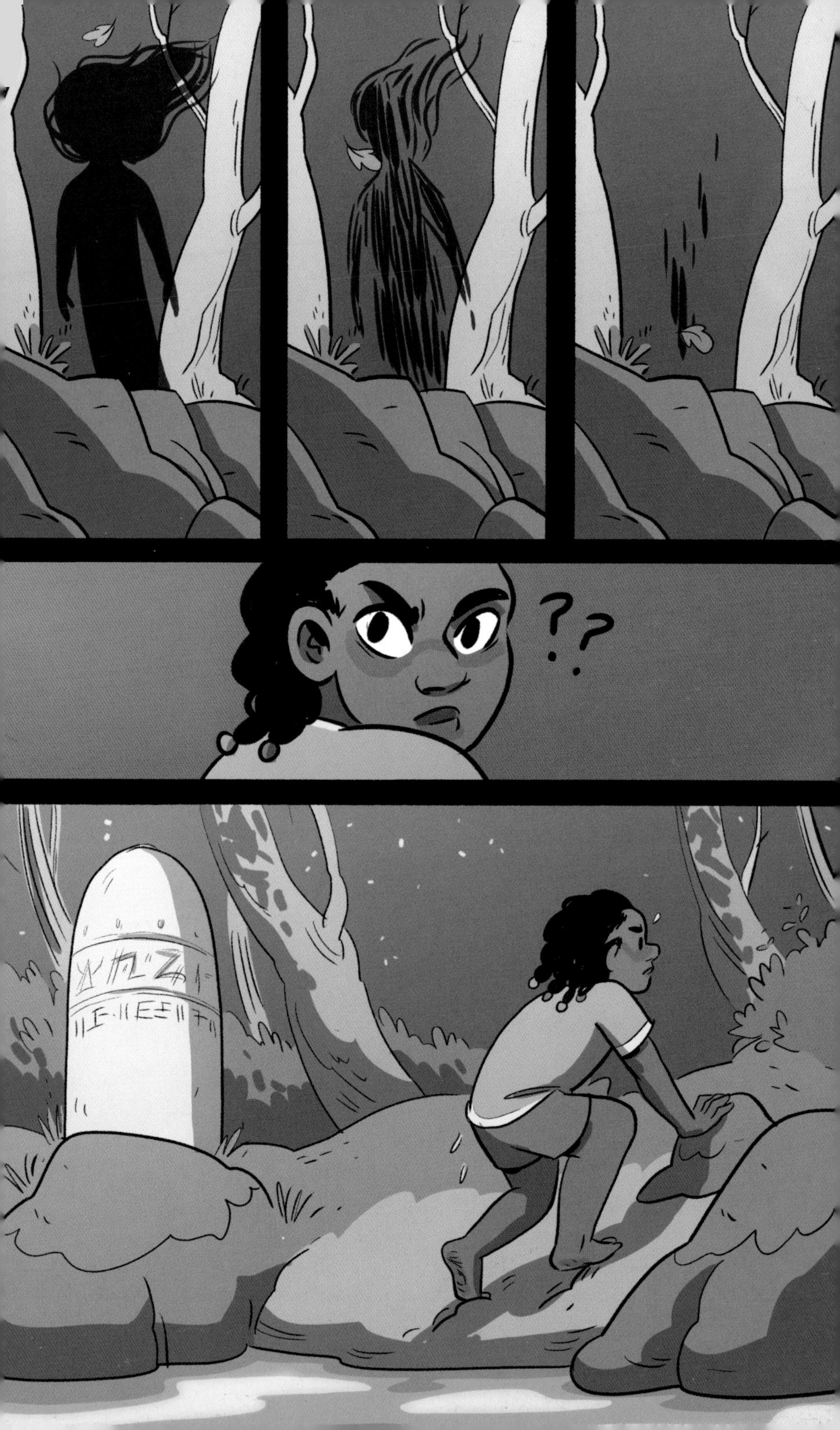
??

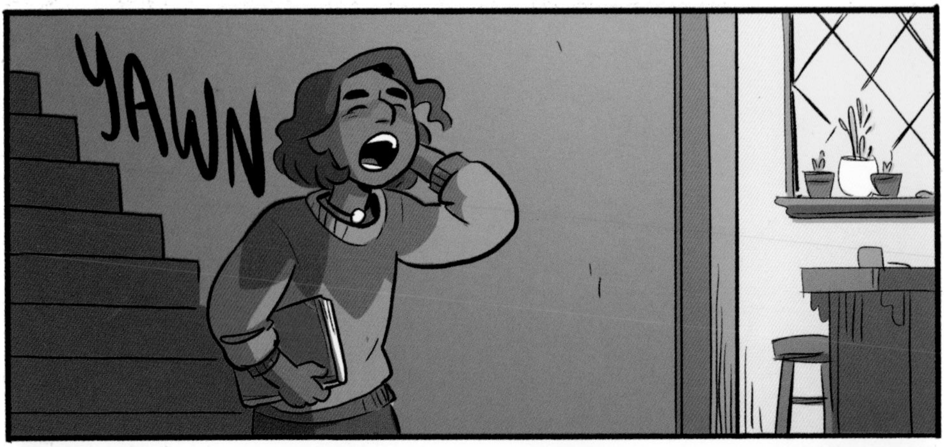
YAWN

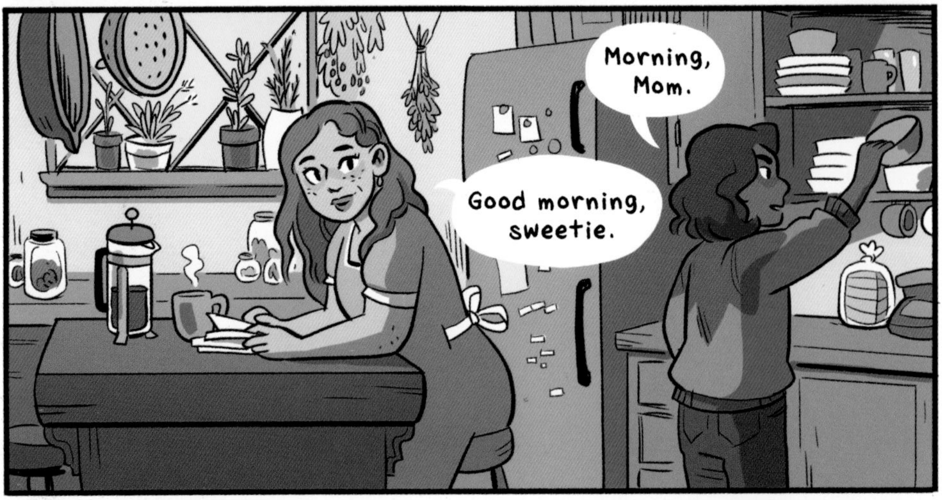
Morning, Mom.
Good morning, sweetie.

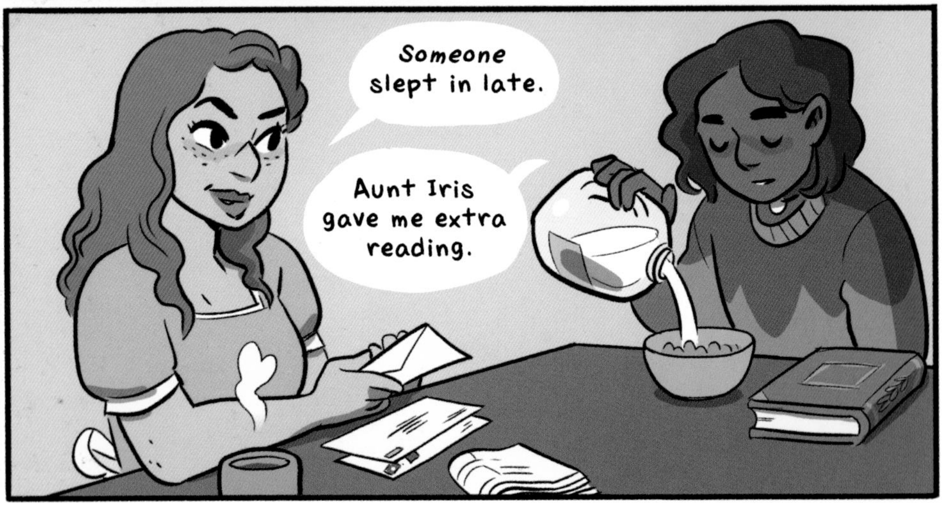
Someone slept in late.
Aunt Iris gave me extra reading.

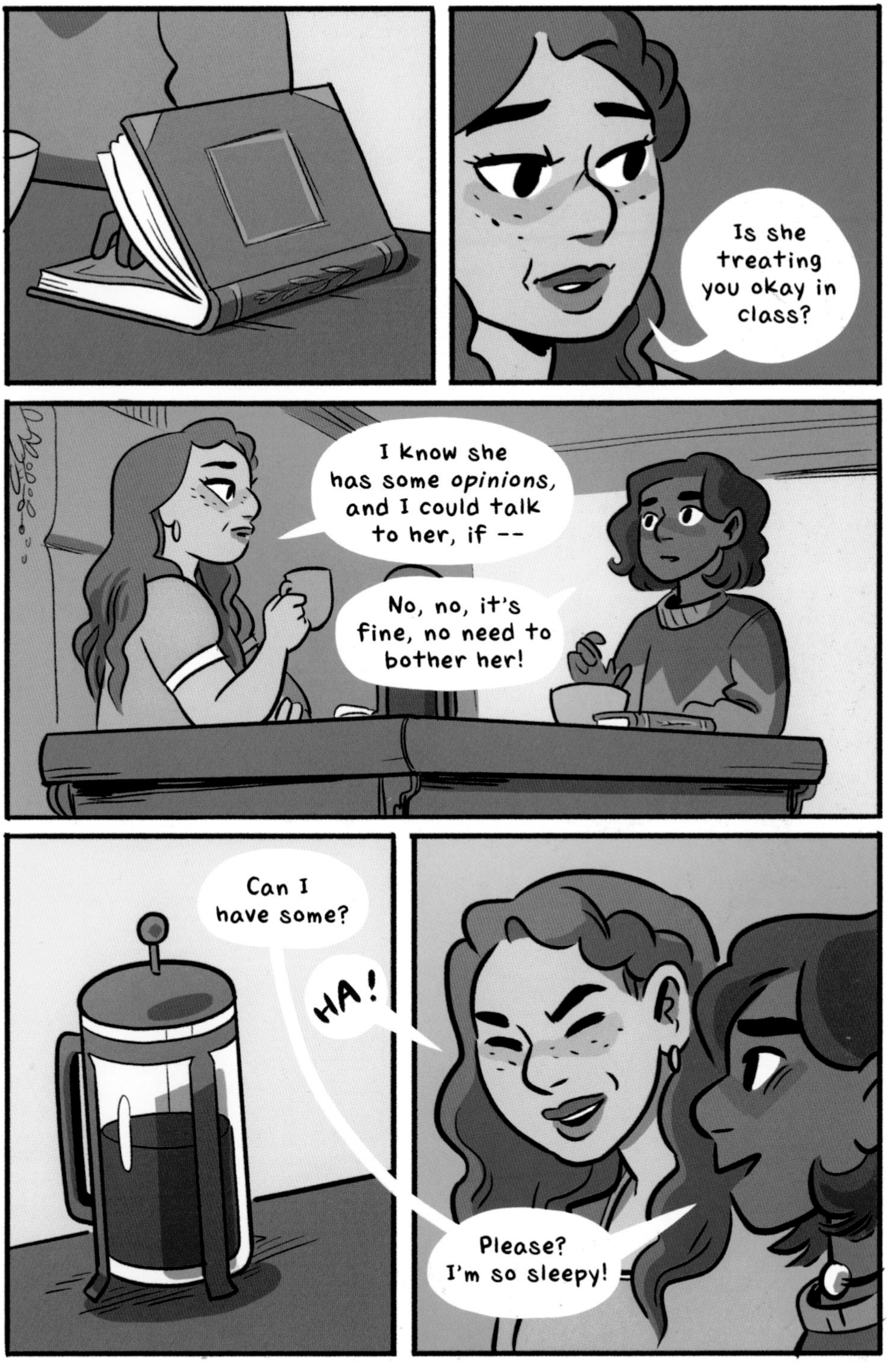
Is she treating you okay in class?
I know she has some *opinions*, and I could talk to her, if --
No, no, it's fine, no need to bother her!
Can I have some?
HA!
Please? I'm so sleepy!

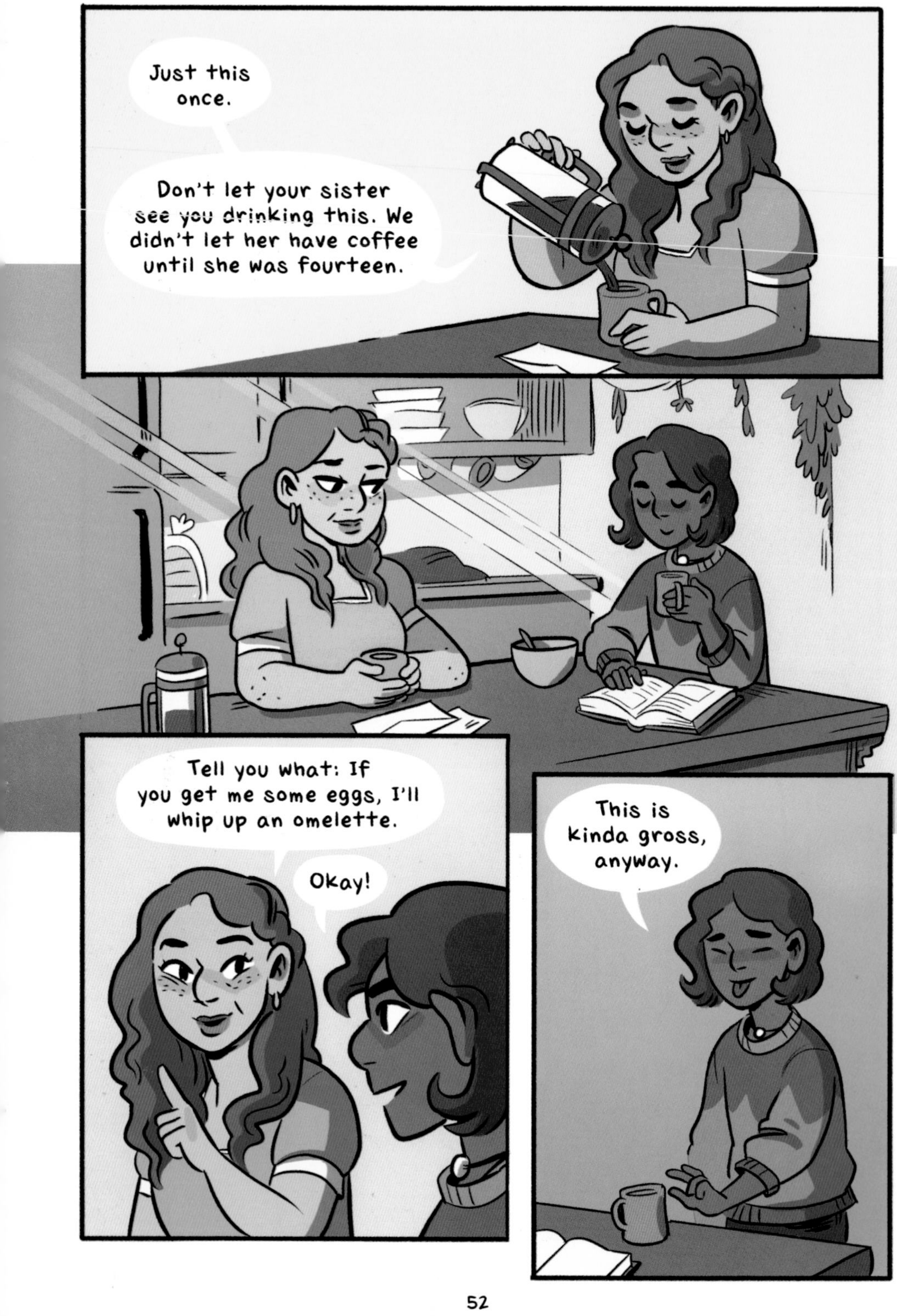
Just this once.
Don't let your sister see you drinking this. We didn't let her have coffee until she was fourteen.
Tell you what: If you get me some eggs, I'll whip up an omelette.
Okay!
This is kinda gross, anyway.

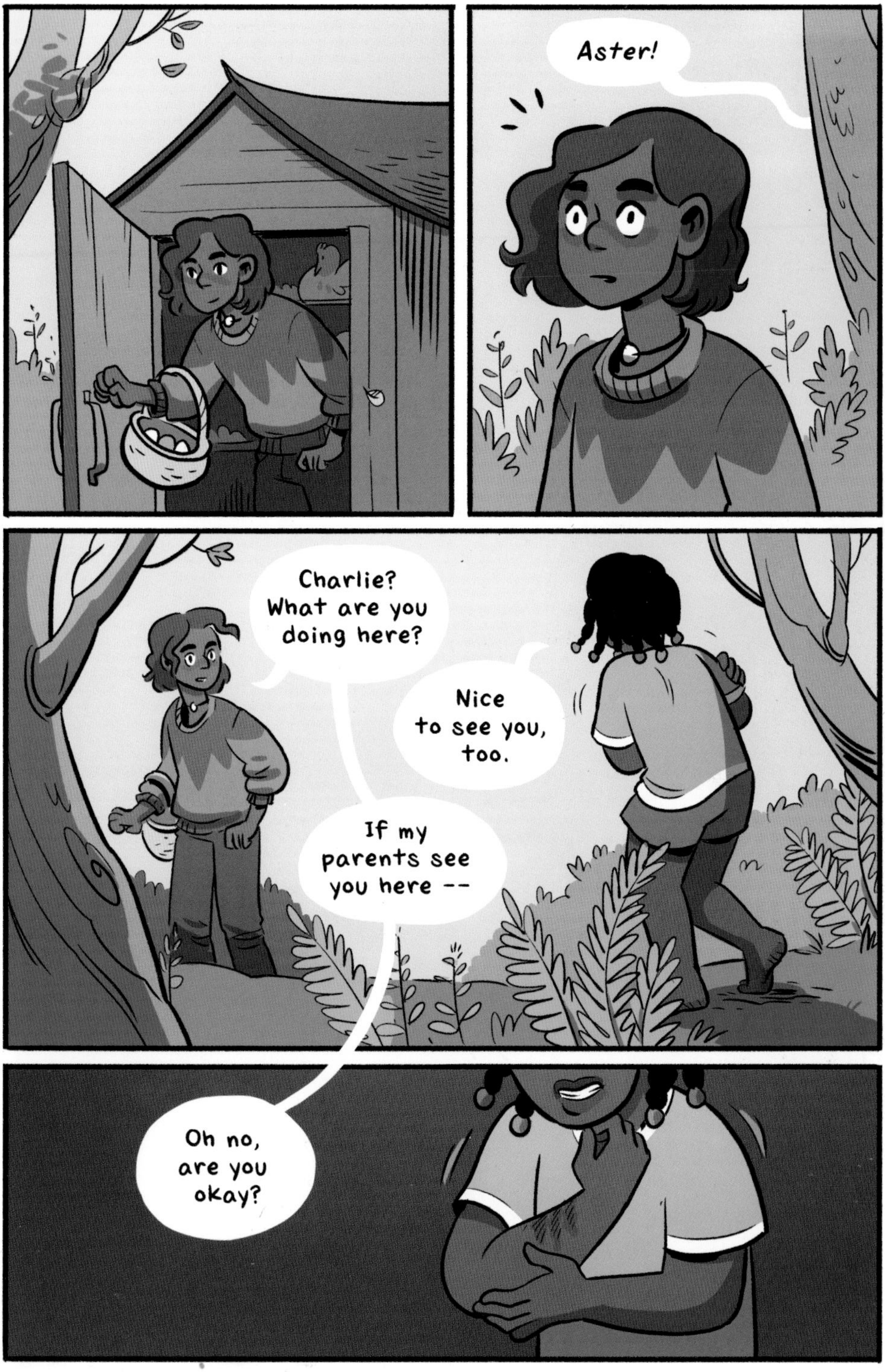
Aster!
Charlie? What are you doing here?
Nice to see you, too.
If my parents see you here --
Oh no, are you okay?

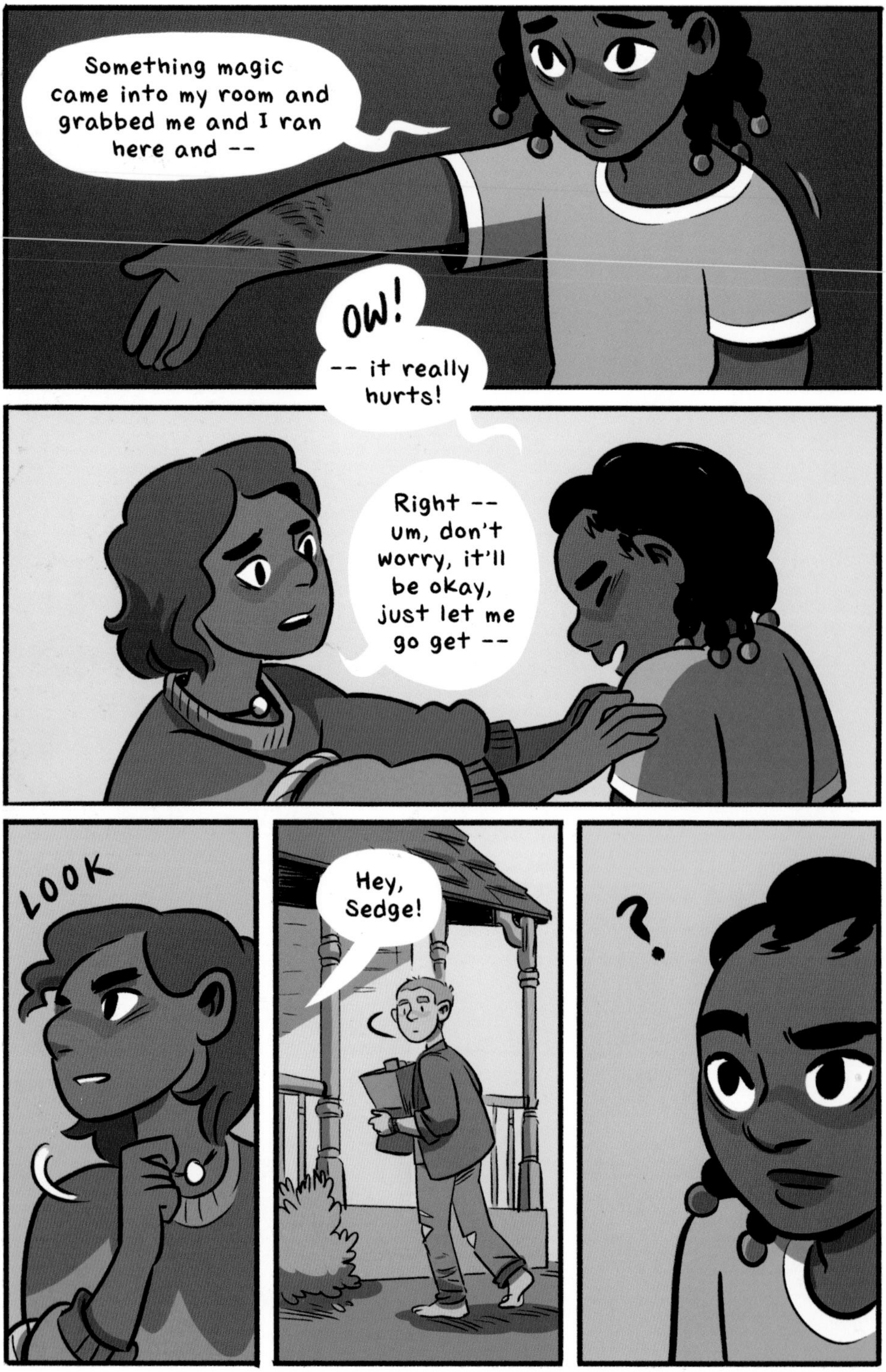
Something magic came into my room and grabbed me and I ran here and --
OW!
-- it really hurts!
Right -- um, don't worry, it'll be okay, just let me go get --
LOOK
Hey, Sedge!
?

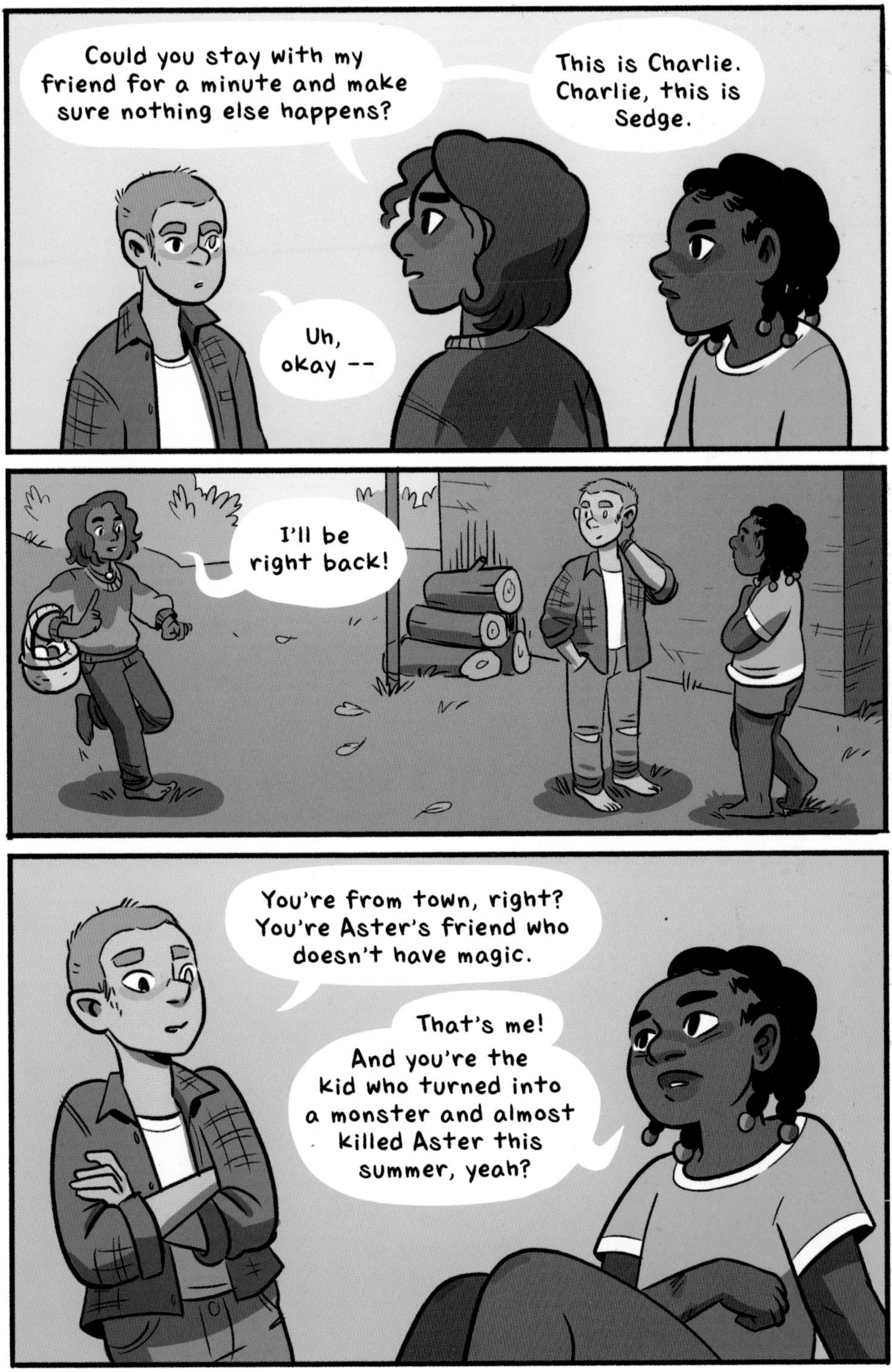
Could you stay with my friend for a minute and make sure nothing else happens?
This is Charlie. Charlie, this is Sedge.
Uh, okay --
I'll be right back!
You're from town, right? You're Aster's friend who doesn't have magic.
That's me!
And you're the kid who turned into a monster and almost killed Aster this summer, yeah?

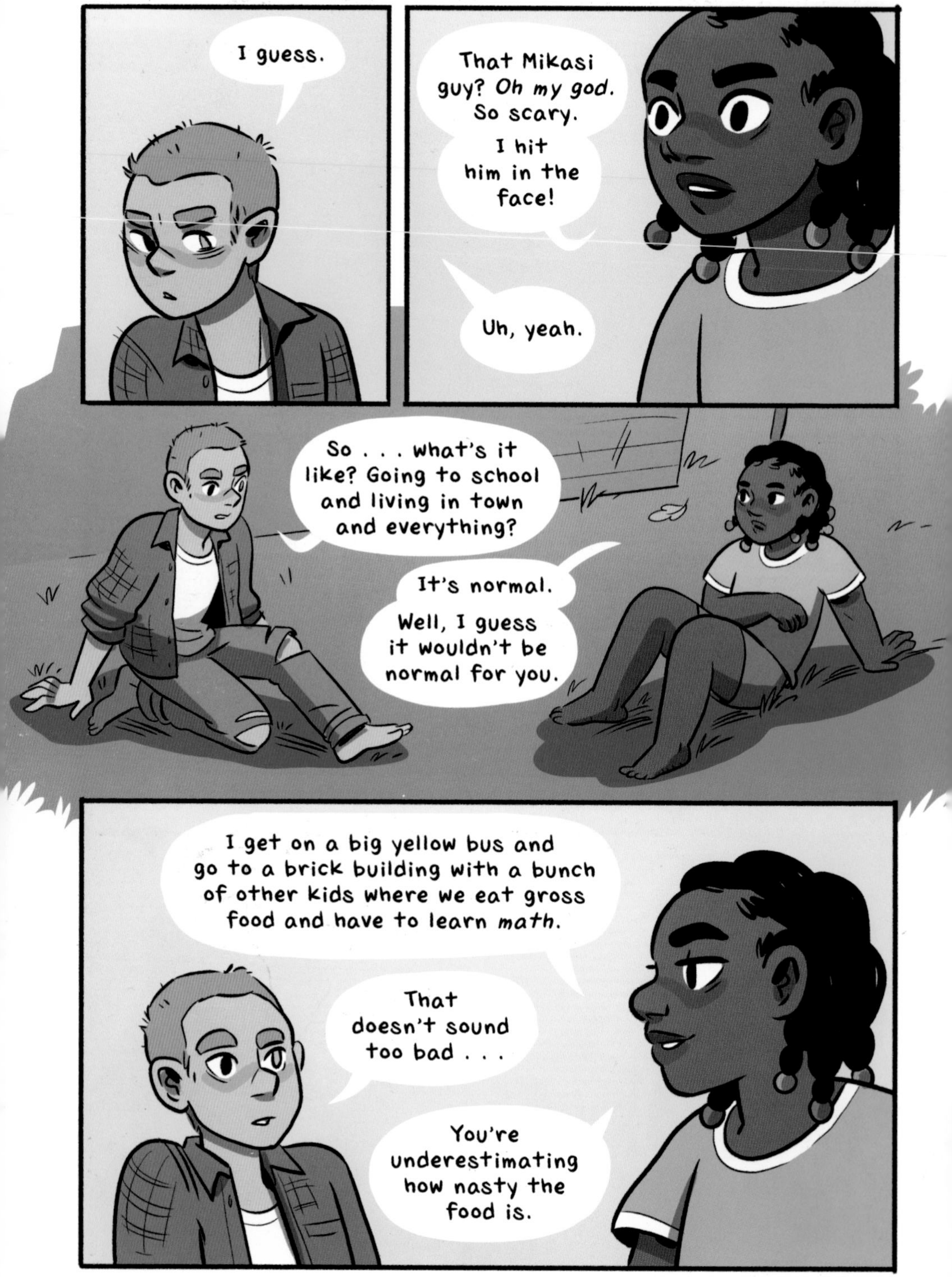
I guess.
That Mikasi guy? *Oh my god.* So scary.
I hit him in the face!
Uh, yeah.
So . . . what's it like? Going to school and living in town and everything?
It's normal.
Well, I guess it wouldn't be normal for you.
I get on a big yellow bus and go to a brick building with a bunch of other kids where we eat gross food and have to learn *math*.
That doesn't sound too bad . . .
You're underestimating how nasty the food is.

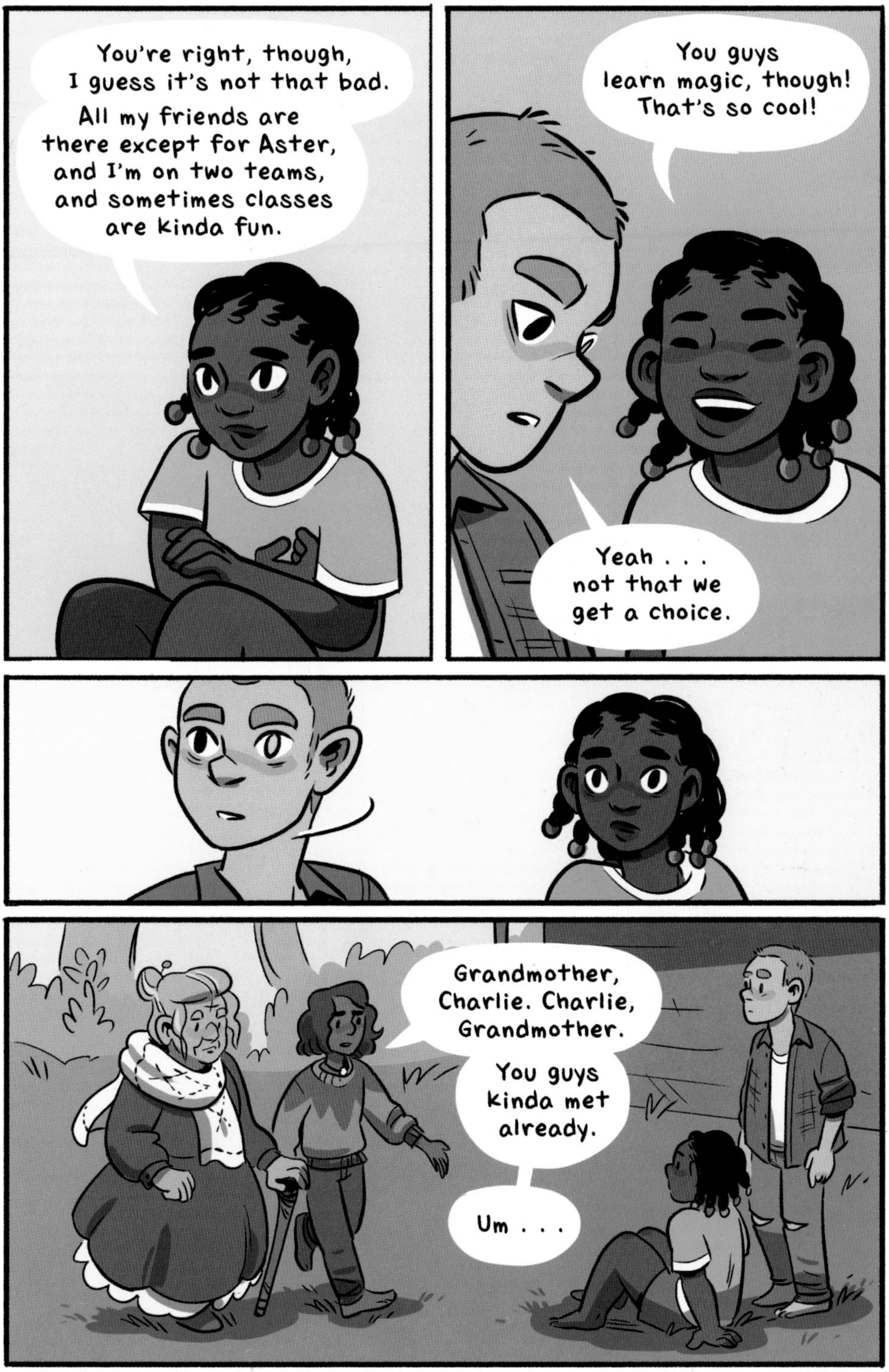
You're right, though, I guess it's not that bad.
All my friends are there except for Aster, and I'm on two teams, and sometimes classes are kinda fun.
You guys learn magic, though! That's so cool!
Yeah . . . not that we get a choice.
Grandmother, Charlie. Charlie, Grandmother.
You guys kinda met already.
Um . . .

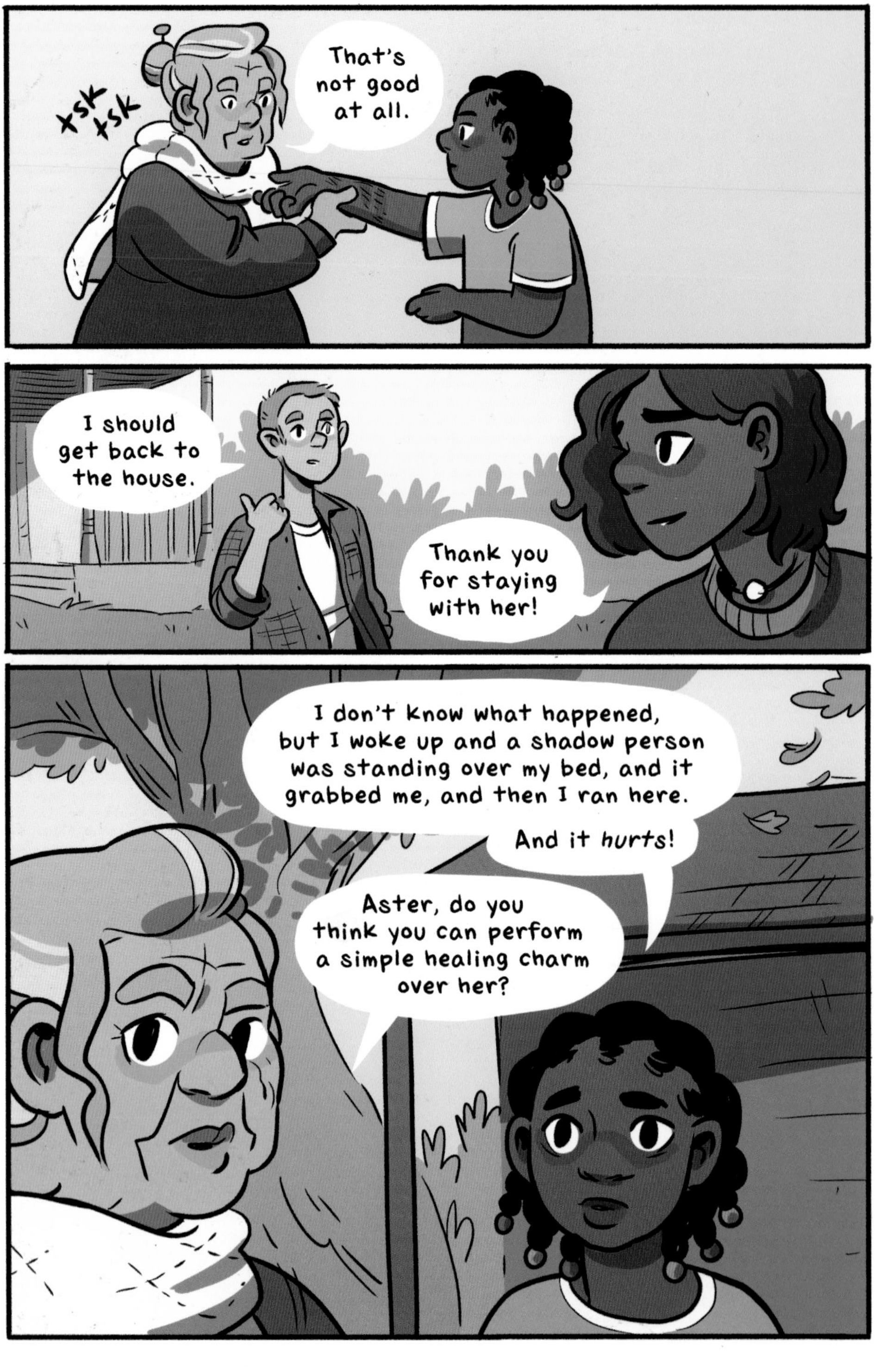
tsk tsk
That's not good at all.
I should get back to the house.
Thank you for staying with her!
I don't know what happened, but I woke up and a shadow person was standing over my bed, and it grabbed me, and then I ran here.
And it *hurts*!
Aster, do you think you can perform a simple healing charm over her?

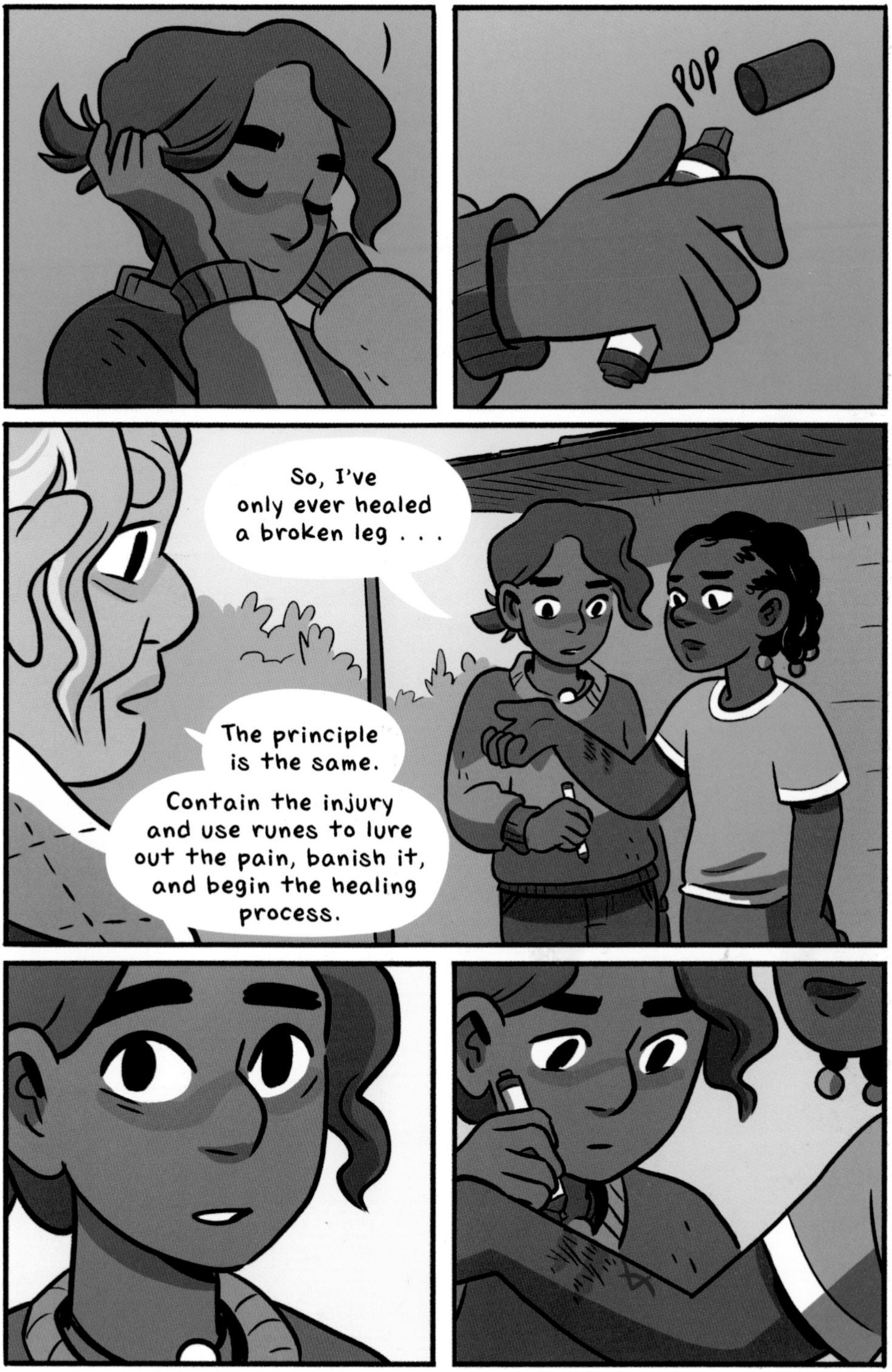
POP
So, I've only ever healed a broken leg . . .
The principle is the same.
Contain the injury and use runes to lure out the pain, banish it, and begin the healing process.

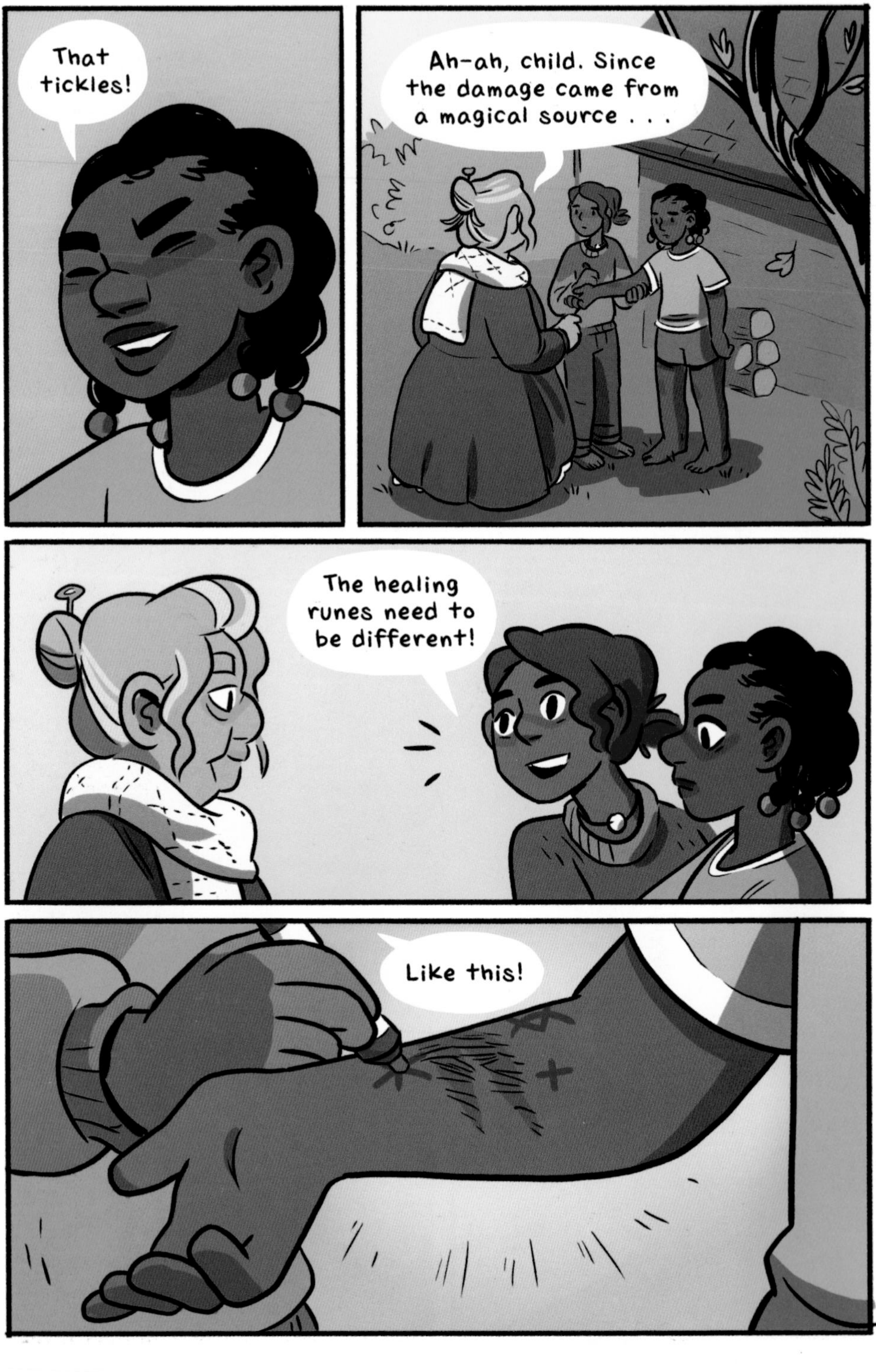
That tickles!
Ah-ah, child. Since the damage came from a magical source . . .
The healing runes need to be different!
Like this!

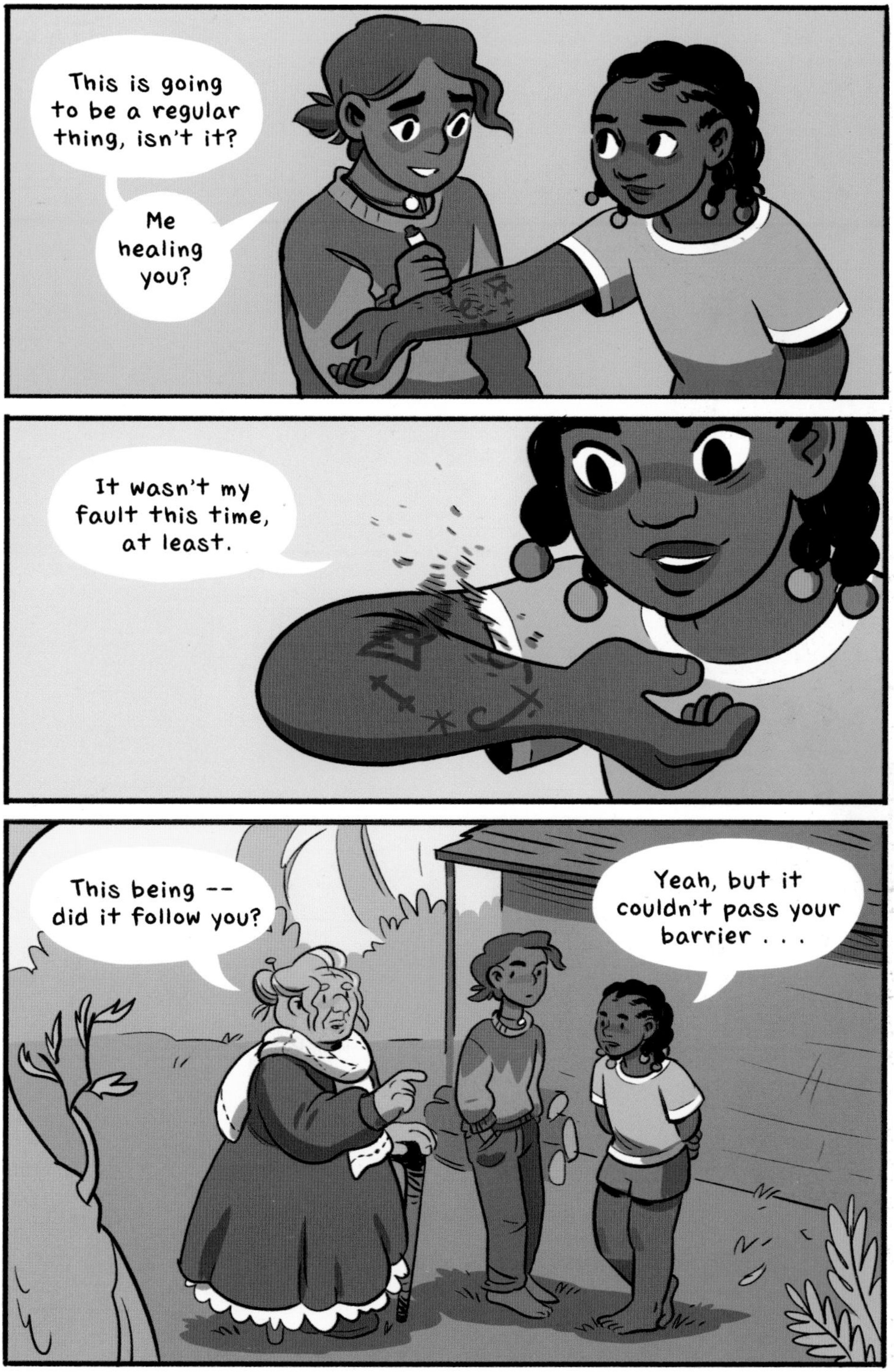
This is going to be a regular thing, isn't it?
Me healing you?
It wasn't my fault this time, at least.
This being -- did it follow you?
Yeah, but it couldn't pass your barrier . . .

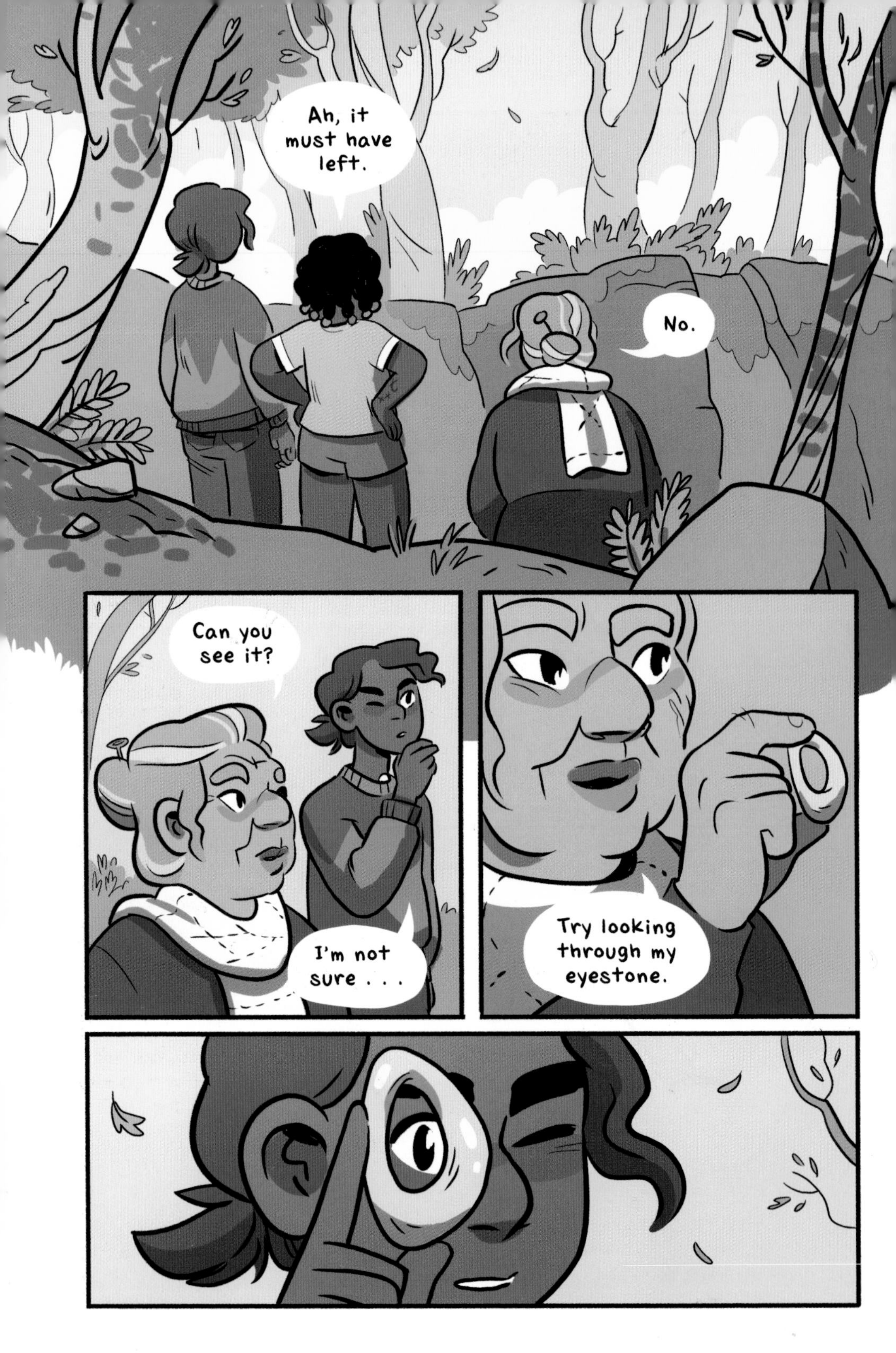

Ah, it must have left.
No.
Can you see it?
I'm not sure . . .
Try looking through my eyestone.

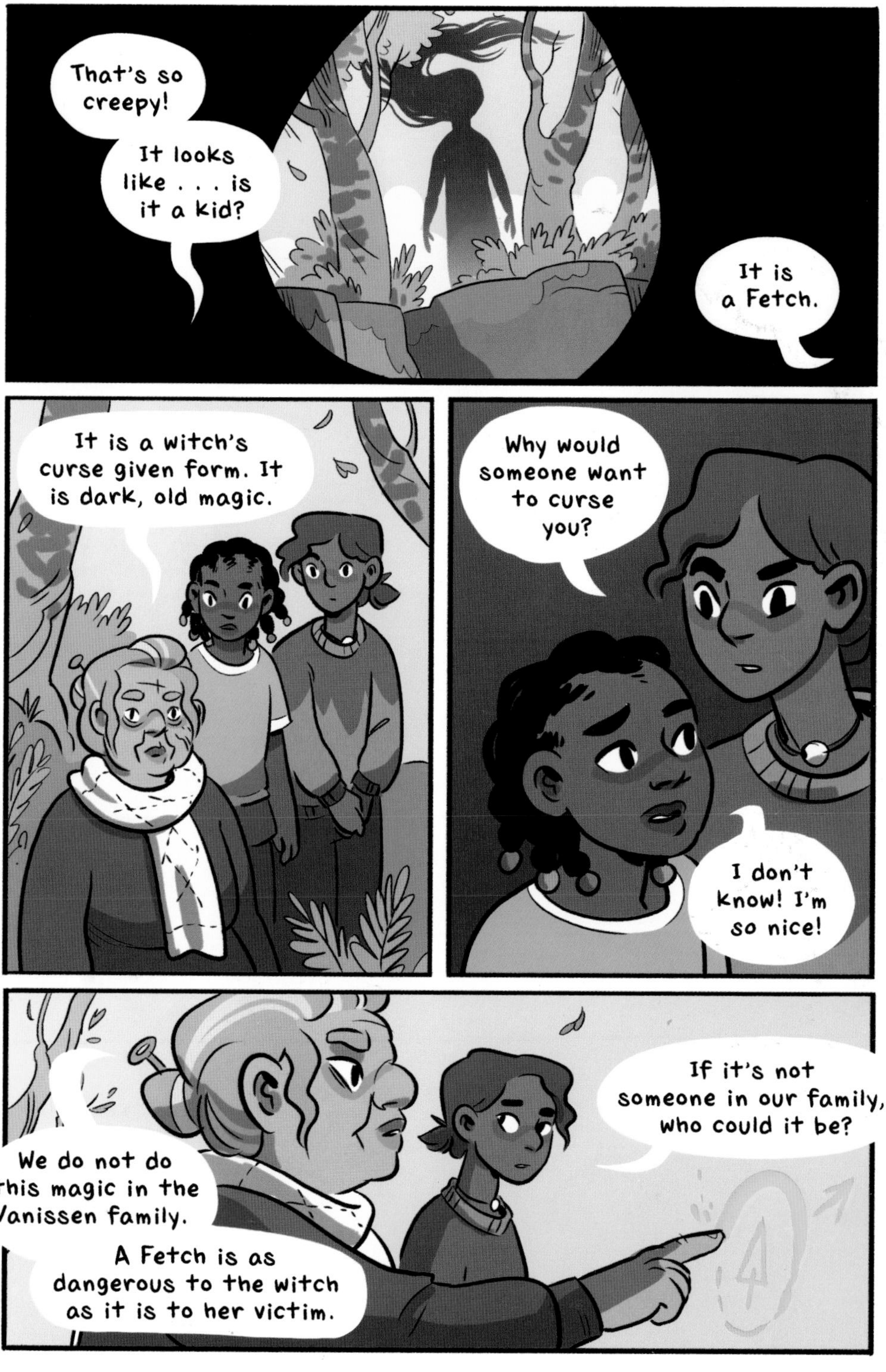
That's so creepy!
It looks like . . . is it a kid?
It is a Fetch.
It is a witch's curse given form. It is dark, old magic.
Why would someone want to curse you?
I don't know! I'm so nice!
If it's not someone in our family, who could it be?
We do not do this magic in the Vanissen family.
A Fetch is as dangerous to the witch as it is to her victim.

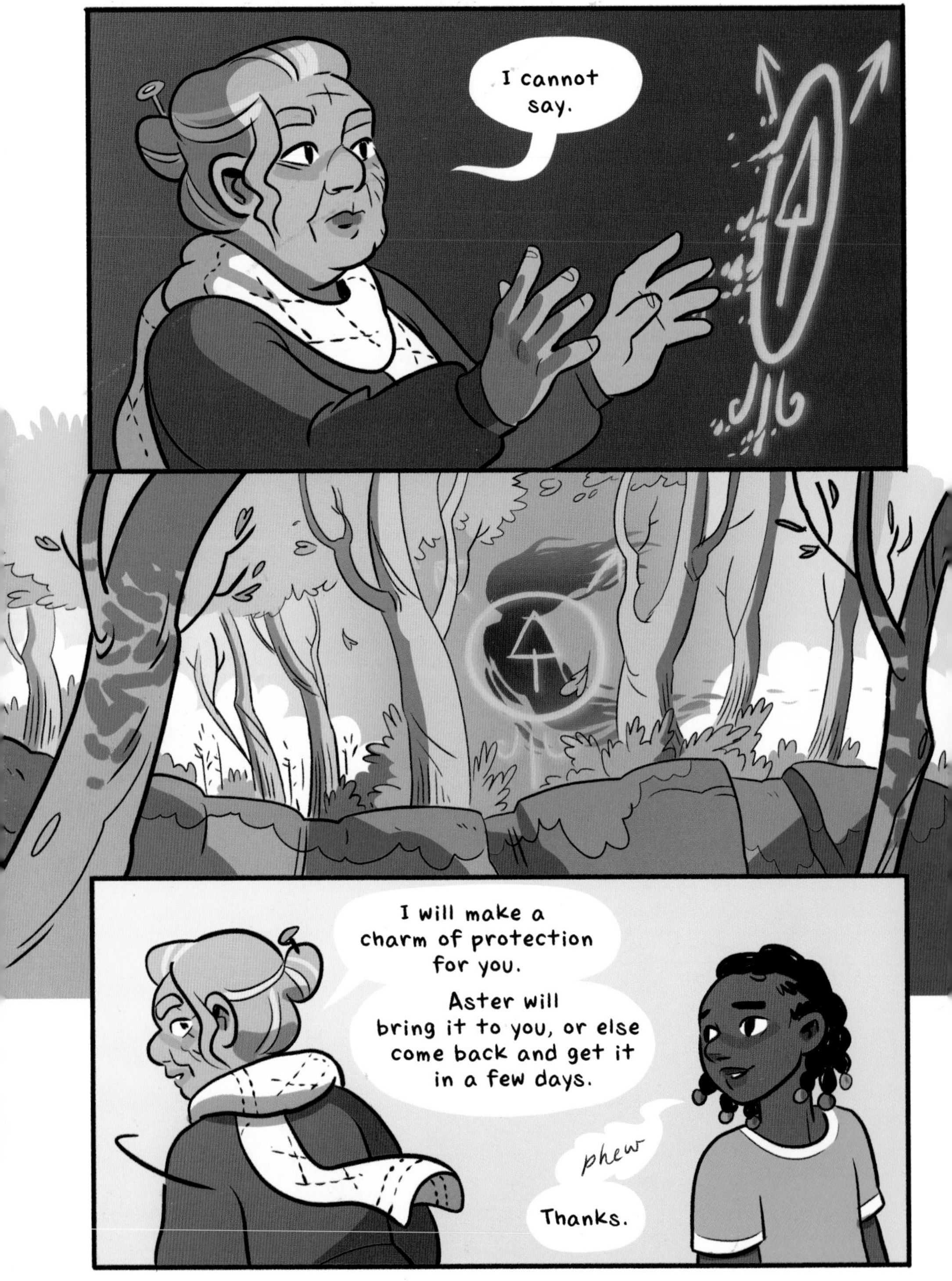
I cannot say.
I will make a charm of protection for you.
Aster will bring it to you, or else come back and get it in a few days.
phew
Thanks.

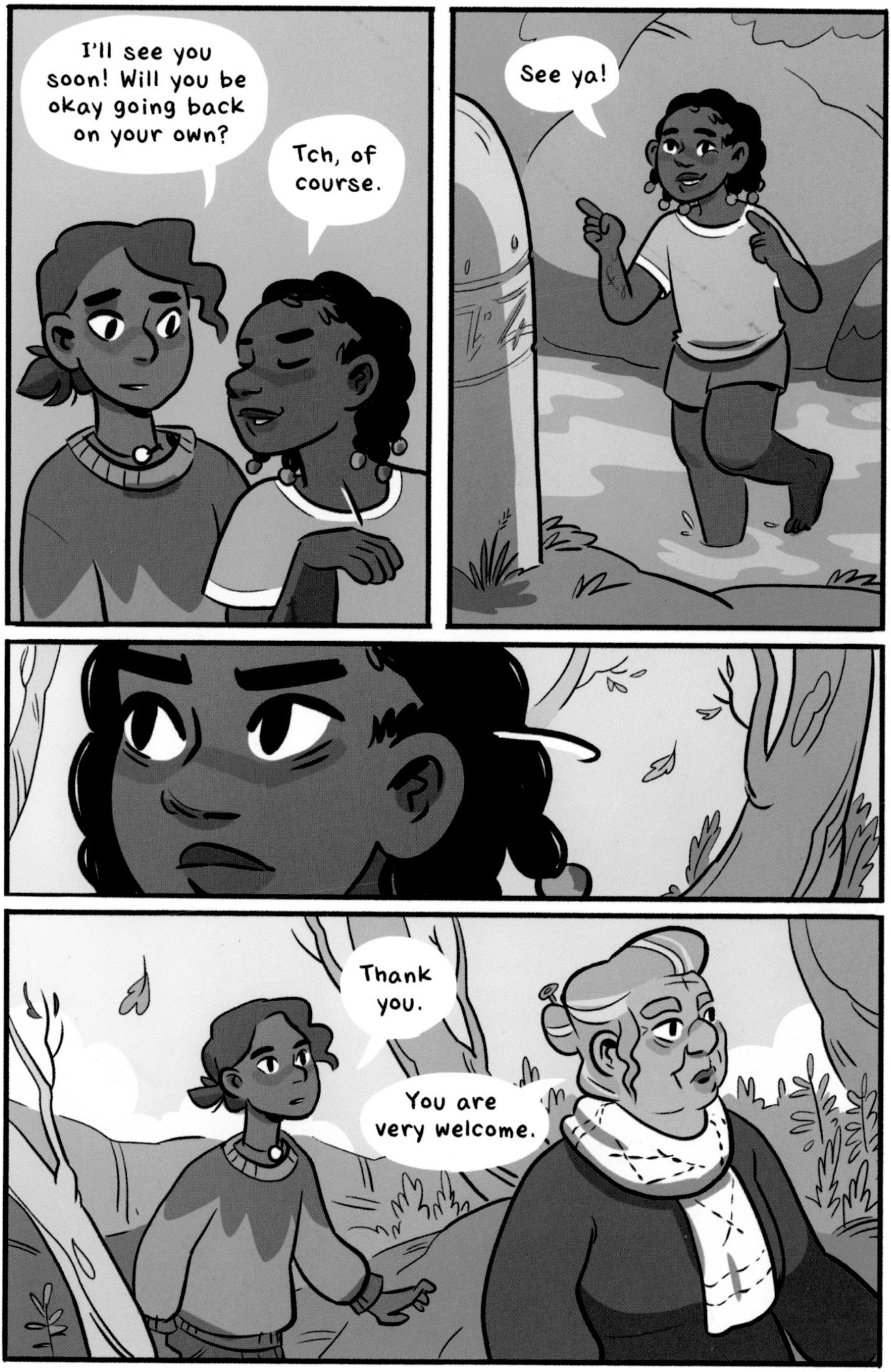
I'll see you soon! Will you be okay going back on your own?
Tch, of course.
See ya!
Thank you.
You are very welcome.

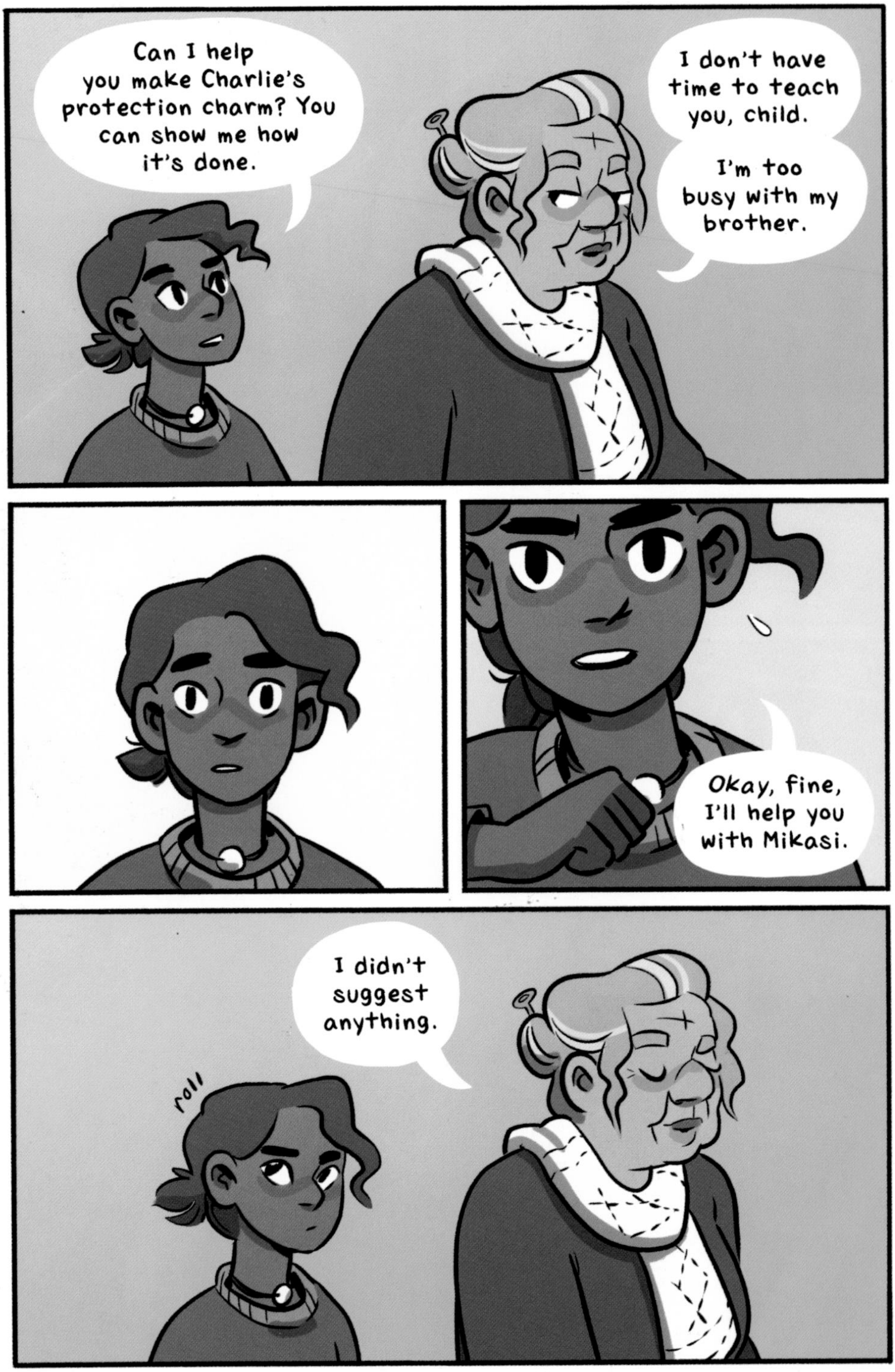
Can I help you make Charlie's protection charm? You can show me how it's done.
I don't have time to teach you, child.
I'm too busy with my brother.
Okay, fine, I'll help you with Mikasi.
I didn't suggest anything.
roll

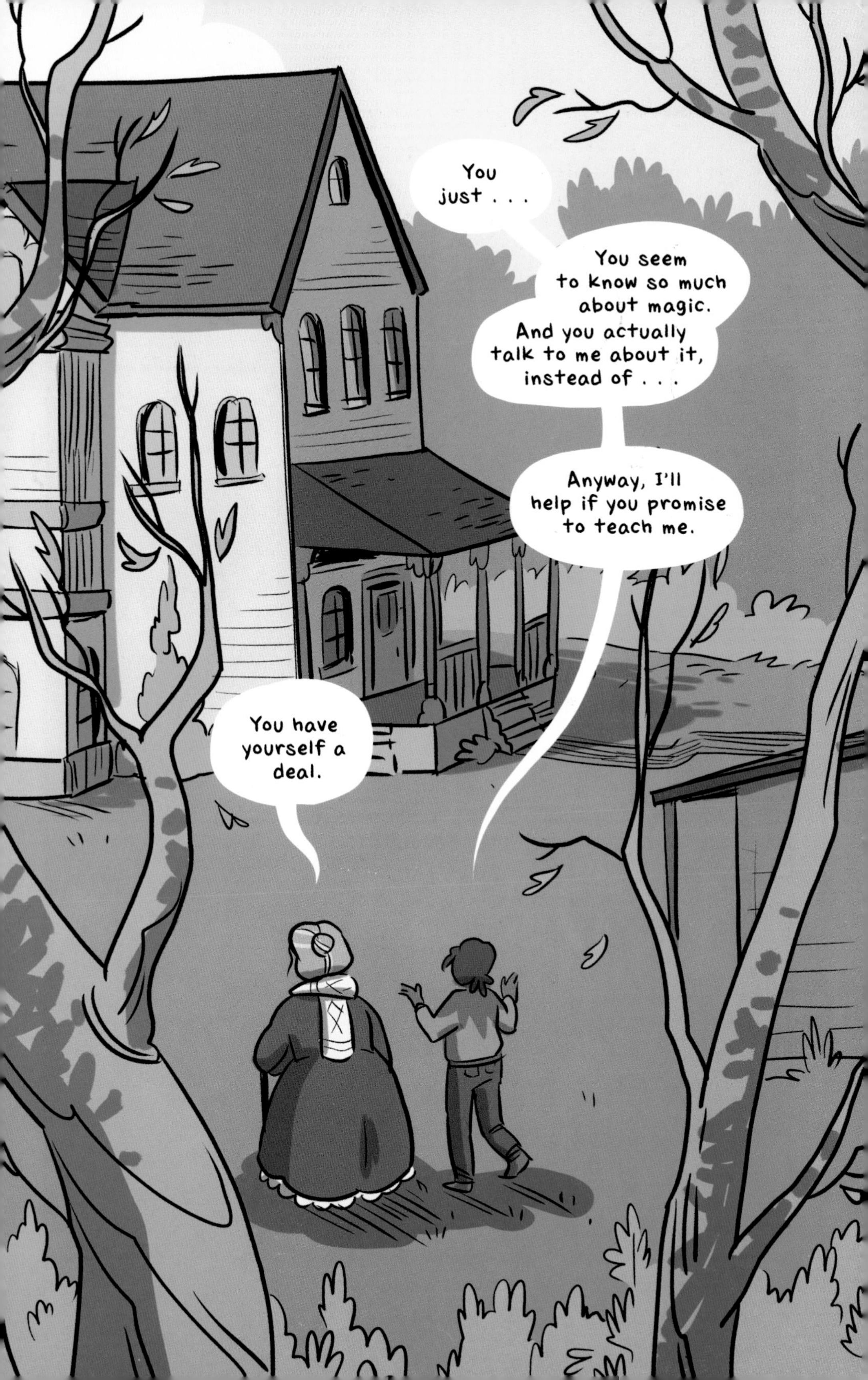
You just . . .
You seem to know so much about magic.
And you actually talk to me about it, instead of . . .
Anyway, I'll help if you promise to teach me.
You have yourself a deal.

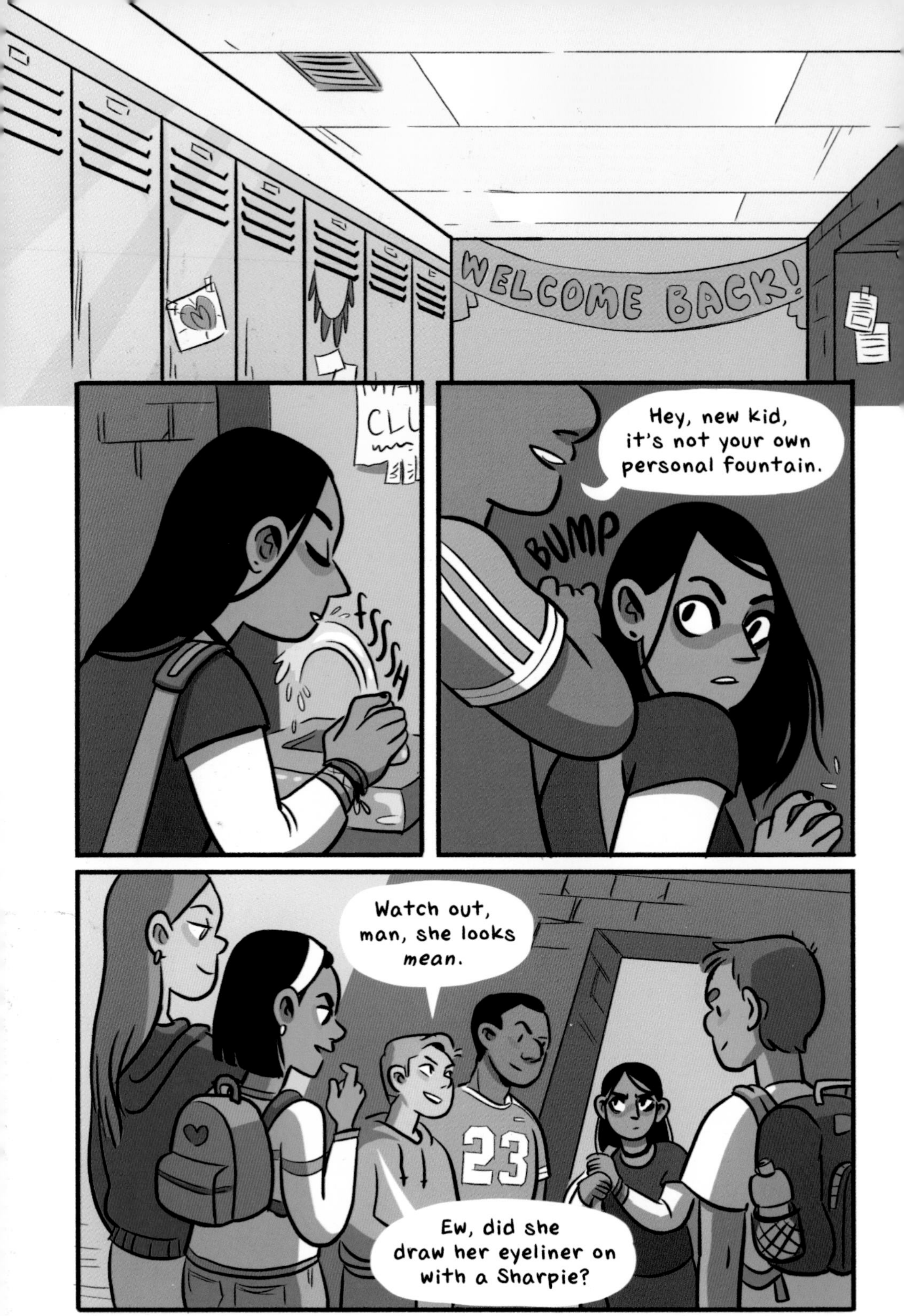
WELCOME BACK!
CLU
FSSSH
Hey, new kid, it's not your own personal fountain.
BUMP
Watch out, man, she looks *mean*.
Ew, did she draw her eyeliner on with a Sharpie?

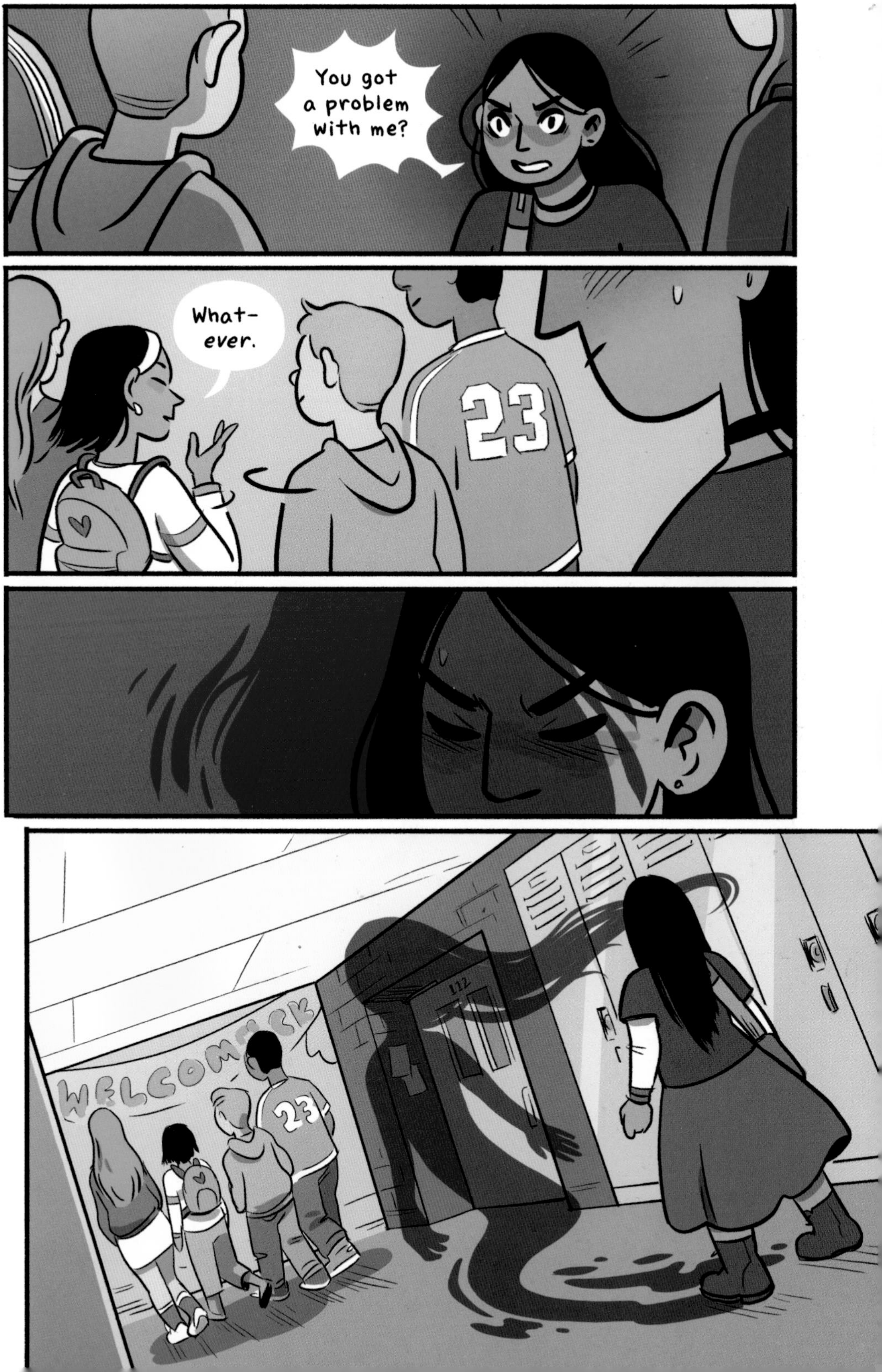
You got a problem with me?
What-ever.
23
WELCOME BACK
23
122

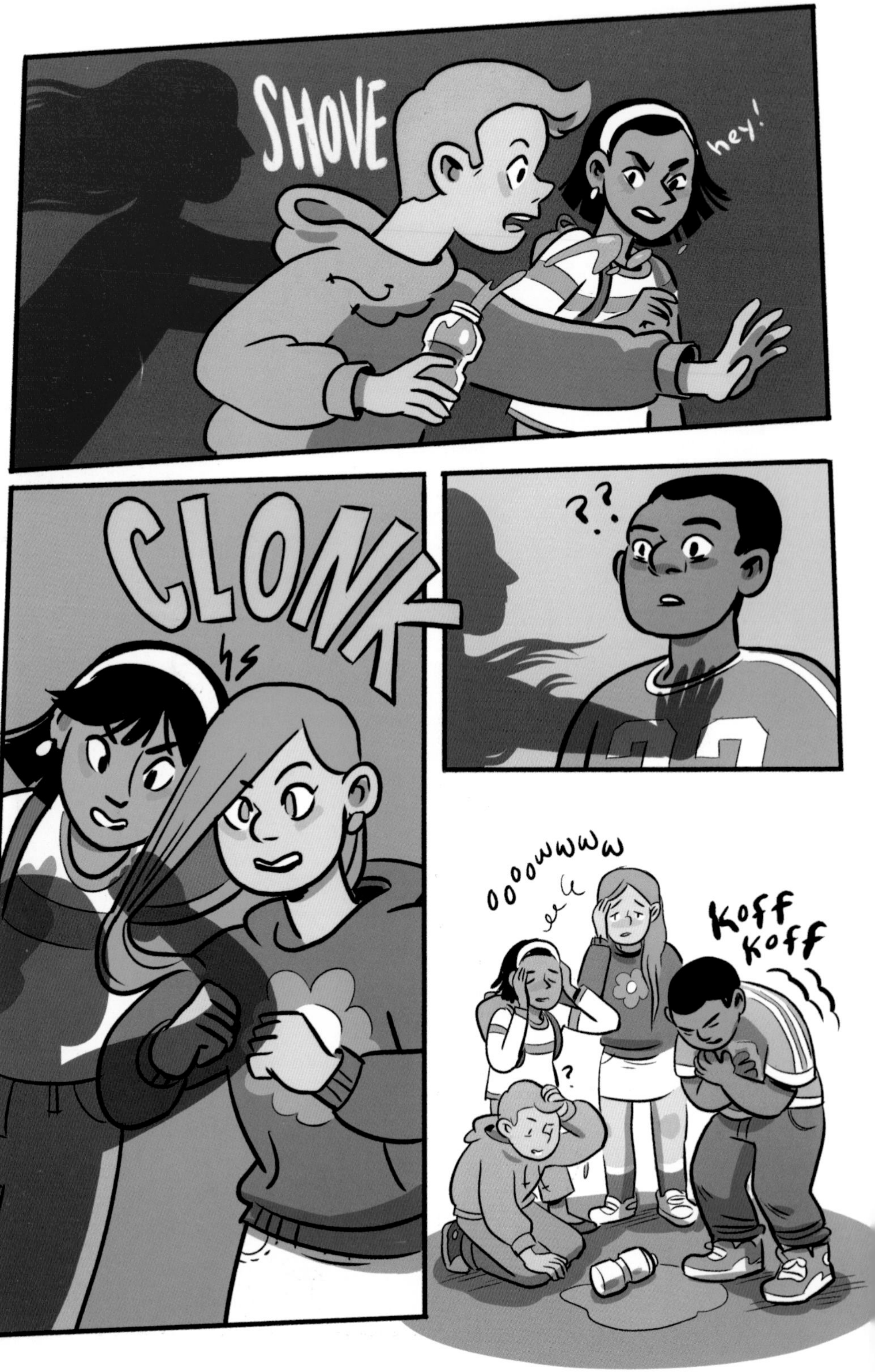
SHOVE
hey!
CLONK
??
OOOOWWWW
KOFF
KOFF
?

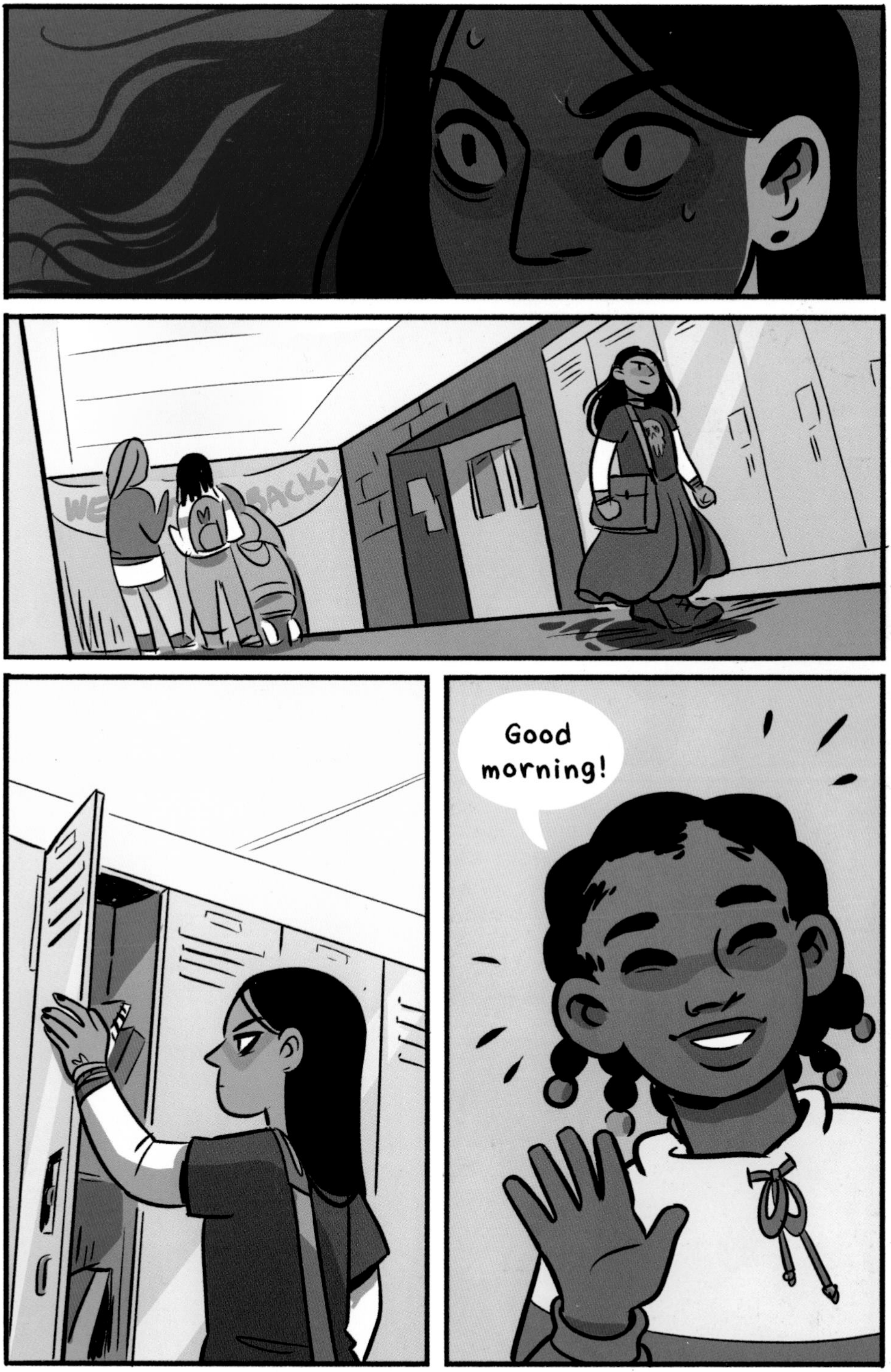
Good morning!

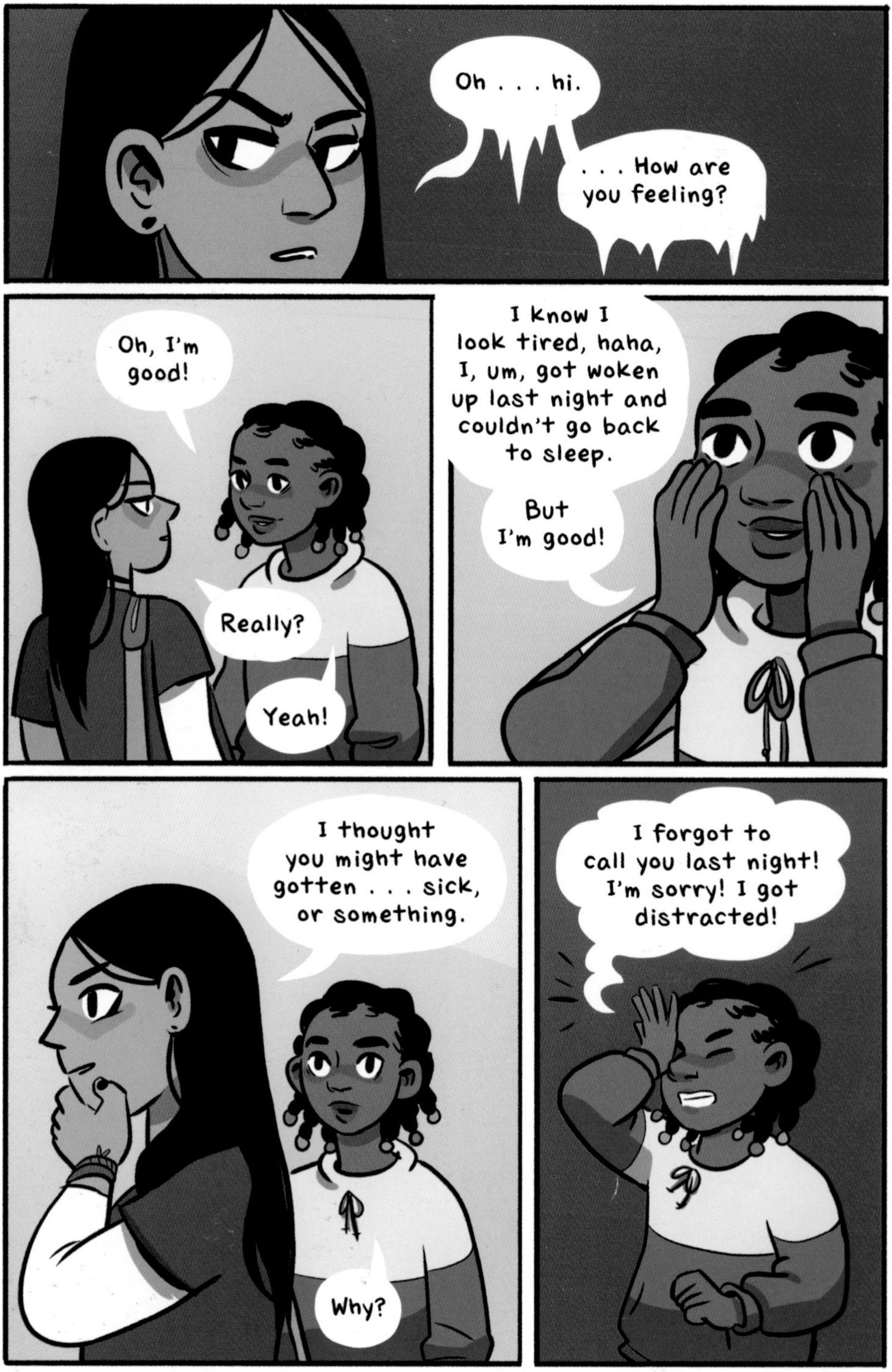

Oh . . . hi.
. . . How are you feeling?
Oh, I'm good!
Really?
Yeah!
I know I look tired, haha, I, um, got woken up last night and couldn't go back to sleep.
But I'm good!
I thought you might have gotten . . . sick, or something.
Why?
I forgot to call you last night! I'm sorry! I got distracted!

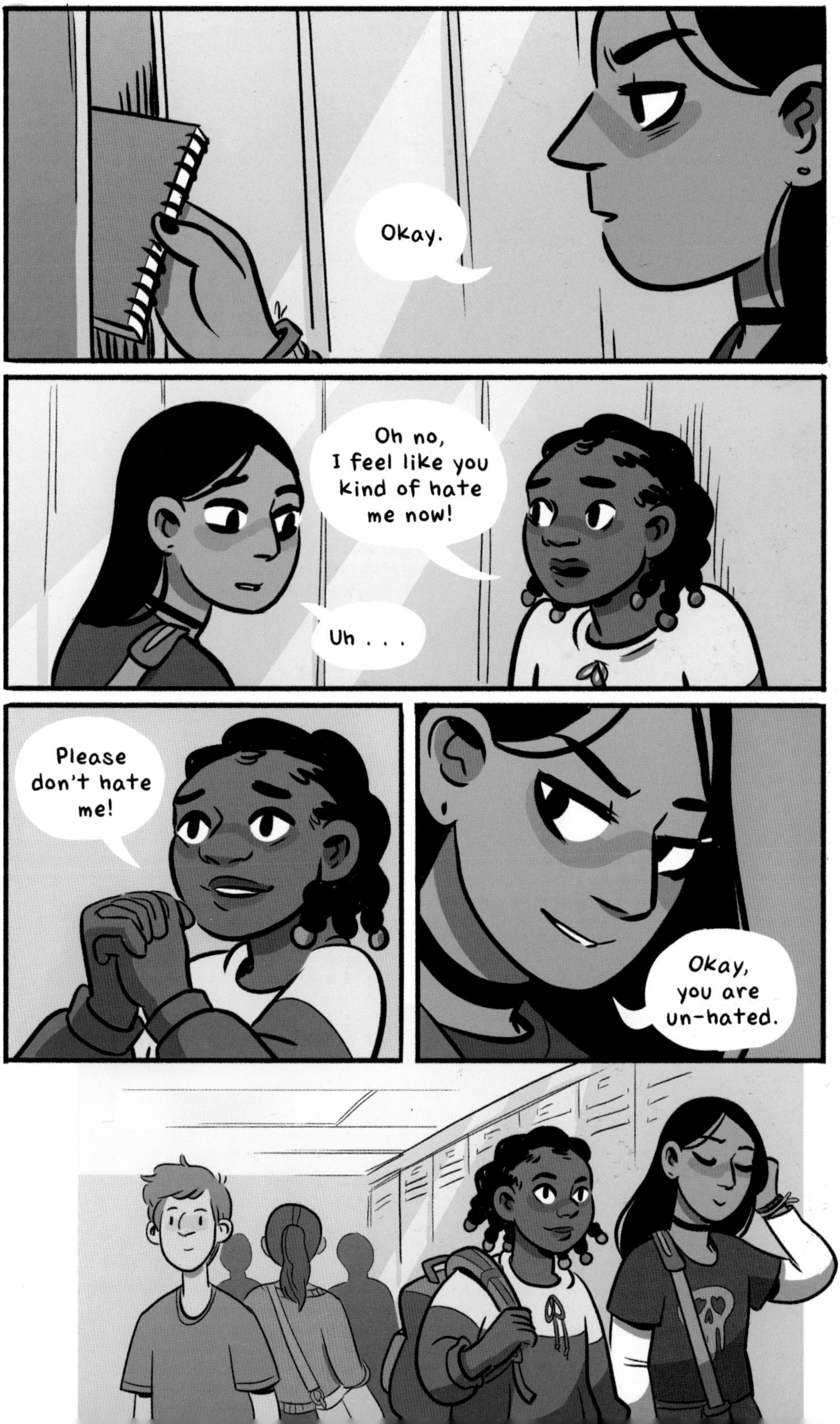
Okay.
Oh no, I feel like you kind of hate me now!
Uh . . .
Please don't hate me!
Okay, you are un-hated.

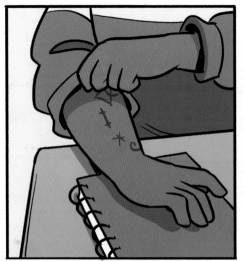

Sooo . . . what woke you up last night?

Oh, just a bad dream. But I dealt with it!

You dealt with it . . . That's never happened before.

What?

It can be our secret.

? ? ?

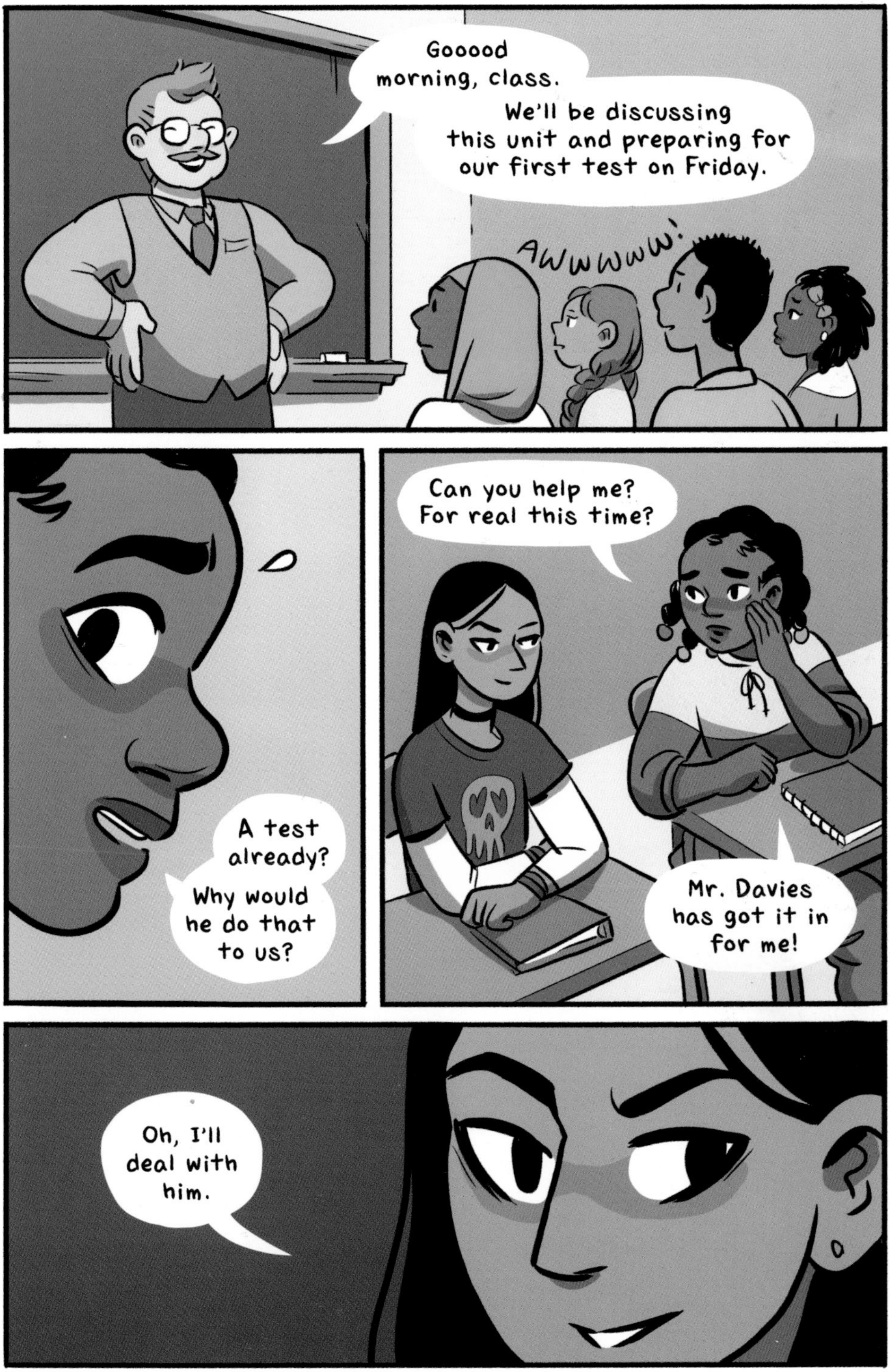
Gooood morning, class.
We'll be discussing this unit and preparing for our first test on Friday.
AWWWWWW!
A test already?
Why would he do that to us?
Can you help me? For real this time?
Mr. Davies has got it in for me!
Oh, I'll deal with him.

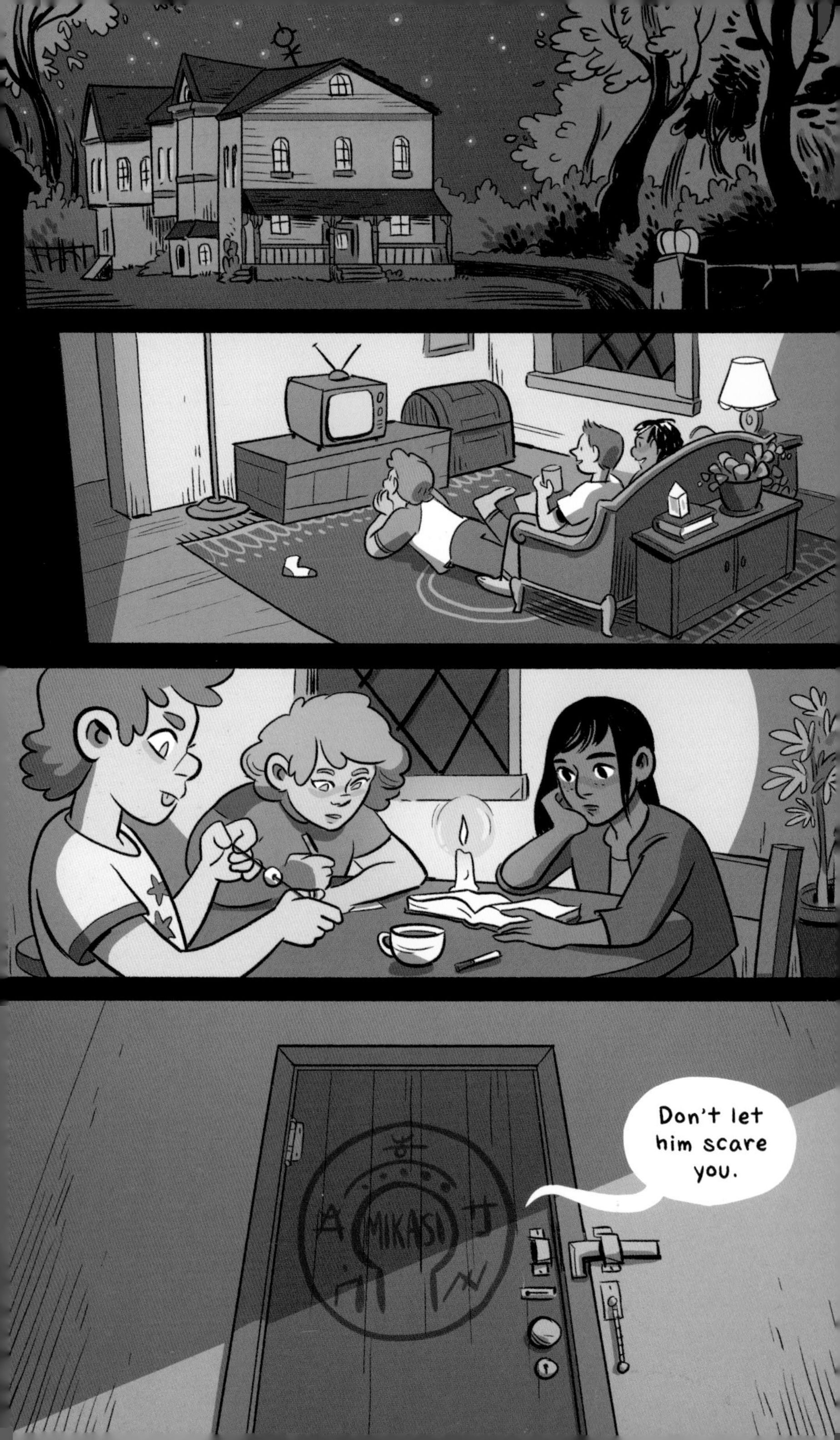
MIKASI
Don't let him scare you.

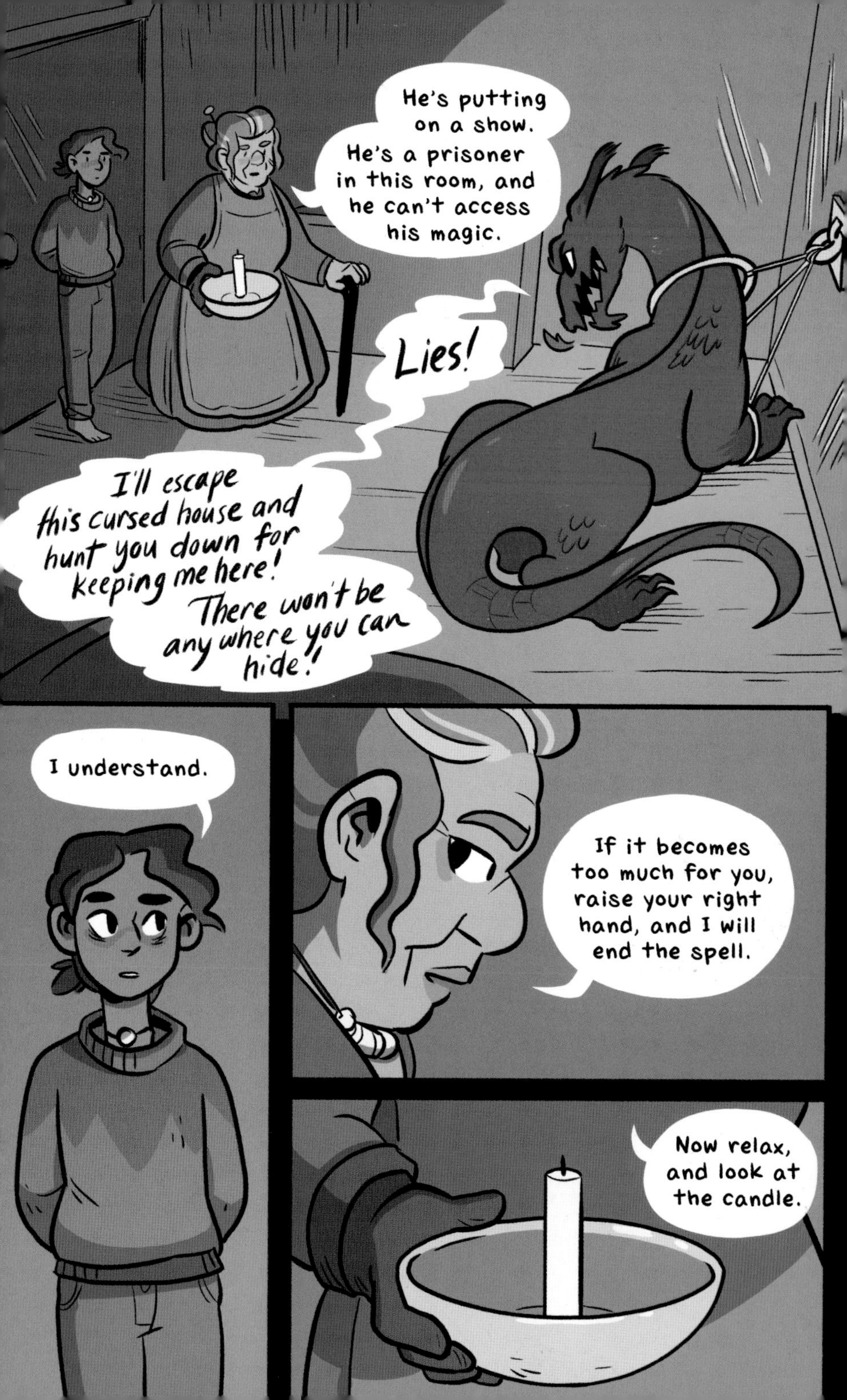
He's putting on a show. He's a prisoner in this room, and he can't access his magic.
Lies!
I'll escape this cursed house and hunt you down for keeping me here!
There won't be anywhere you can hide!
I understand.
If it becomes too much for you, raise your right hand, and I will end the spell.
Now relax, and look at the candle.

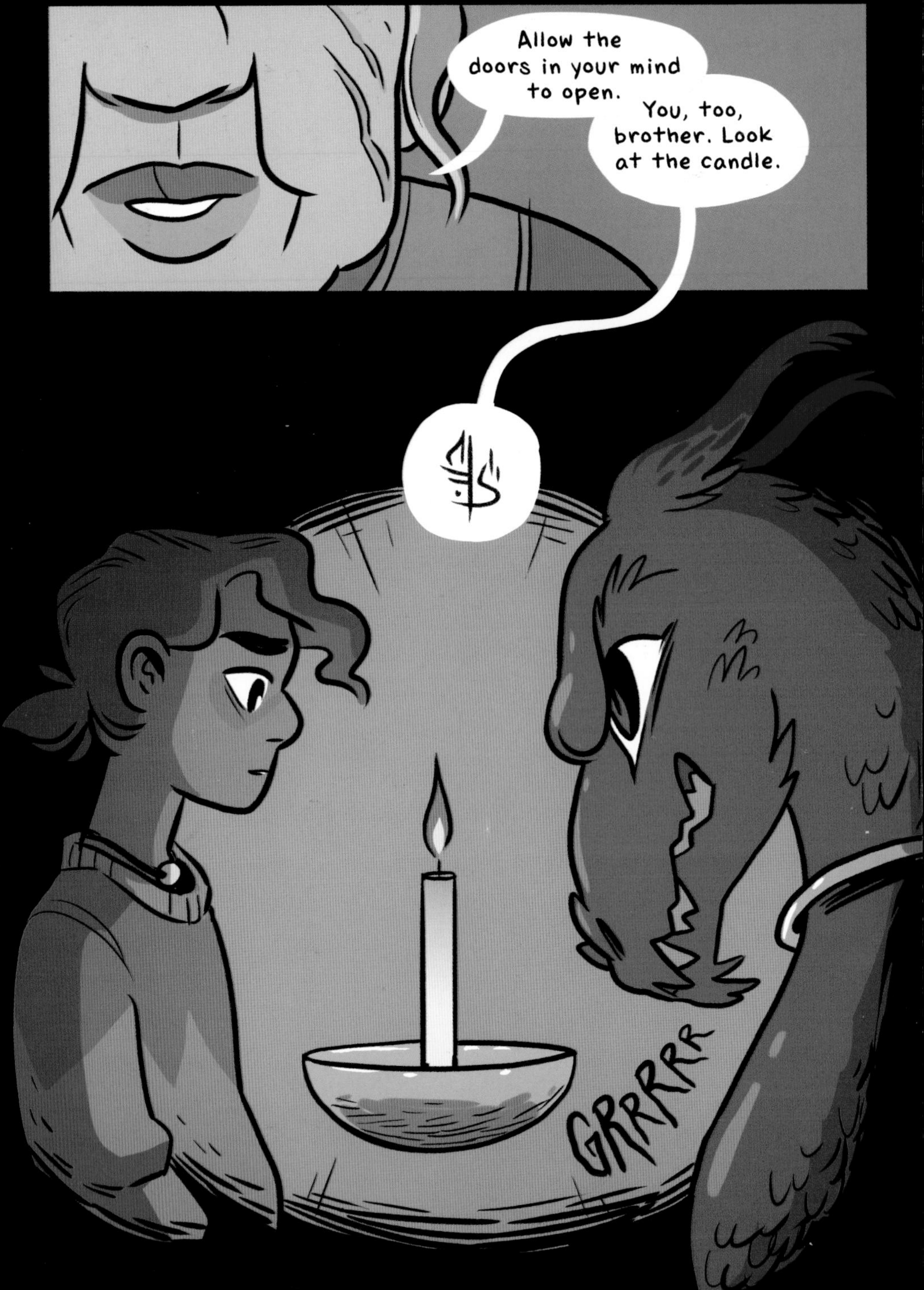
Allow the doors in your mind to open.
You, too, brother. Look at the candle.
GRRRRR

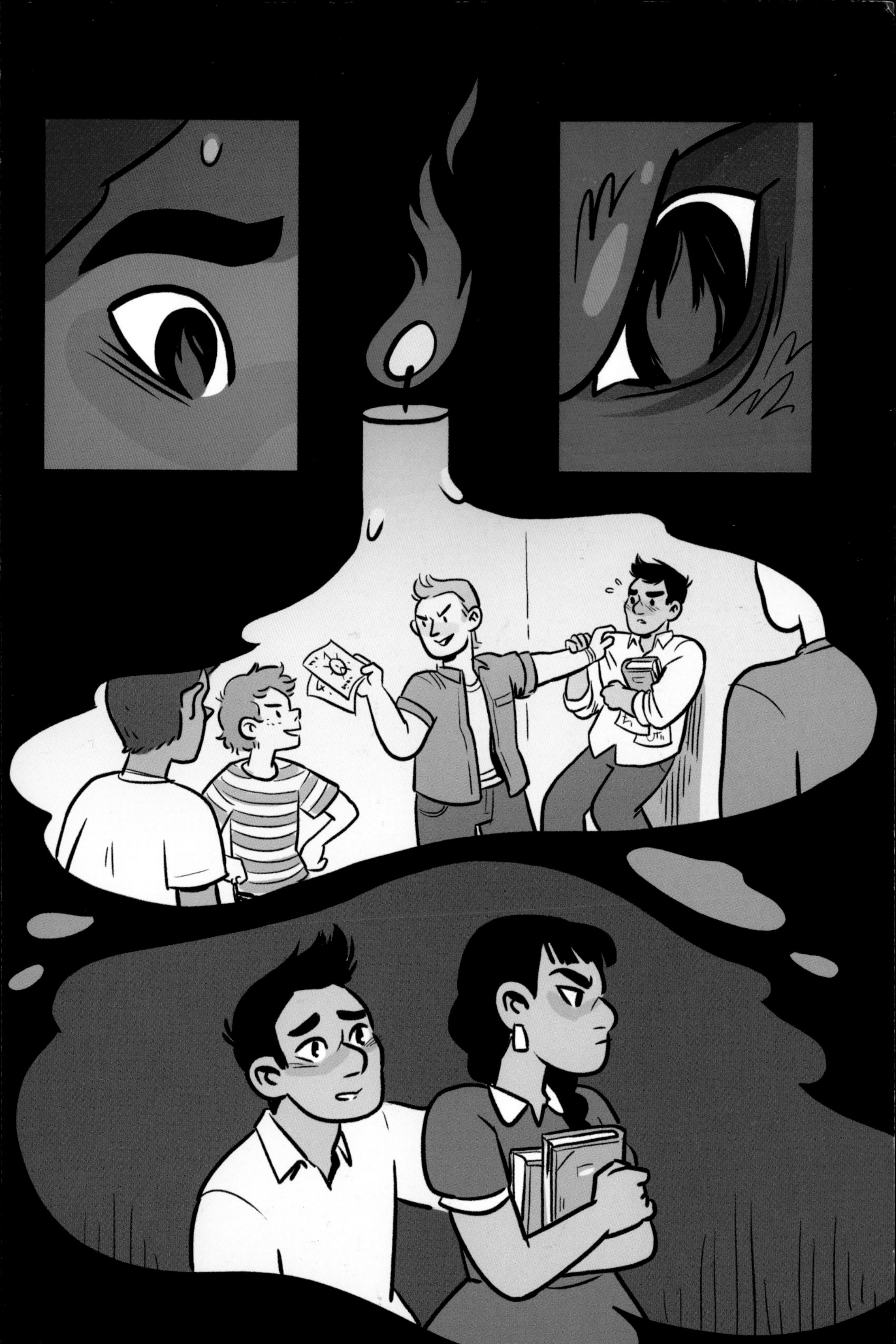

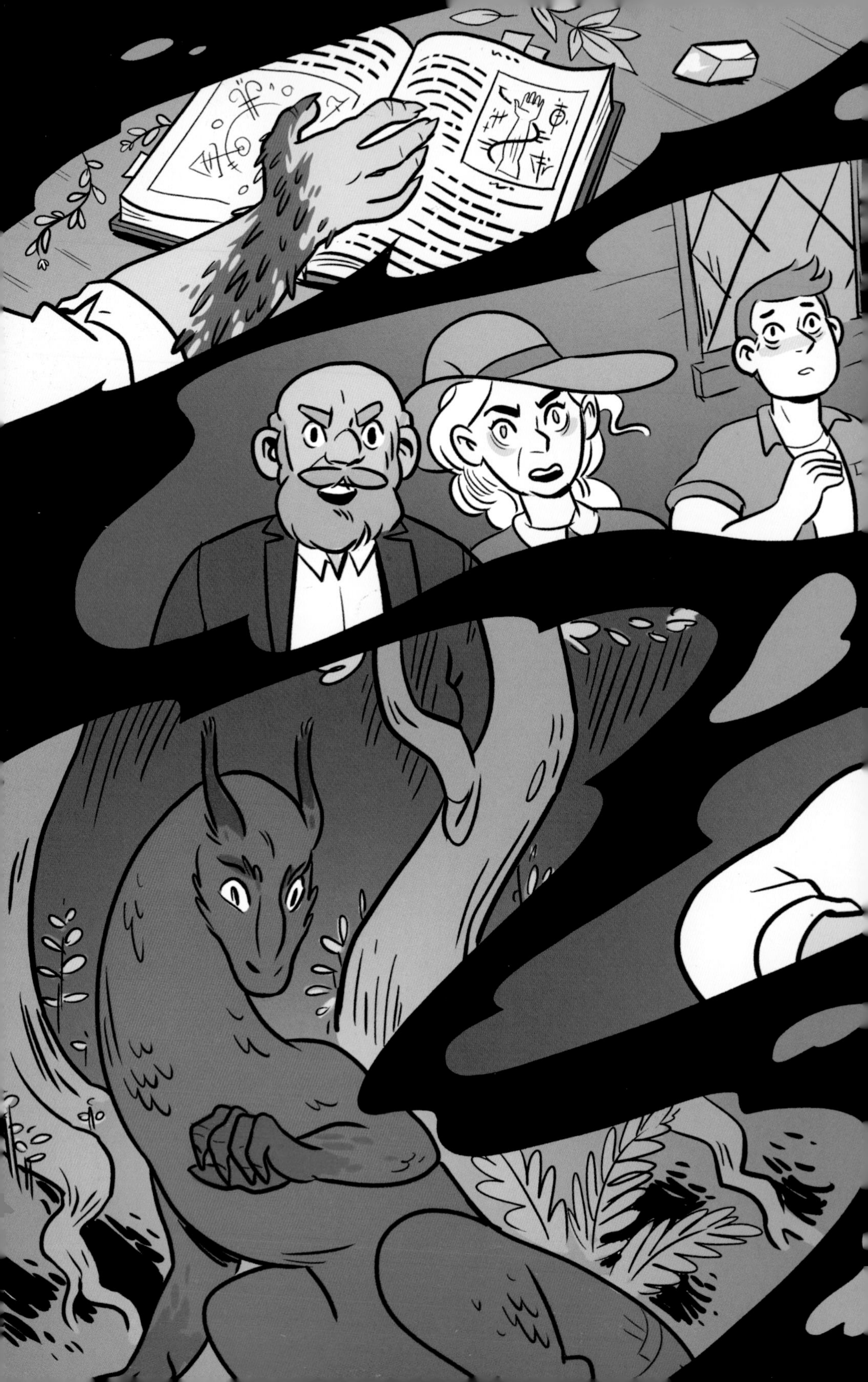

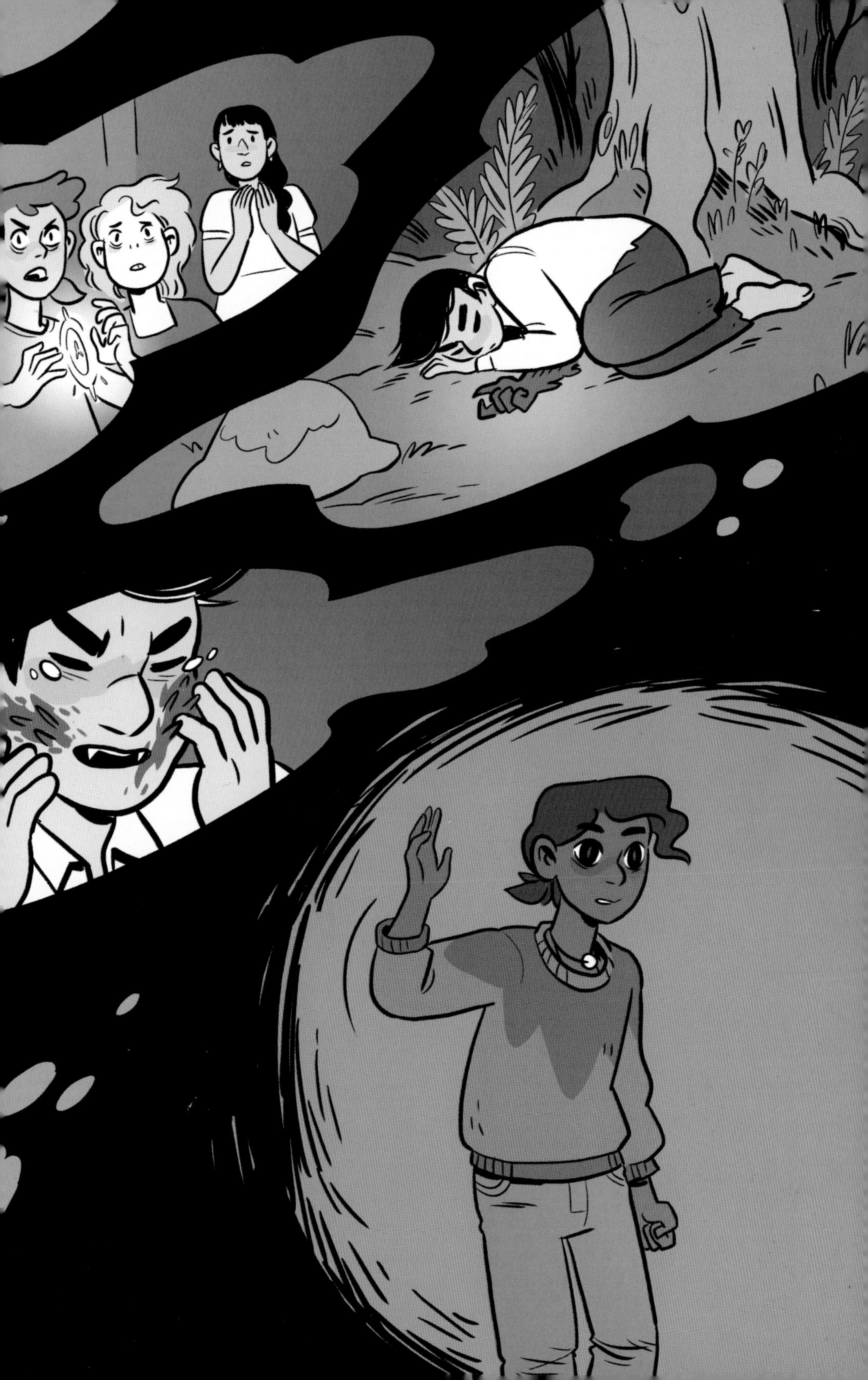

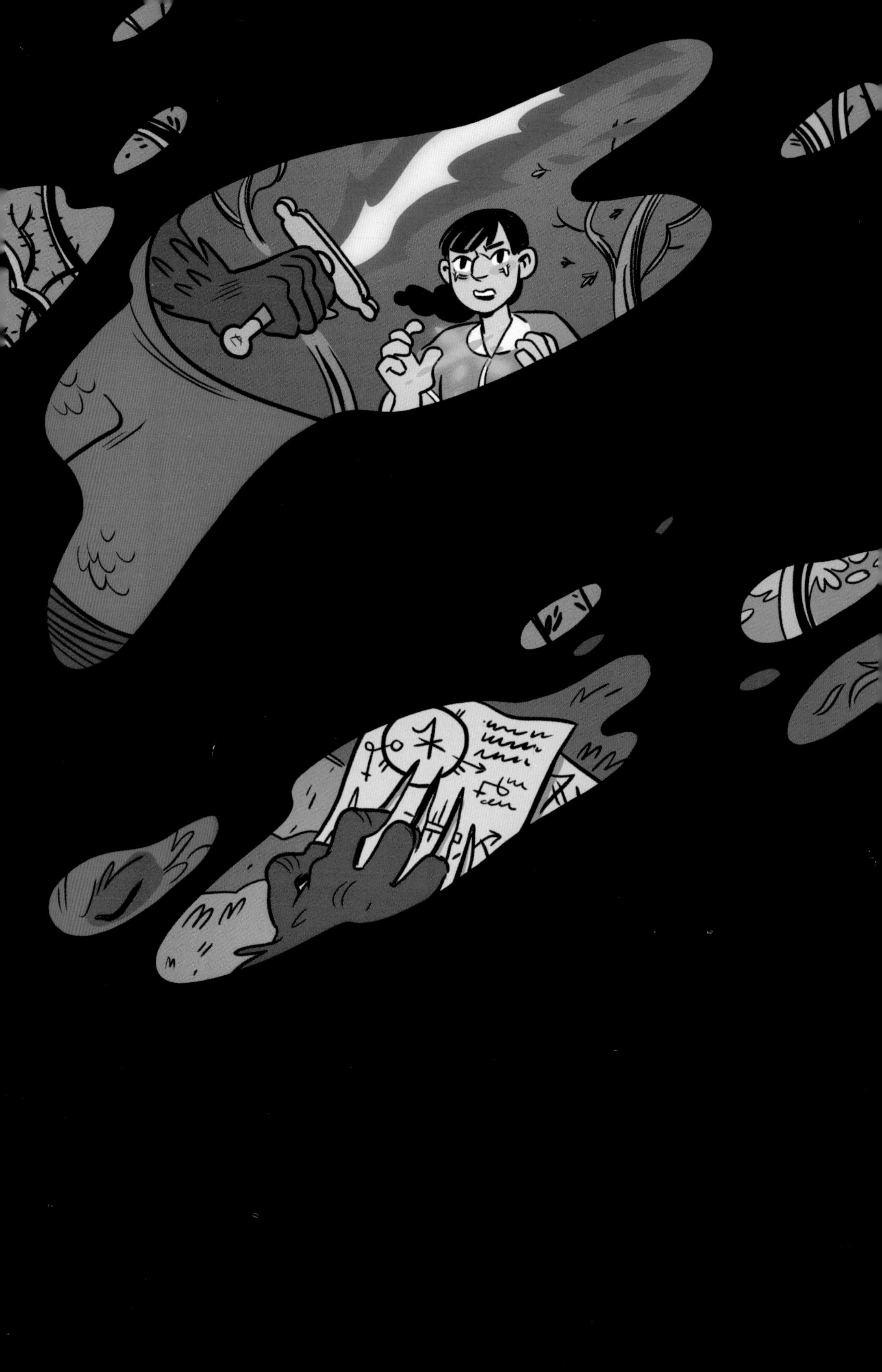

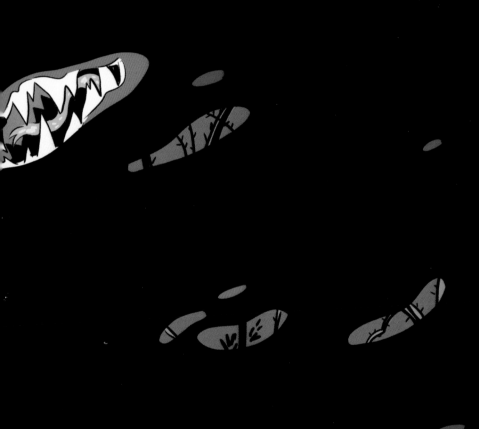

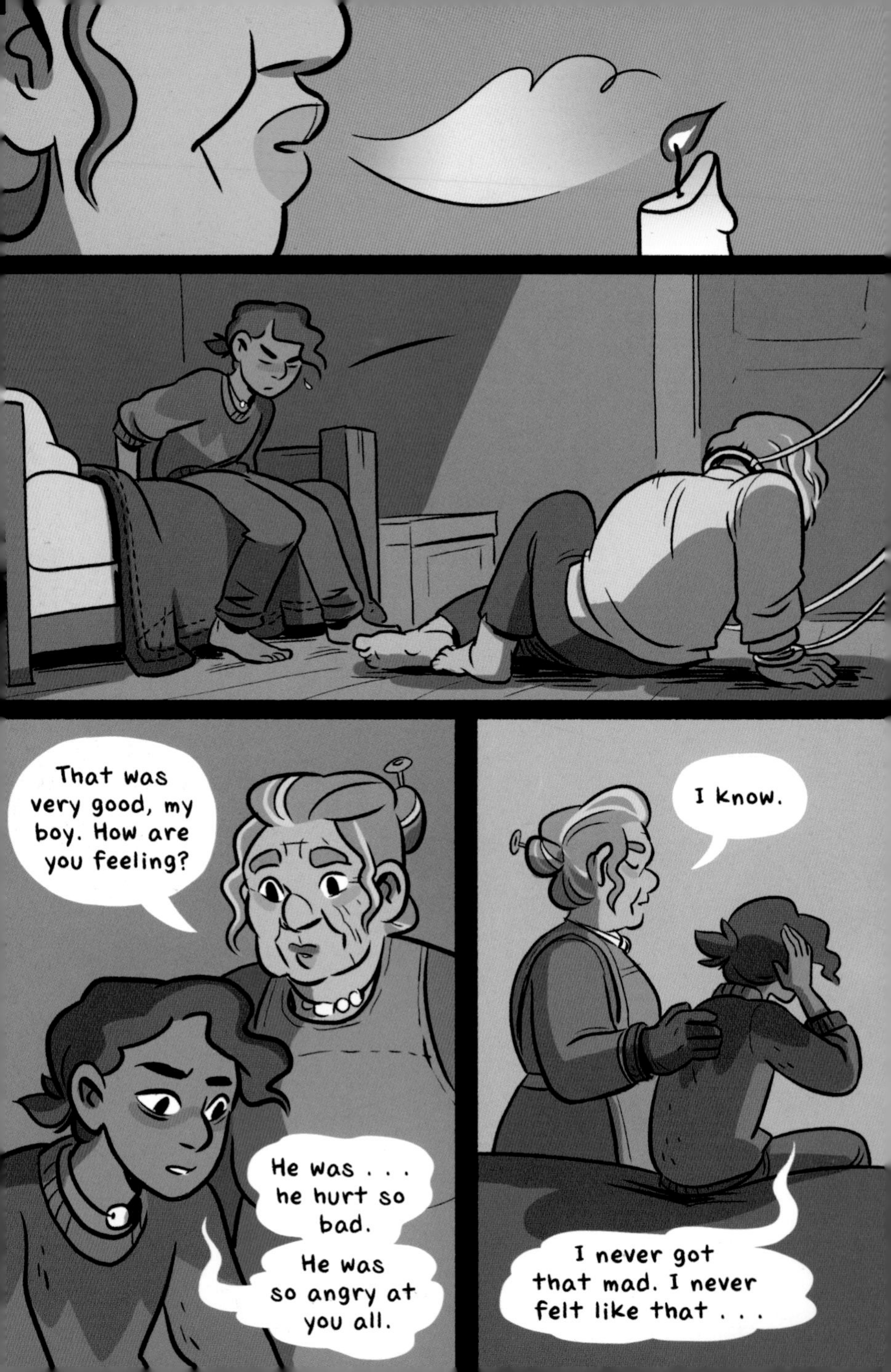
That was very good, my boy. How are you feeling?
He was . . . he hurt so bad.
He was so angry at you all.
I know.
I never got that mad. I never felt like that . . .

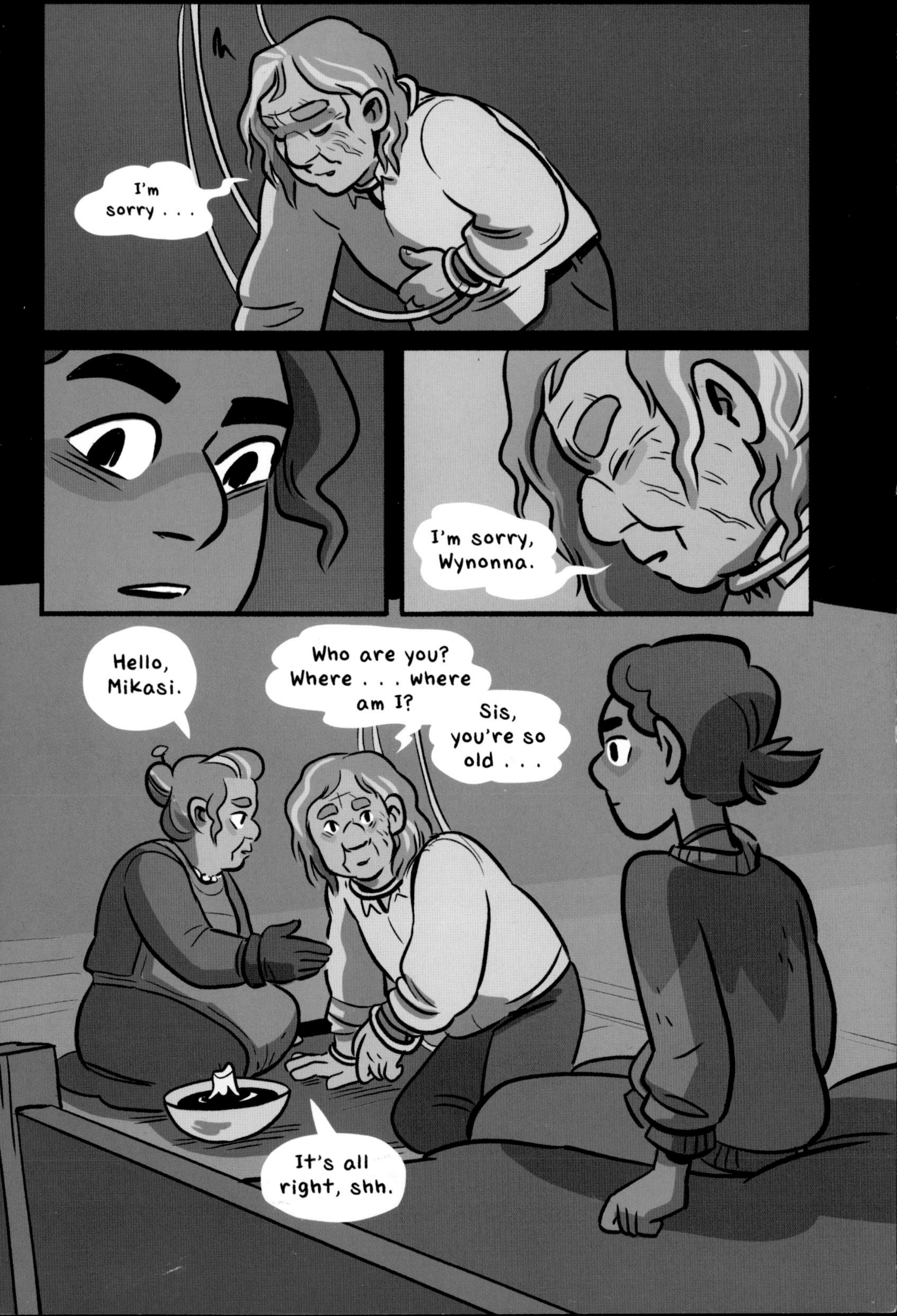
I'm sorry . . .
I'm sorry, Wynonna.
Hello, Mikasi.
Who are you? Where . . . where am I?
Sis, you're so old . . .
It's all right, shh.

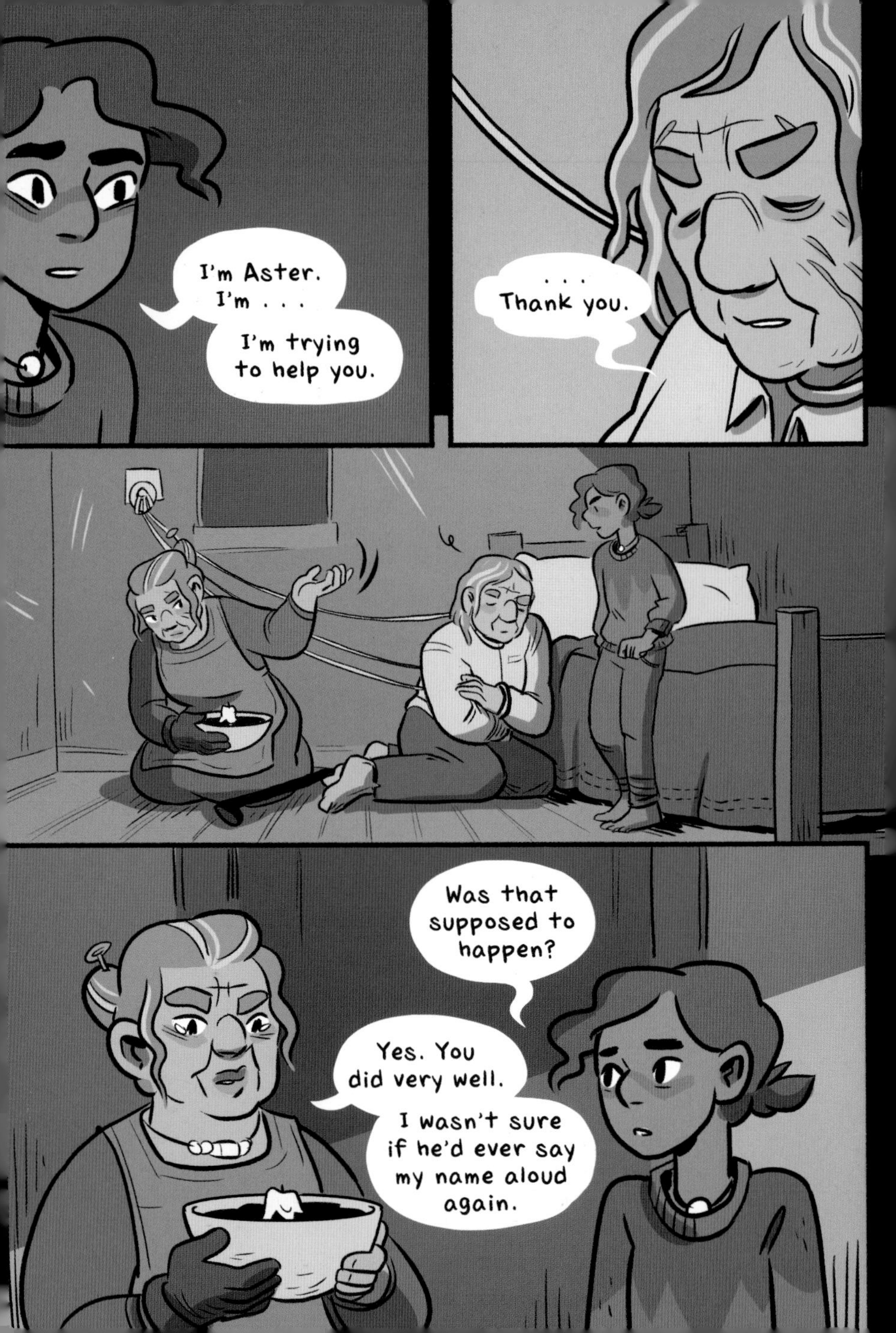
I'm Aster. I'm . . .
I'm trying to help you.
. . . Thank you.
Was that supposed to happen?
Yes. You did very well.
I wasn't sure if he'd ever say my name aloud again.

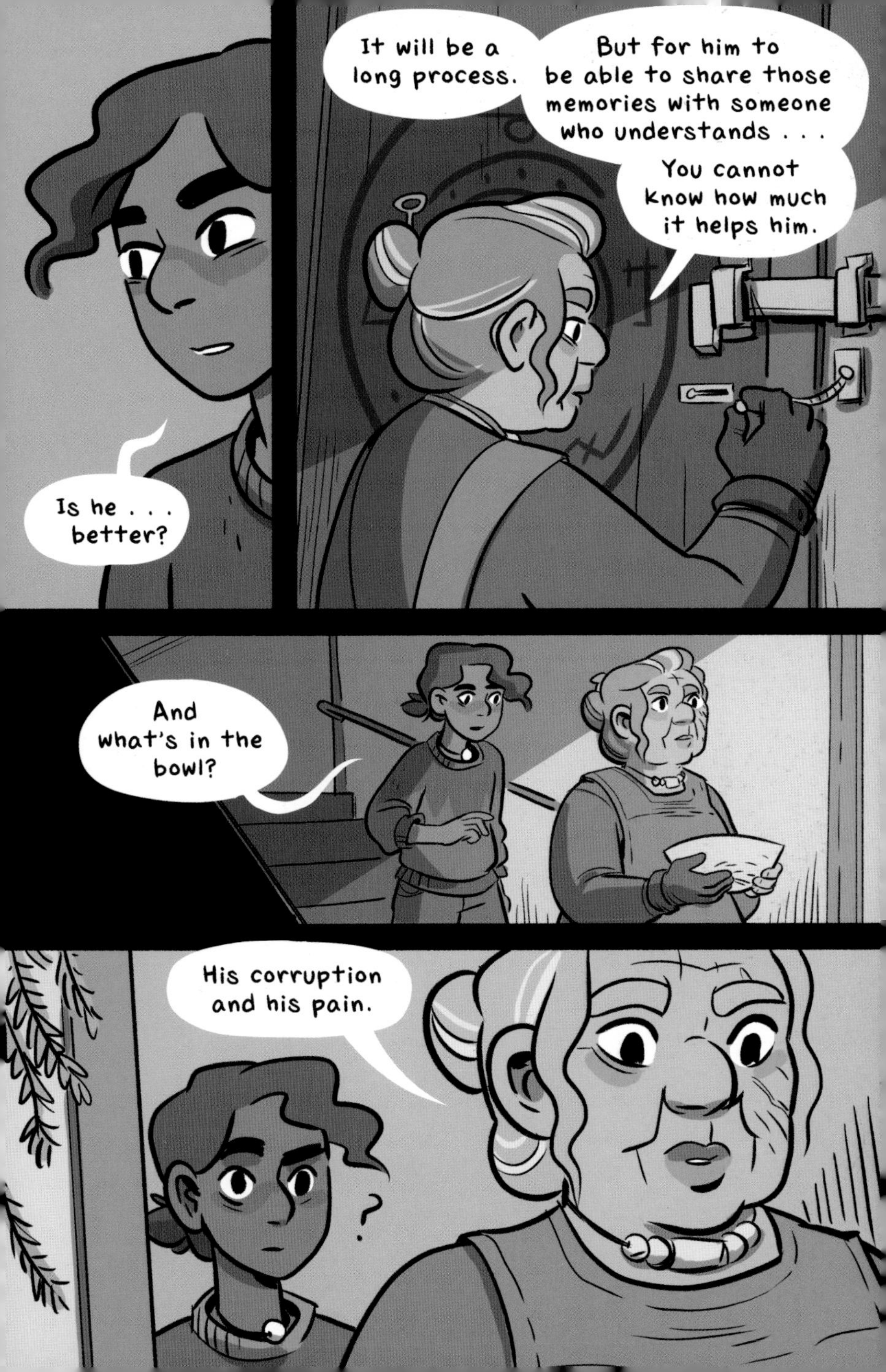
Is he . . . better?
It will be a long process.
But for him to be able to share those memories with someone who understands . . .
You cannot know how much it helps him.
And what's in the bowl?
His corruption and his pain.
?

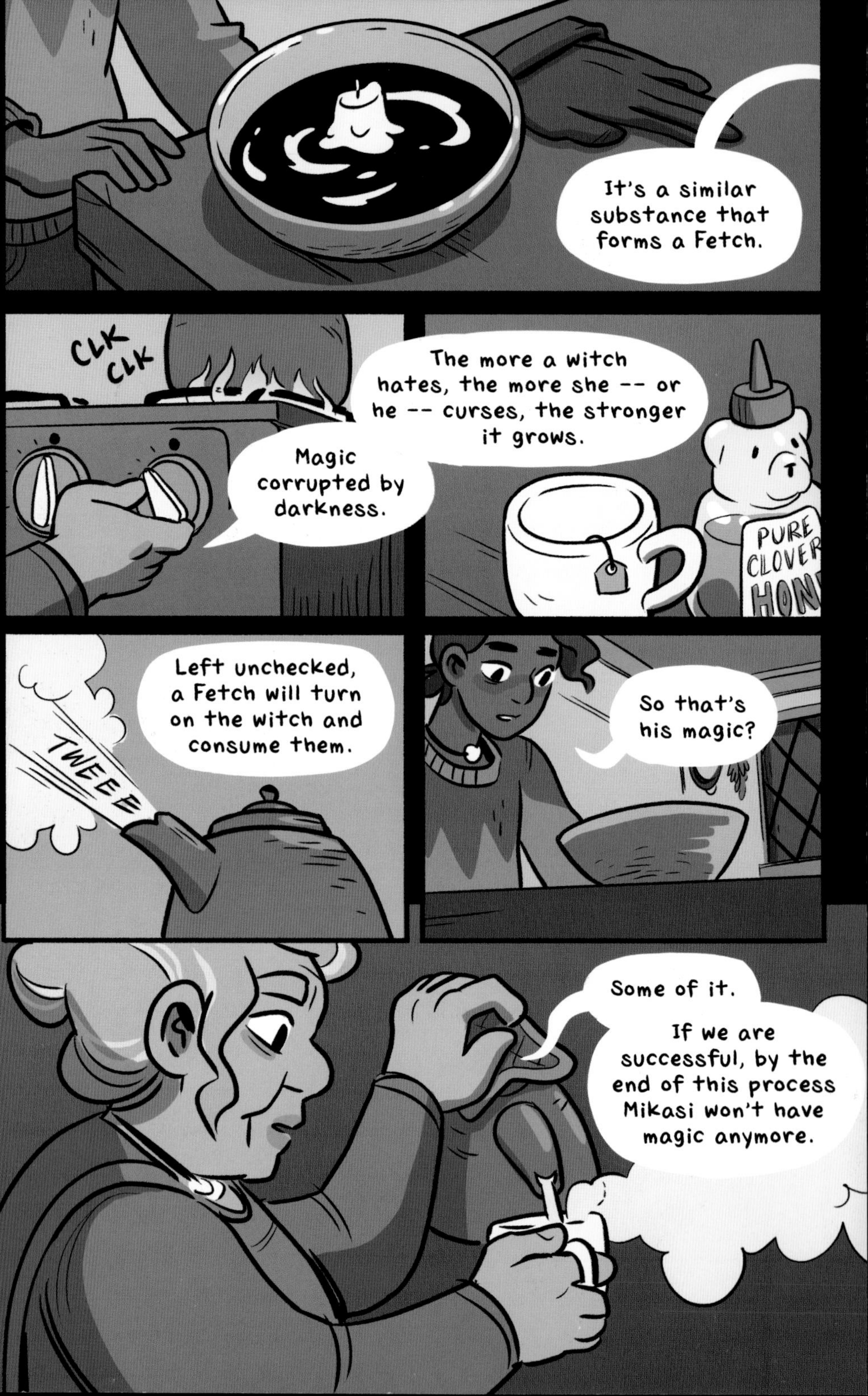
It's a similar substance that forms a Fetch.
CLK CLK
Magic corrupted by darkness.
The more a witch hates, the more she -- or he -- curses, the stronger it grows.
PURE CLOVER HON
TWEEE
Left unchecked, a Fetch will turn on the witch and consume them.
So that's his magic?
Some of it.
If we are successful, by the end of this process Mikasi won't have magic anymore.

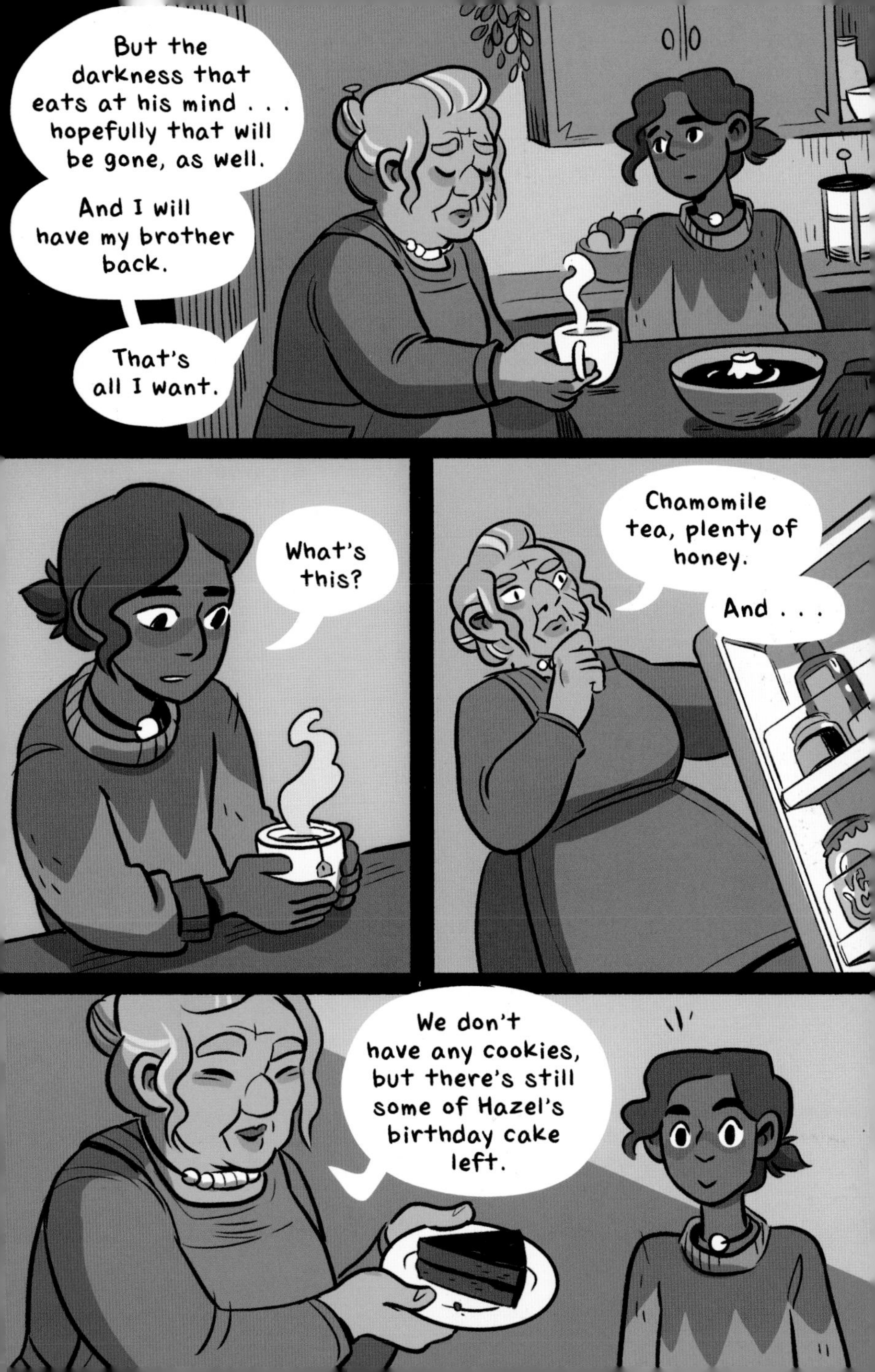

But the darkness that eats at his mind . . . hopefully that will be gone, as well.
And I will have my brother back.
That's all I want.
What's this?
Chamomile tea, plenty of honey.
And . . .
We don't have any cookies, but there's still some of Hazel's birthday cake left.

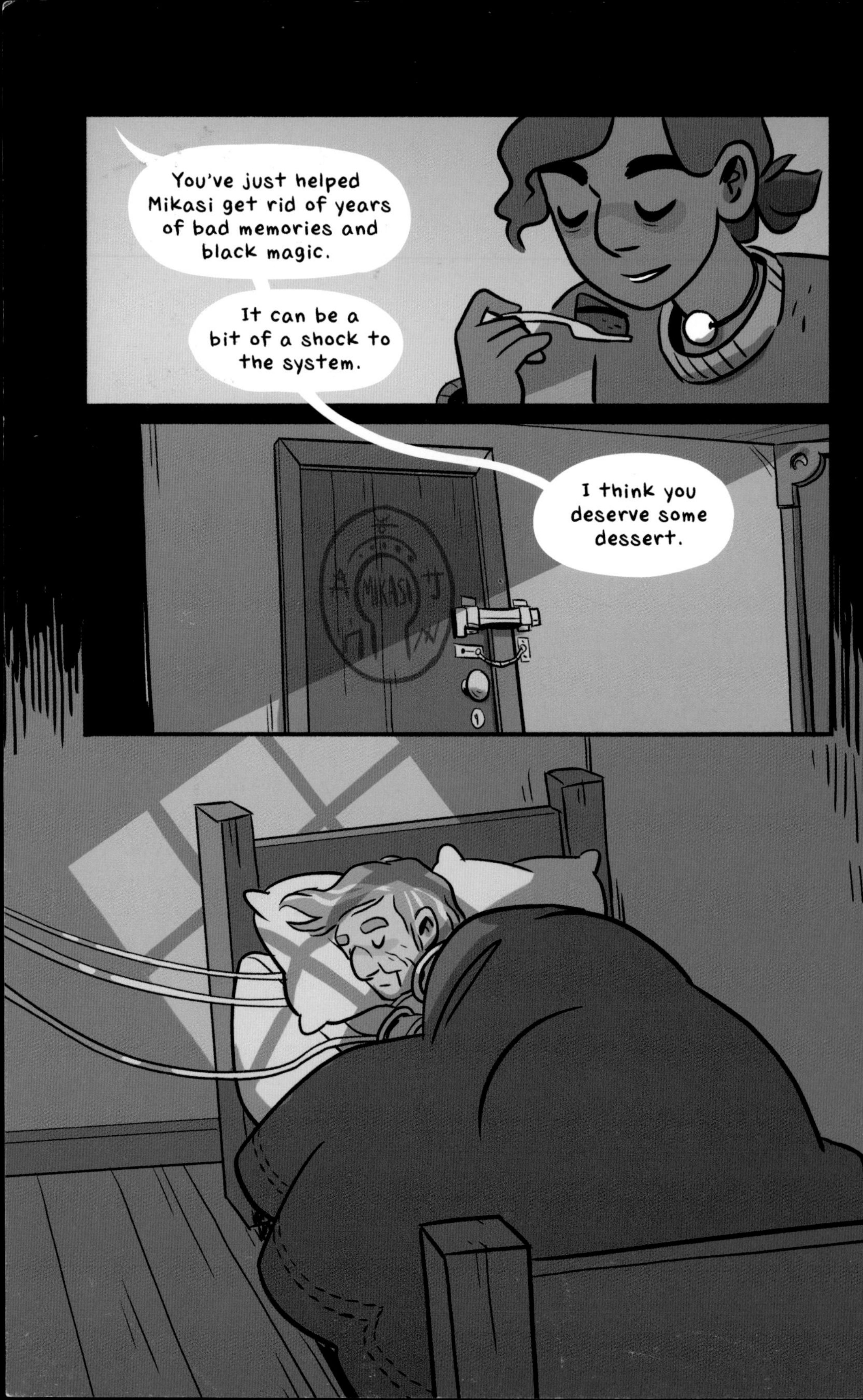
You've just helped Mikasi get rid of years of bad memories and black magic.
It can be a bit of a shock to the system.
MIKASI
I think you deserve some dessert.

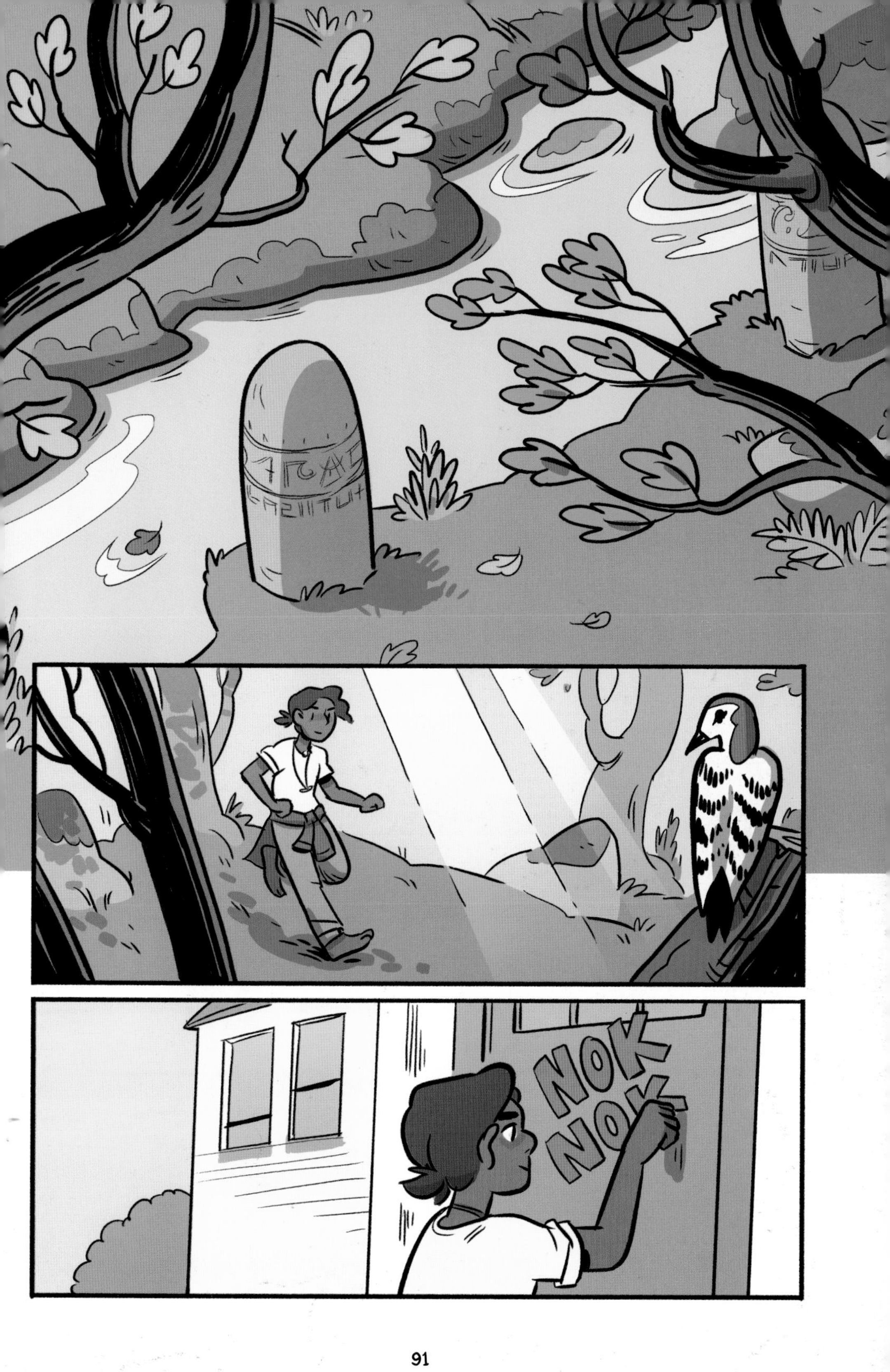
NOK
NOK

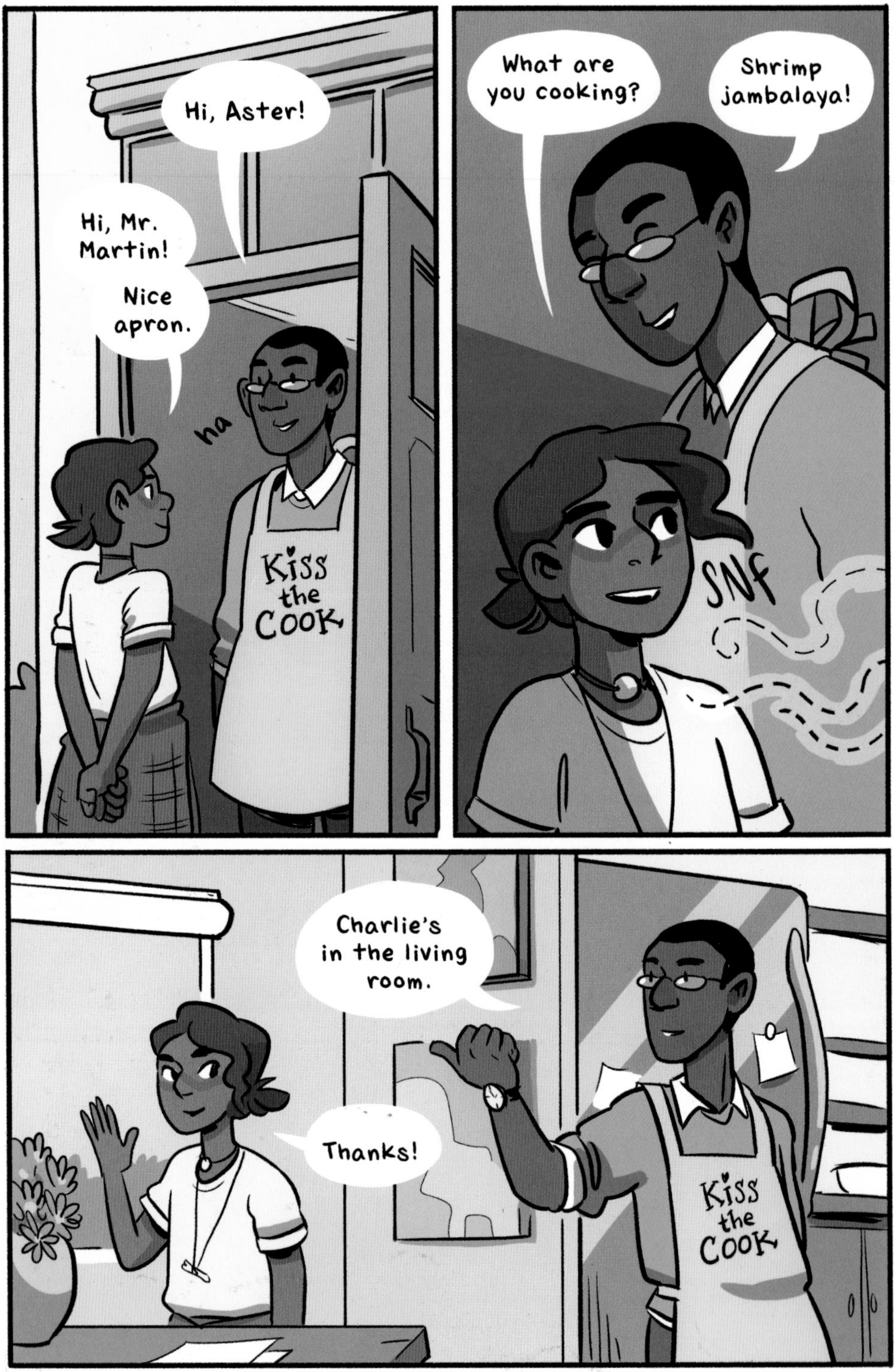
Hi, Aster!
Hi, Mr. Martin!
Nice apron.
ha
Kiss the COOK
What are you cooking?
Shrimp jambalaya!
SNF
Charlie's in the living room.
Thanks!
Kiss the COOK

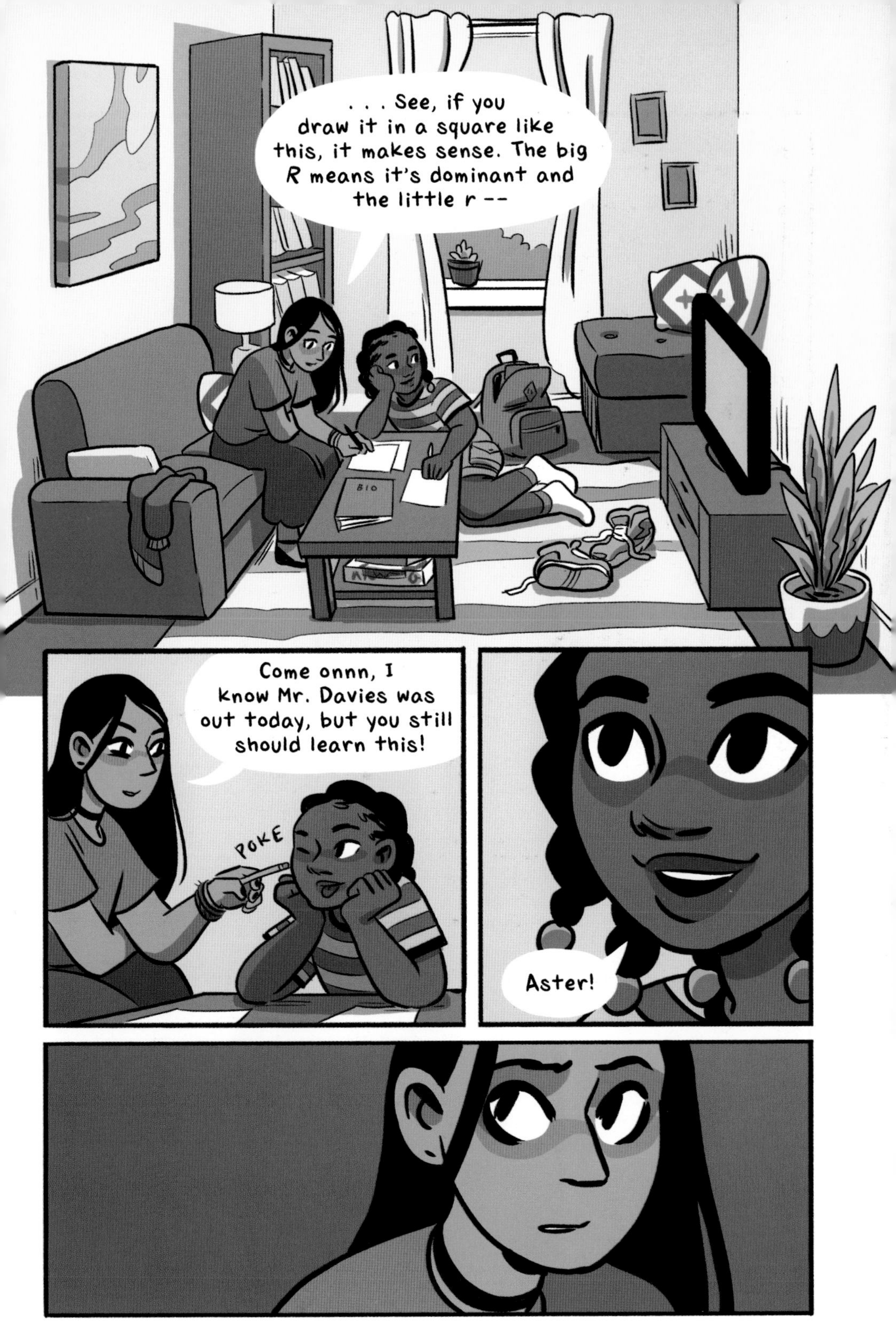
. . . See, if you draw it in a square like this, it makes sense. The big R means it's dominant and the little r --
BIO
Come onnn, I know Mr. Davies was out today, but you still should learn this!
POKE
Aster!

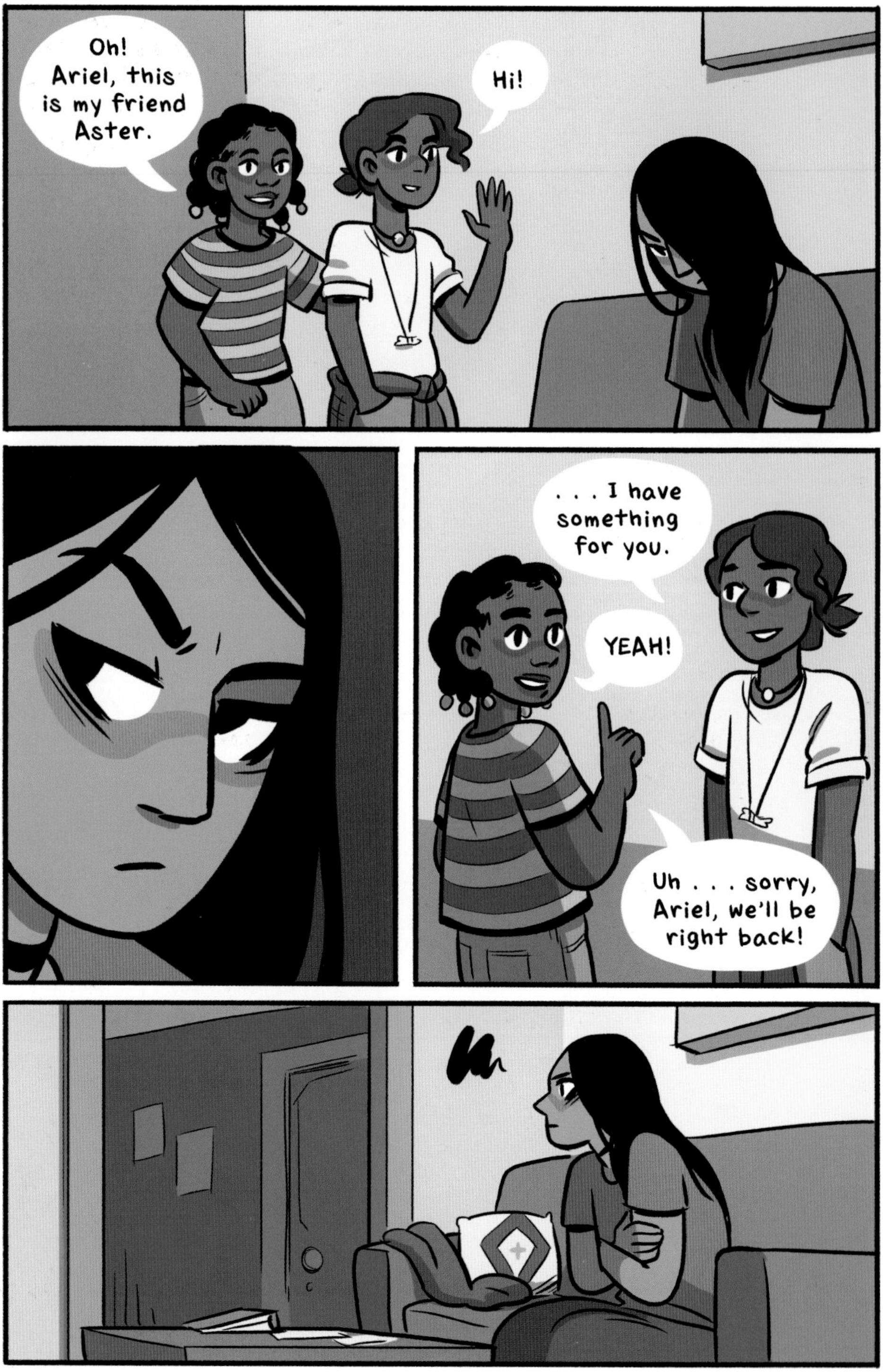
Oh! Ariel, this is my friend Aster.
Hi!
. . . I have something for you.
YEAH!
Uh . . . sorry, Ariel, we'll be right back!

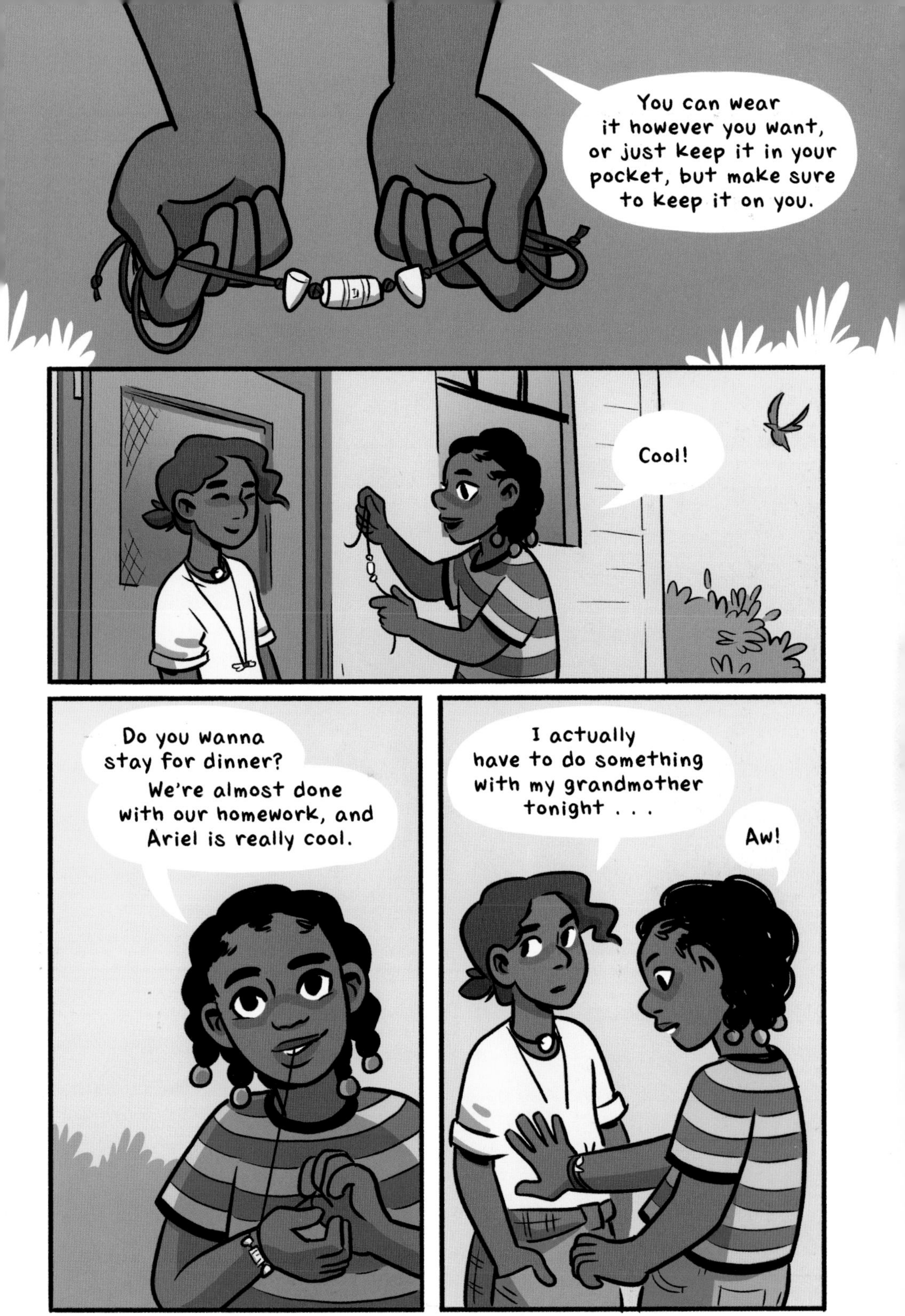
You can wear it however you want, or just keep it in your pocket, but make sure to keep it on you.
Cool!
Do you wanna stay for dinner?
We're almost done with our homework, and Ariel is really cool.
I actually have to do something with my grandmother tonight . . .
Aw!

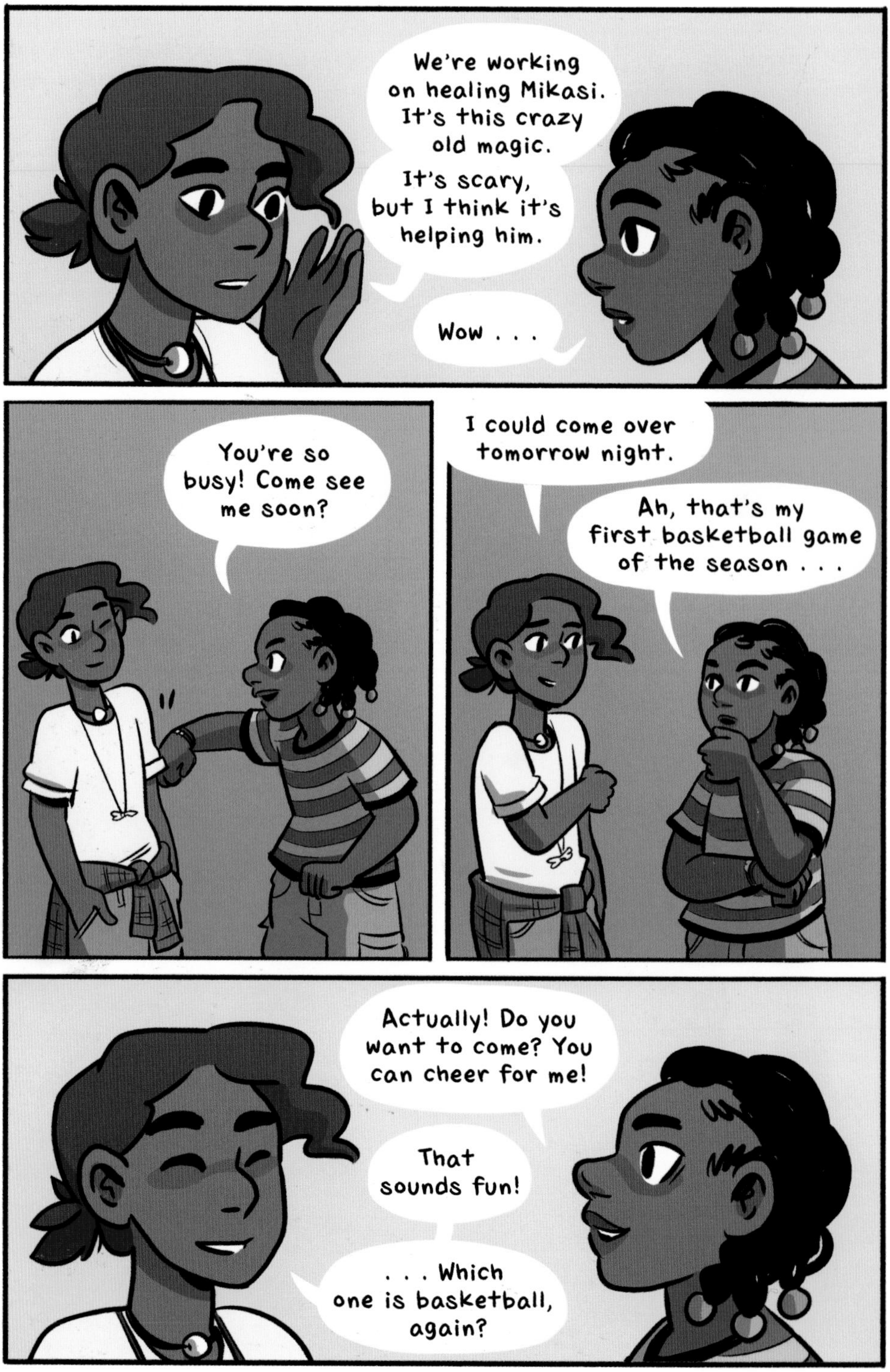
We're working on healing Mikasi. It's this crazy old magic.
It's scary, but I think it's helping him.
Wow . . .
You're so busy! Come see me soon?
I could come over tomorrow night.
Ah, that's my first basketball game of the season . . .
Actually! Do you want to come? You can cheer for me!
That sounds fun!
. . . Which one is basketball, again?

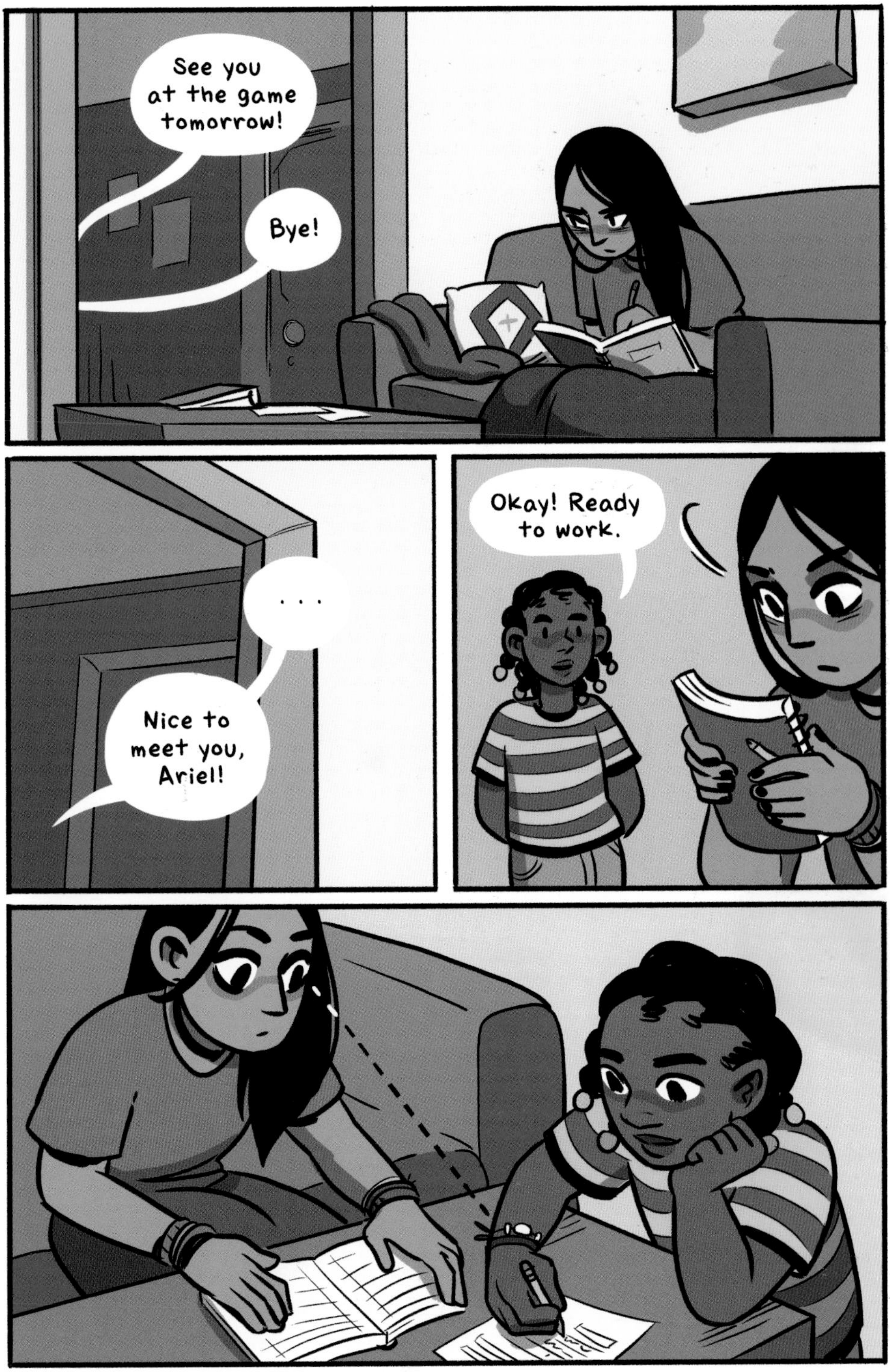
See you at the game tomorrow!
Bye!
. . .
Nice to meet you, Ariel!
Okay! Ready to work.

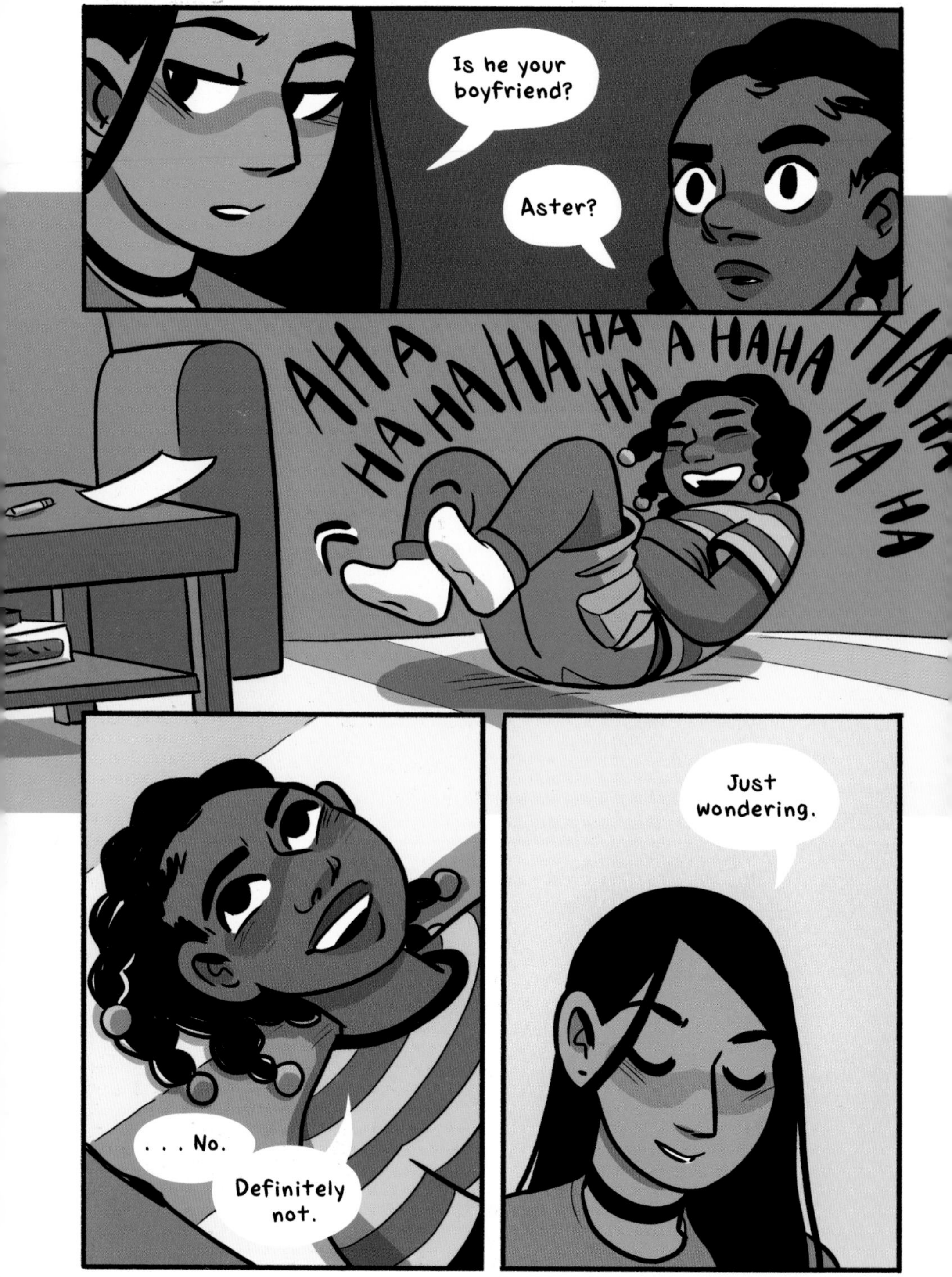
Is he your boyfriend?
Aster?
AHA HAHAHAHA HA HA A HAHA HA HA HA HA HA
. . . No.
Definitely not.
Just wondering.

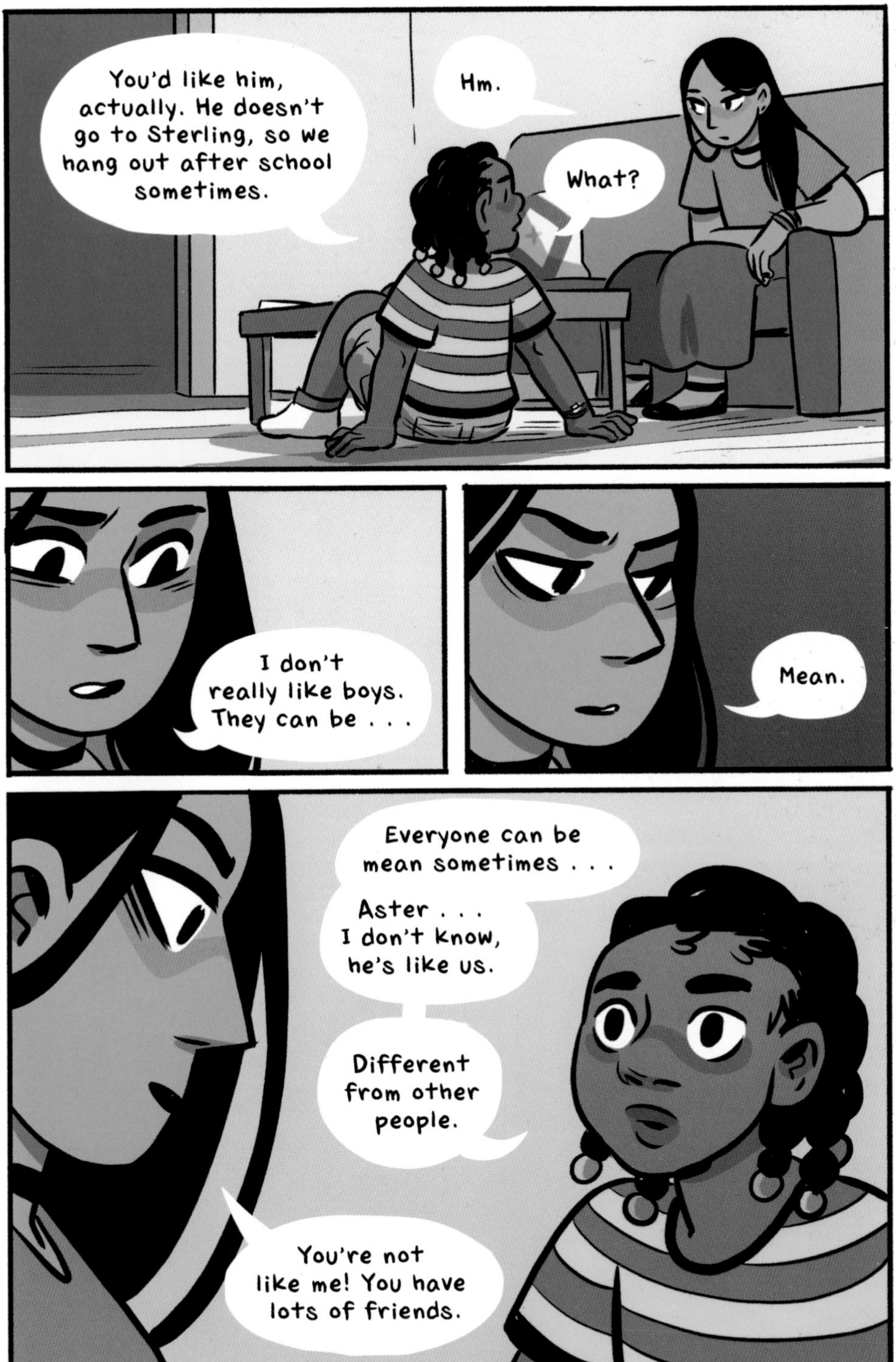
You'd like him, actually. He doesn't go to Sterling, so we hang out after school sometimes.
Hm.
What?
I don't really like boys. They can be . . .
Mean.
Everyone can be mean sometimes . . .
Aster . . . I don't know, he's like us.
Different from other people.
You're not like me! You have lots of friends.

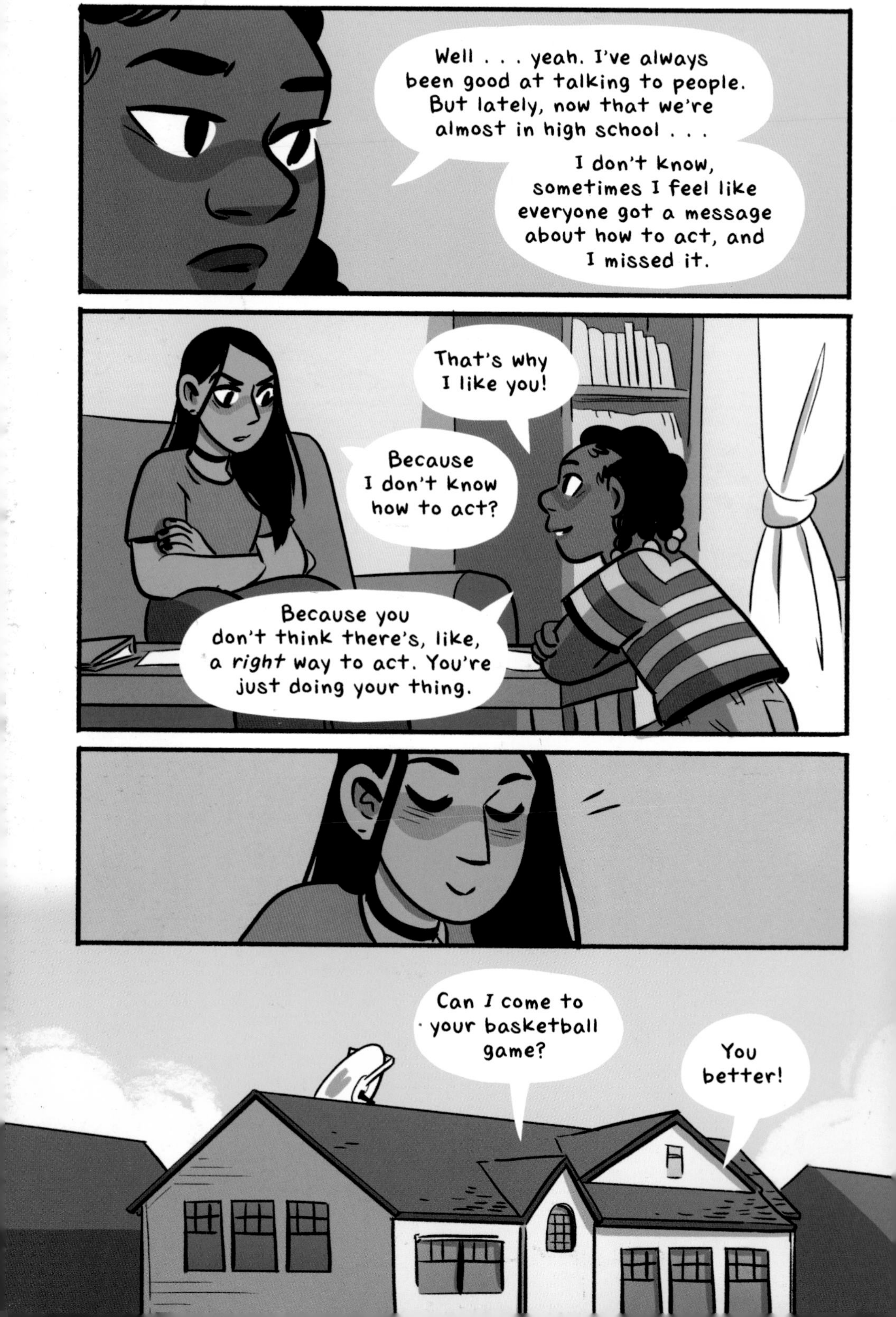
Well . . . yeah. I've always been good at talking to people. But lately, now that we're almost in high school . . .
I don't know, sometimes I feel like everyone got a message about how to act, and I missed it.
That's why I like you!
Because I don't know how to act?
Because you don't think there's, like, a *right* way to act. You're just doing your thing.
Can *I* come to your basketball game?
You better!

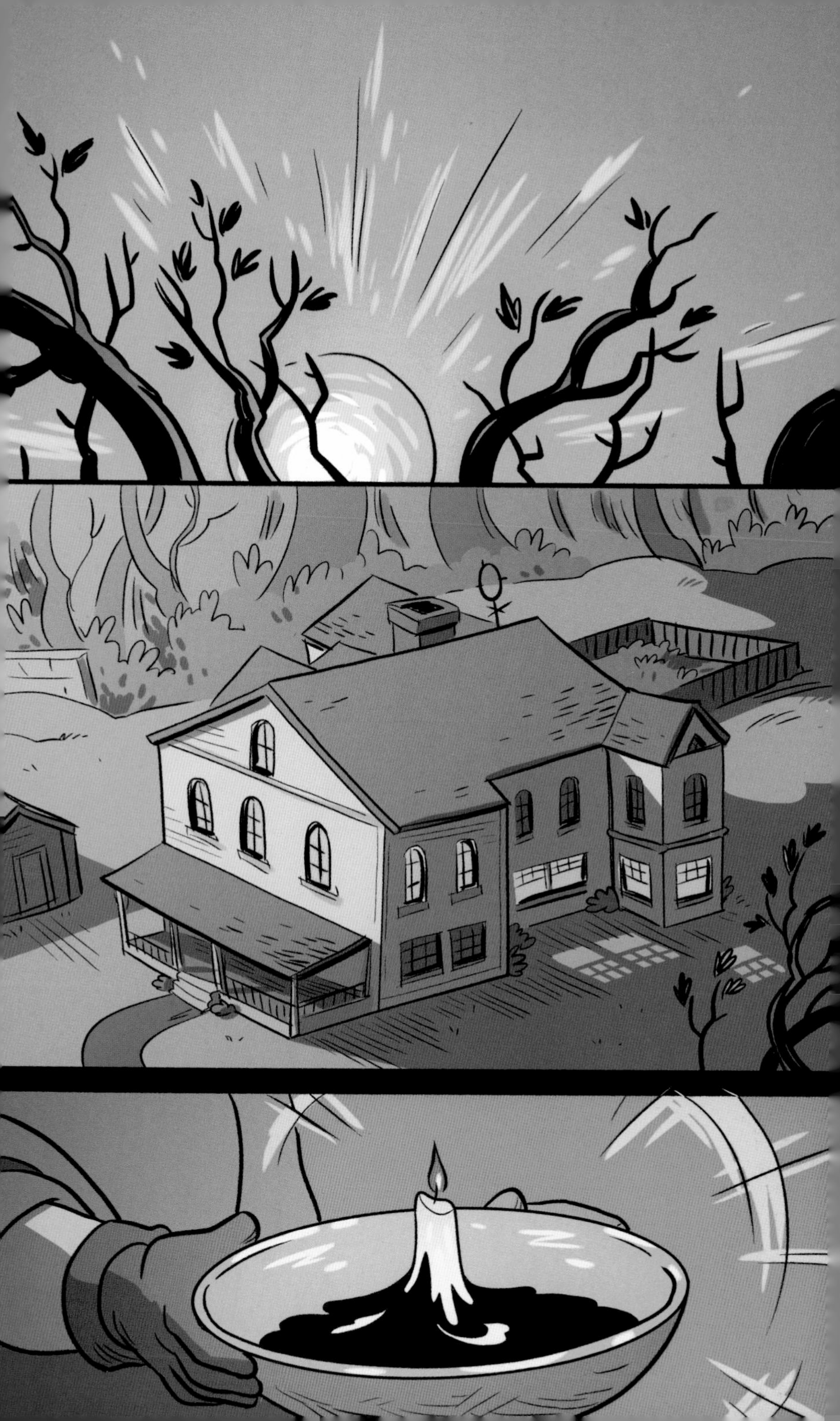

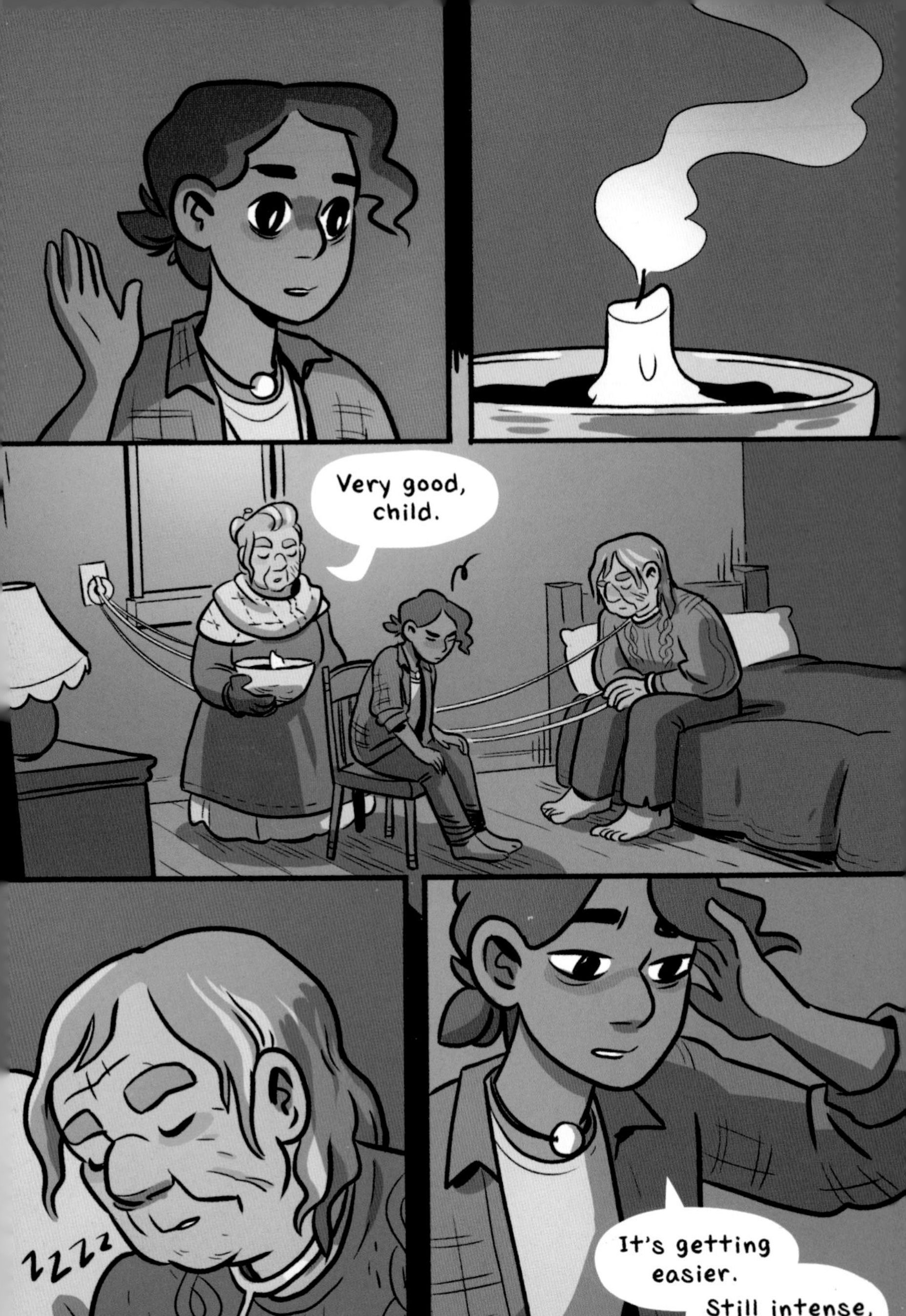
Very good, child.
ZZZZ
It's getting easier.
Still intense, though.

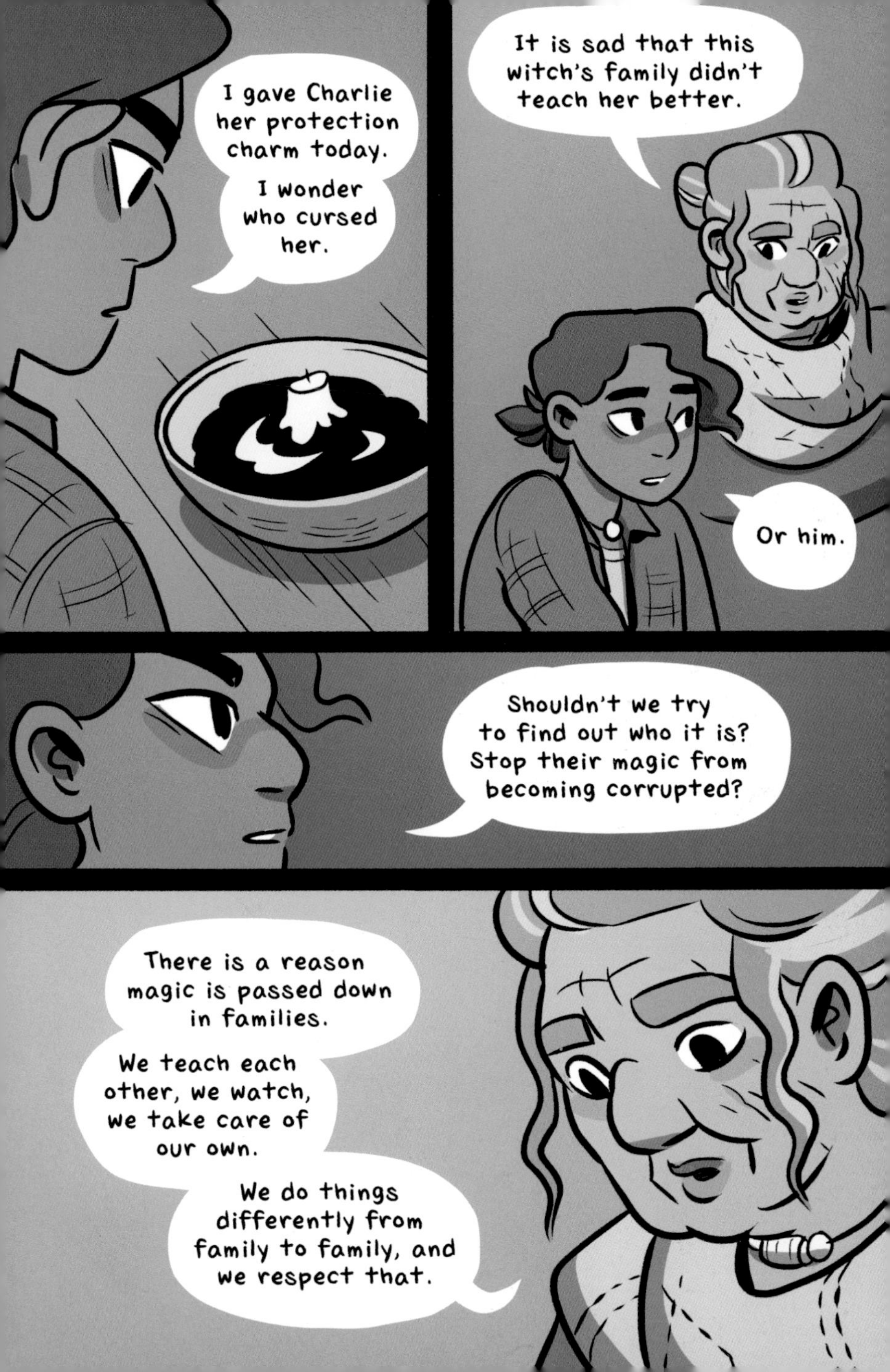
I gave Charlie her protection charm today.
I wonder who cursed her.
It is sad that this witch's family didn't teach her better.
Or him.
Shouldn't we try to find out who it is? Stop their magic from becoming corrupted?
There is a reason magic is passed down in families.
We teach each other, we watch, we take care of our own.
We do things differently from family to family, and we respect that.

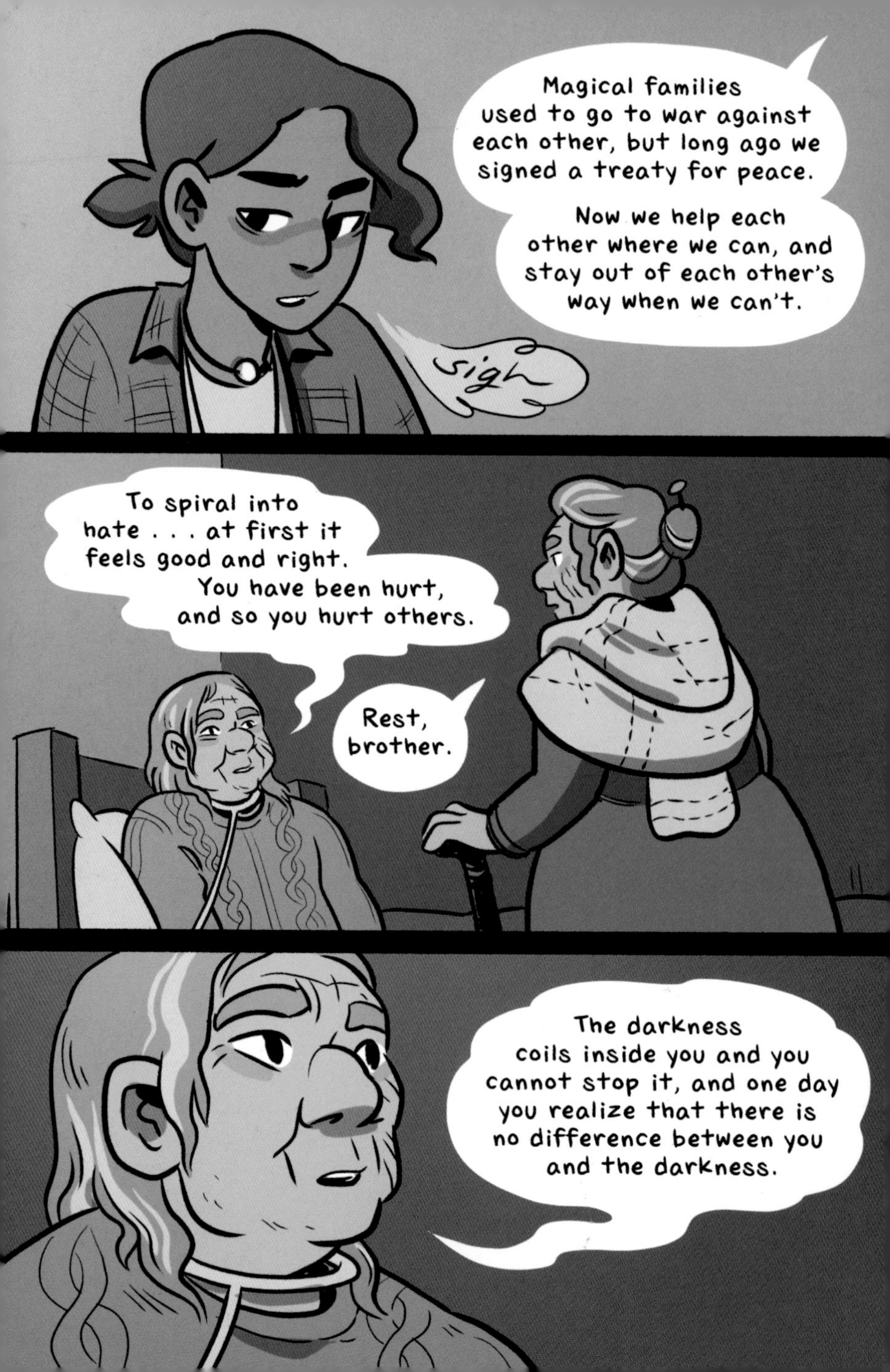
Magical families used to go to war against each other, but long ago we signed a treaty for peace.
Now we help each other where we can, and stay out of each other's way when we can't.
sigh
To spiral into hate . . . at first it feels good and right. You have been hurt, and so you hurt others.
Rest, brother.
The darkness coils inside you and you cannot stop it, and one day you realize that there is no difference between you and the darkness.

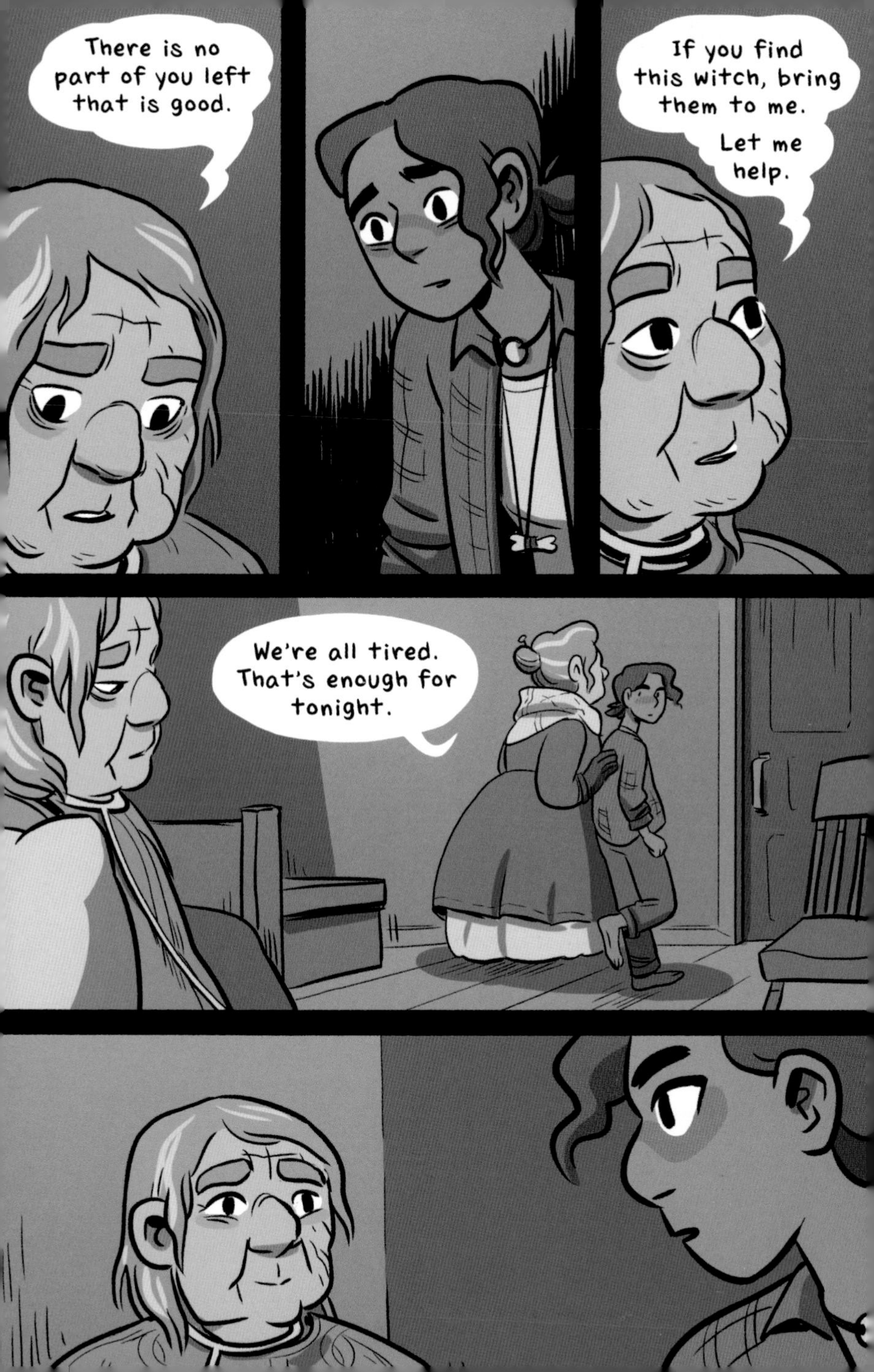
There is no part of you left that is good.
If you find this witch, bring them to me.
Let me help.
We're all tired. That's enough for tonight.

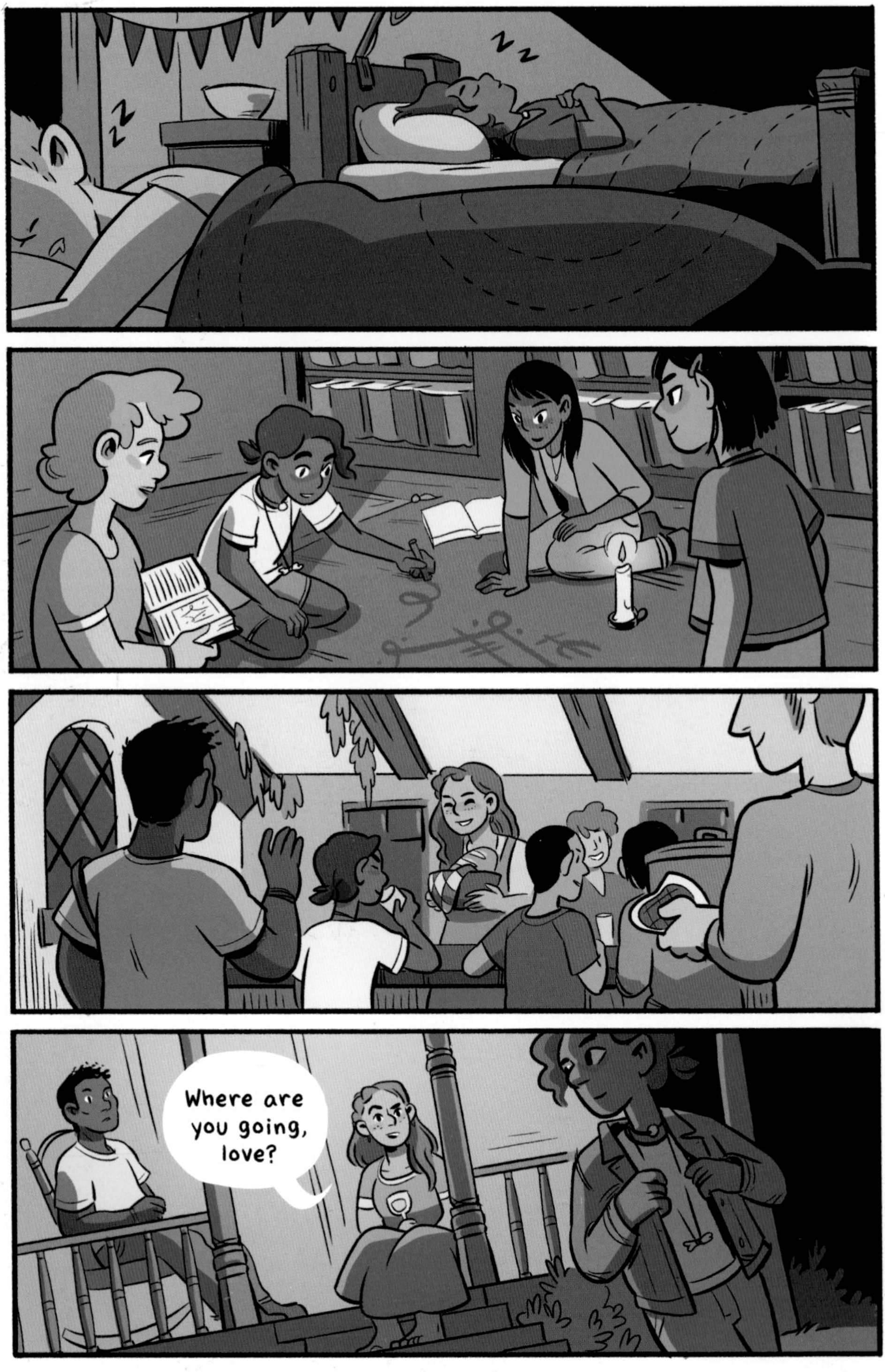
Where are you going, love?

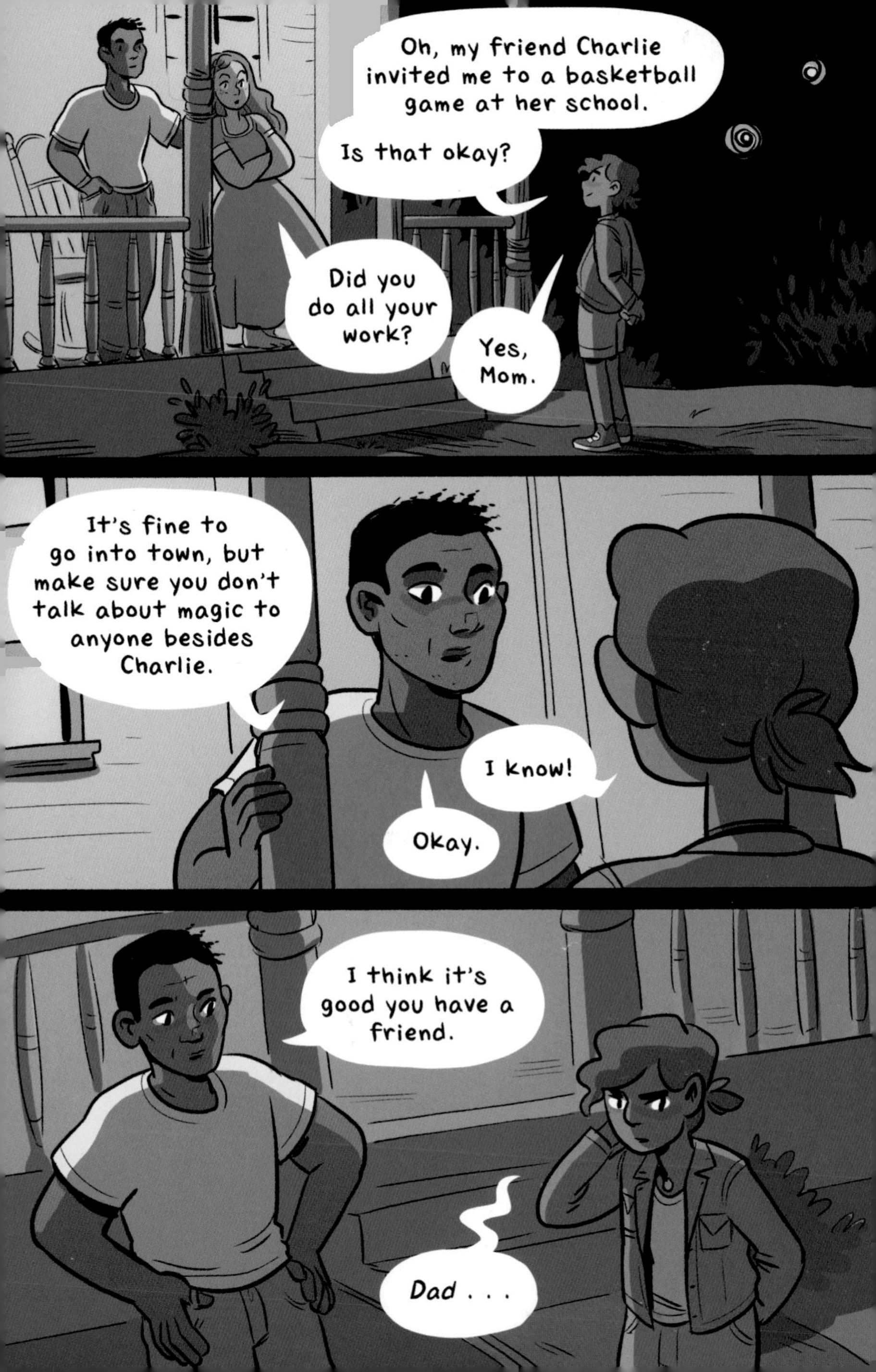

Oh, my friend Charlie invited me to a basketball game at her school.
Is that okay?
Did you do all your work?
Yes, Mom.
It's fine to go into town, but make sure you don't talk about magic to anyone besides Charlie.
I know!
Okay.
I think it's good you have a friend.
Dad . . .

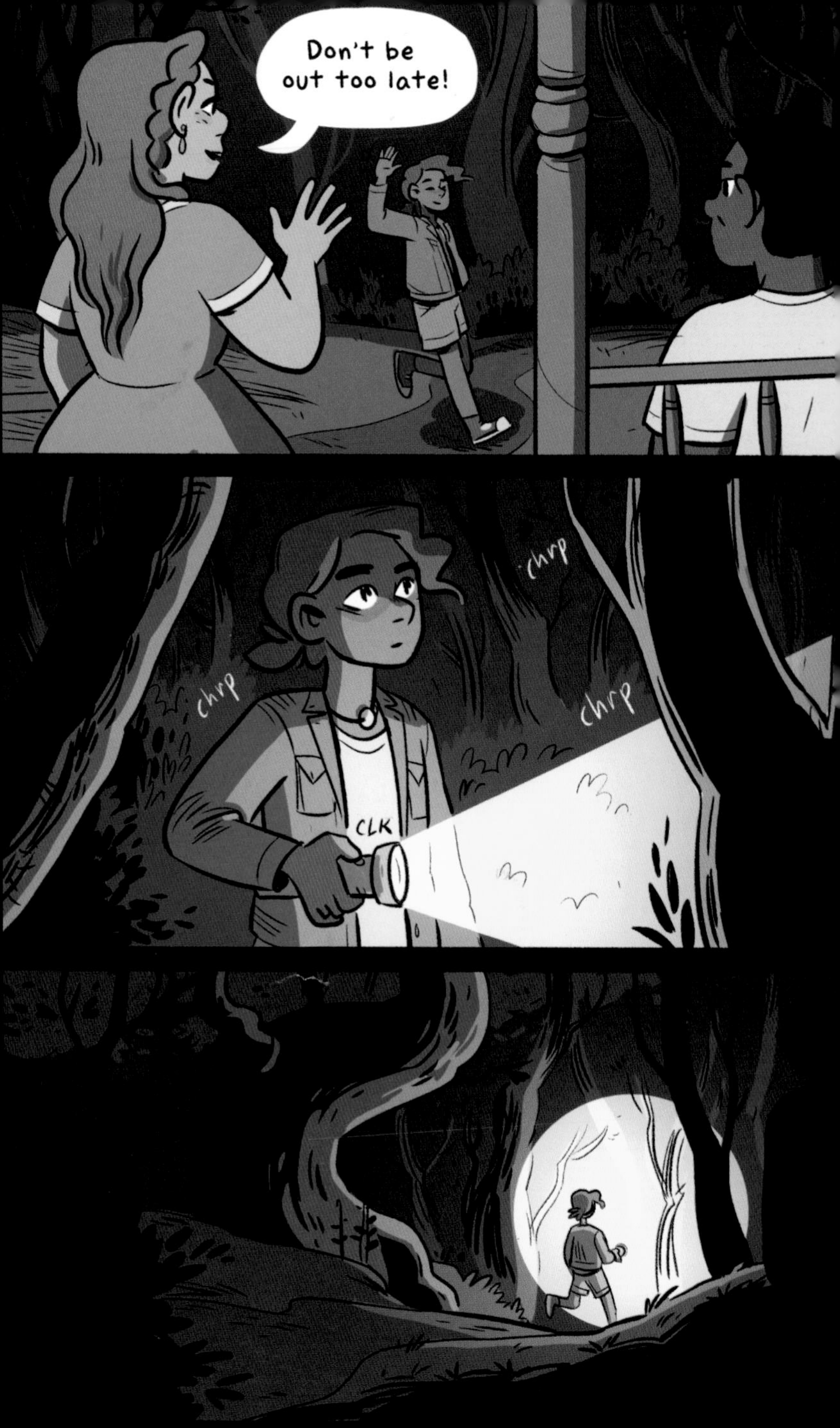
Don't be out too late!
chrp
chrp
chrp
CLK

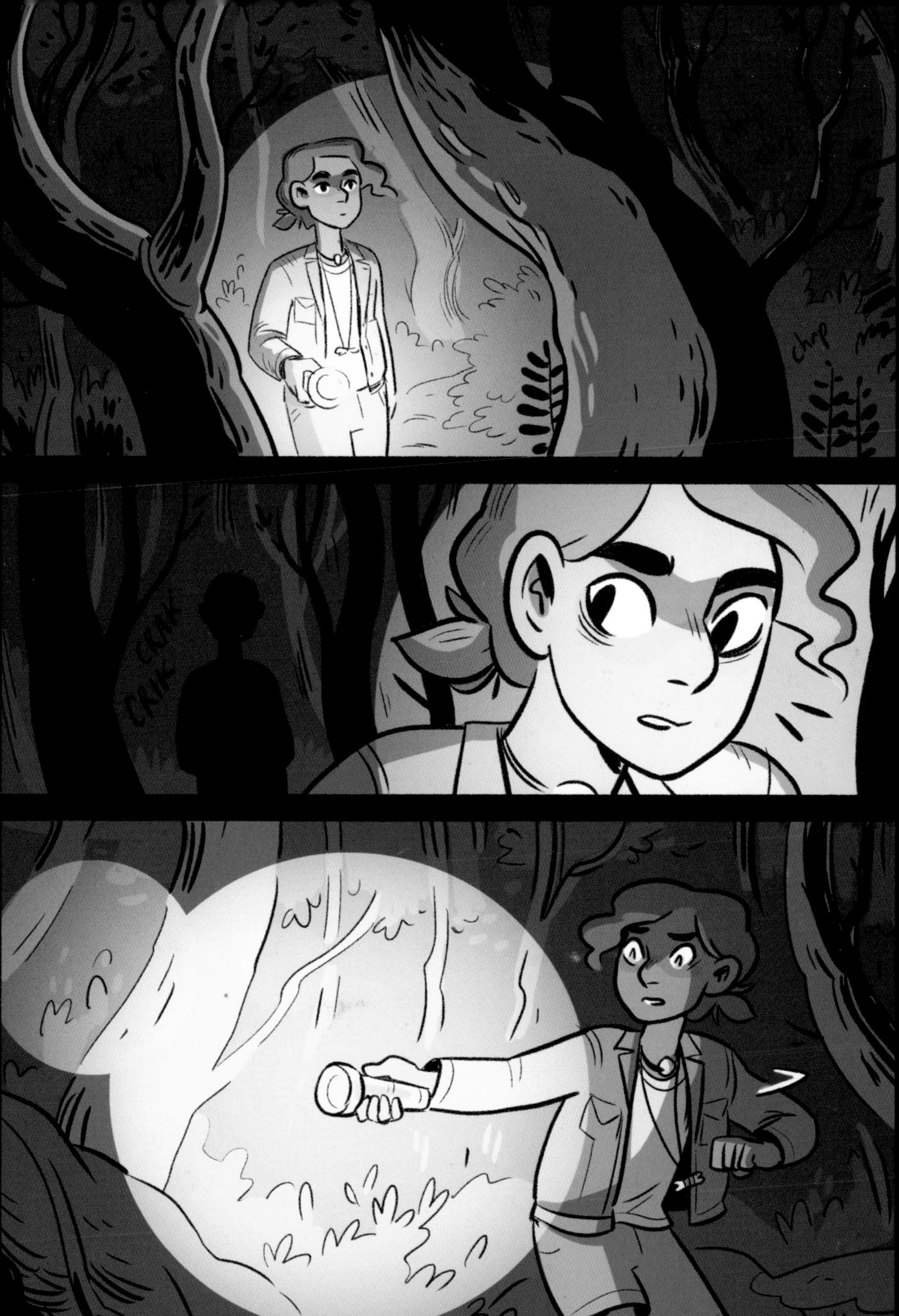
chirp
CRAK
CRIK

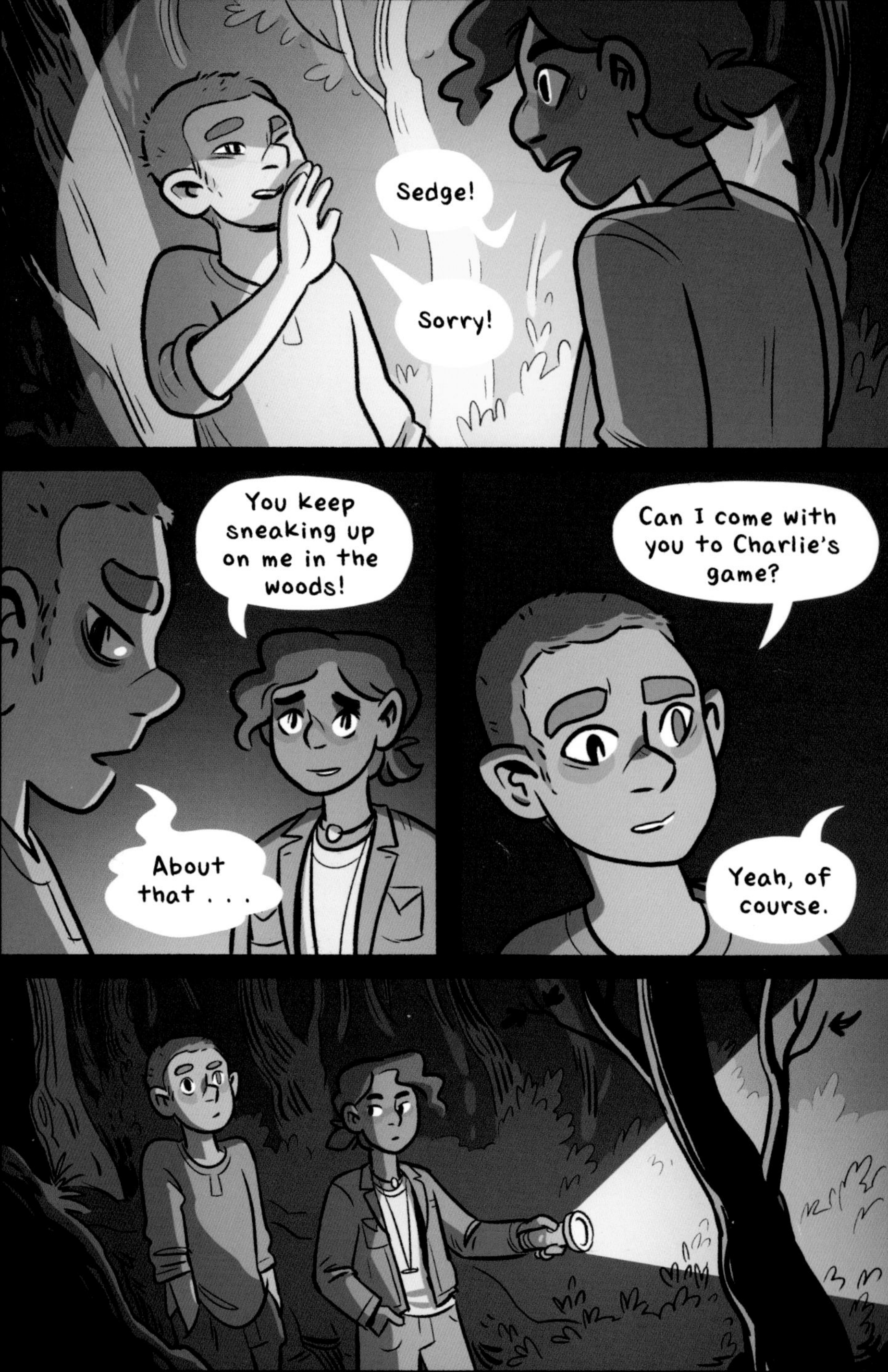
Sedge!
Sorry!
You keep sneaking up on me in the woods!
About that . . .
Can I come with you to Charlie's game?
Yeah, of course.

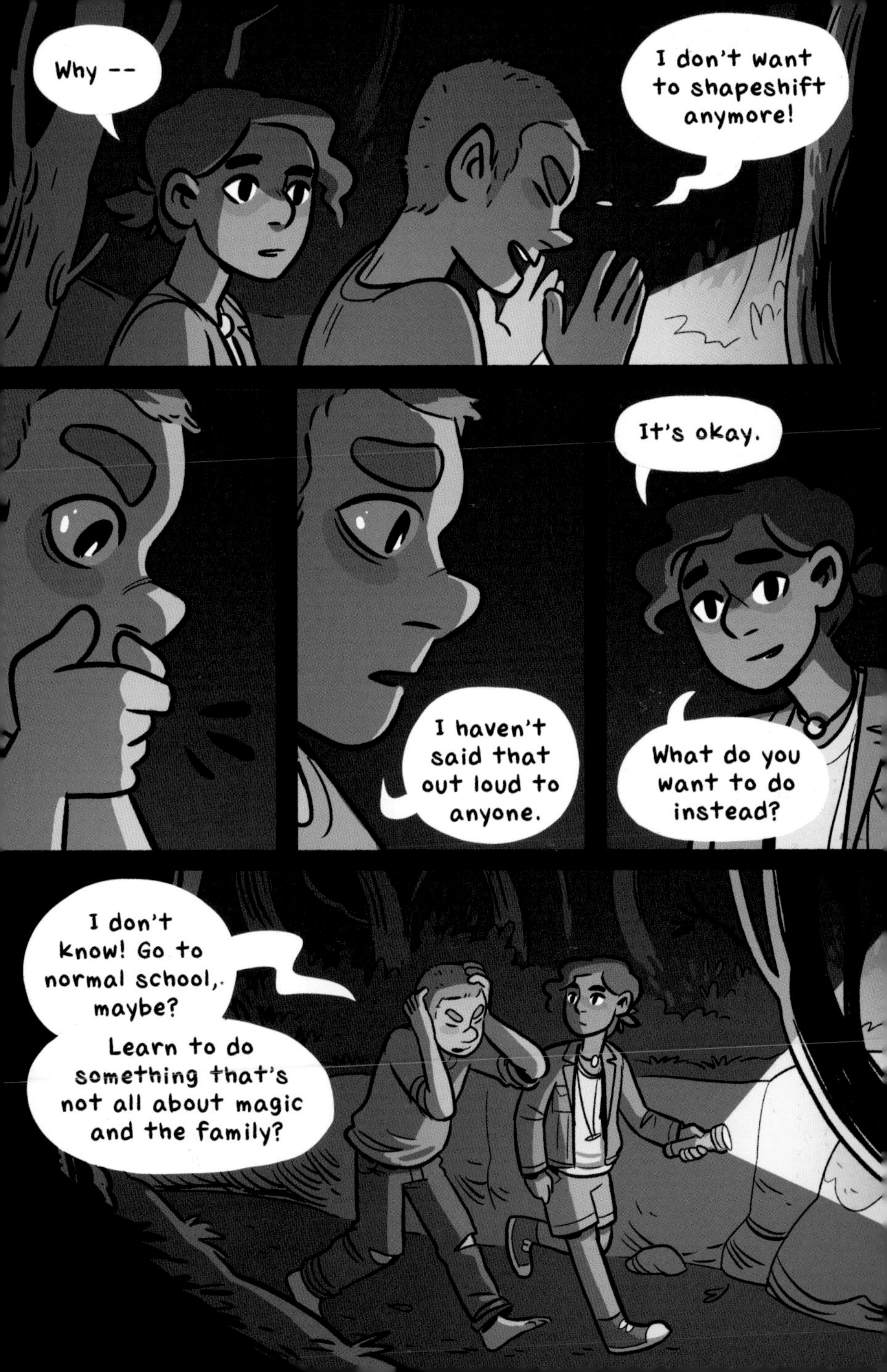
Why --
I don't want to shapeshift anymore!
I haven't said that out loud to anyone.
It's okay.
What do you want to do instead?
I don't know! Go to normal school, maybe?
Learn to do something that's not all about magic and the family?

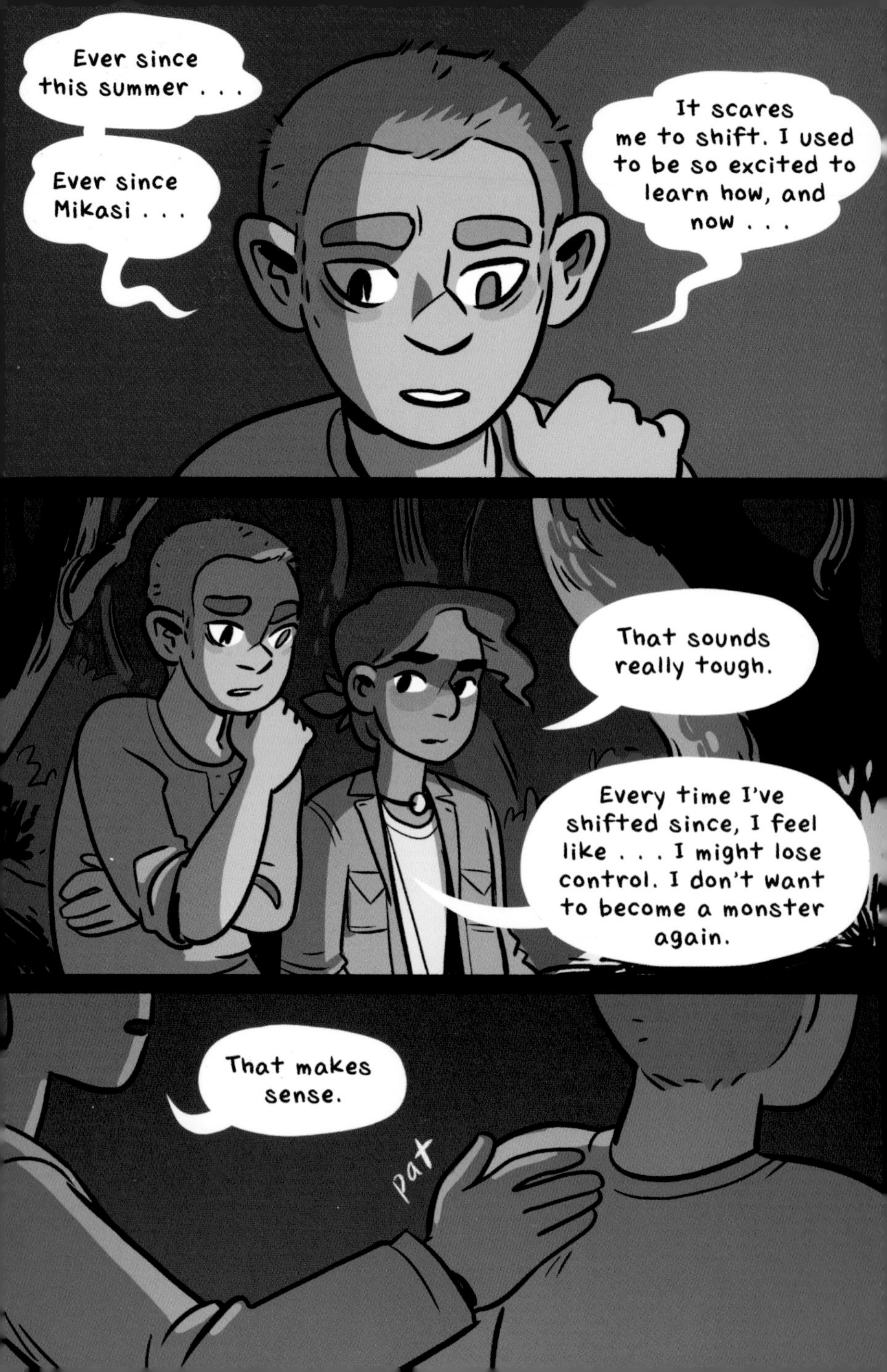
Ever since this summer . . .
Ever since Mikasi . . .
It scares me to shift. I used to be so excited to learn how, and now . . .
That sounds really tough.
Every time I've shifted since, I feel like . . . I might lose control. I don't want to become a monster again.
That makes sense.
pat

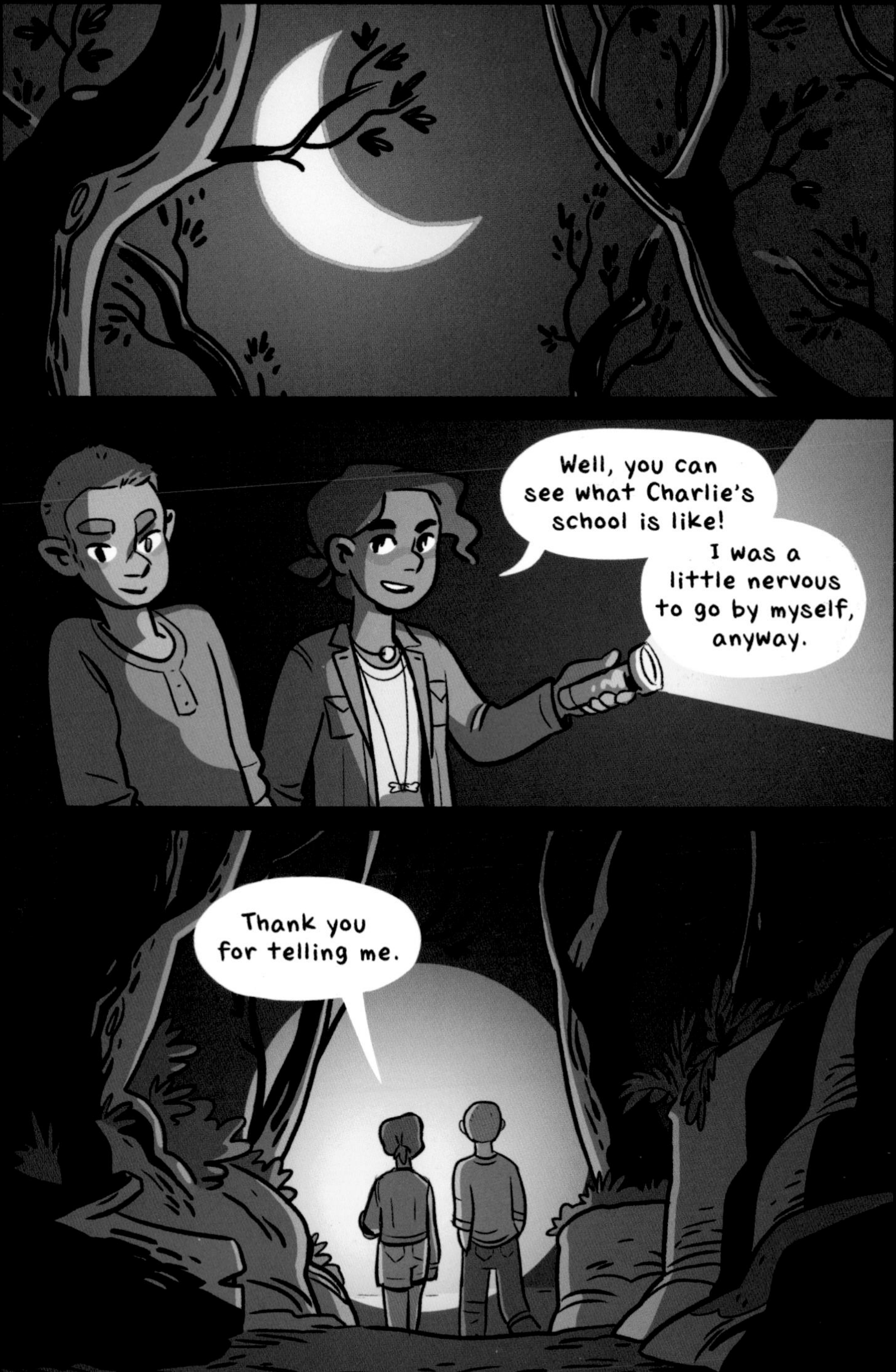
Well, you can see what Charlie's school is like!
I was a little nervous to go by myself, anyway.
Thank you for telling me.

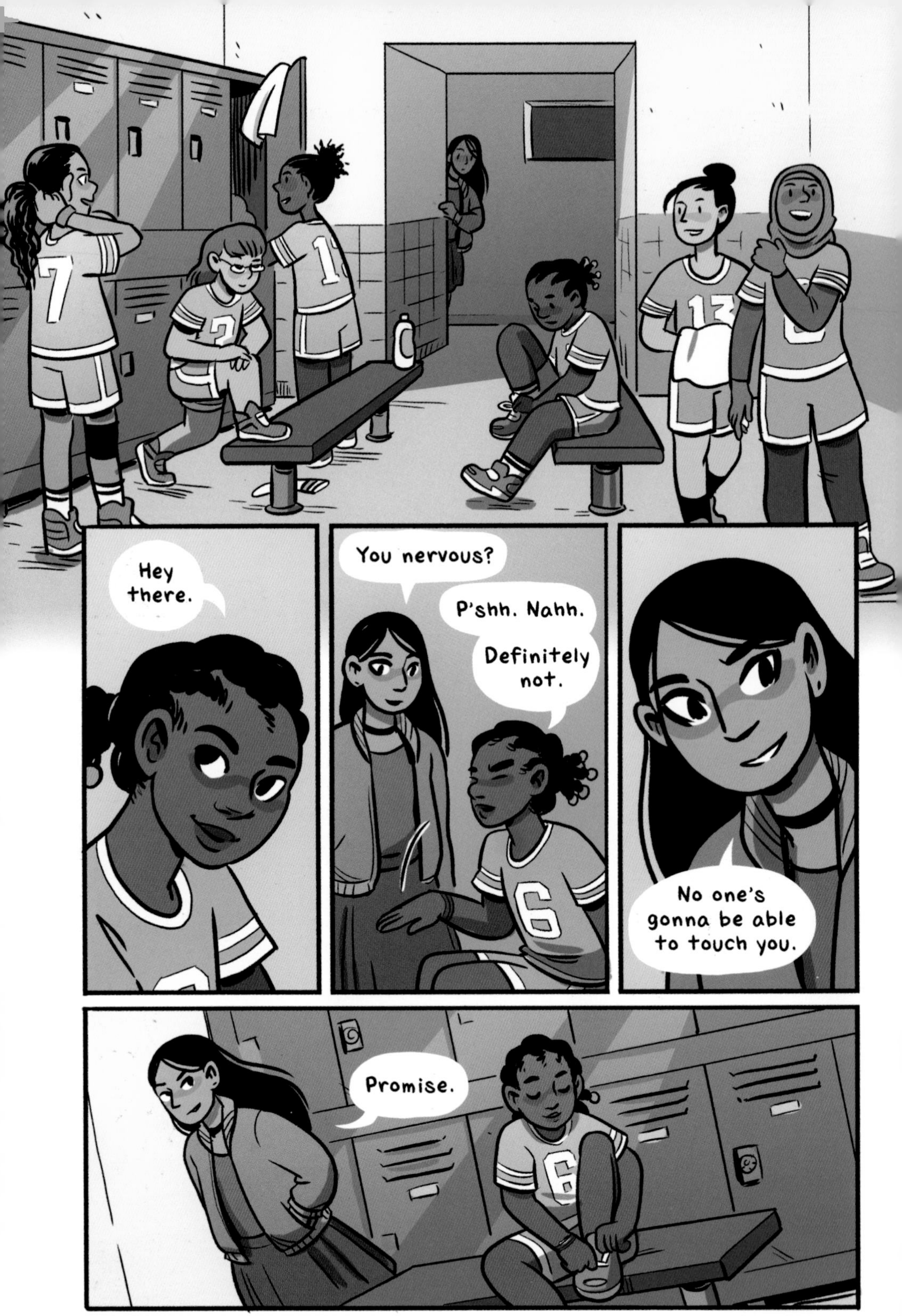
Hey there.
You nervous?
P'shh. Nahh.
Definitely not.
No one's gonna be able to touch you.
Promise.

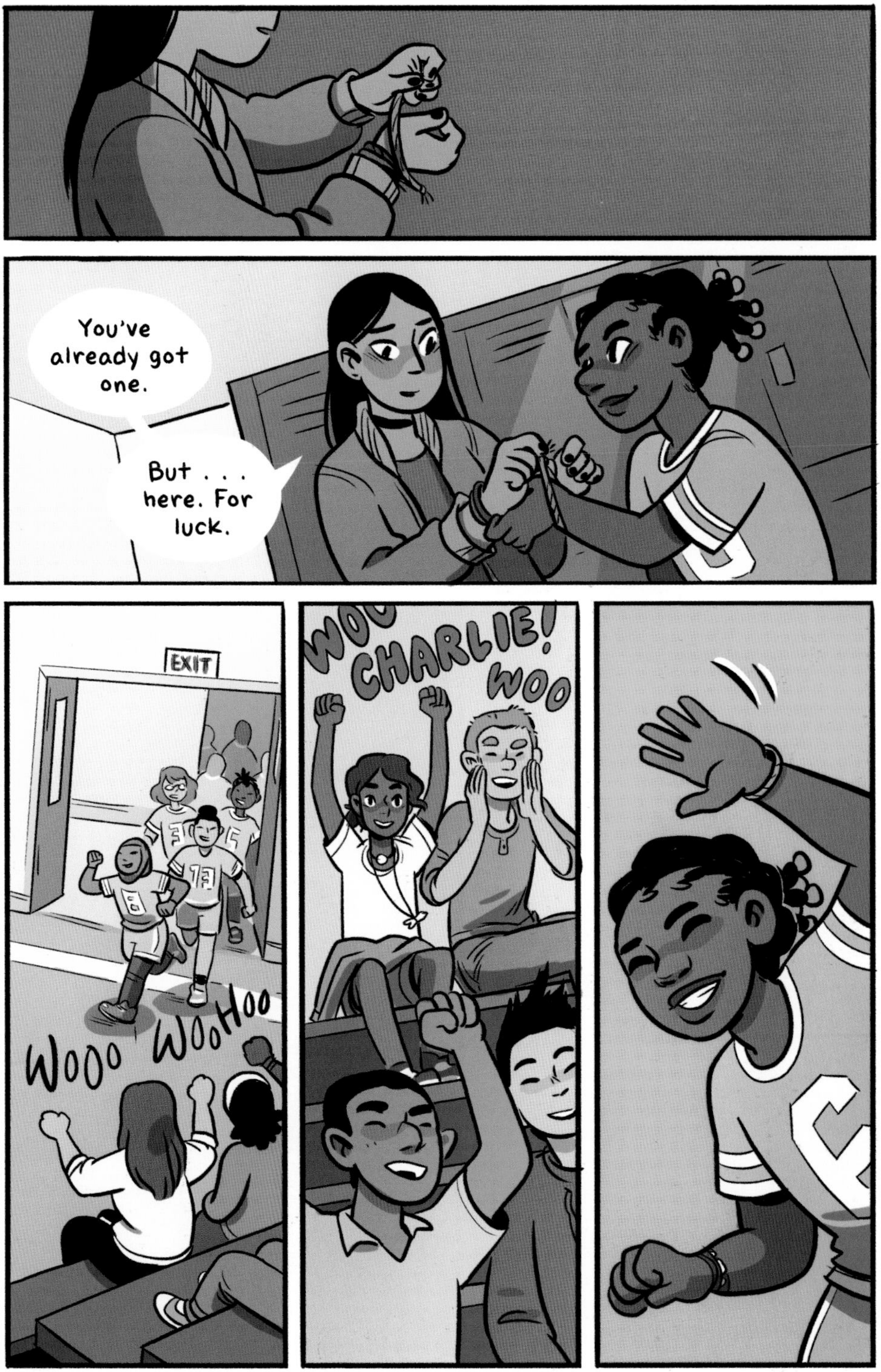
You've already got one.
But . . . here. For luck.
EXIT
WOOO WOOHOO
WOO CHARLIE! WOO

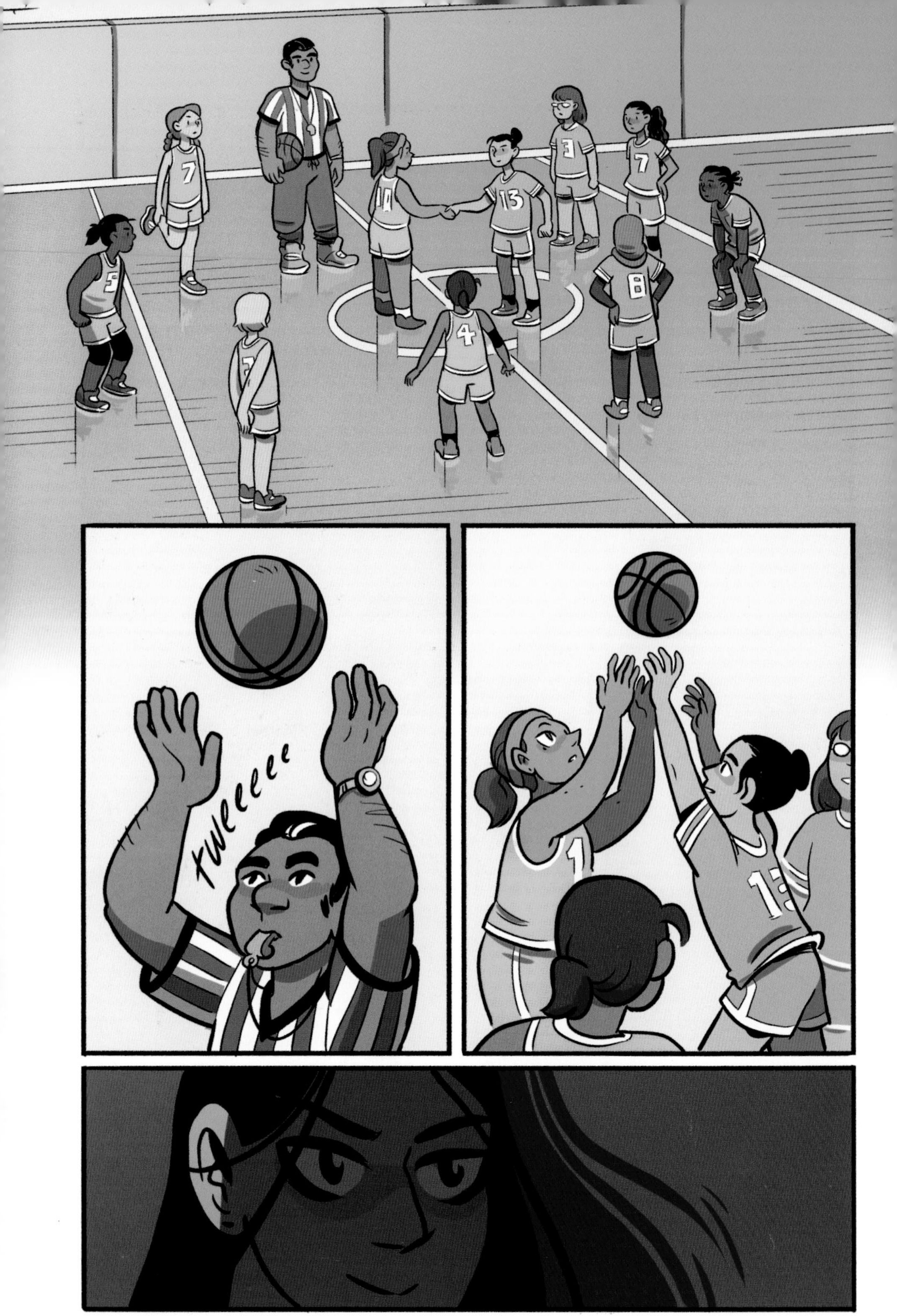
tweeeee

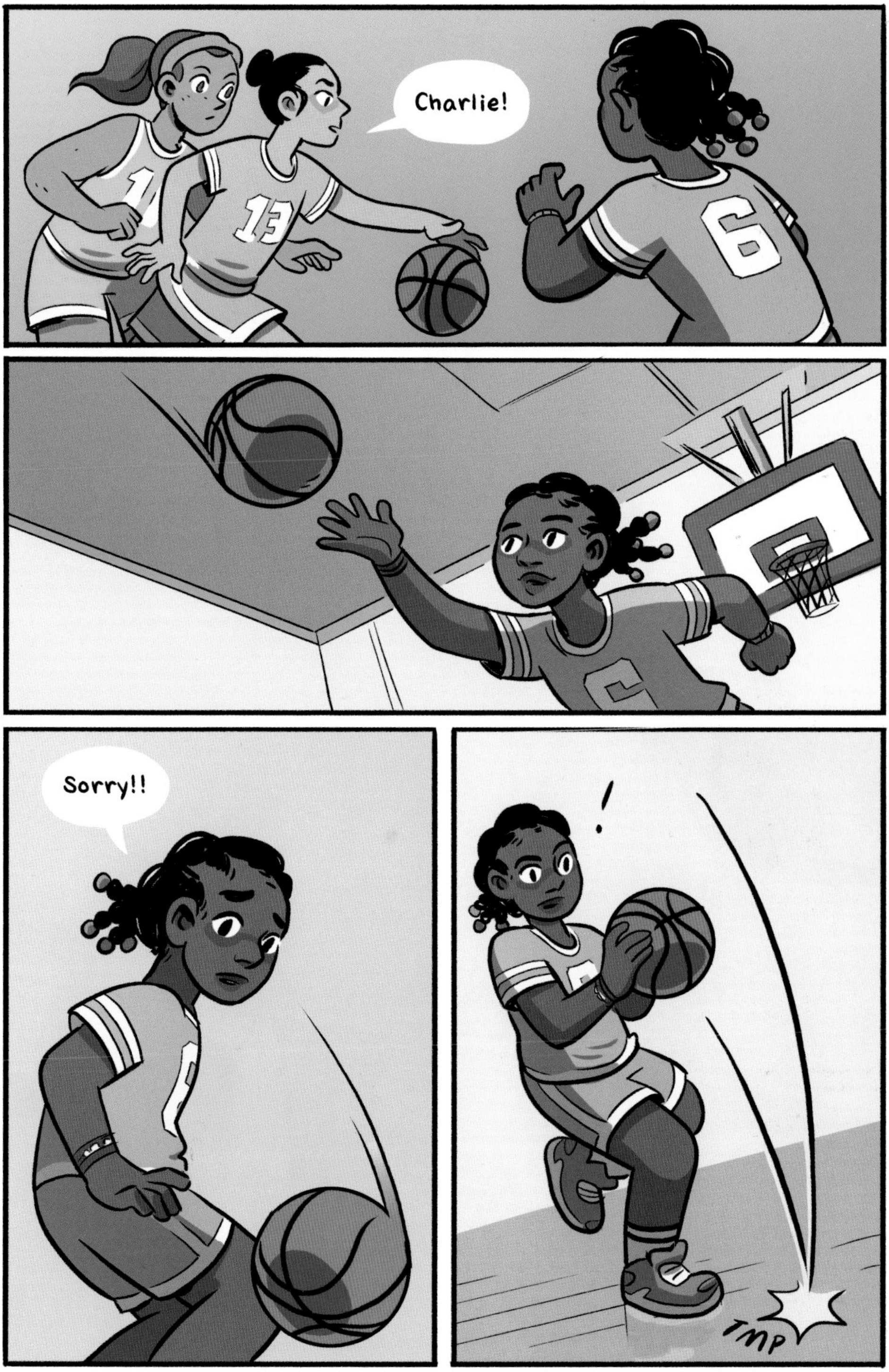

Charlie!
Sorry!!
!
TMP

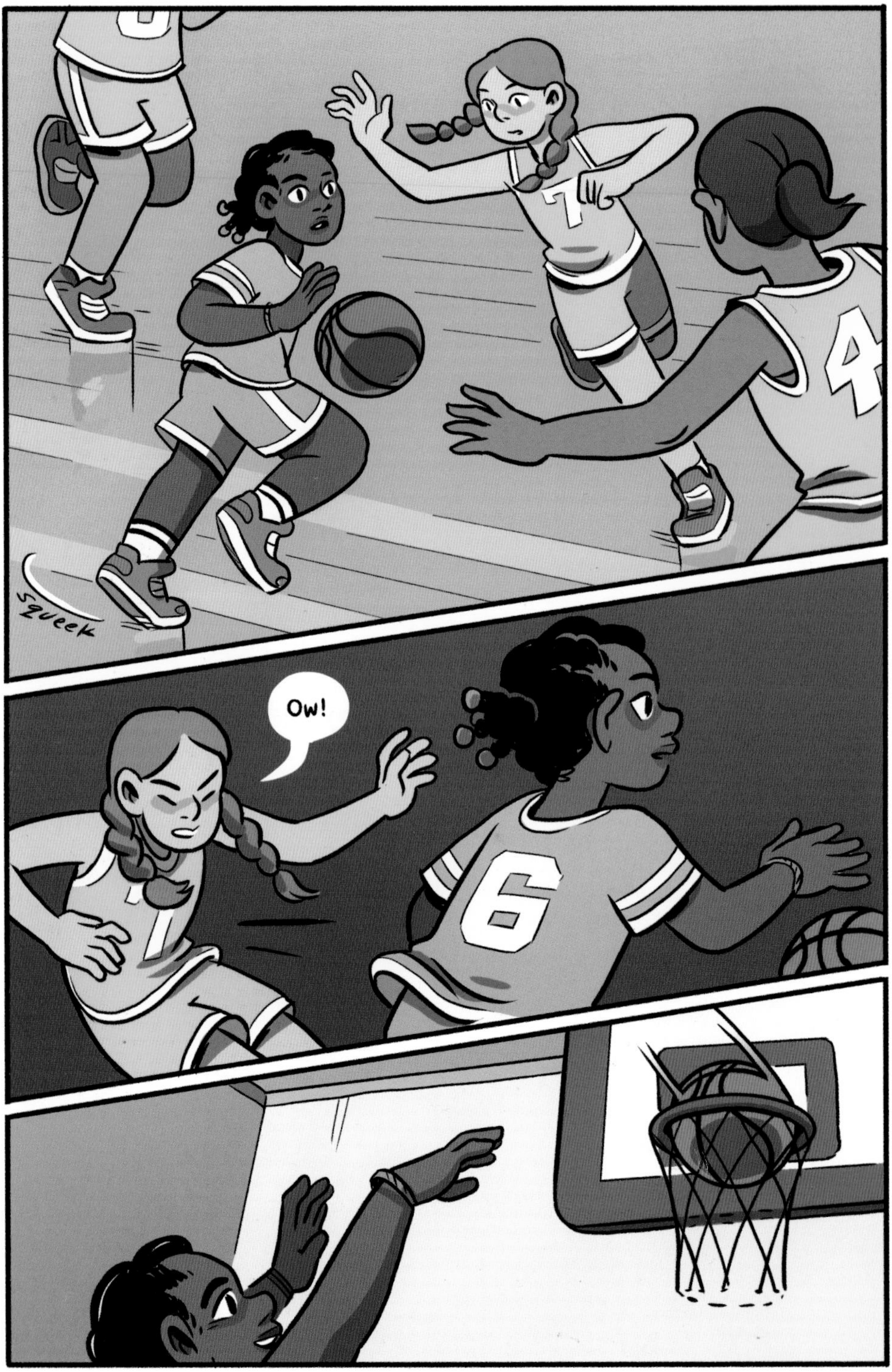
squeek
Ow!

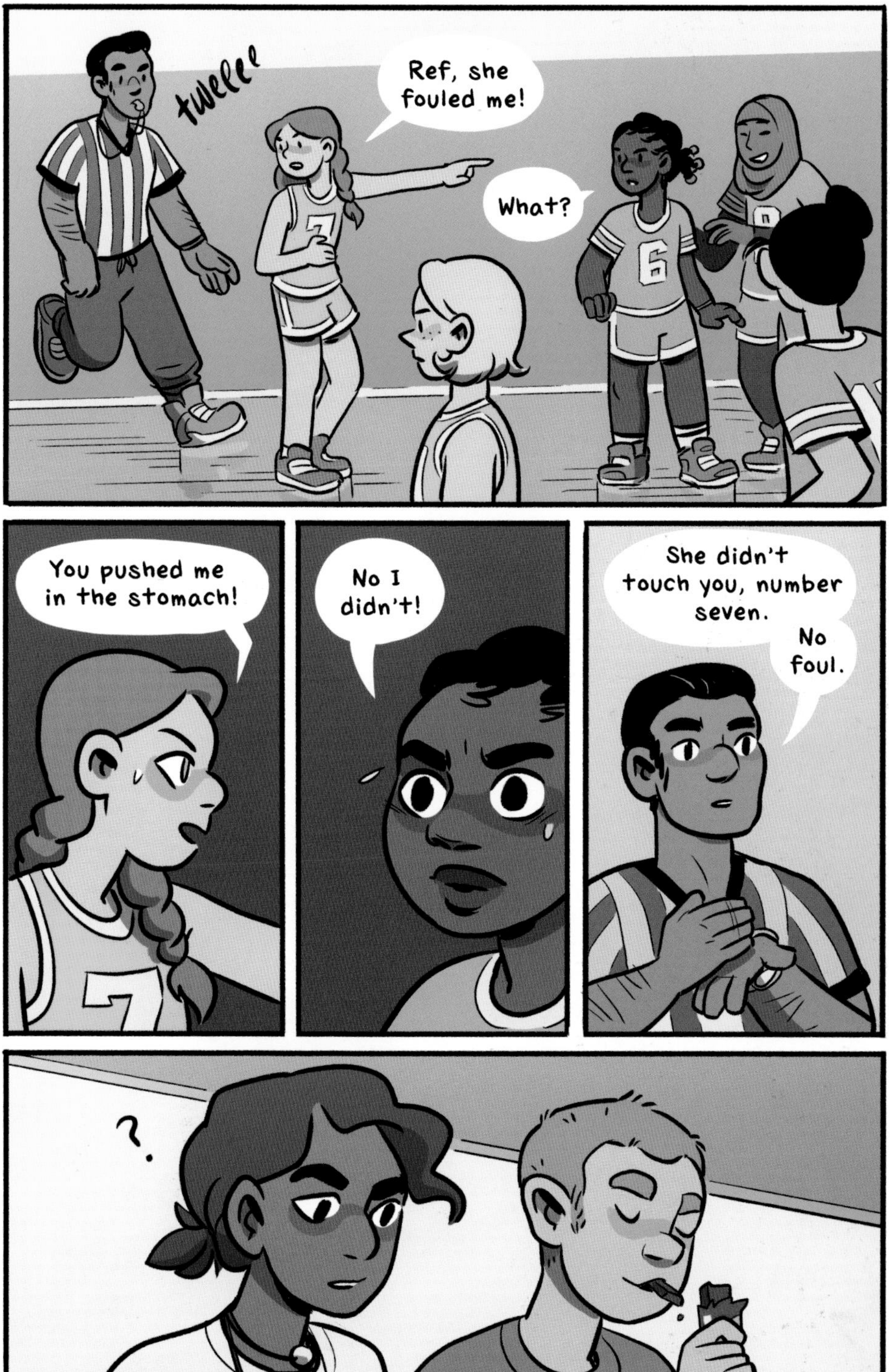
TWEEE
Ref, she fouled me!
What?
You pushed me in the stomach!
No I didn't!
She didn't touch you, number seven.
No foul.
?

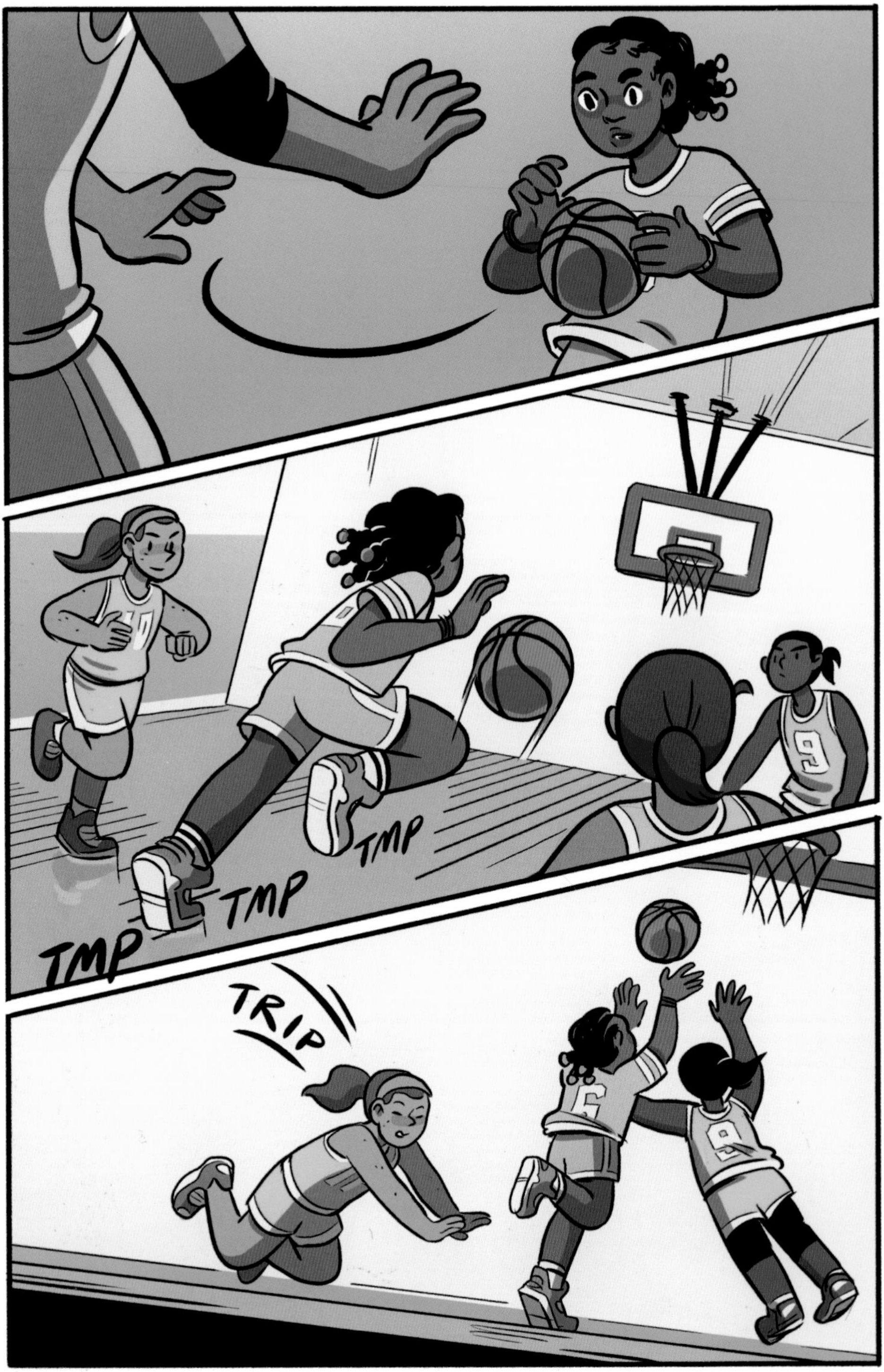
TMP
TMP
TMP
TRIP

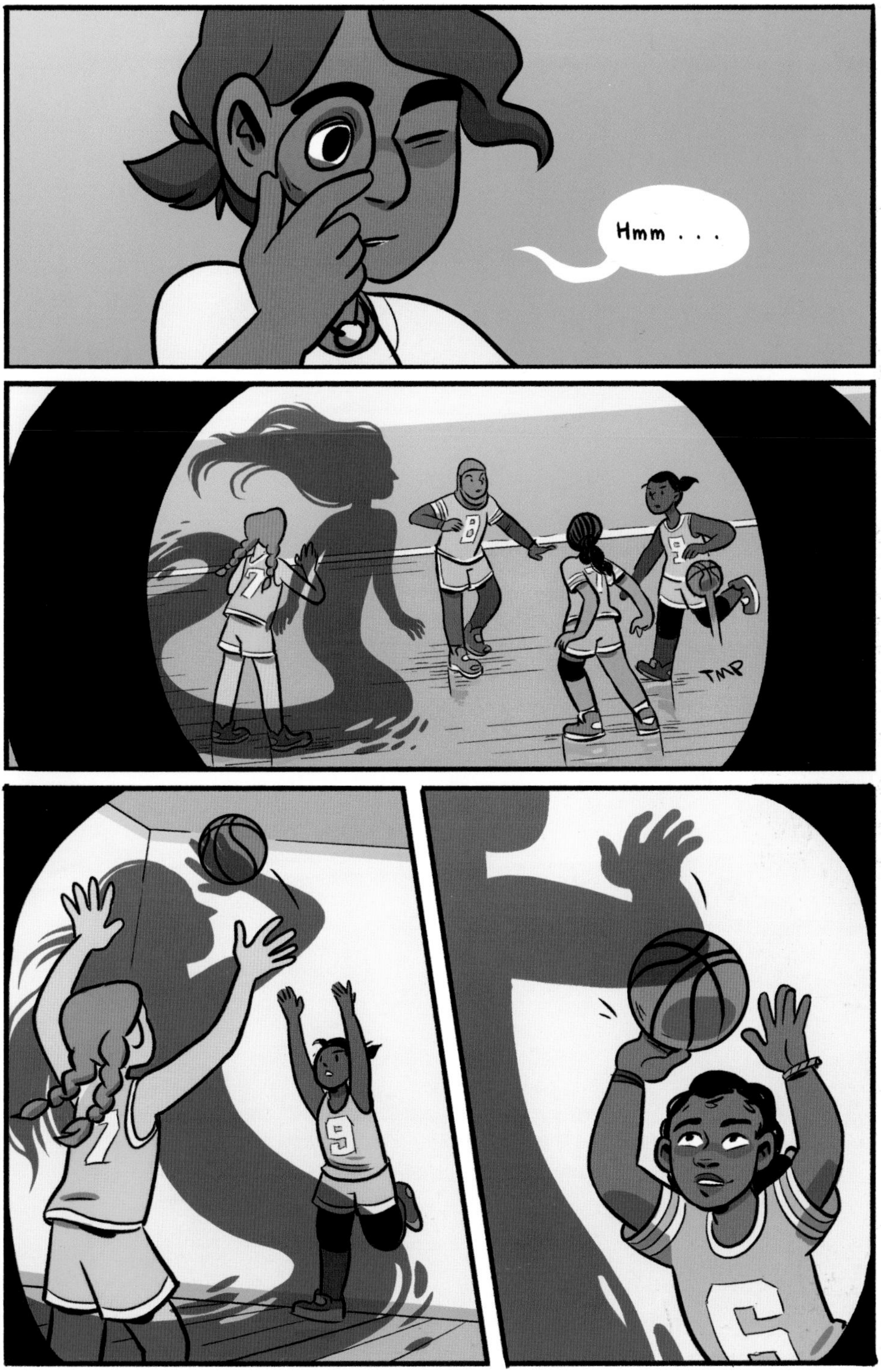
Hmm . . .
TMP

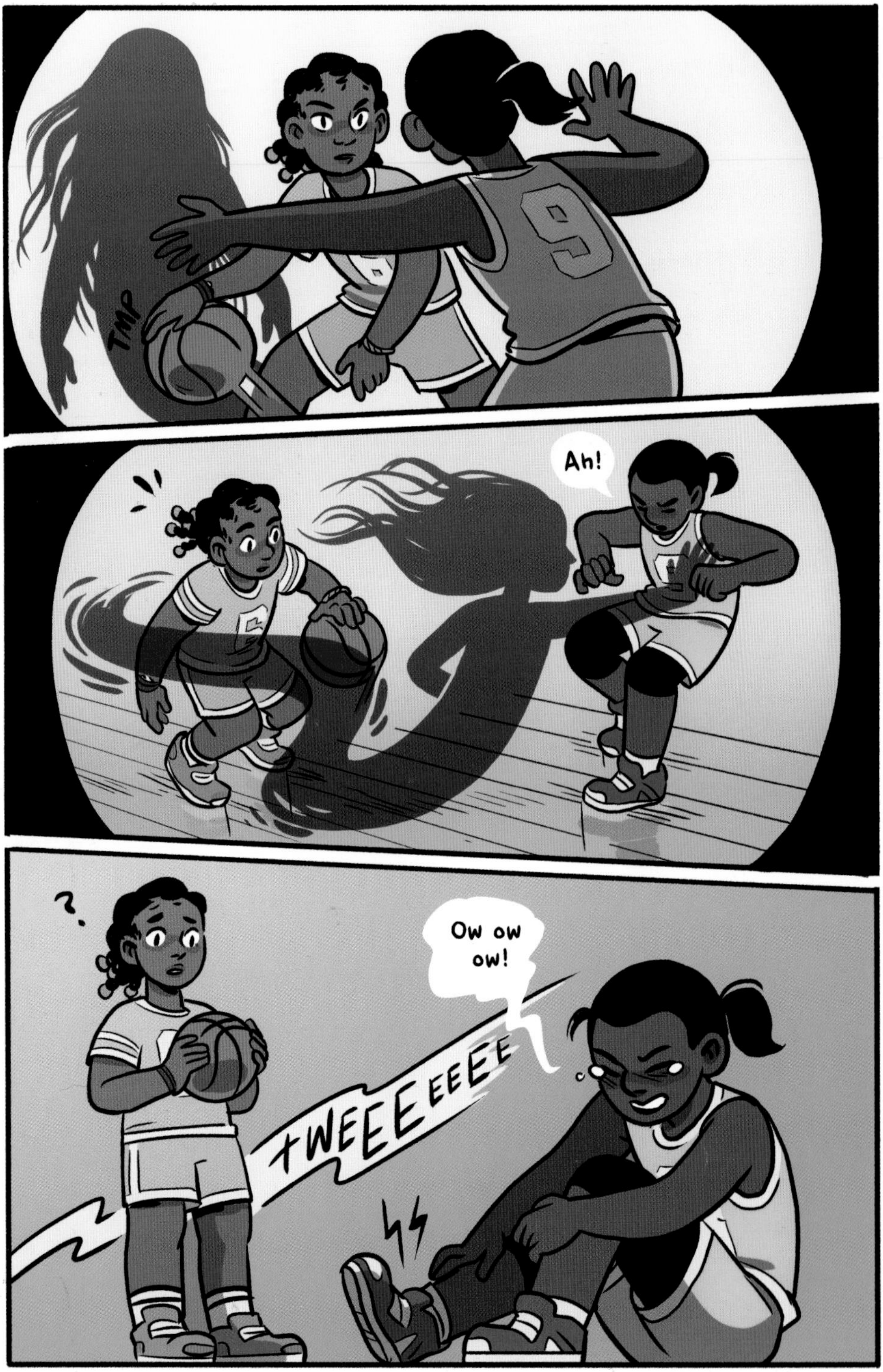
TMP
Ah!
?
Ow ow ow!
TWEEEeeeee

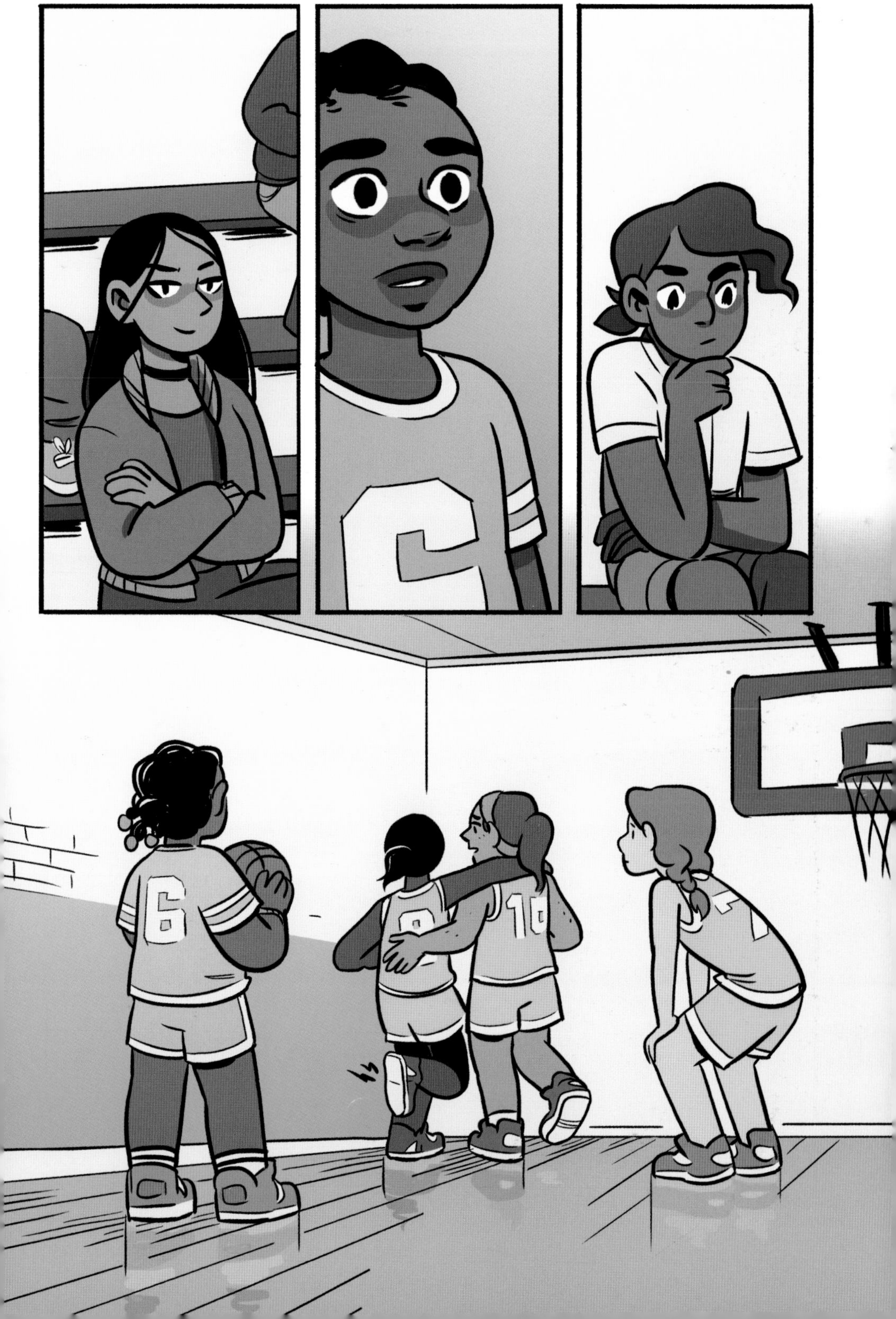

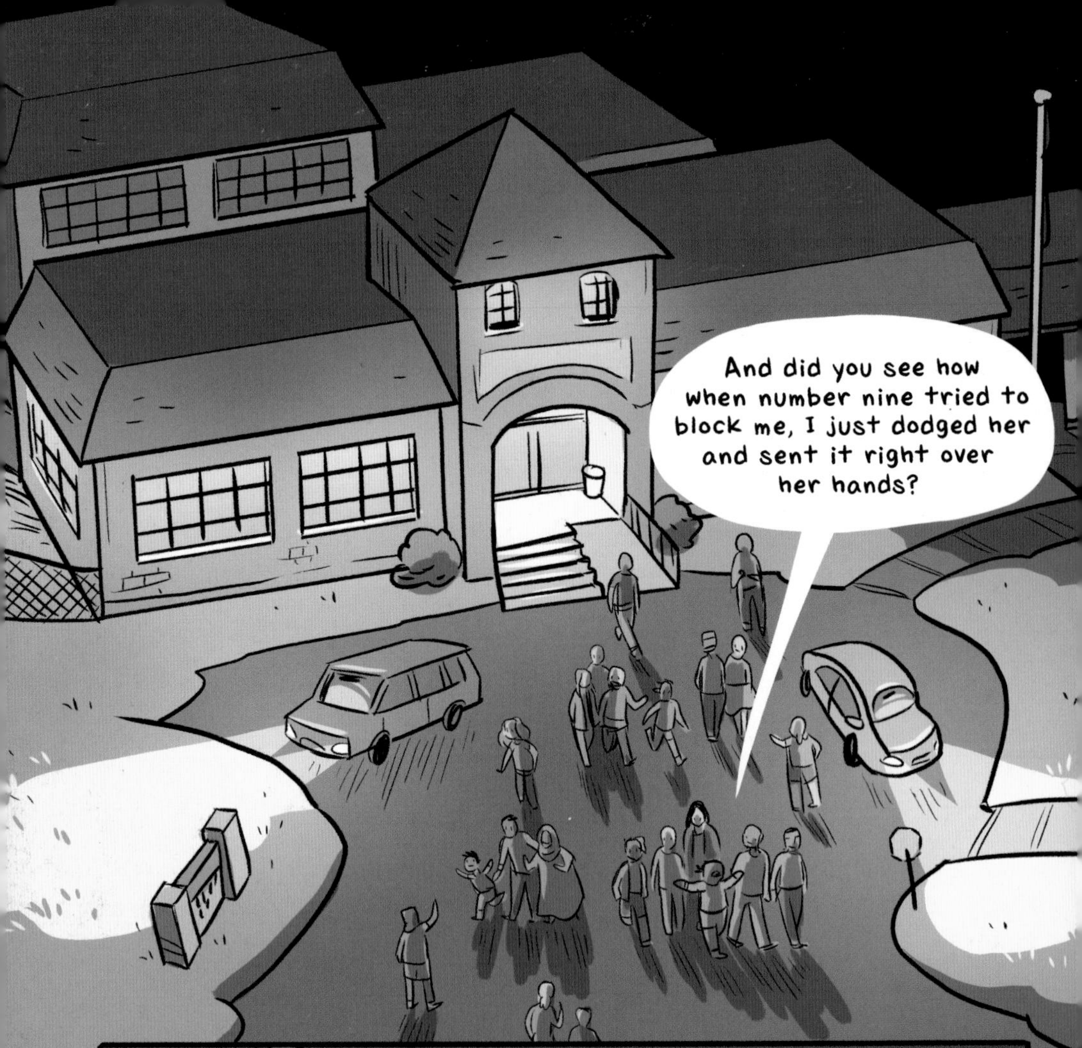
And did you see how when number nine tried to block me, I just dodged her and sent it right over her hands?

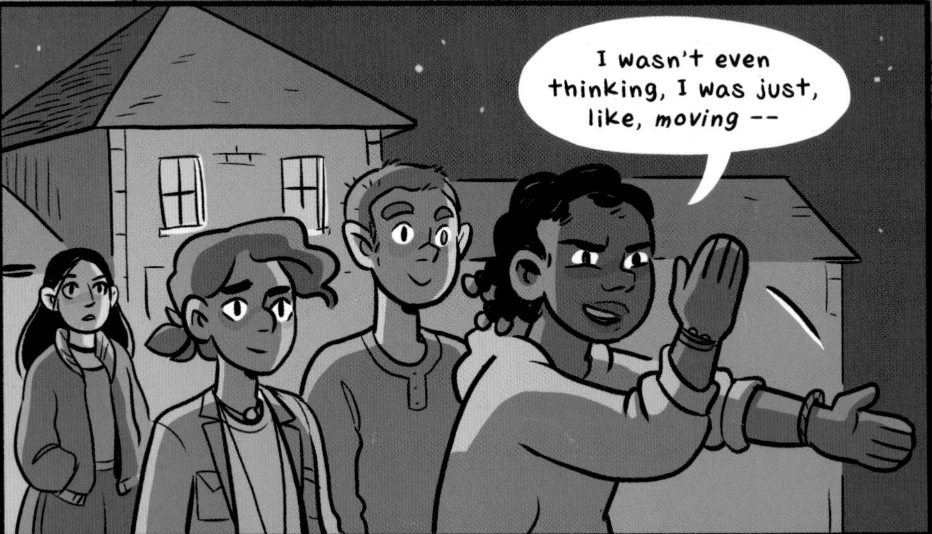
I wasn't even thinking, I was just, like, *moving* --

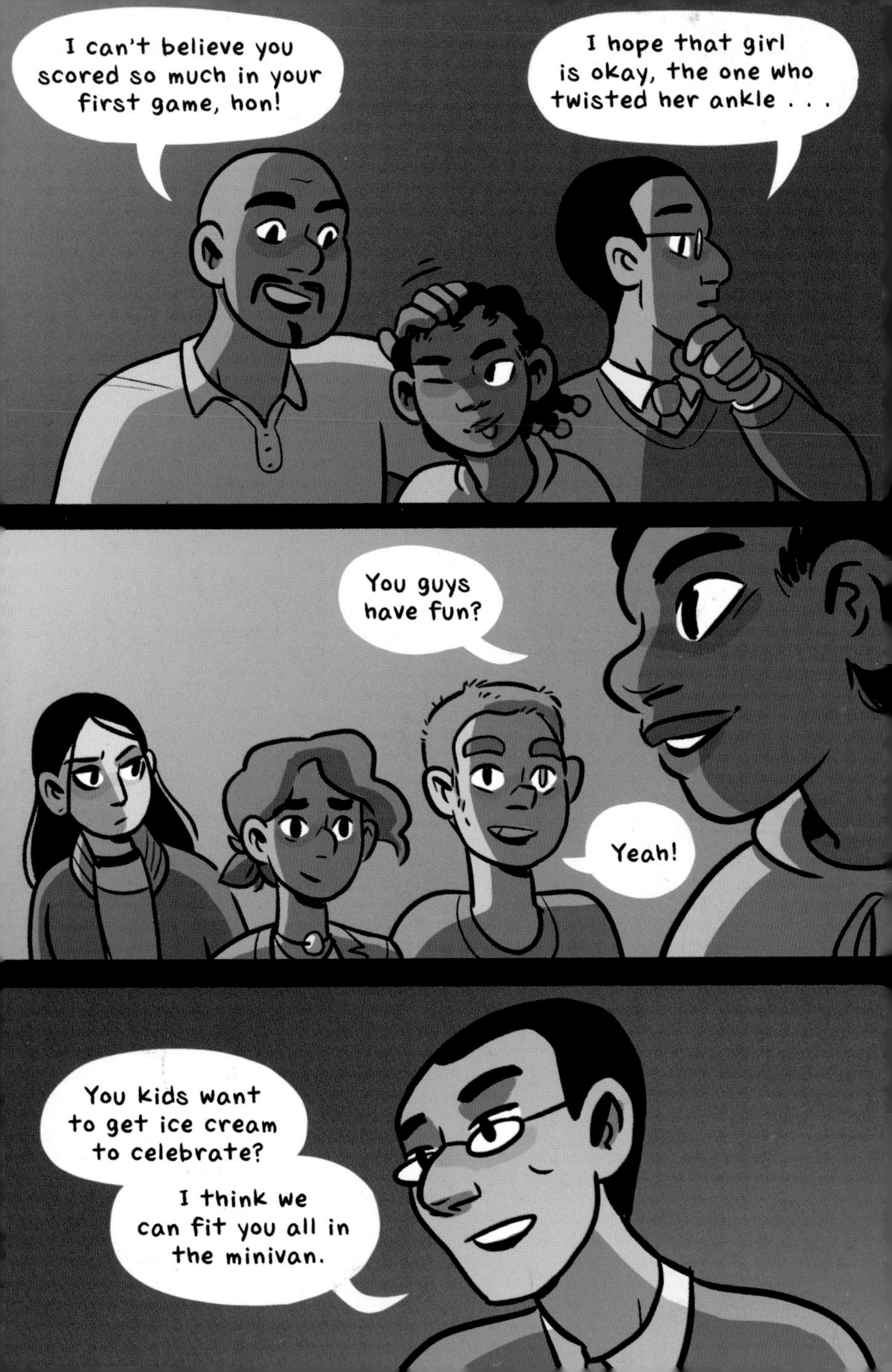

I can't believe you scored so much in your first game, hon!
I hope that girl is okay, the one who twisted her ankle . . .
You guys have fun?
Yeah!
You kids want to get ice cream to celebrate?
I think we can fit you all in the minivan.

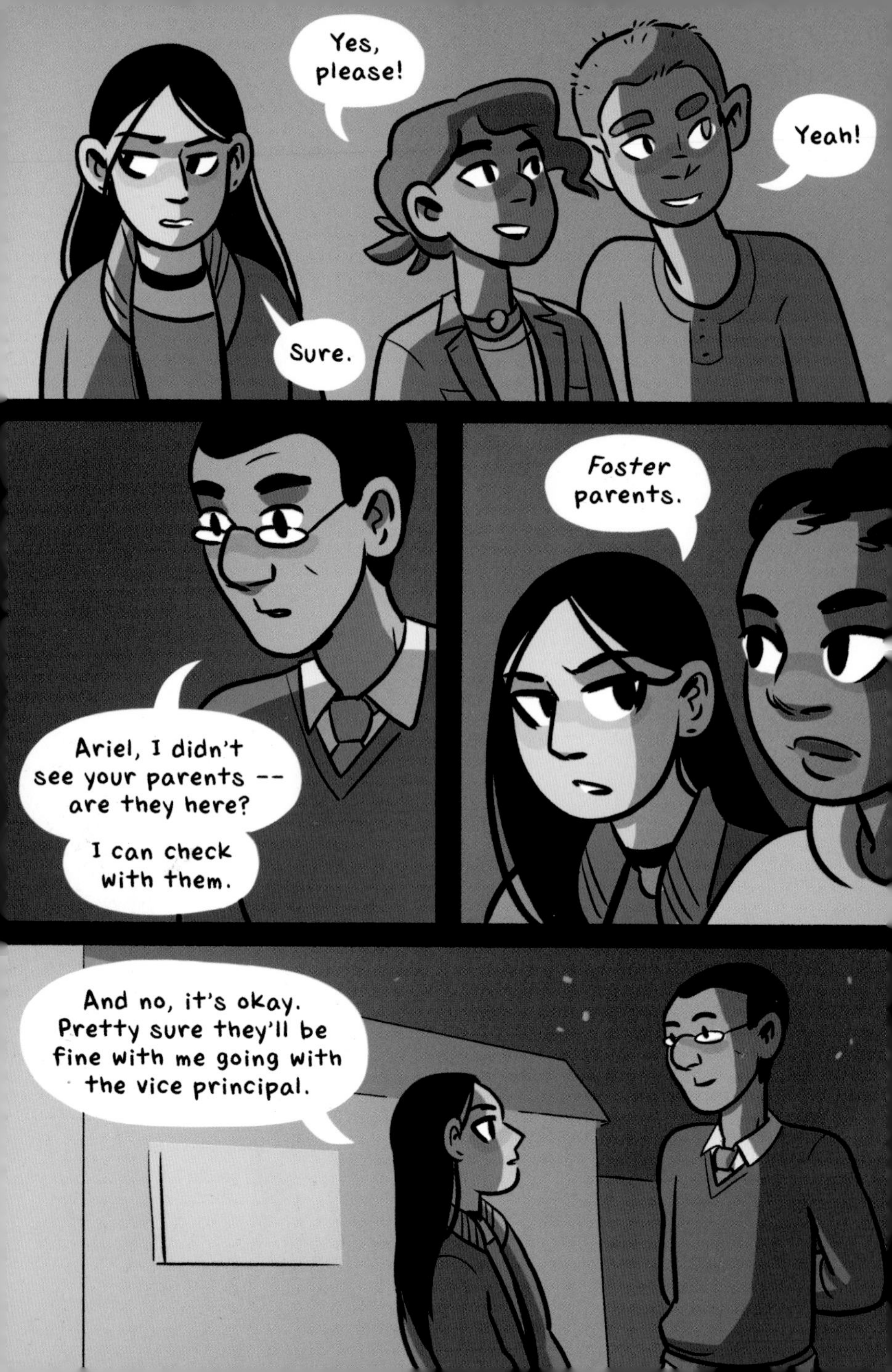
Yes, please!
Yeah!
Sure.
Ariel, I didn't see your parents -- are they here?
I can check with them.
Foster parents.
And no, it's okay. Pretty sure they'll be fine with me going with the vice principal.

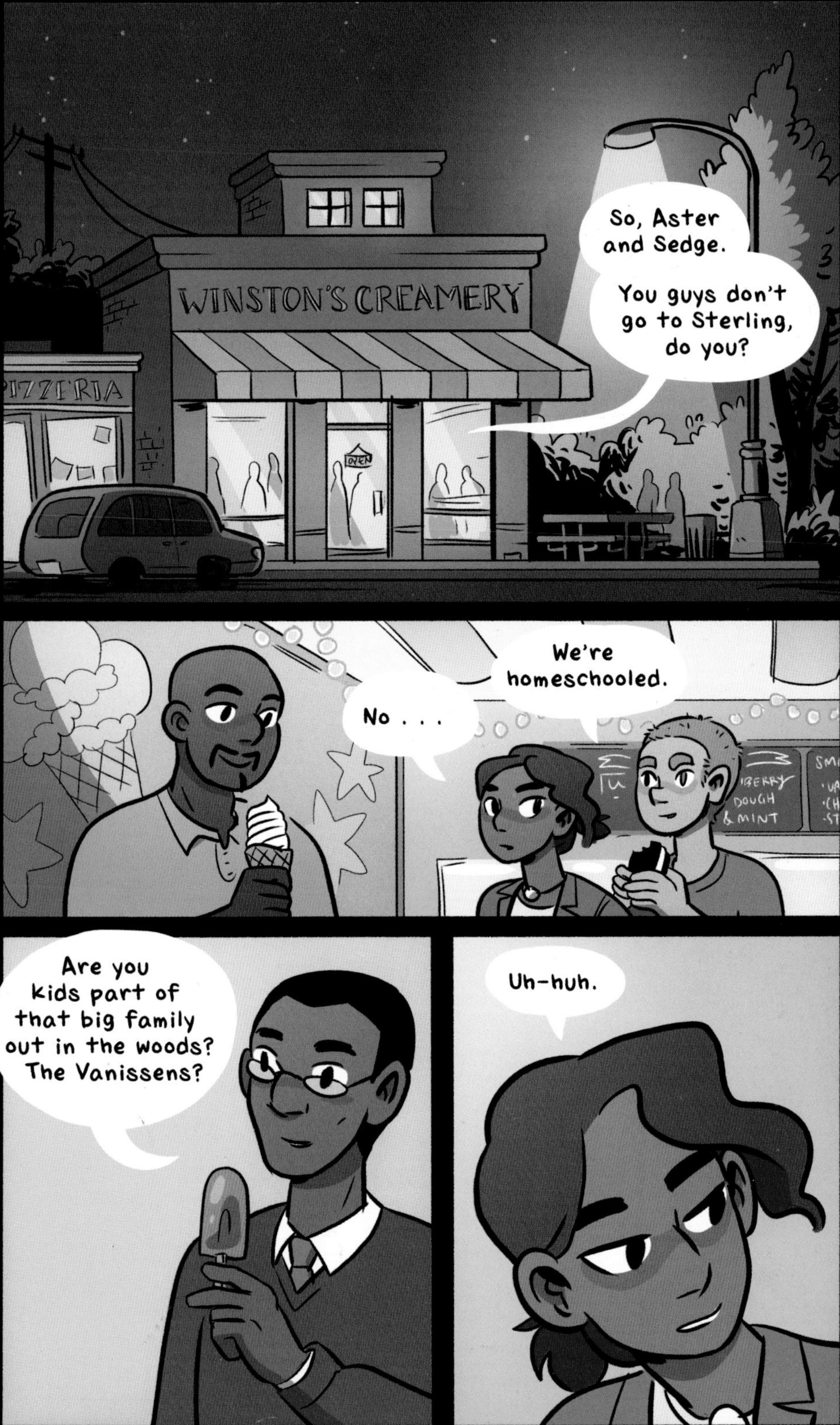
WINSTON'S CREAMERY
PIZZERIA
So, Aster and Sedge.
You guys don't go to Sterling, do you?
No . . .
We're homeschooled.
Are you kids part of that big family out in the woods? The Vanissens?
Uh-huh.

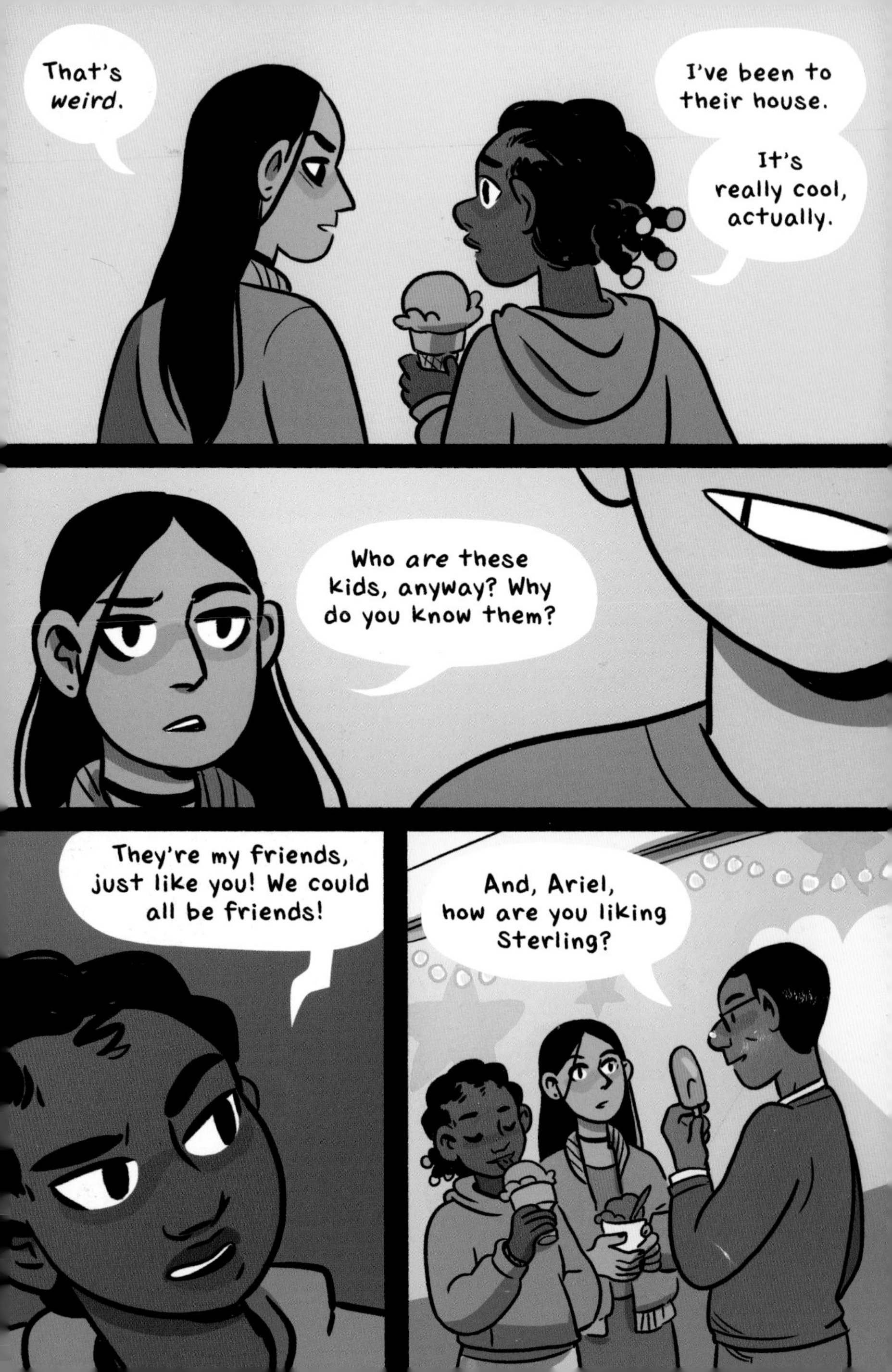

That's weird.
I've been to their house.
It's really cool, actually.
Who are these kids, anyway? Why do you know them?
They're my friends, just like you! We could all be friends!
And, Ariel, how are you liking Sterling?

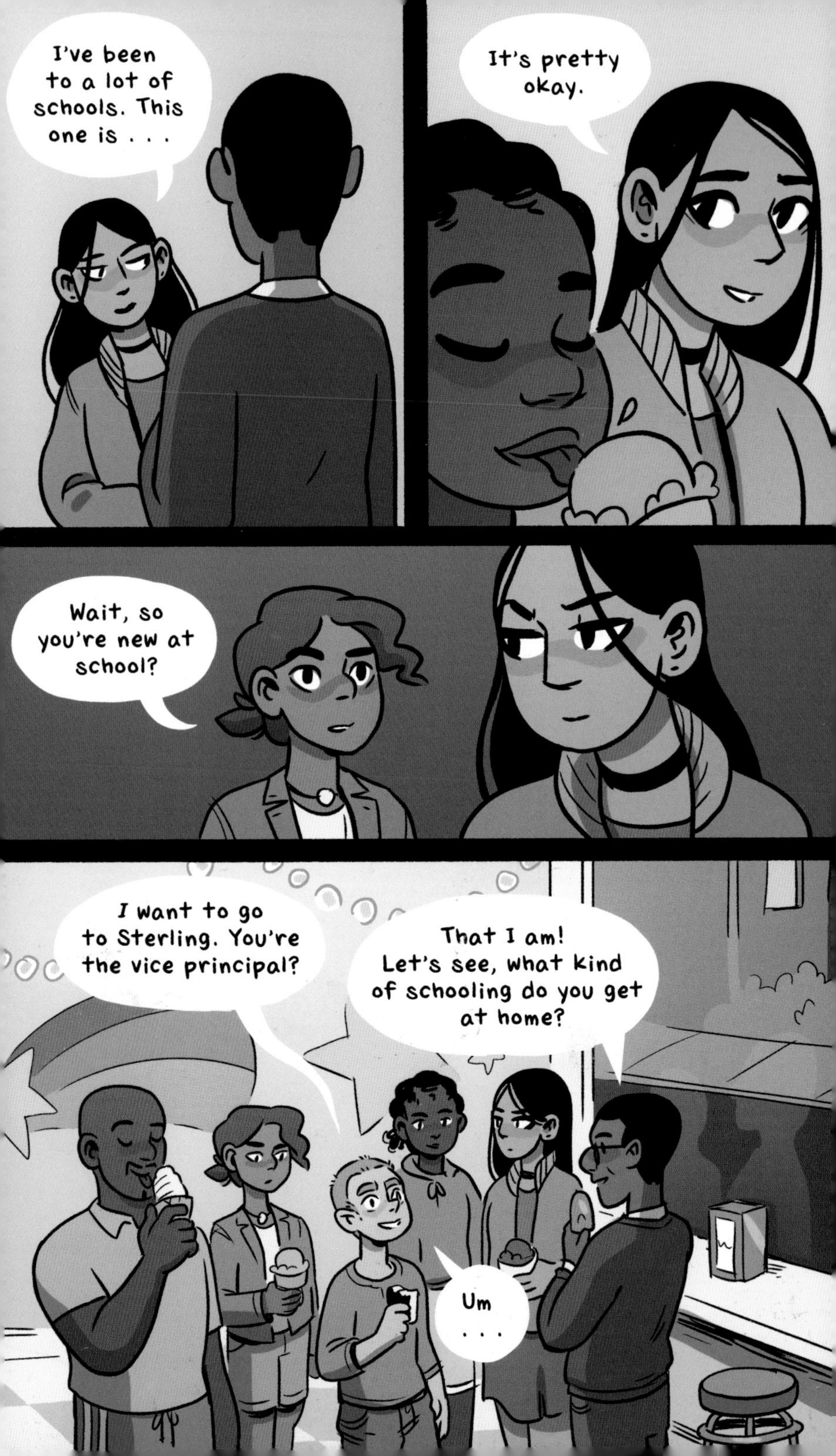
I've been to a lot of schools. This one is . . .
It's pretty okay.
Wait, so you're new at school?
I want to go to Sterling. You're the vice principal?
That I am! Let's see, what kind of schooling do you get at home?
Um . . .

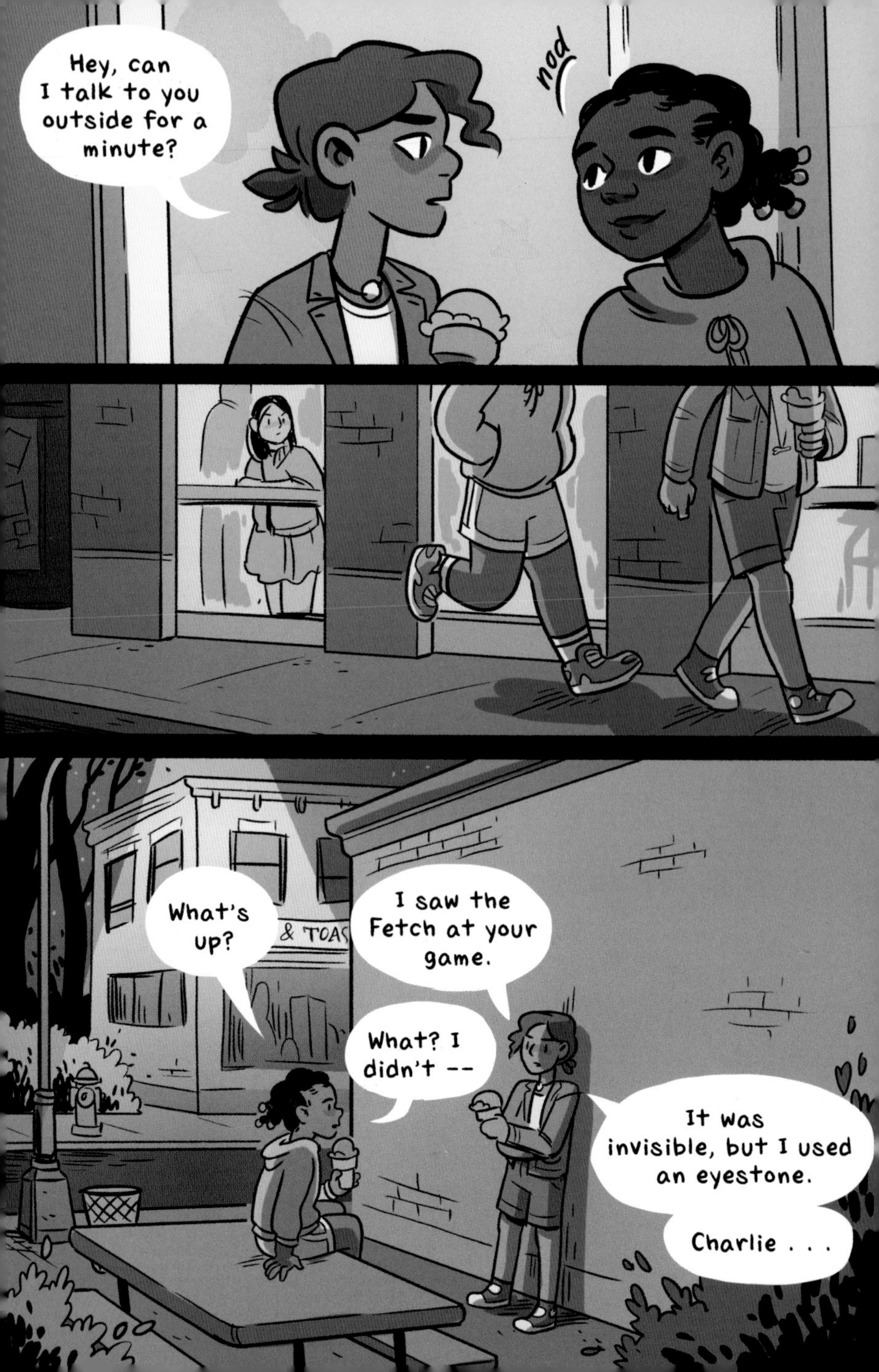
Hey, can I talk to you outside for a minute?
nod
What's up?
& TOAS
I saw the Fetch at your game.
What? I didn't --
It was invisible, but I used an eyestone.
Charlie . . .

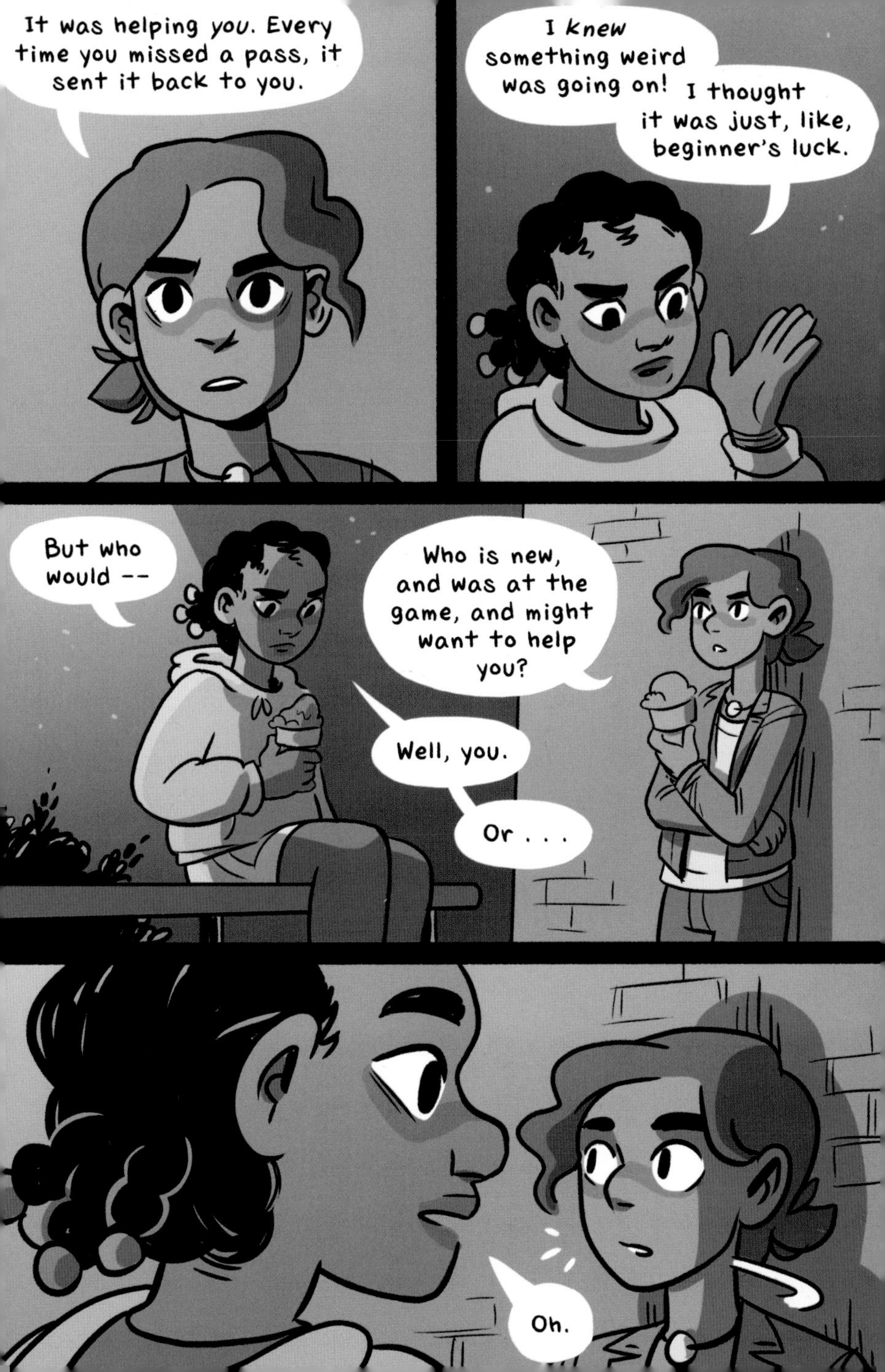
It was helping you. Every time you missed a pass, it sent it back to you.
I knew something weird was going on!
I thought it was just, like, beginner's luck.
But who would --
Who is new, and was at the game, and might want to help you?
Well, you.
Or . . .
Oh.

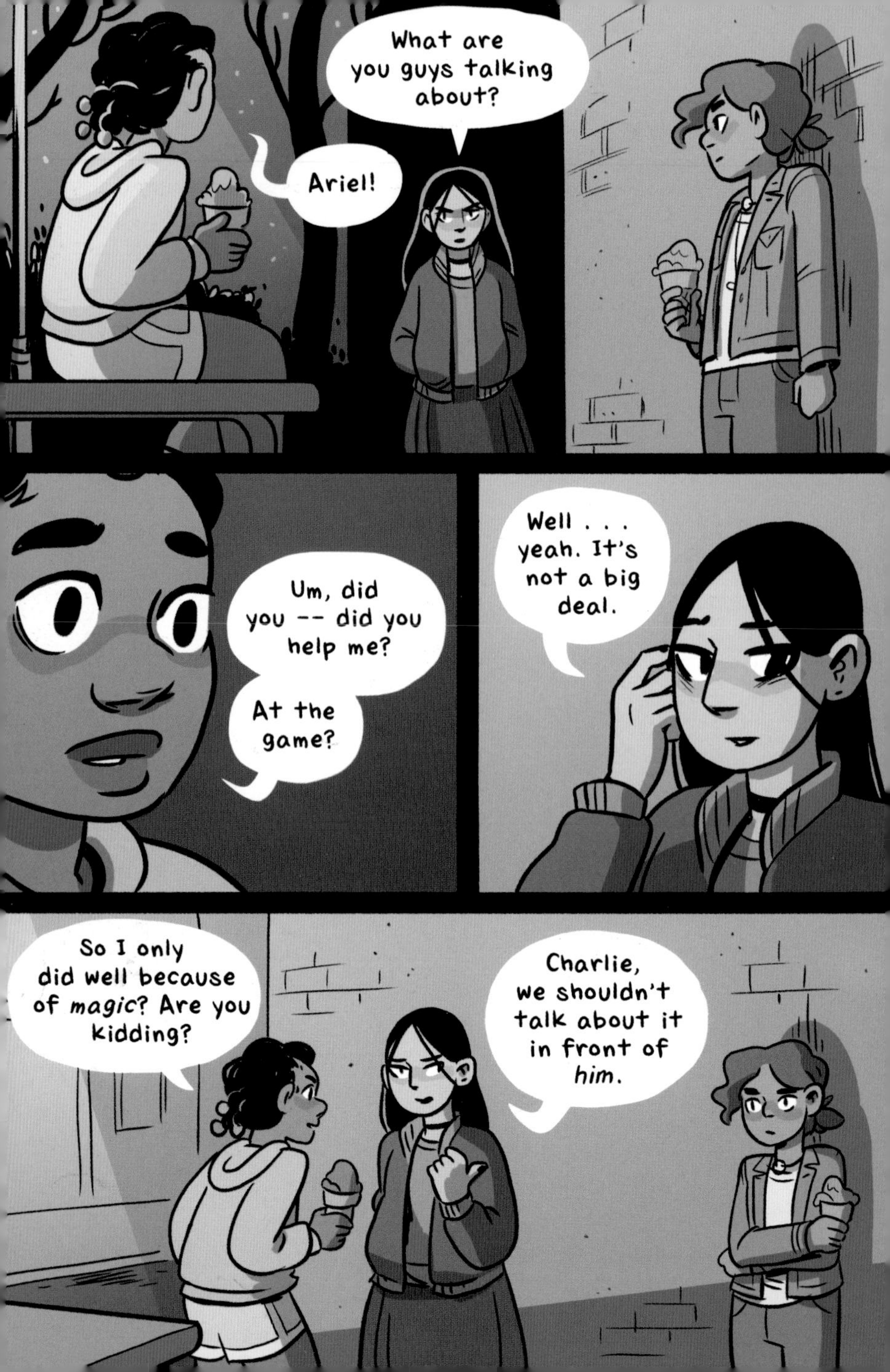
What are you guys talking about?
Ariel!
Um, did you -- did you help me?
At the game?
Well . . . yeah. It's not a big deal.
So I only did well because of *magic*? Are you kidding?
Charlie, we shouldn't talk about it in front of *him*.

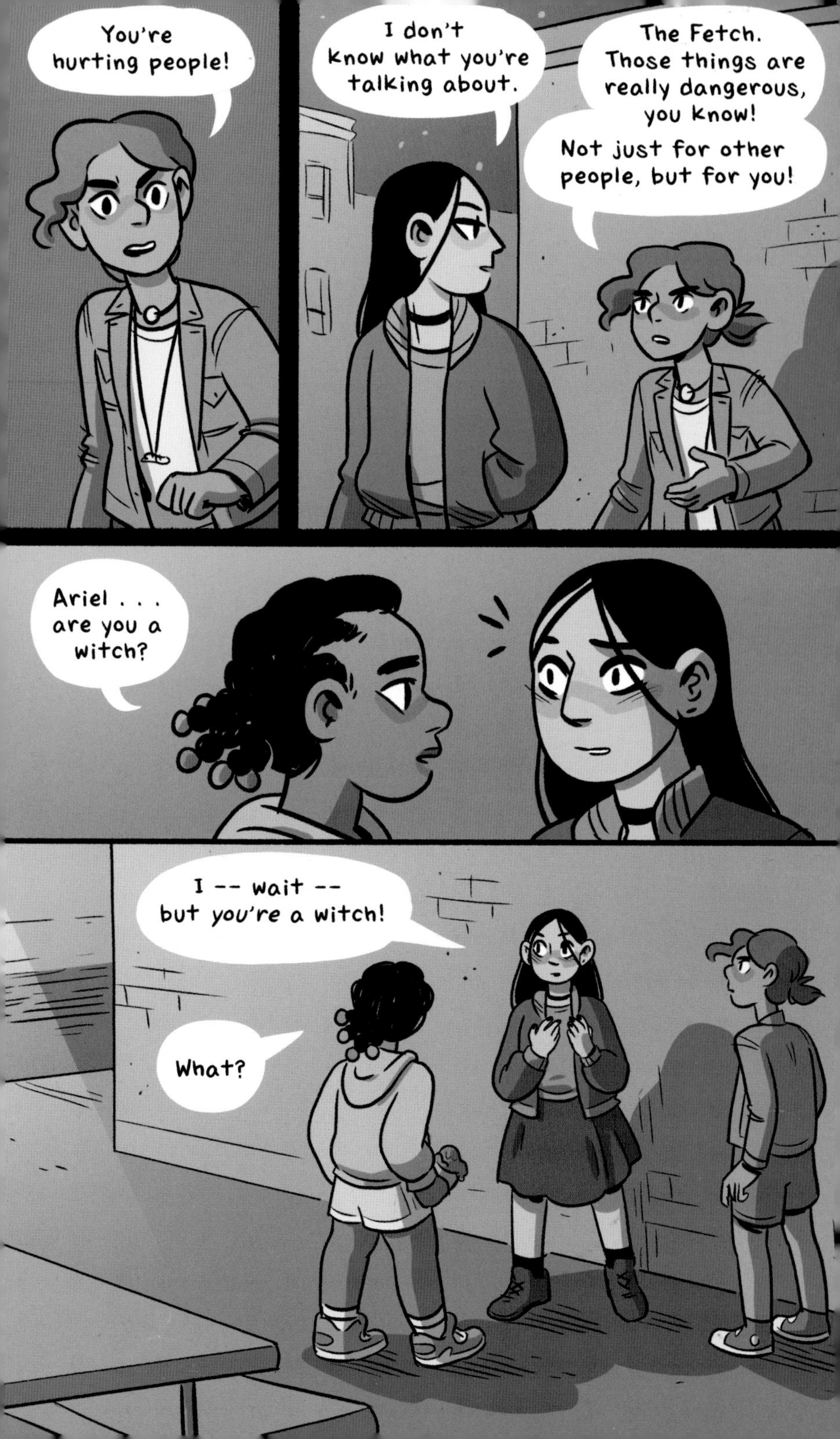

You're hurting people!
I don't know what you're talking about.
The Fetch. Those things are really dangerous, you know!
Not just for other people, but for you!
Ariel . . . are you a witch?
I -- wait -- but *you're* a witch!
What?

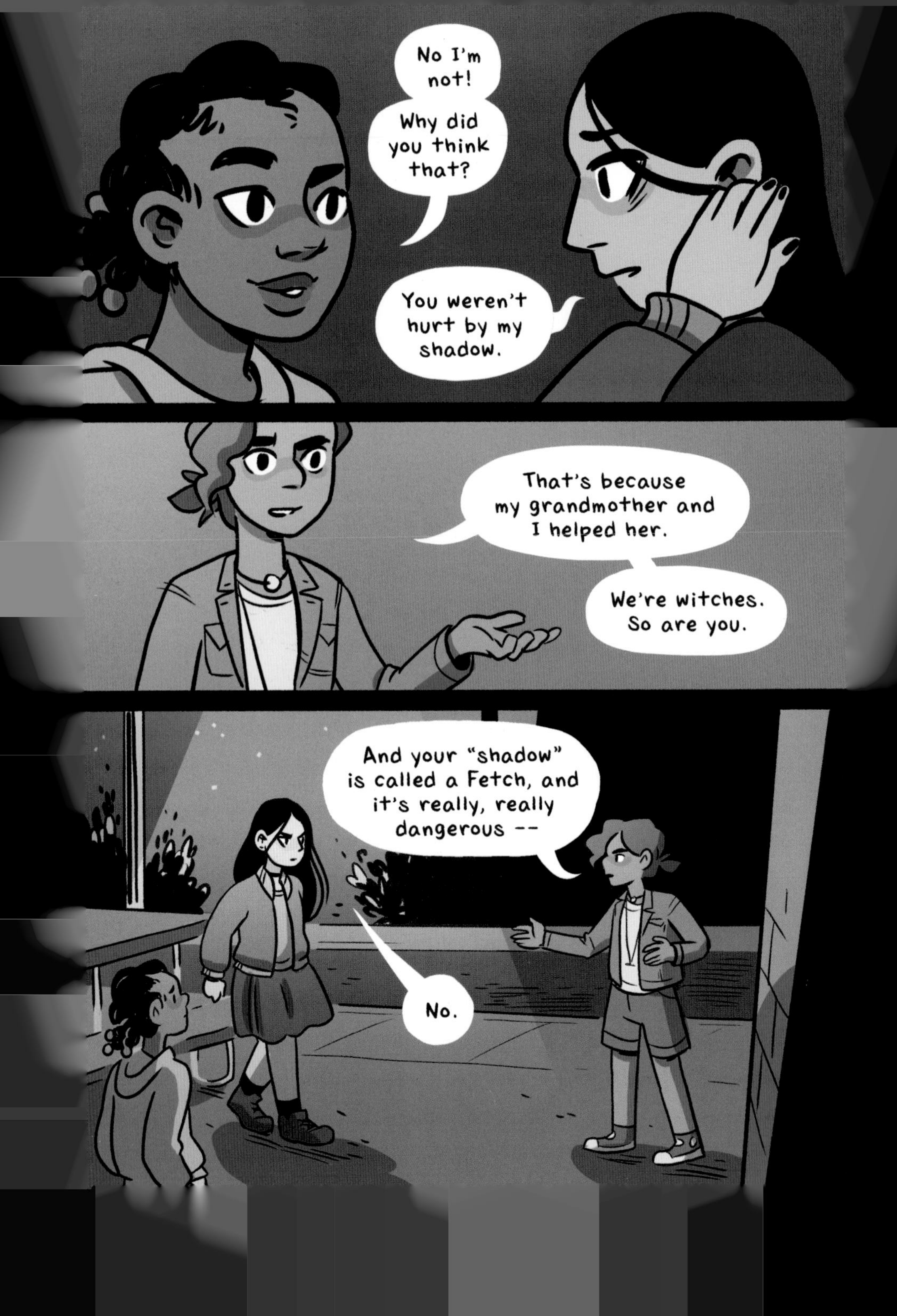
No I'm not!
Why did you think that?
You weren't hurt by my shadow.
That's because my grandmother and I helped her.
We're witches. So are you.
And your "shadow" is called a Fetch, and it's really, really dangerous --
No.

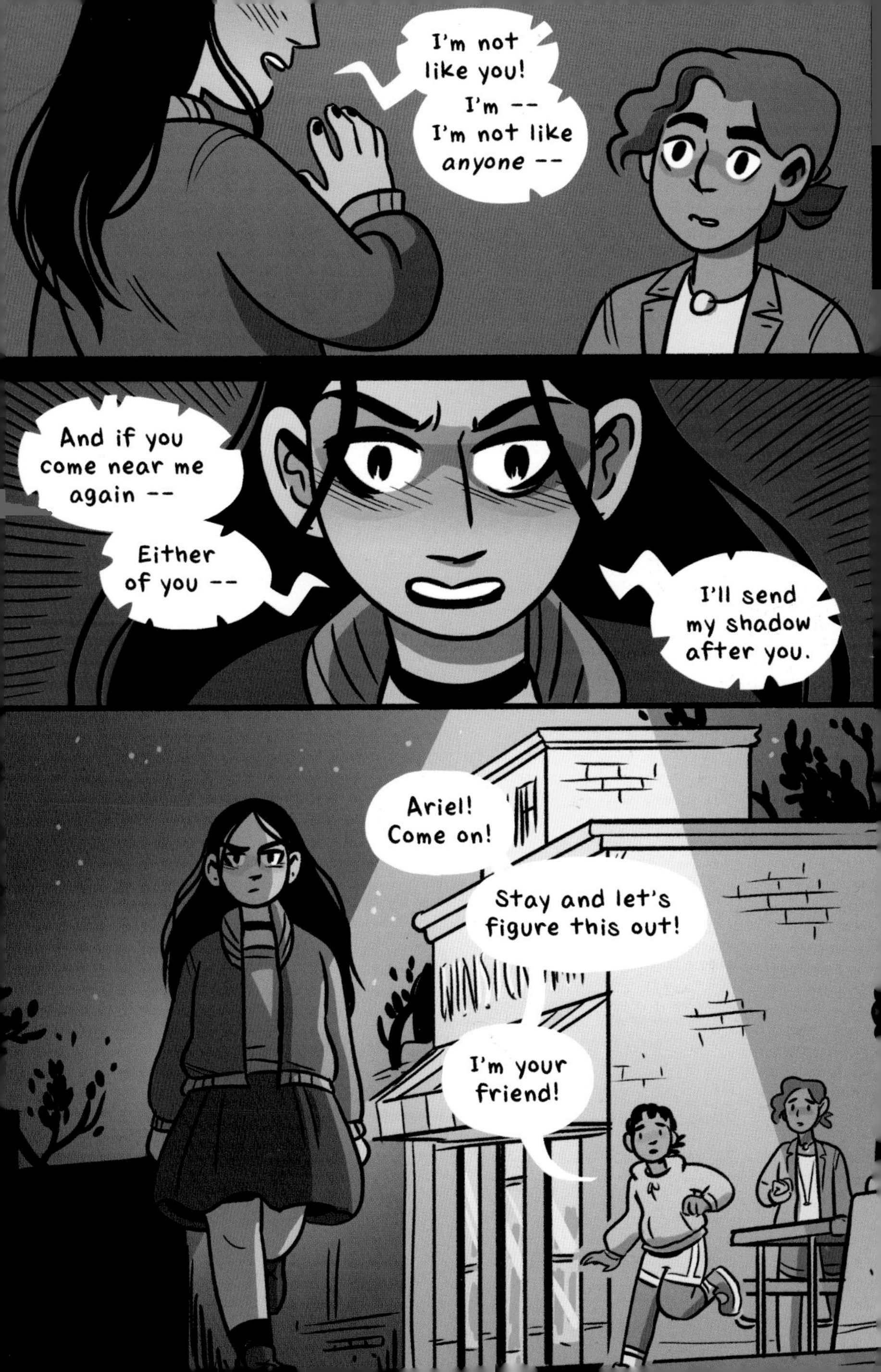
I'm not like you!
I'm -- I'm not like *anyone* --
And if you come near me again --
Either of you --
I'll send my shadow after you.
Ariel! Come on!
Stay and let's figure this out!
I'm your friend!

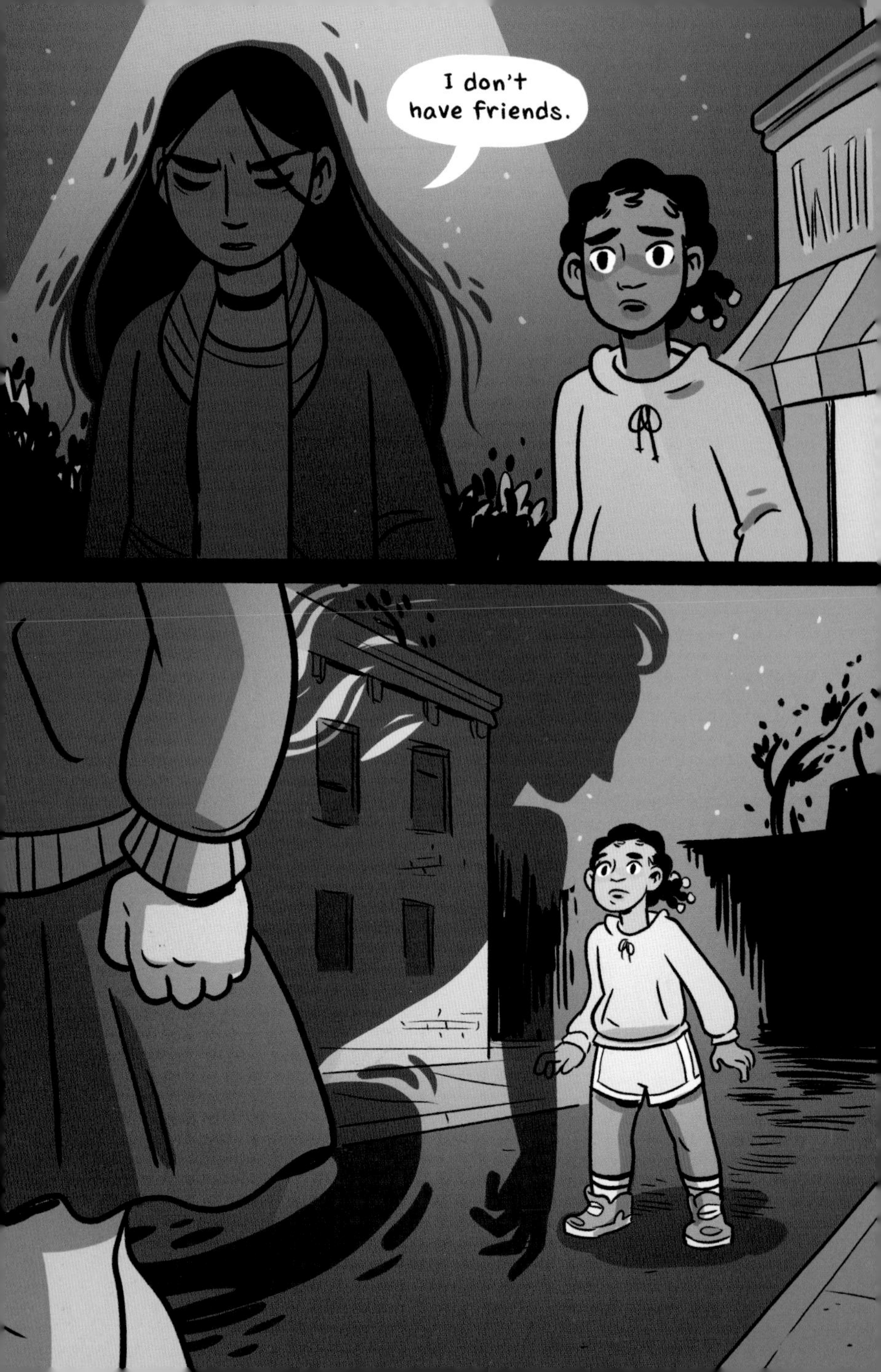
I don't have friends.

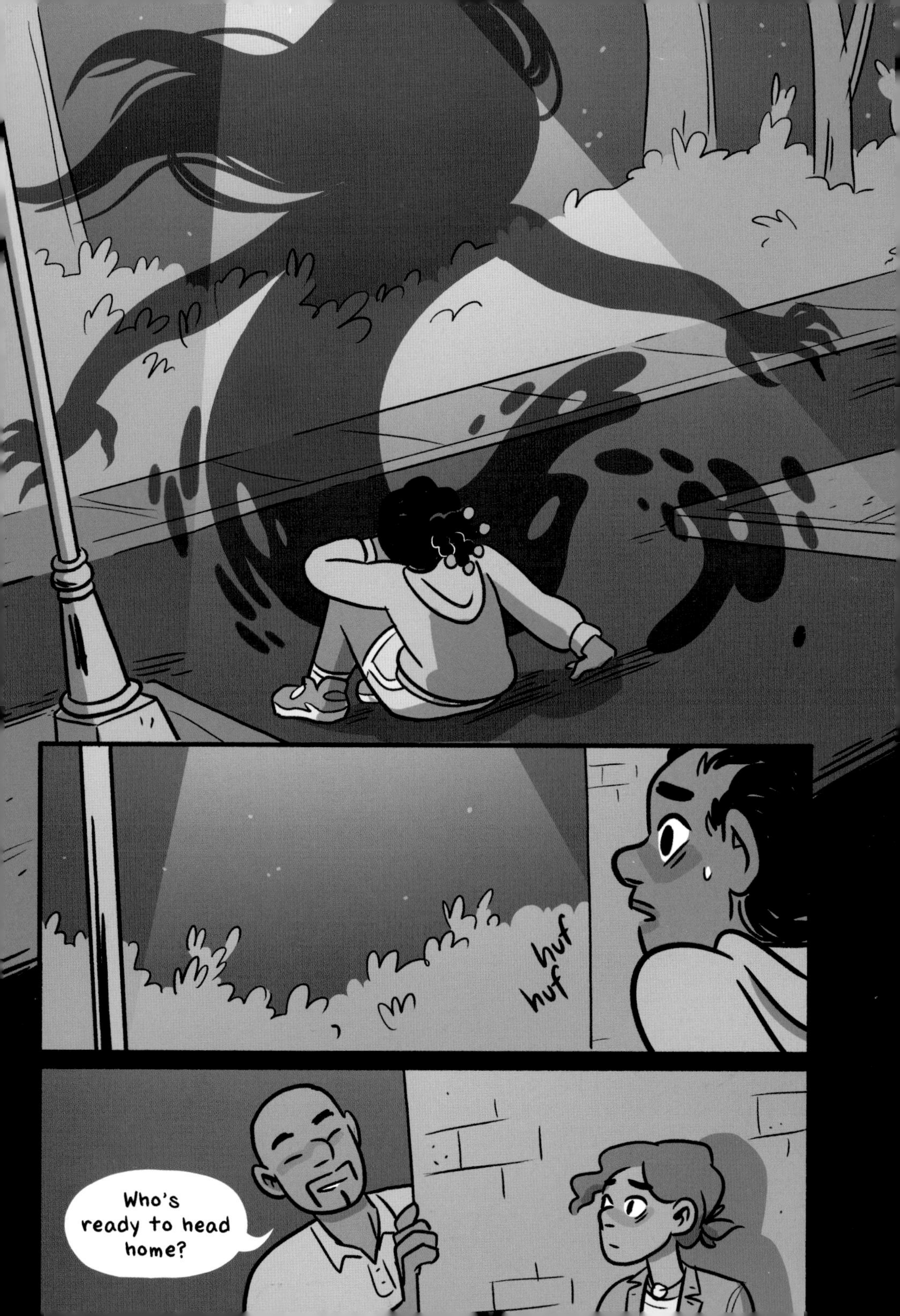
huf huf
Who's ready to head home?

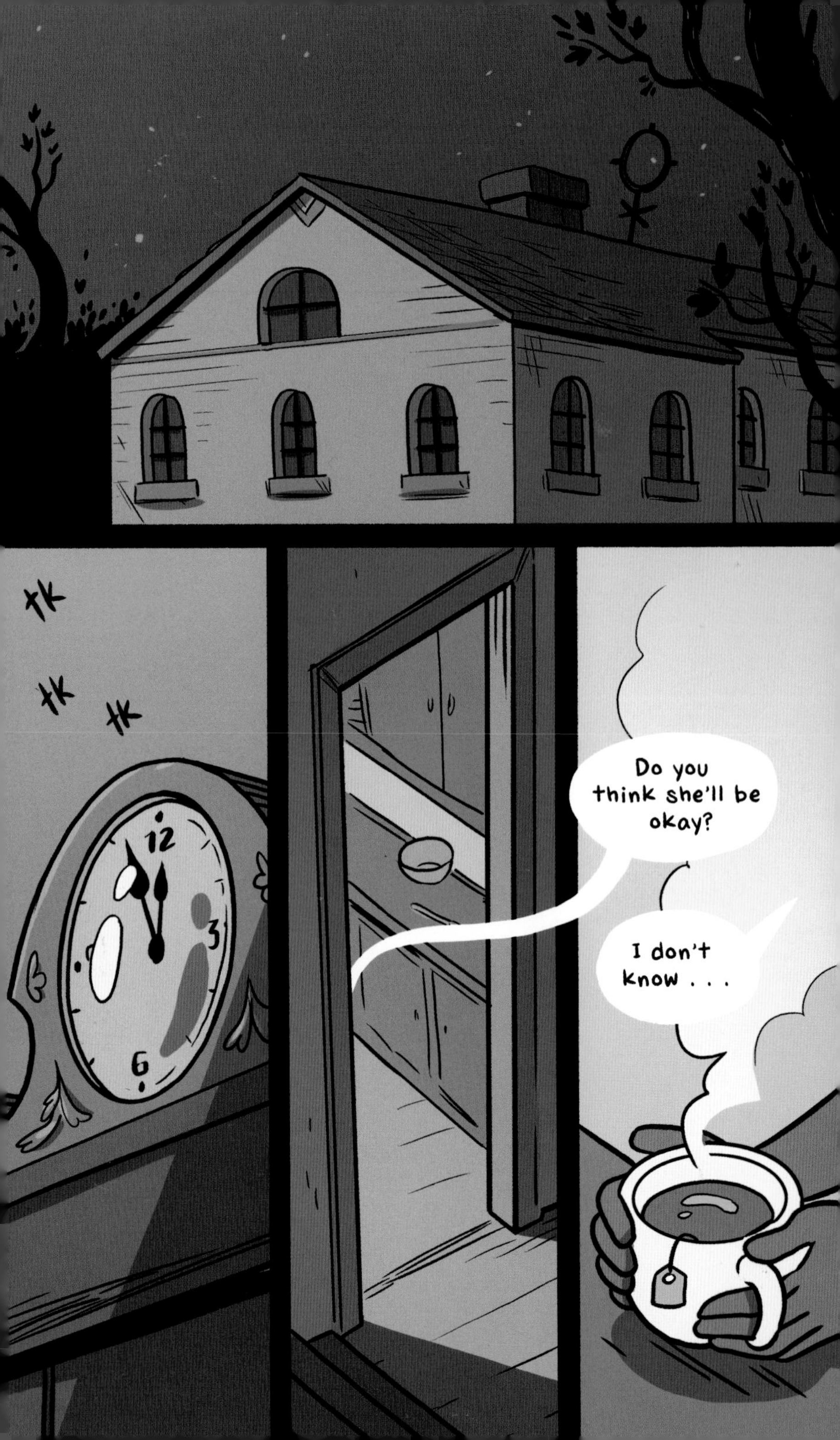
tk
tk
tk
Do you think she'll be okay?
I don't know . . .

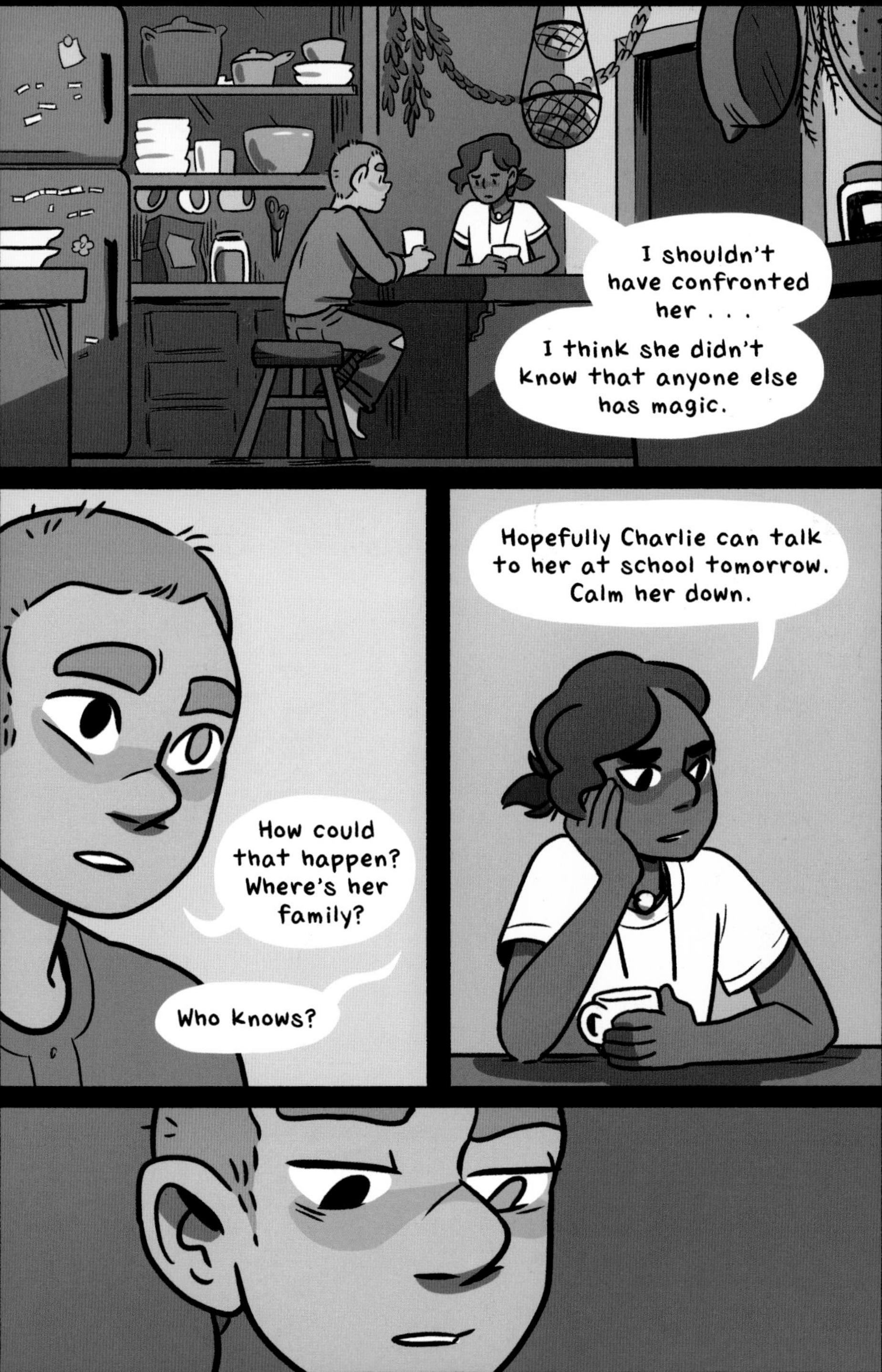
I shouldn't have confronted her . . .
I think she didn't know that anyone else has magic.
Hopefully Charlie can talk to her at school tomorrow. Calm her down.
How could that happen? Where's her family?
Who knows?

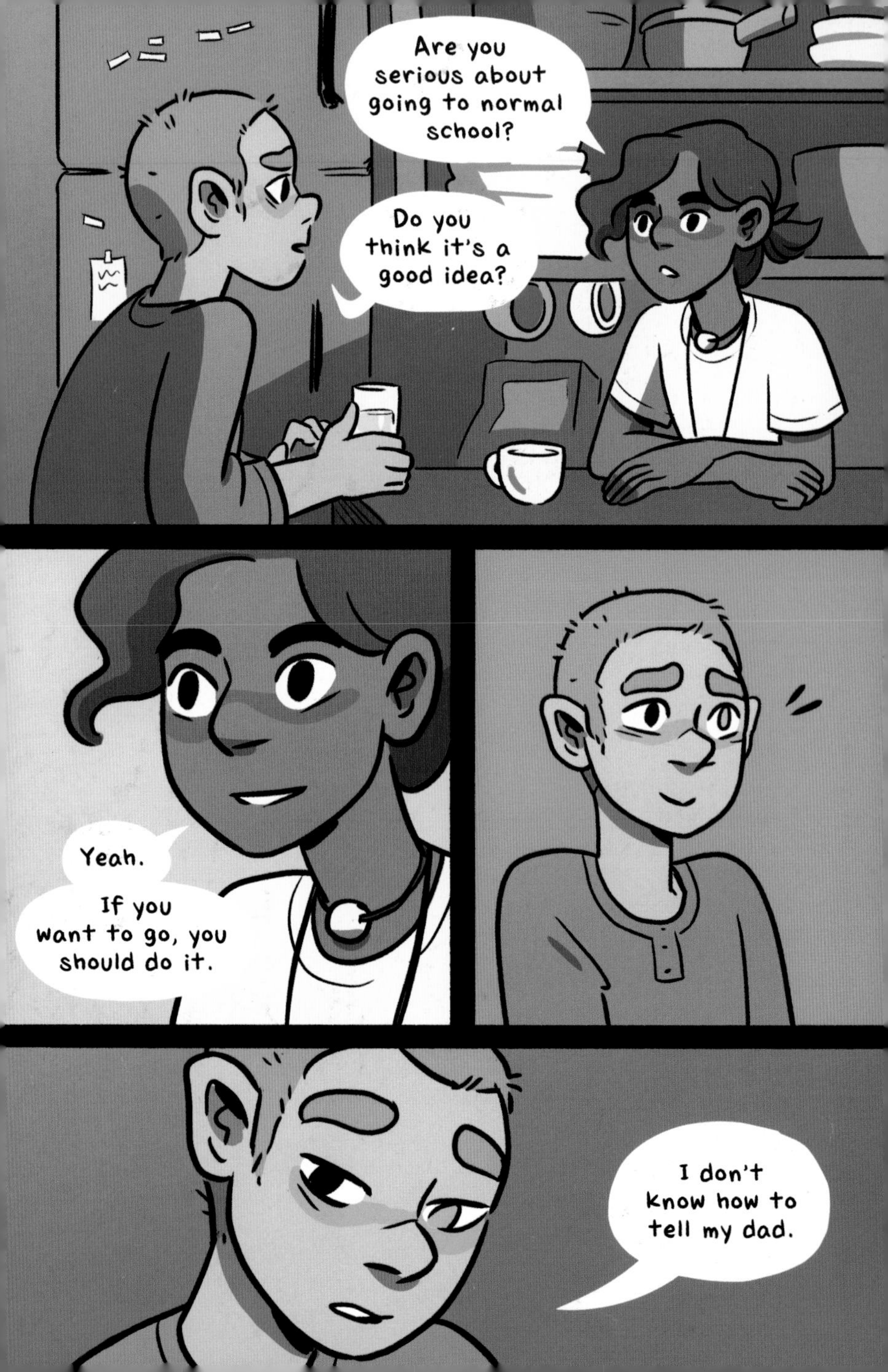
Are you serious about going to normal school?
Do you think it's a good idea?
Yeah.
If you want to go, you should do it.
I don't know how to tell my dad.

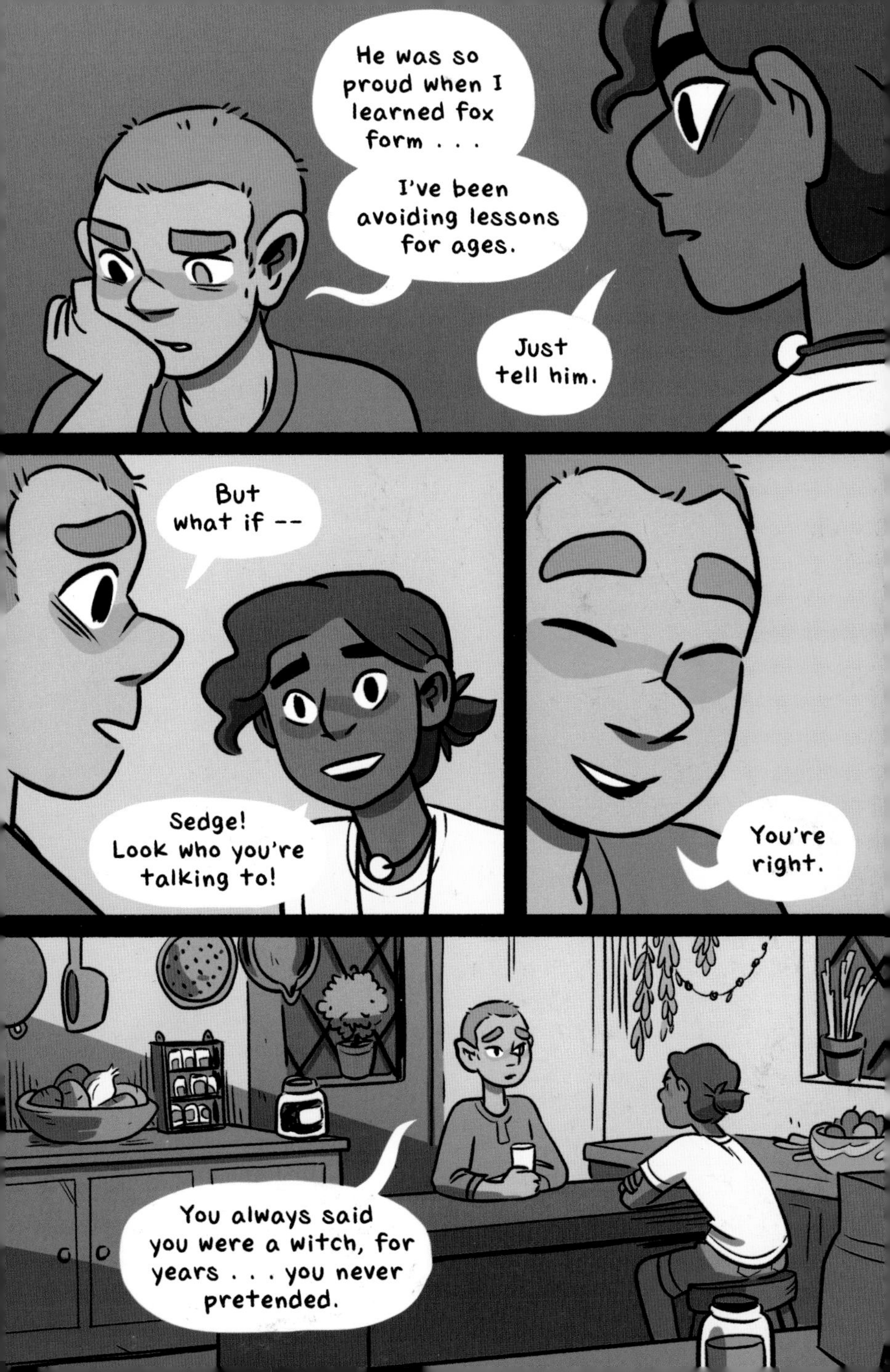
He was so proud when I learned fox form . . .
I've been avoiding lessons for ages.
Just tell him.
But what if --
Sedge! Look who you're talking to!
You're right.
You always said you were a witch, for years . . . you never pretended.

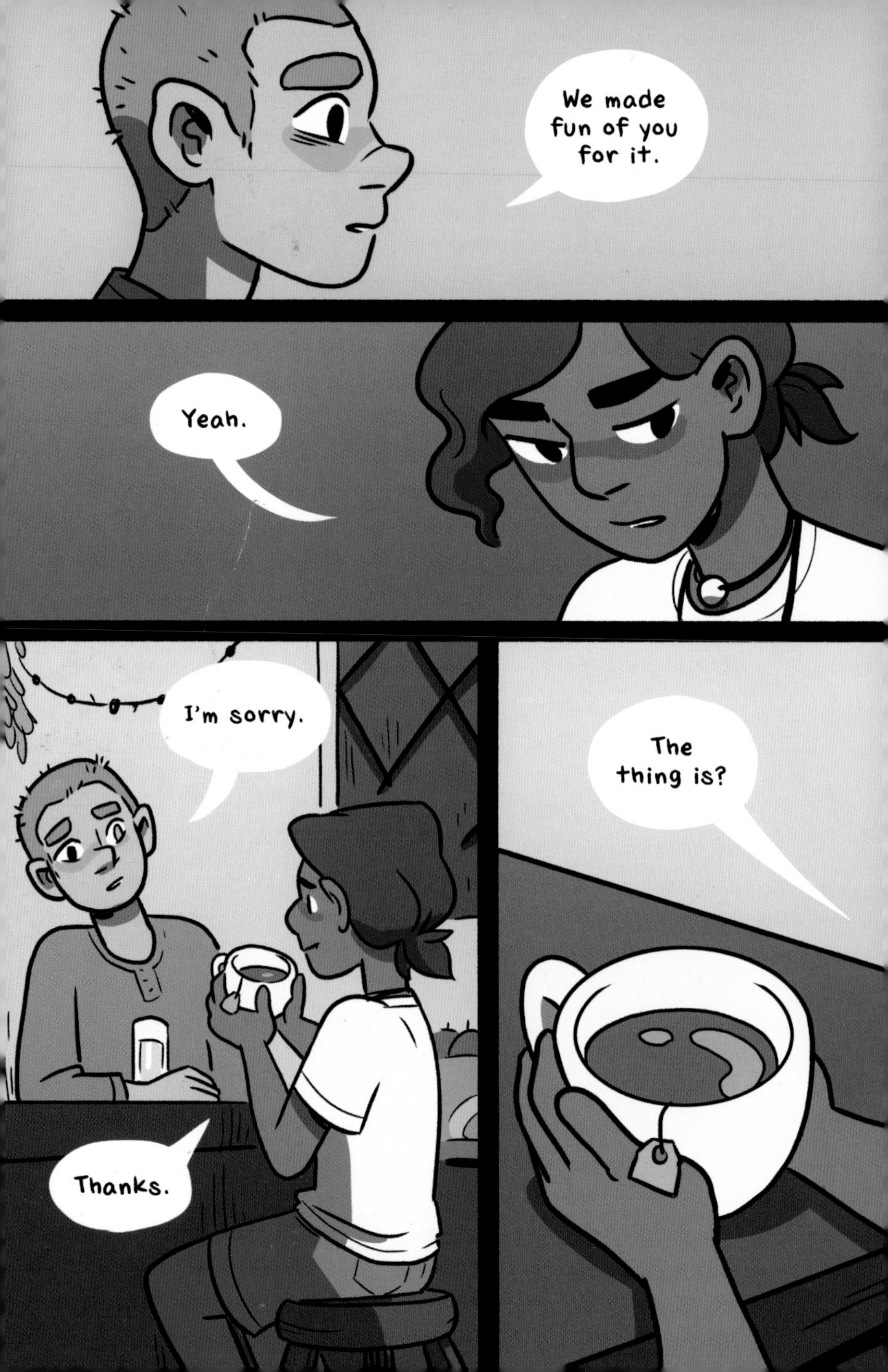
We made fun of you for it.
Yeah.
I'm sorry.
Thanks.
The thing is?

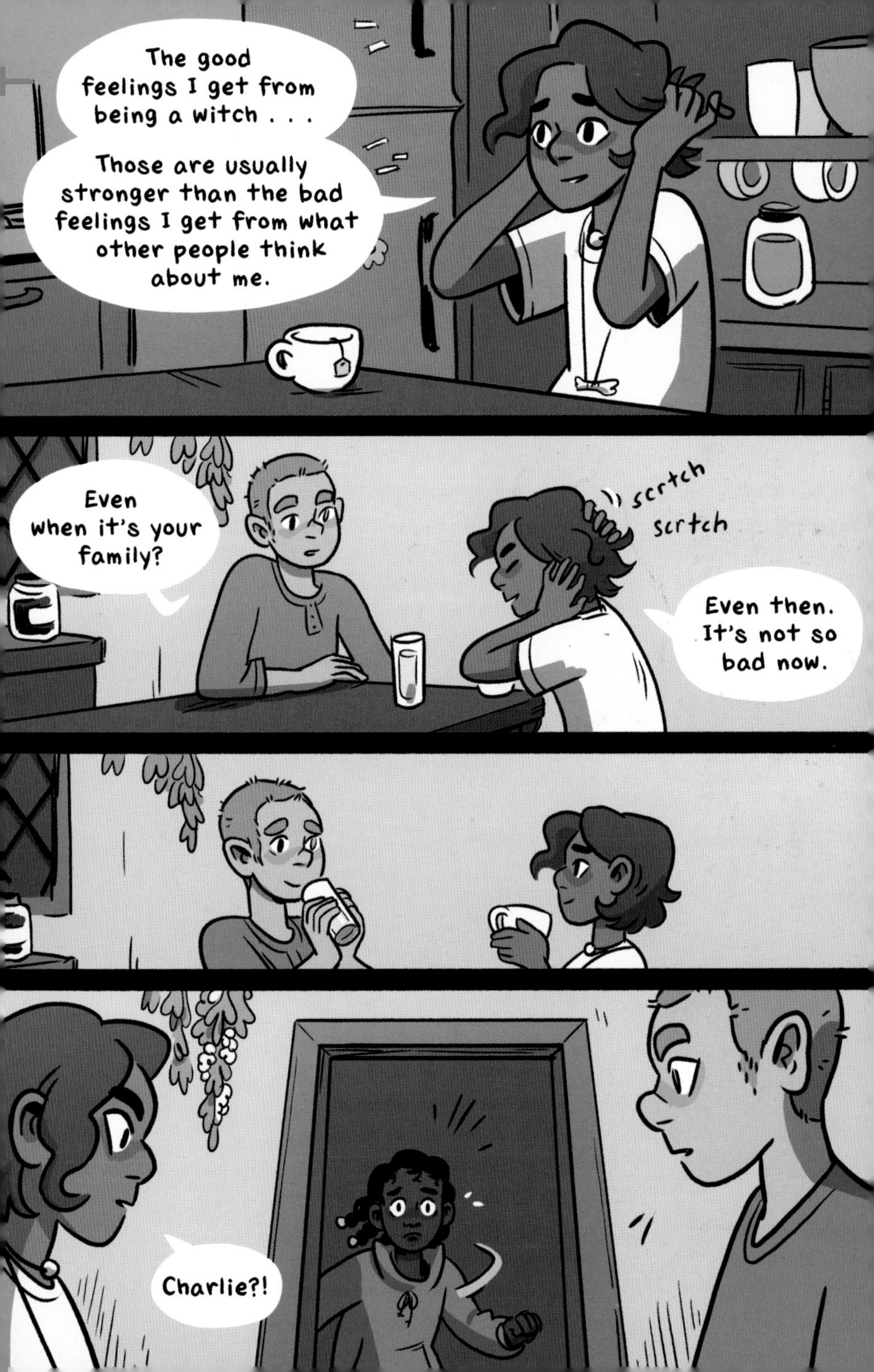
The good feelings I get from being a witch . . .
Those are usually stronger than the bad feelings I get from what other people think about me.
Even when it's your family?
scrtch scrtch
Even then. It's not so bad now.
Charlie?!

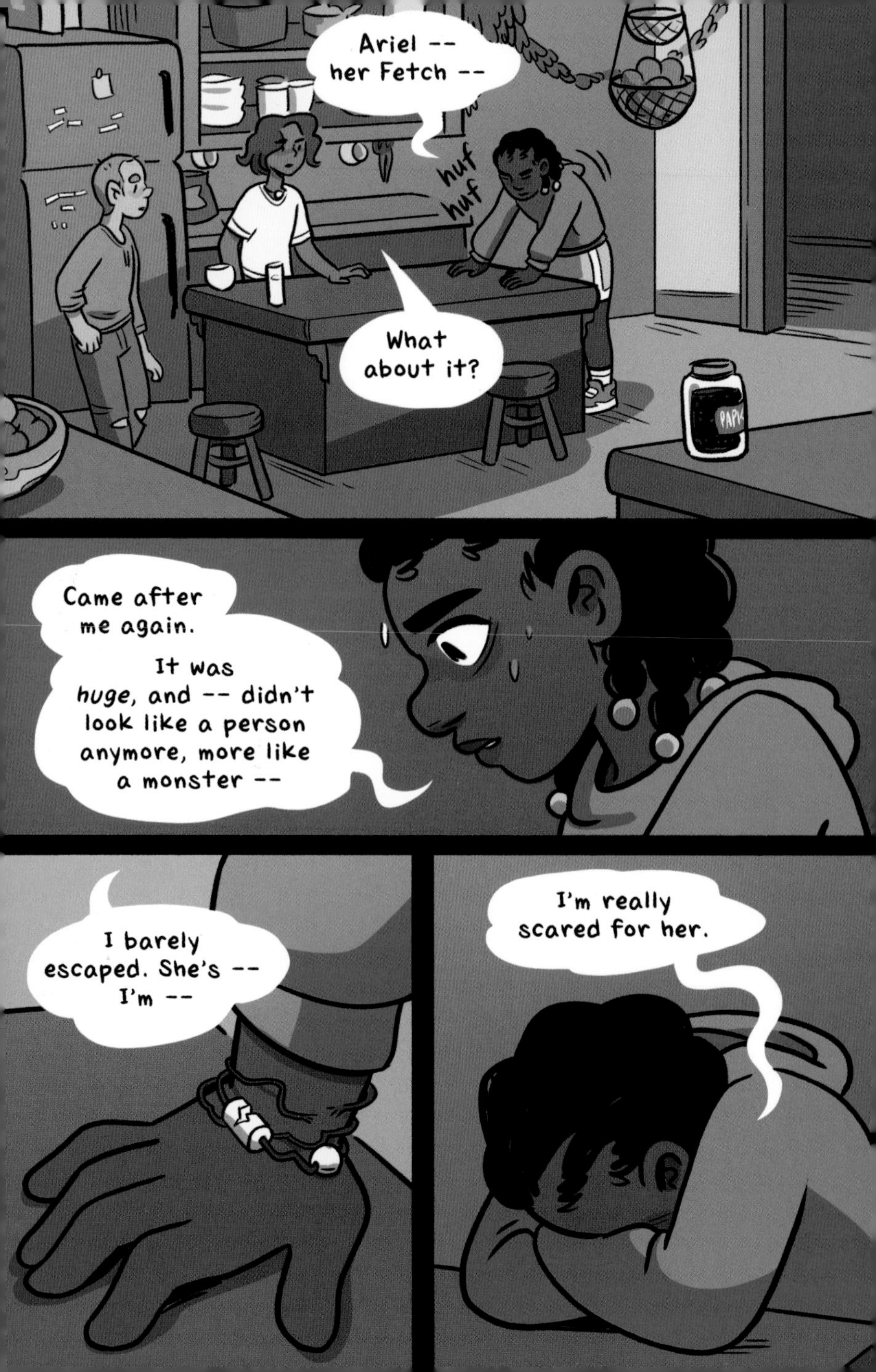
Ariel -- her Fetch --
huf huf
What about it?
Came after me again.
It was *huge*, and -- didn't look like a person anymore, more like a monster --
I barely escaped. She's -- I'm --
I'm really scared for her.

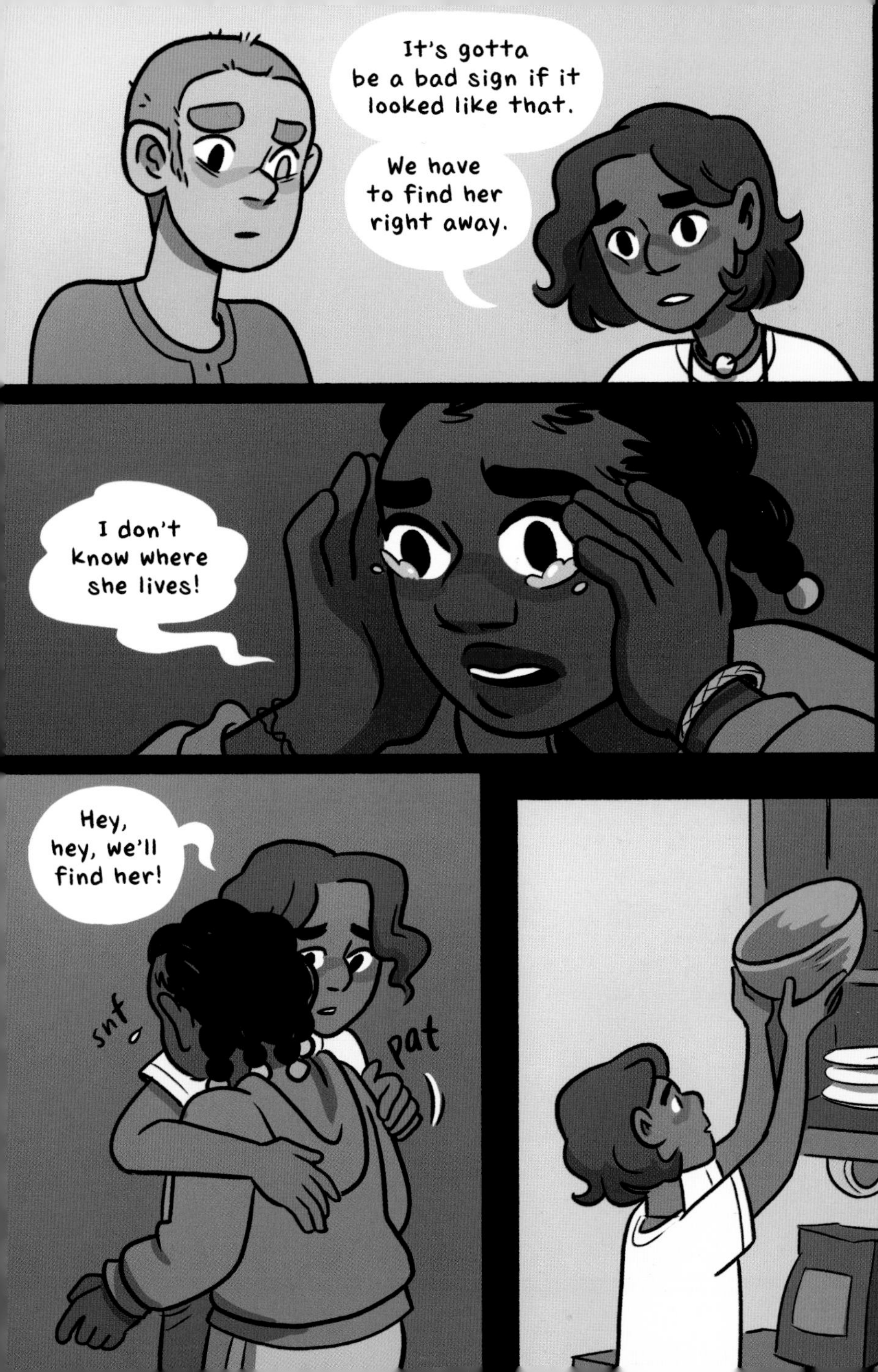
It's gotta be a bad sign if it looked like that.
We have to find her right away.
I don't know where she lives!
Hey, hey, we'll find her!
snf
pat

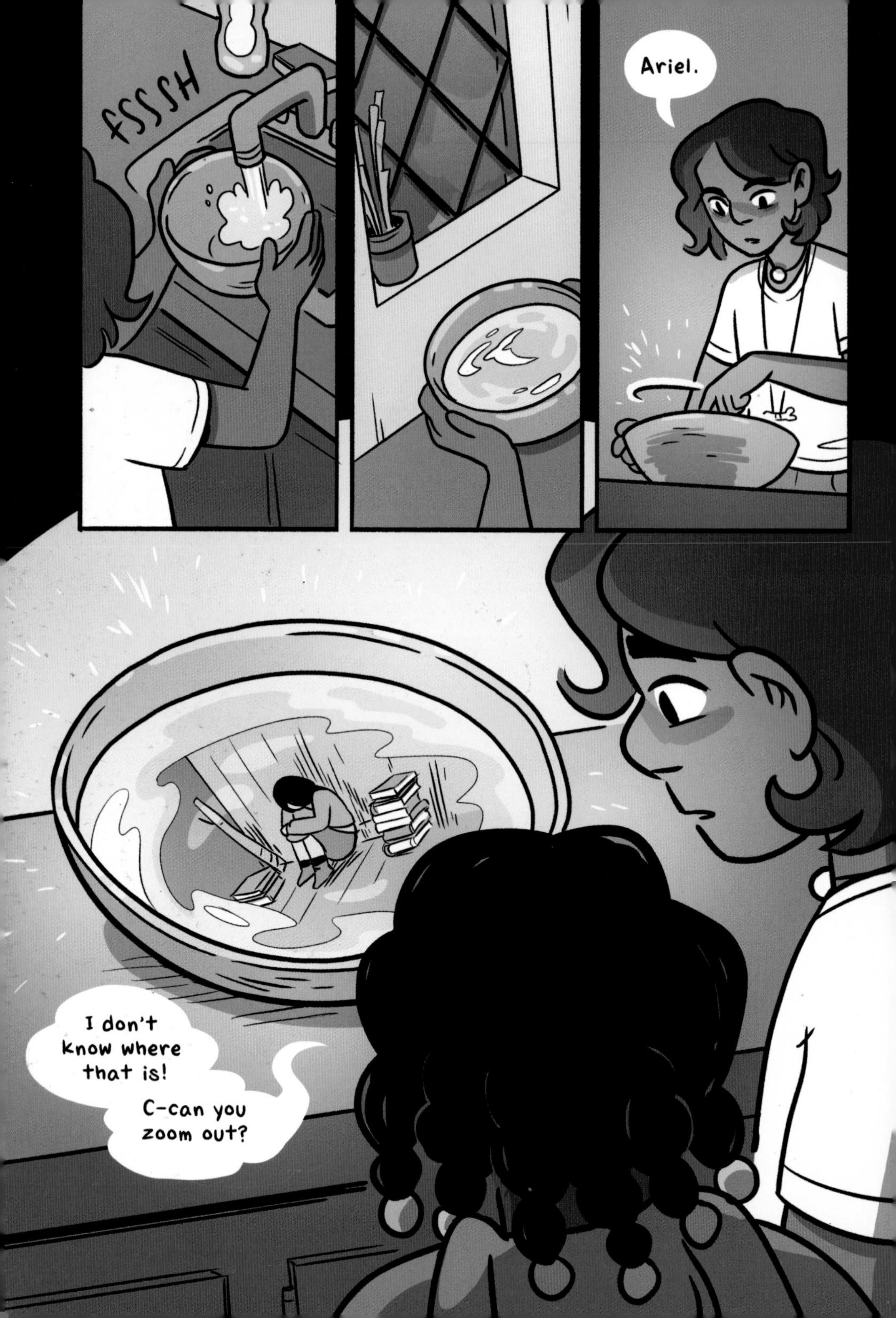
FSSSH
Ariel.
I don't know where that is!
C-can you zoom out?

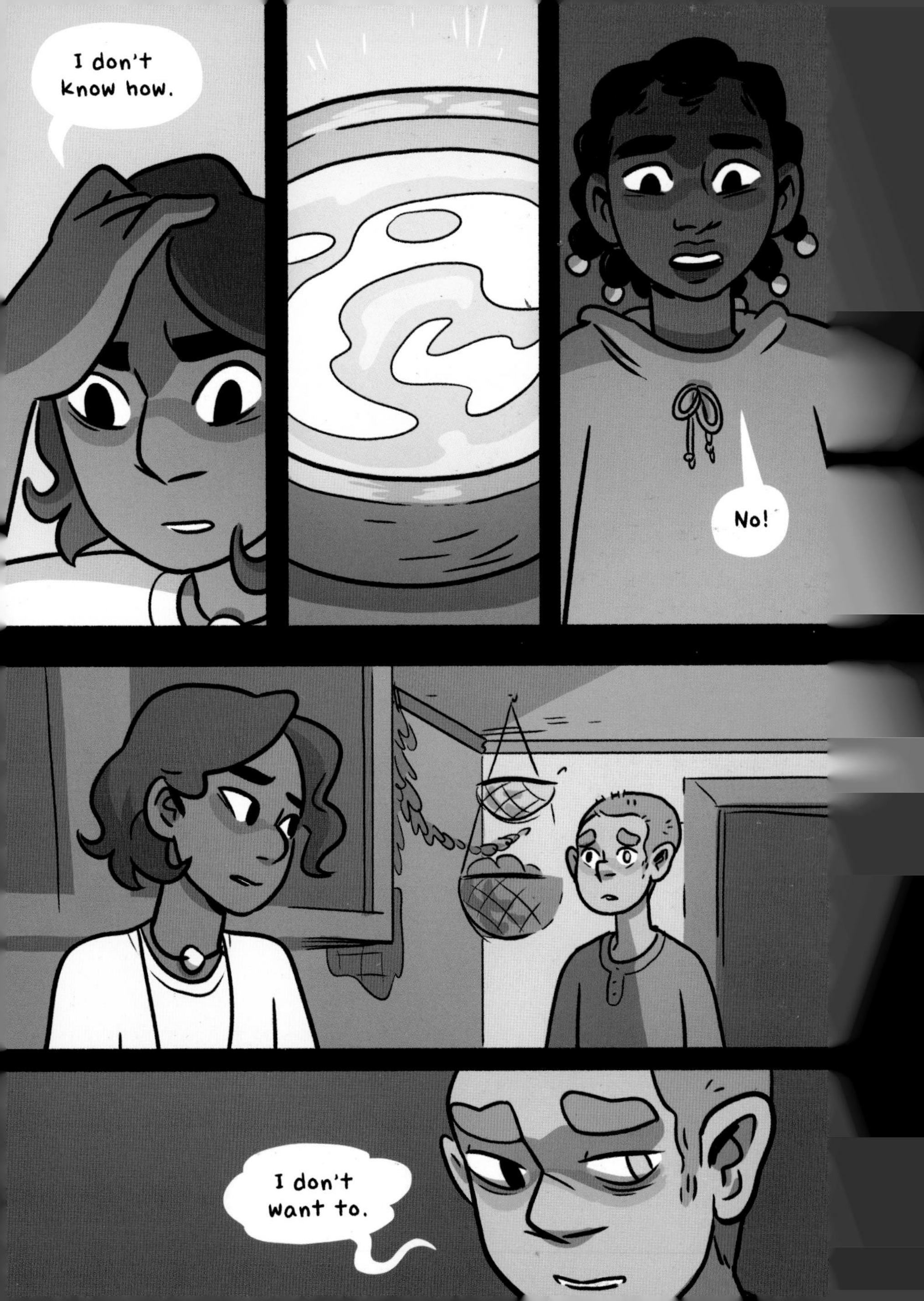
I don't know how.
No!
I don't want to.

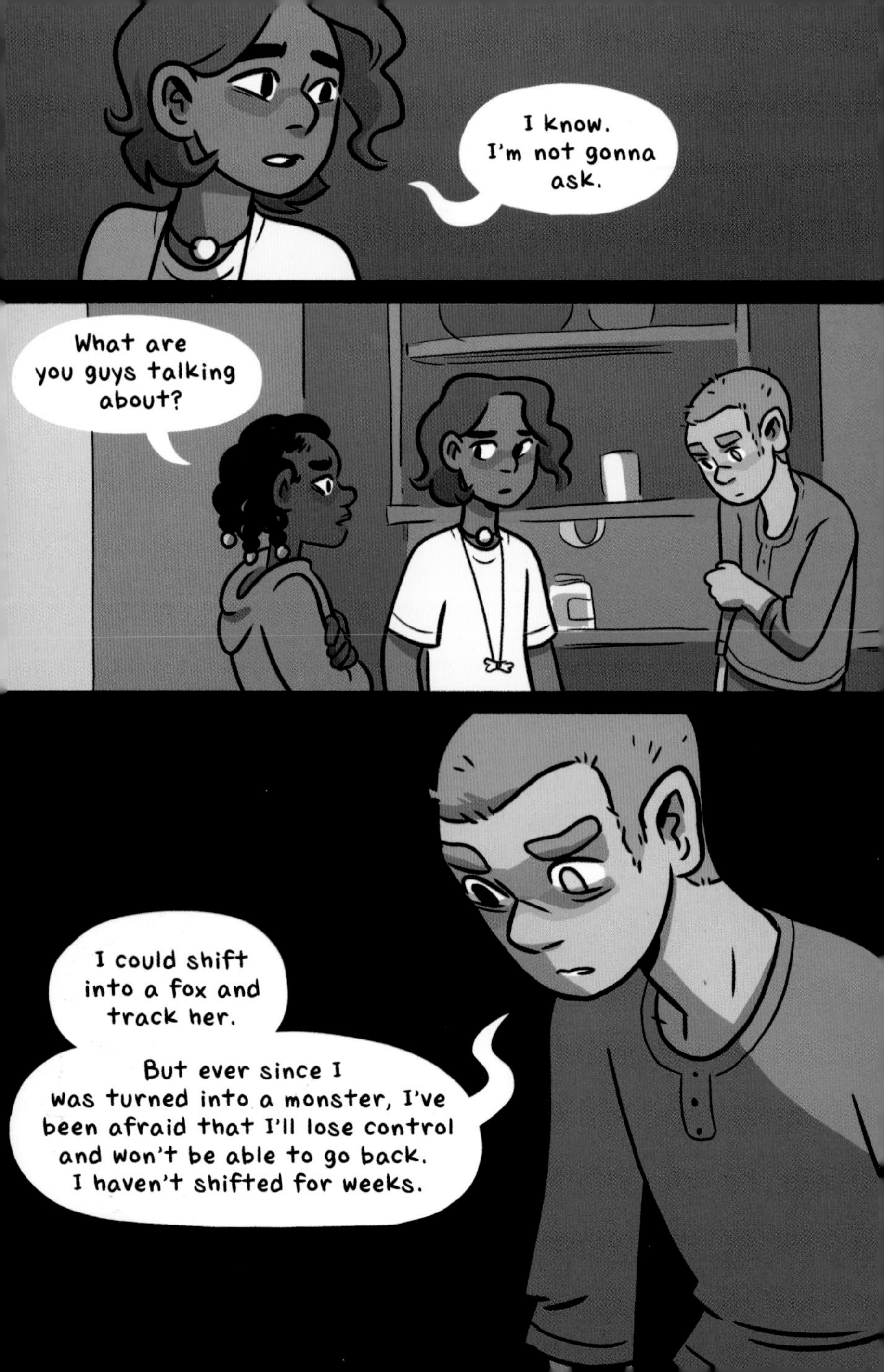
I know. I'm not gonna ask.
What are you guys talking about?
I could shift into a fox and track her.
But ever since I was turned into a monster, I've been afraid that I'll lose control and won't be able to go back. I haven't shifted for weeks.

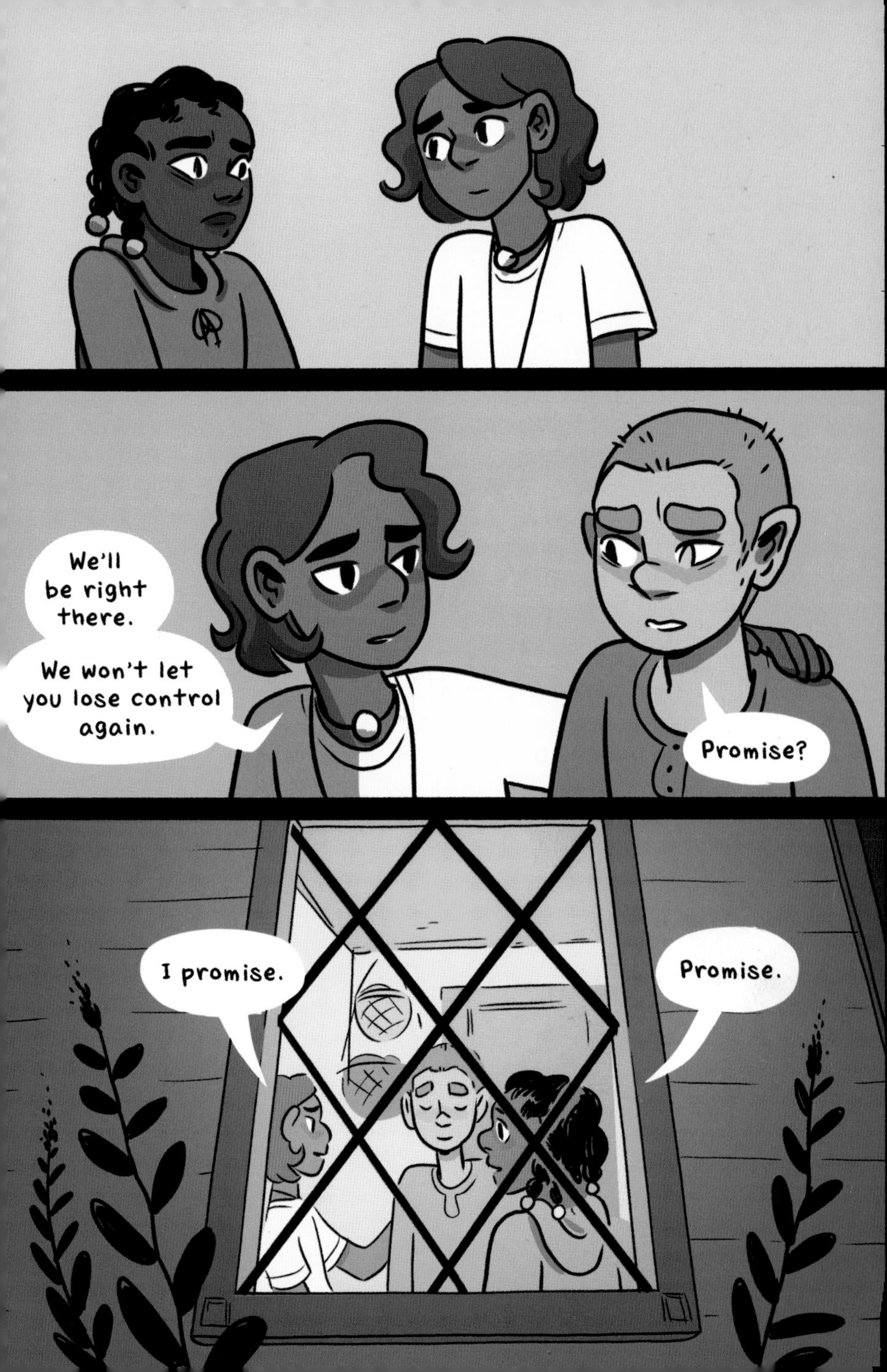
We'll be right there.
We won't let you lose control again.
Promise?
I promise.
Promise.

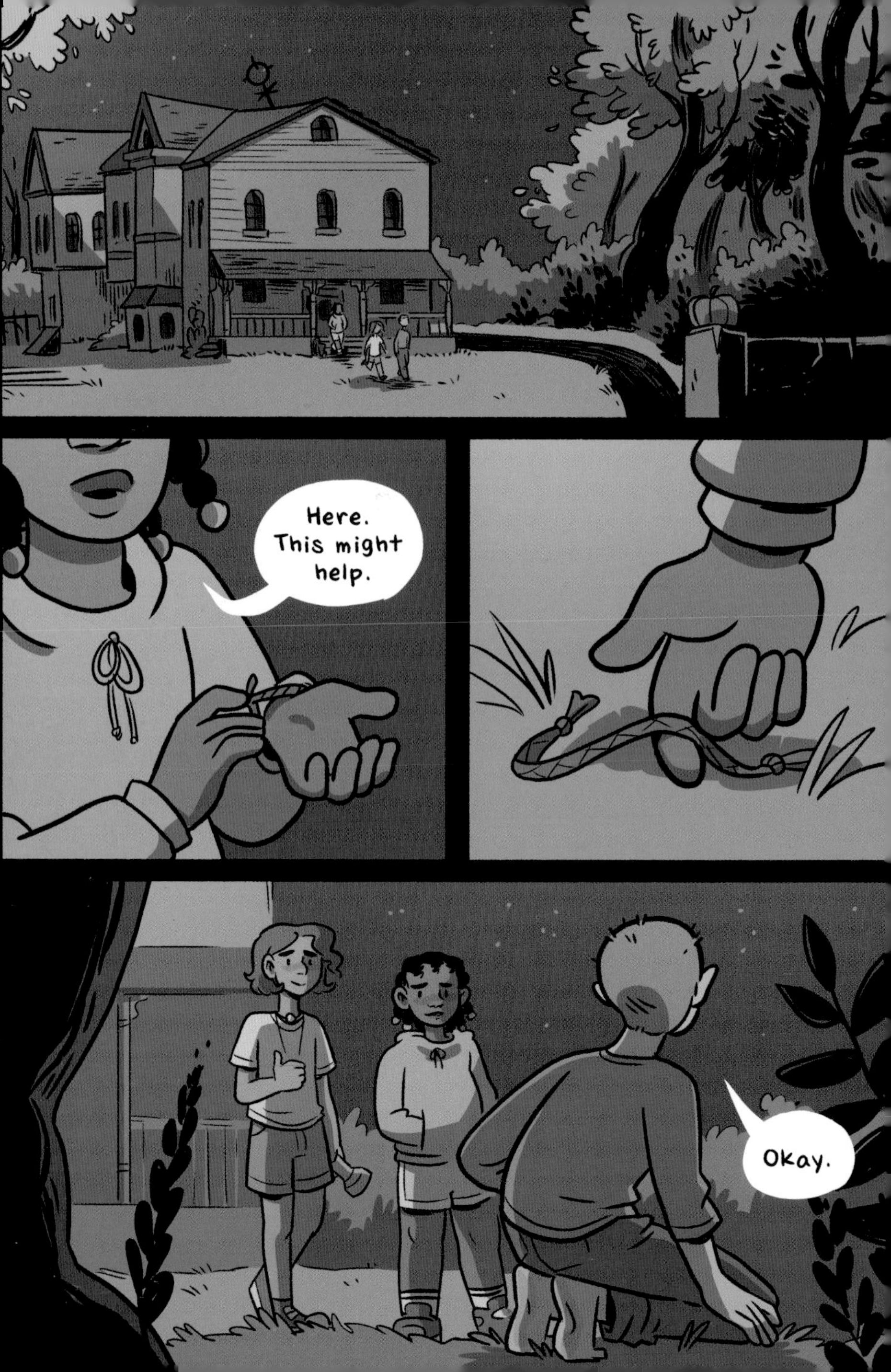
Here. This might help.
Okay.

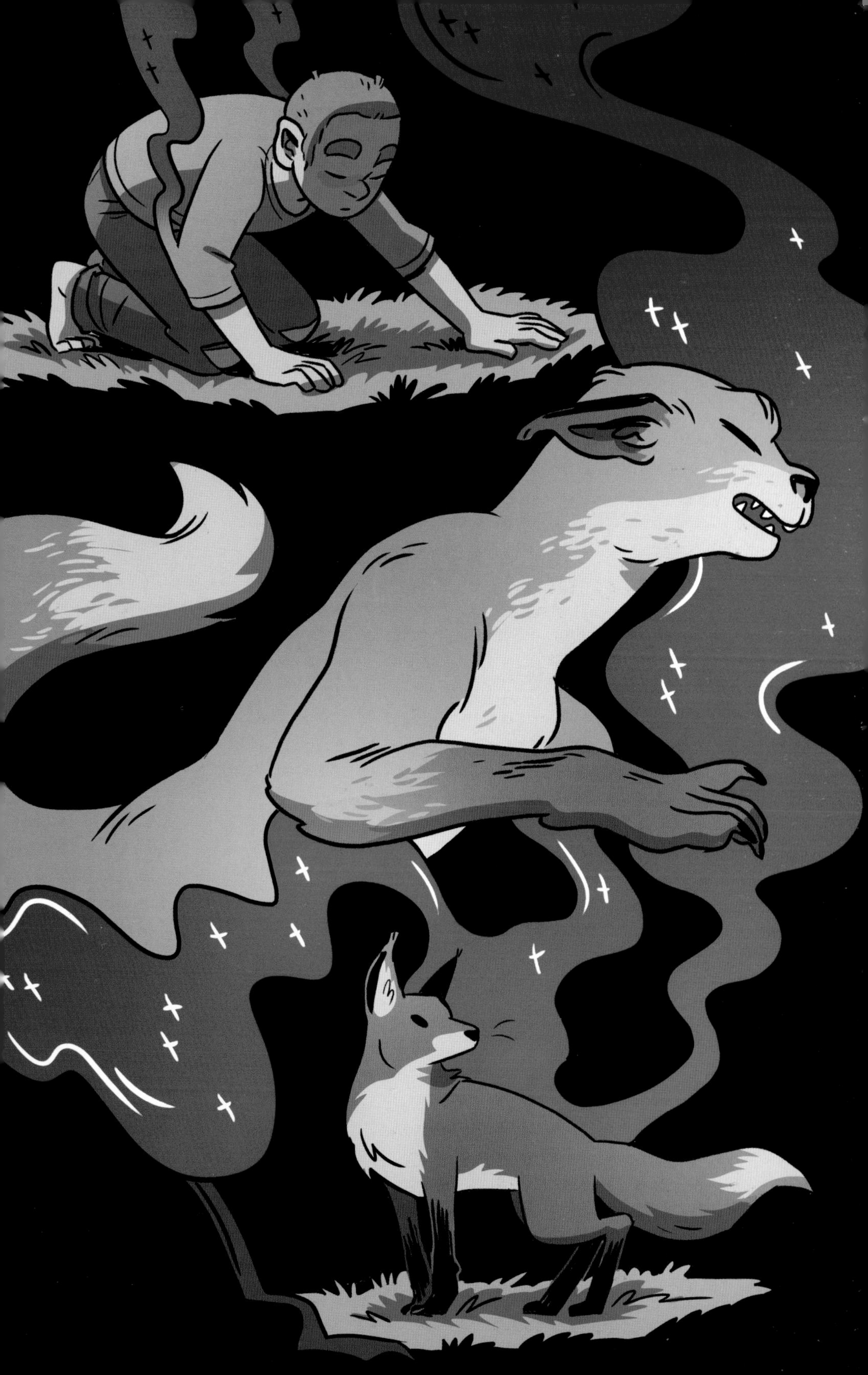

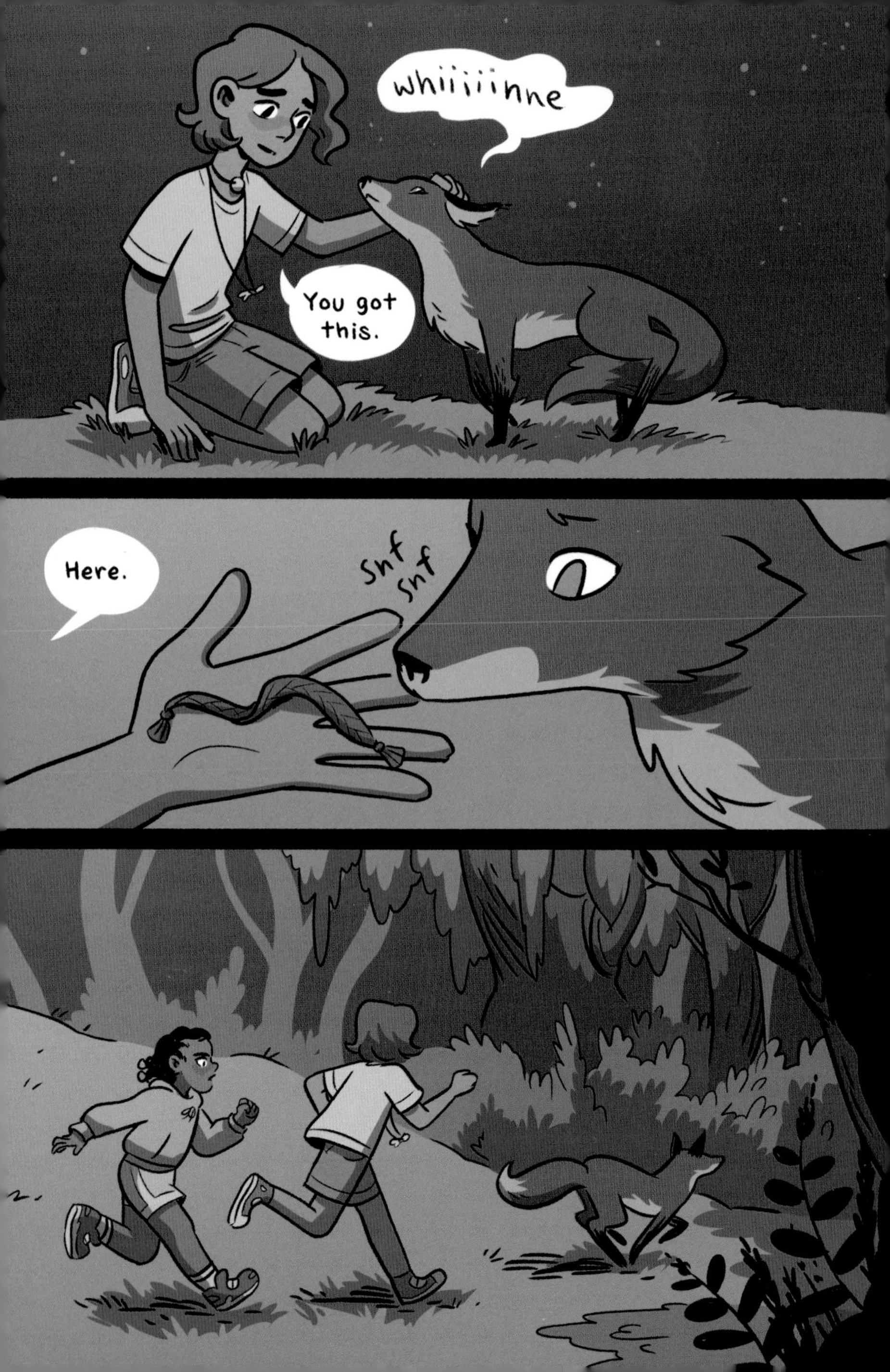
whiiiiinne
You got this.
Here.
snf
snf

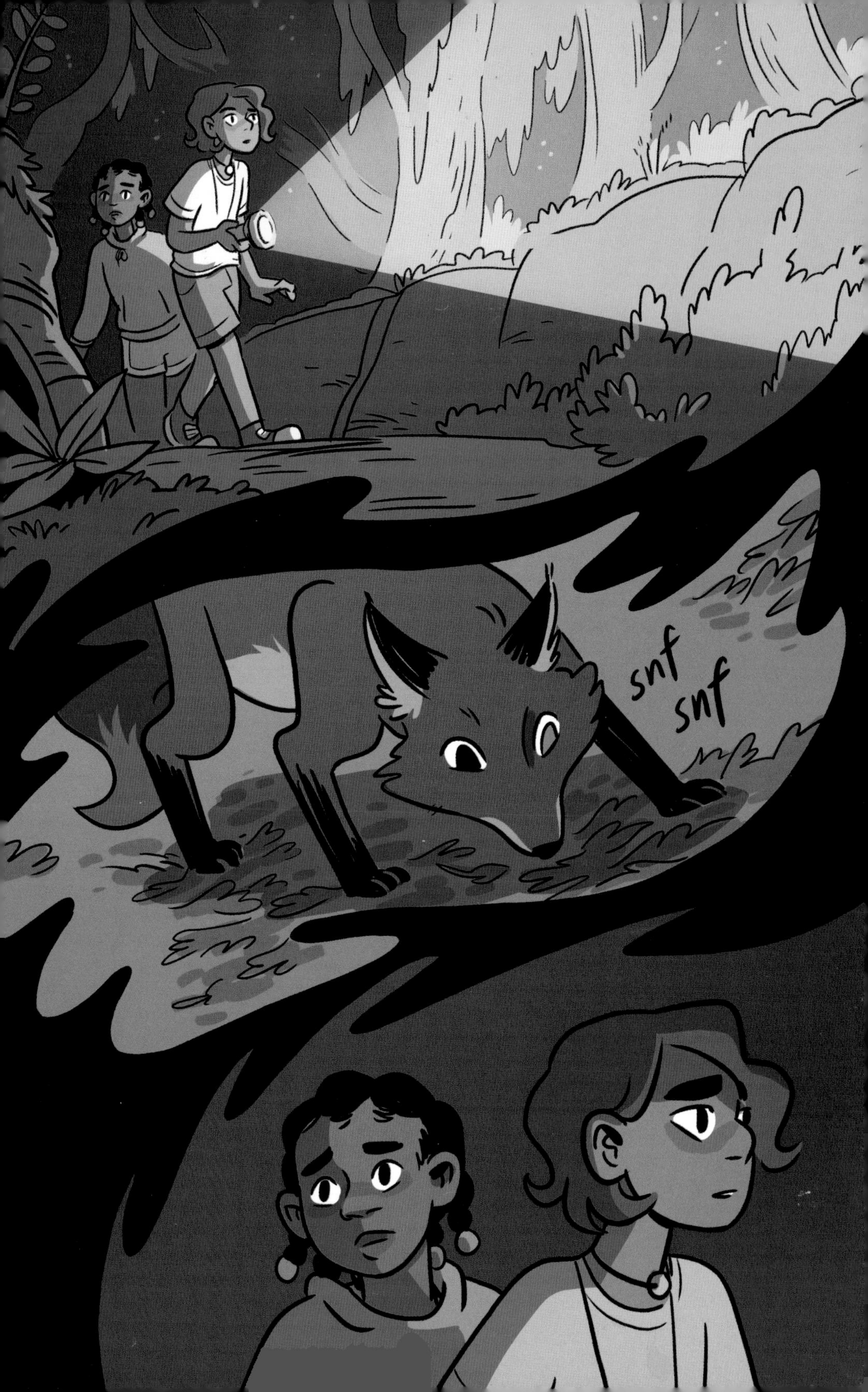
snf
snf

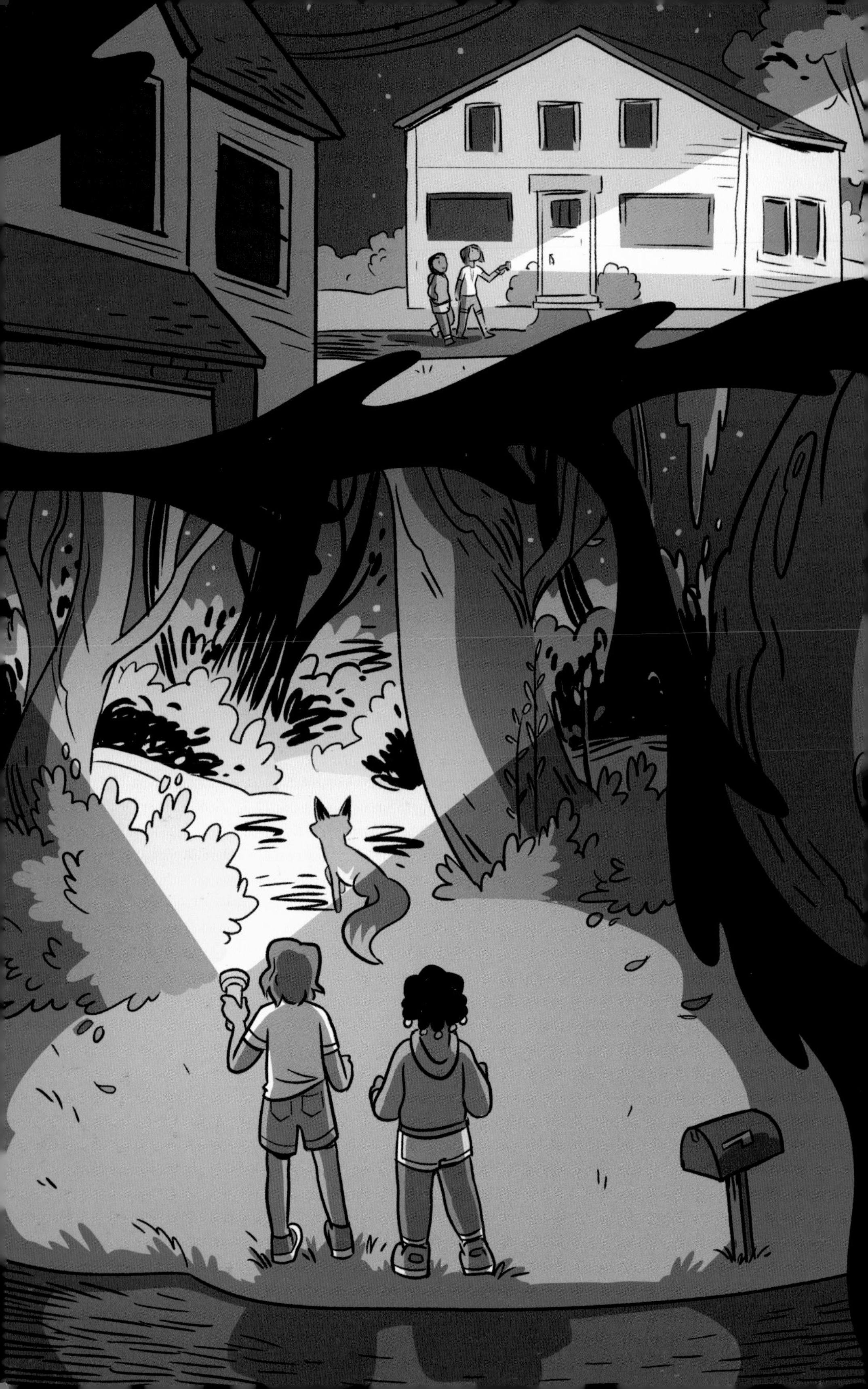

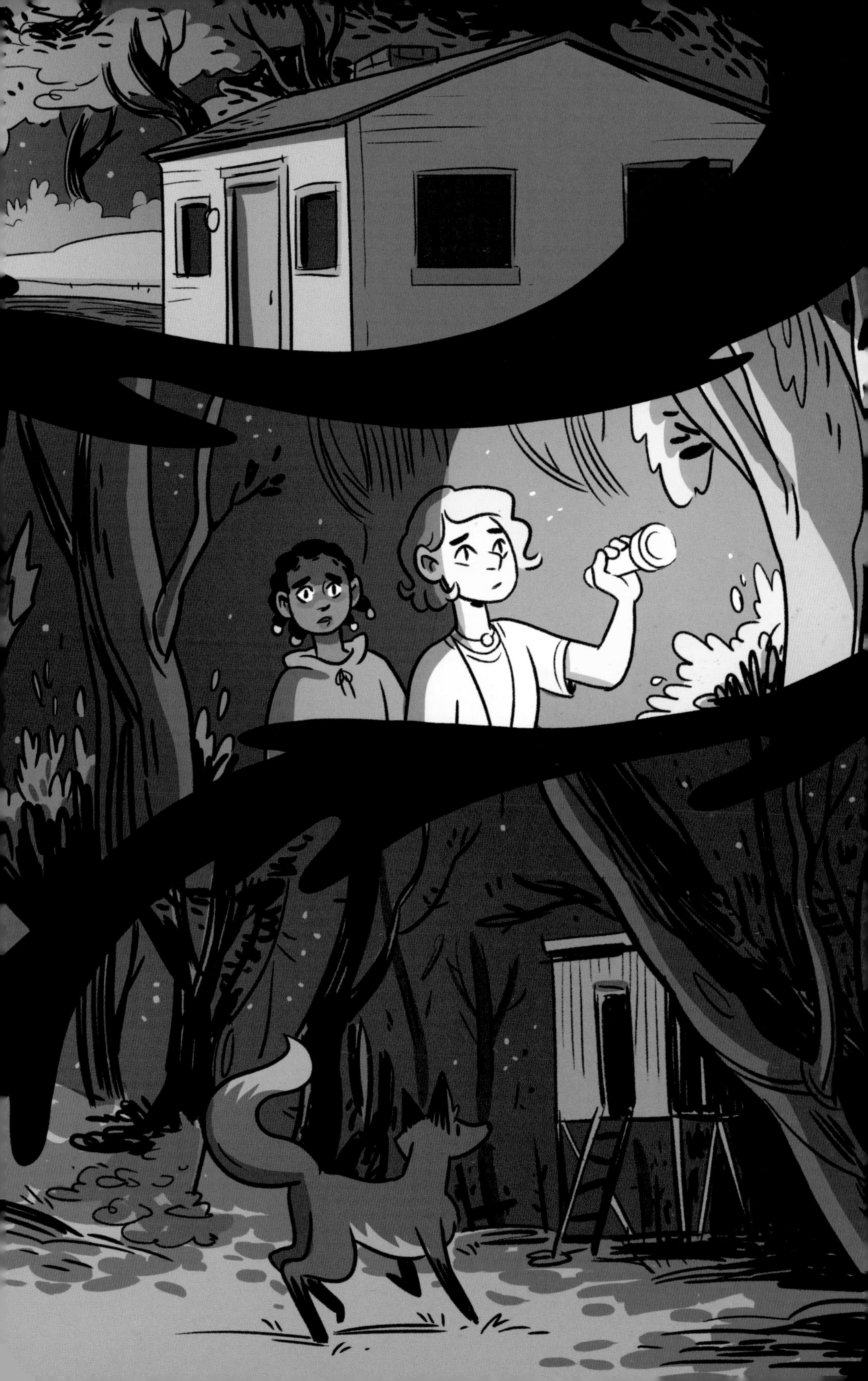

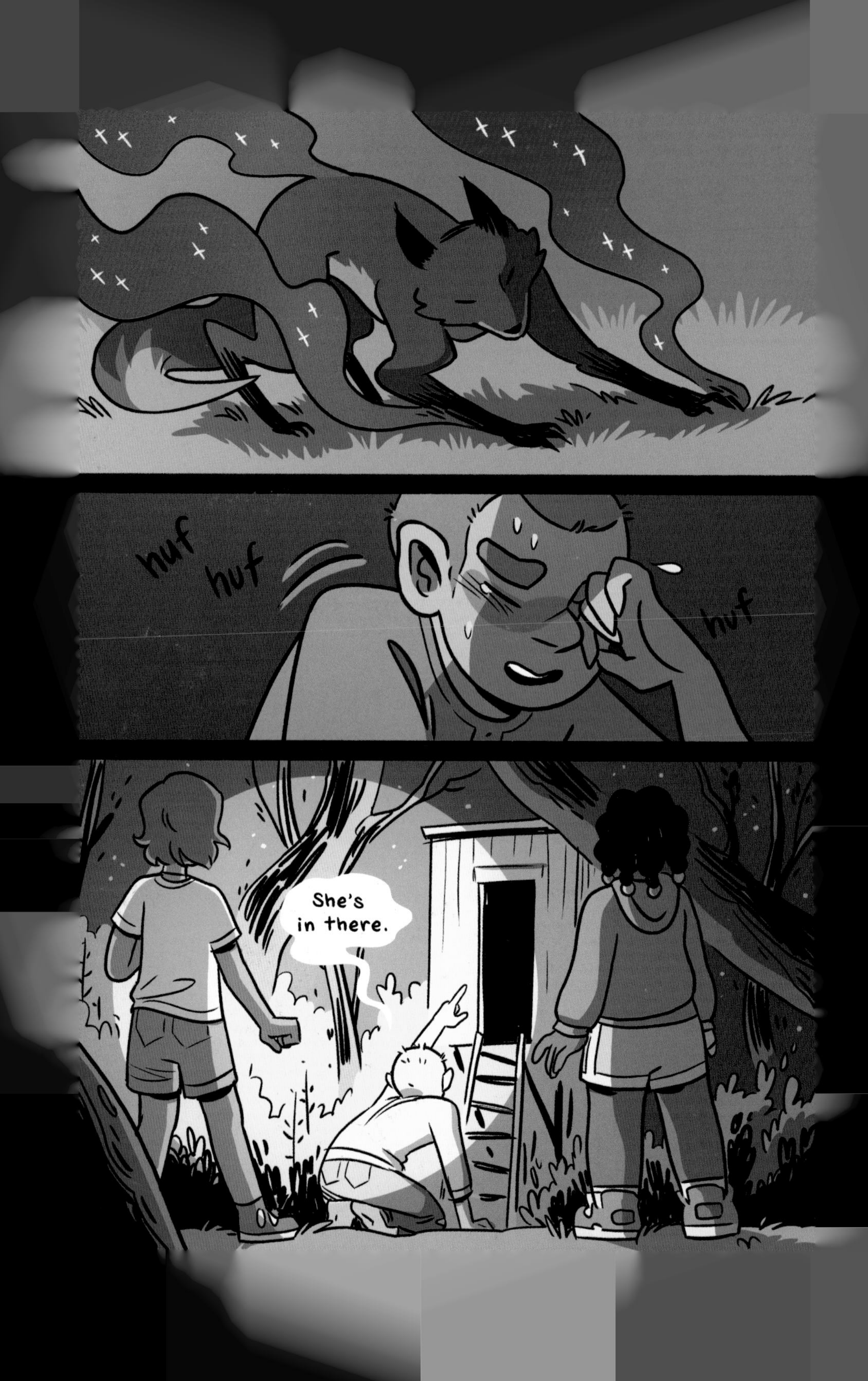
huf
huf
huf
She's in there.

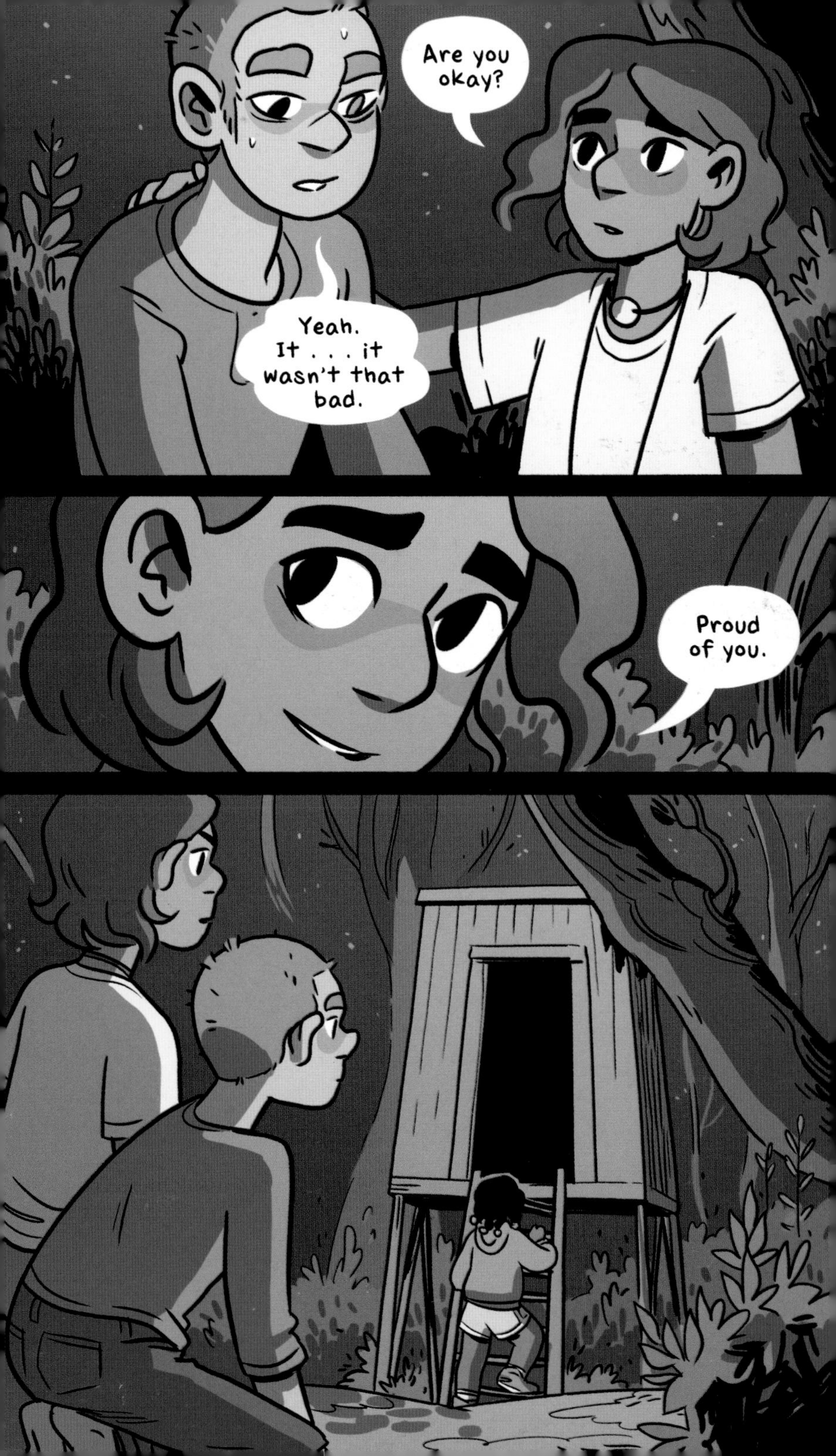
Are you okay?
Yeah. It . . . it wasn't that bad.
Proud of you.

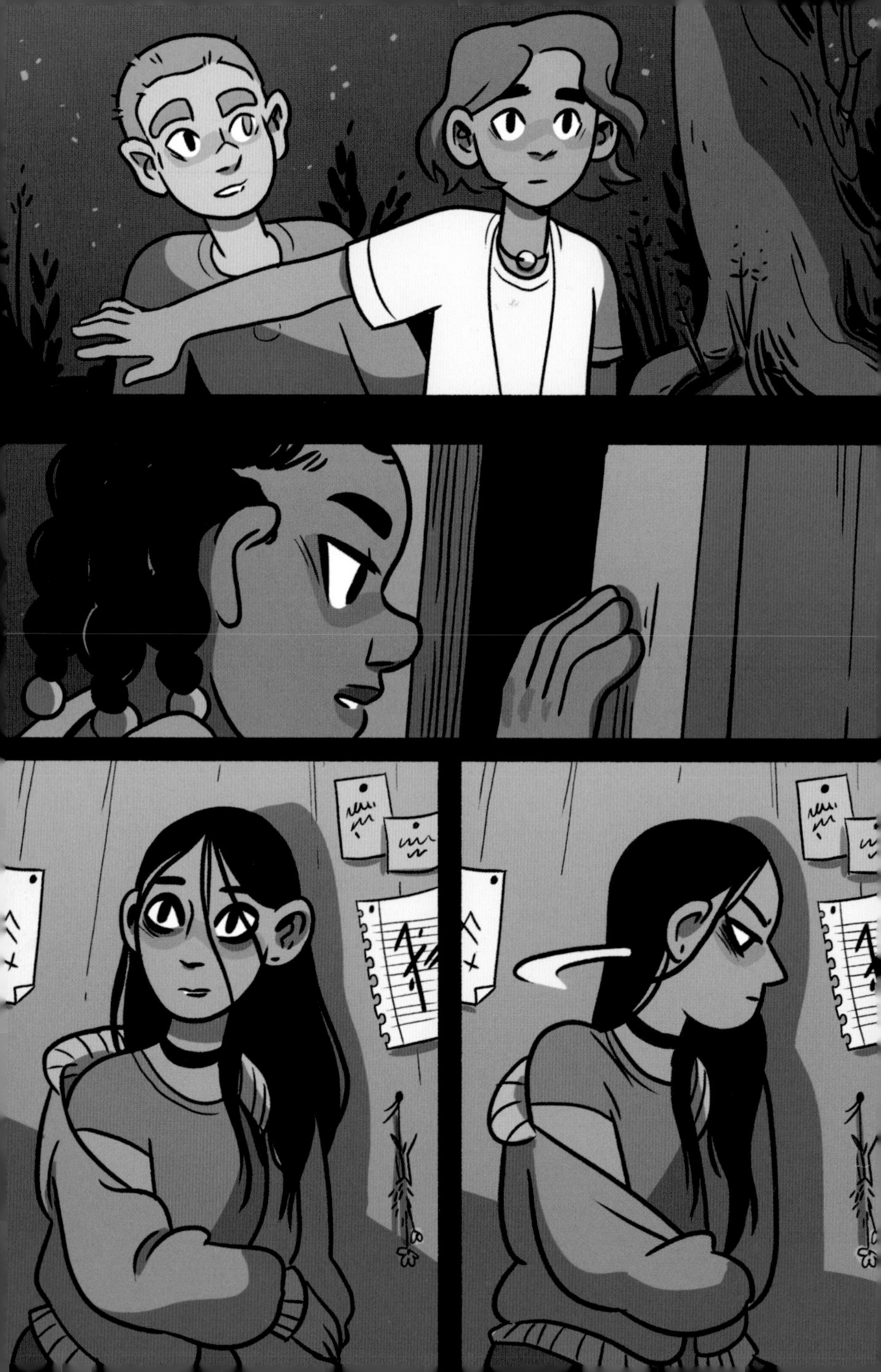

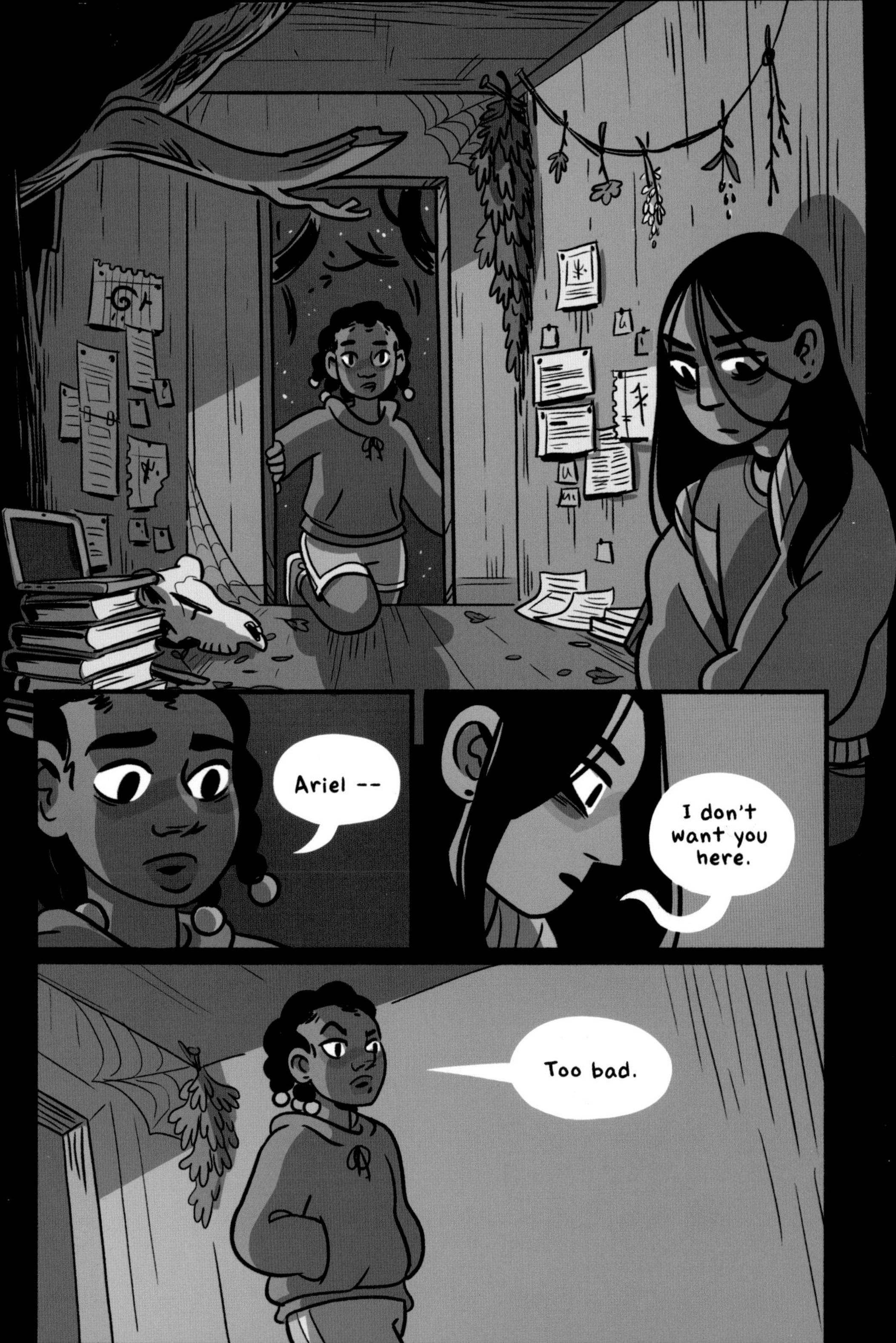
Ariel --
I don't want you here.
Too bad.

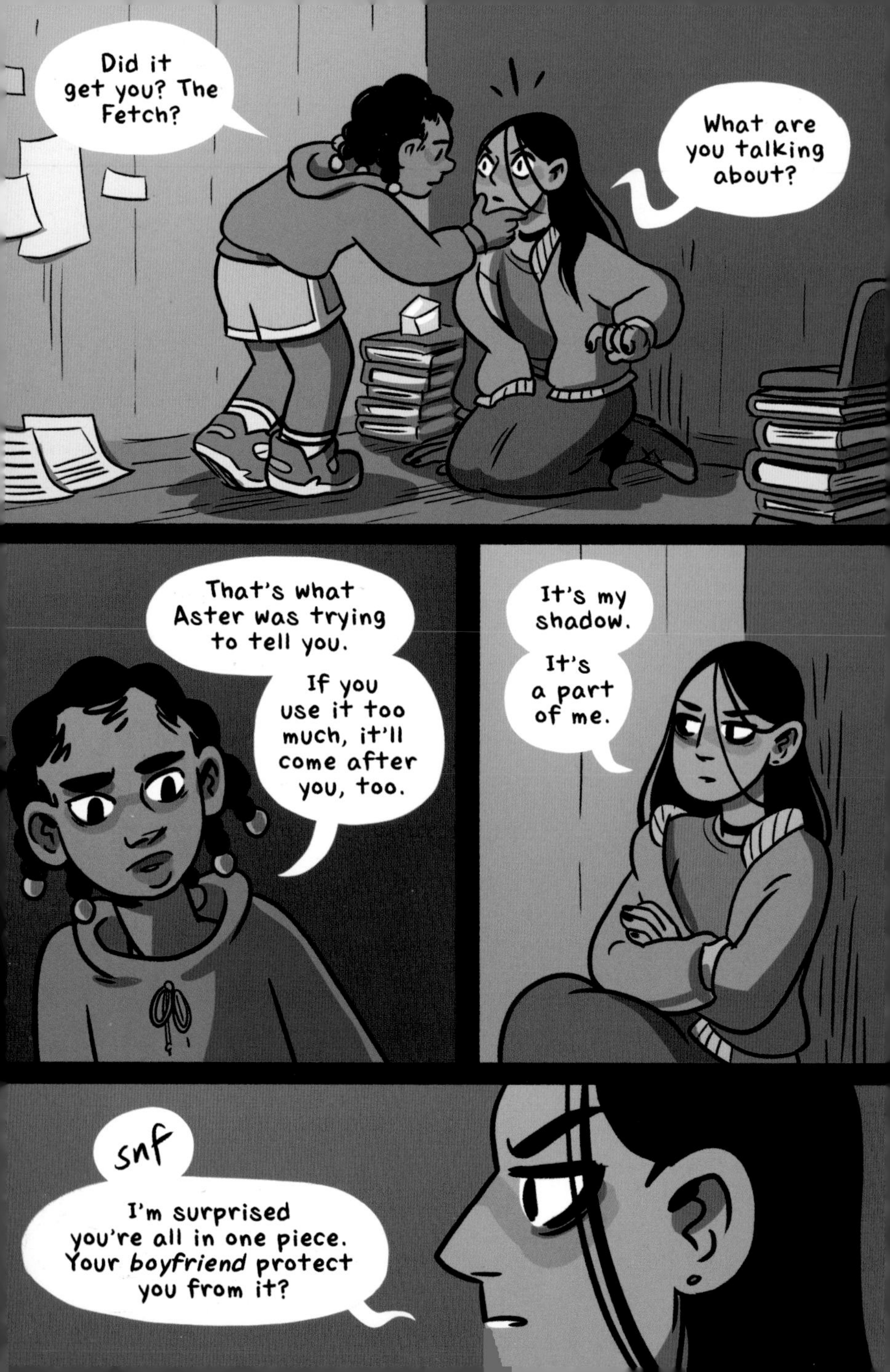
Did it get you? The Fetch?
What are you talking about?
That's what Aster was trying to tell you.
If you use it too much, it'll come after you, too.
It's my shadow.
It's a part of me.
snf
I'm surprised you're all in one piece. Your *boyfriend* protect you from it?

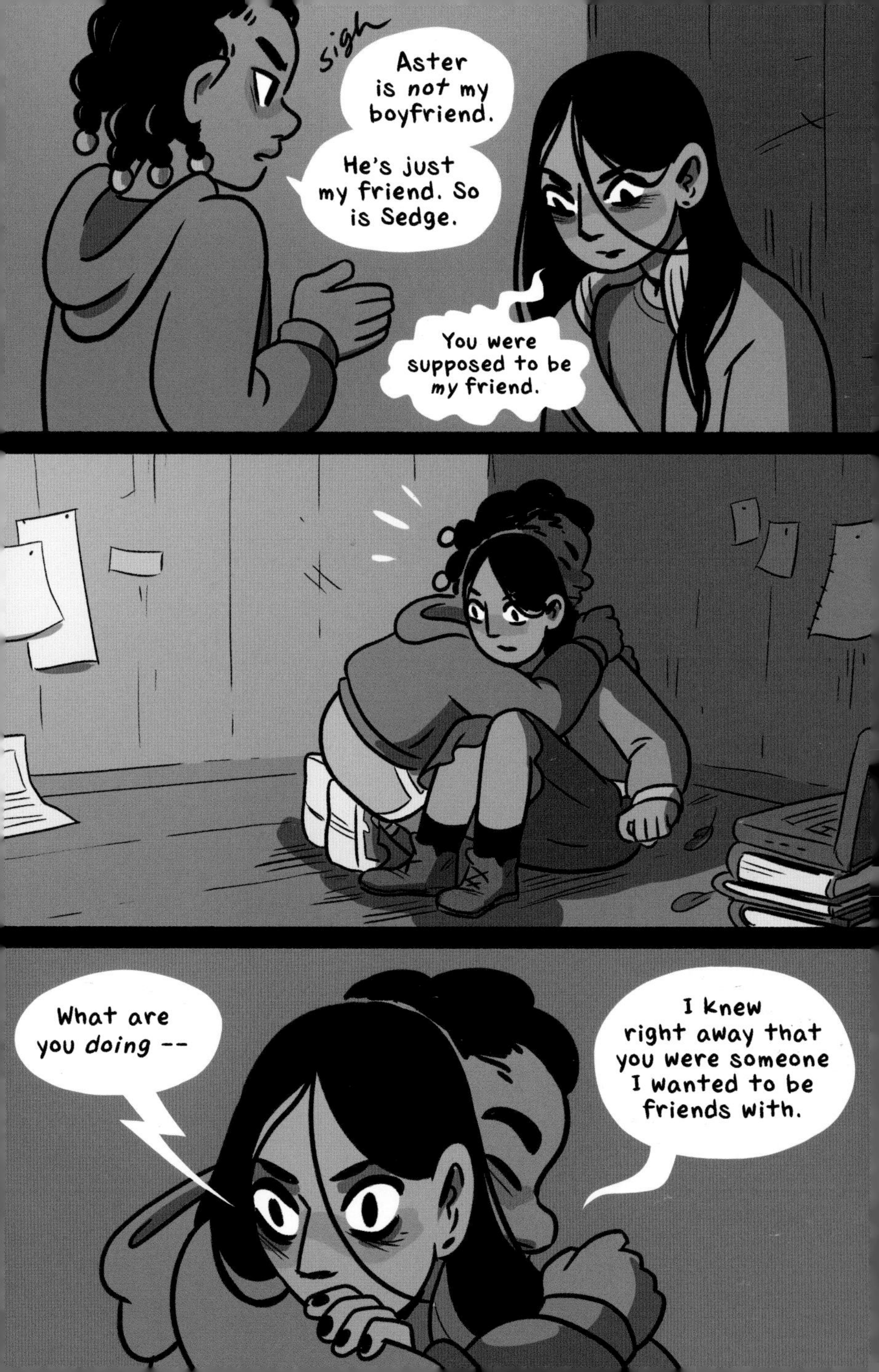
sigh
Aster is *not* my boyfriend.
He's just my friend. So is Sedge.
You were supposed to be *my* friend.
What are you *doing* --
I knew right away that you were someone I wanted to be friends with.

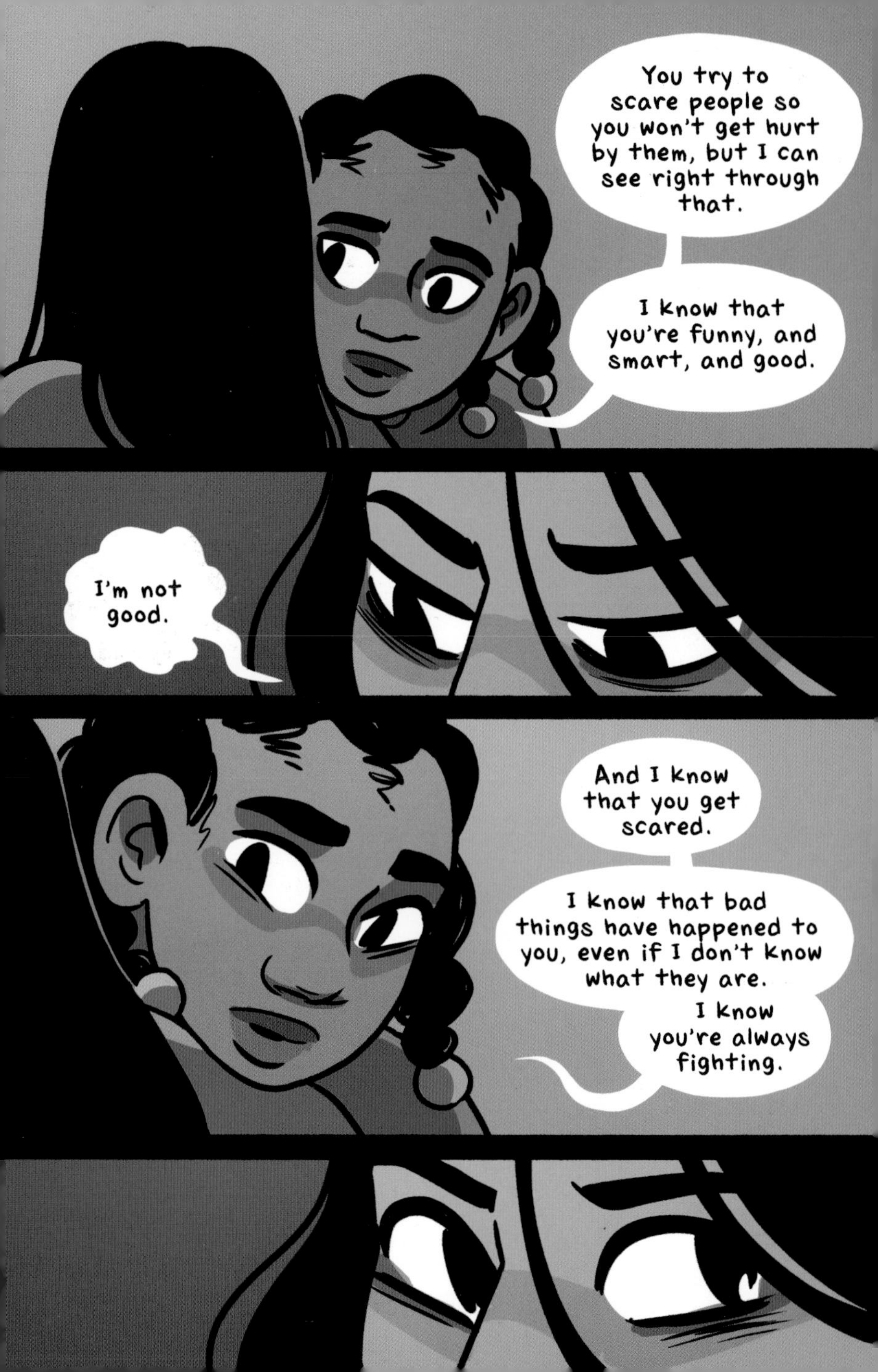
You try to scare people so you won't get hurt by them, but I can see right through that.
I know that you're funny, and smart, and good.
I'm not good.
And I know that you get scared.
I know that bad things have happened to you, even if I don't know what they are.
I know you're always fighting.

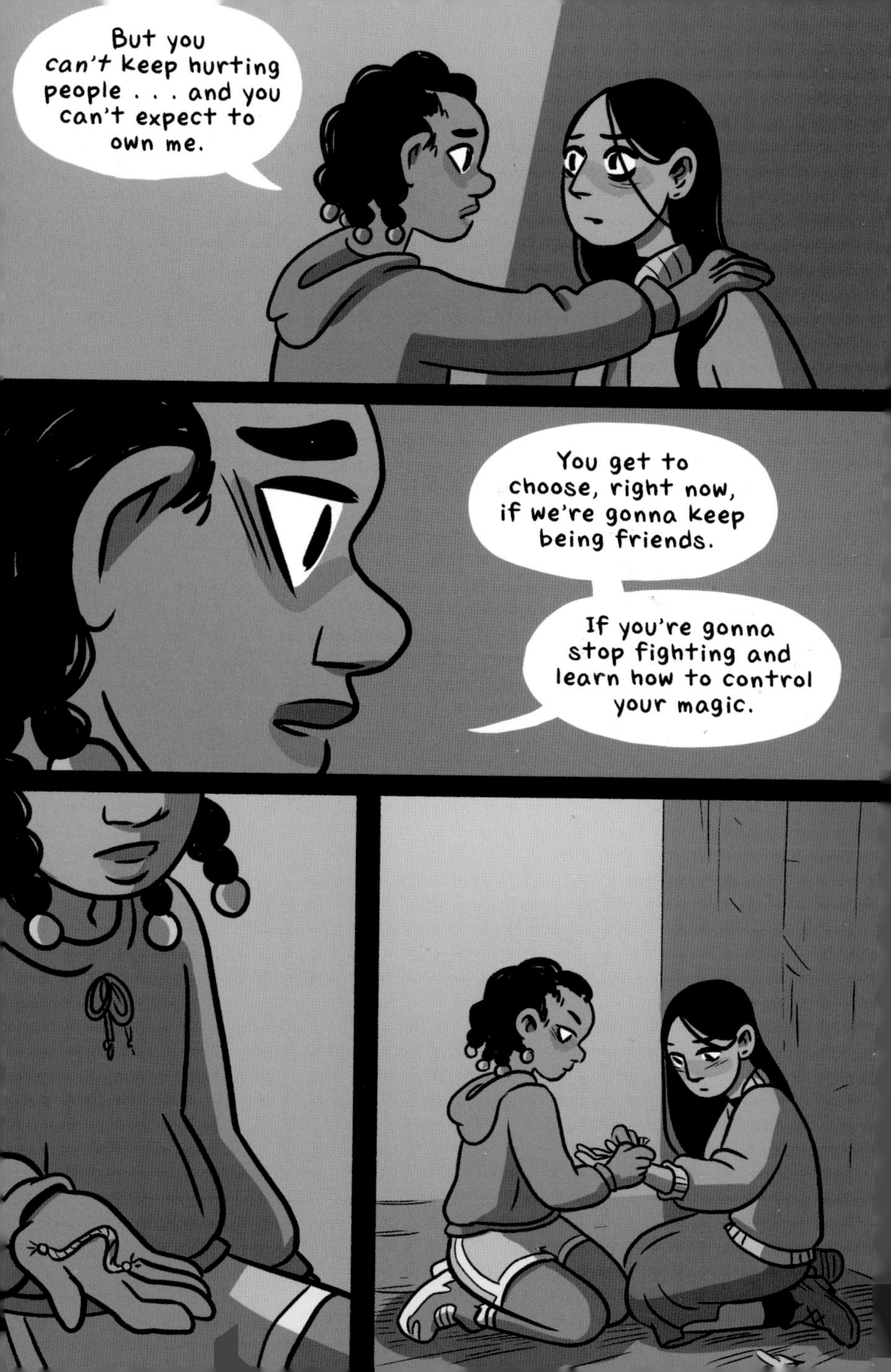
But you can't keep hurting people . . . and you can't expect to own me.
You get to choose, right now, if we're gonna keep being friends.
If you're gonna stop fighting and learn how to control your magic.

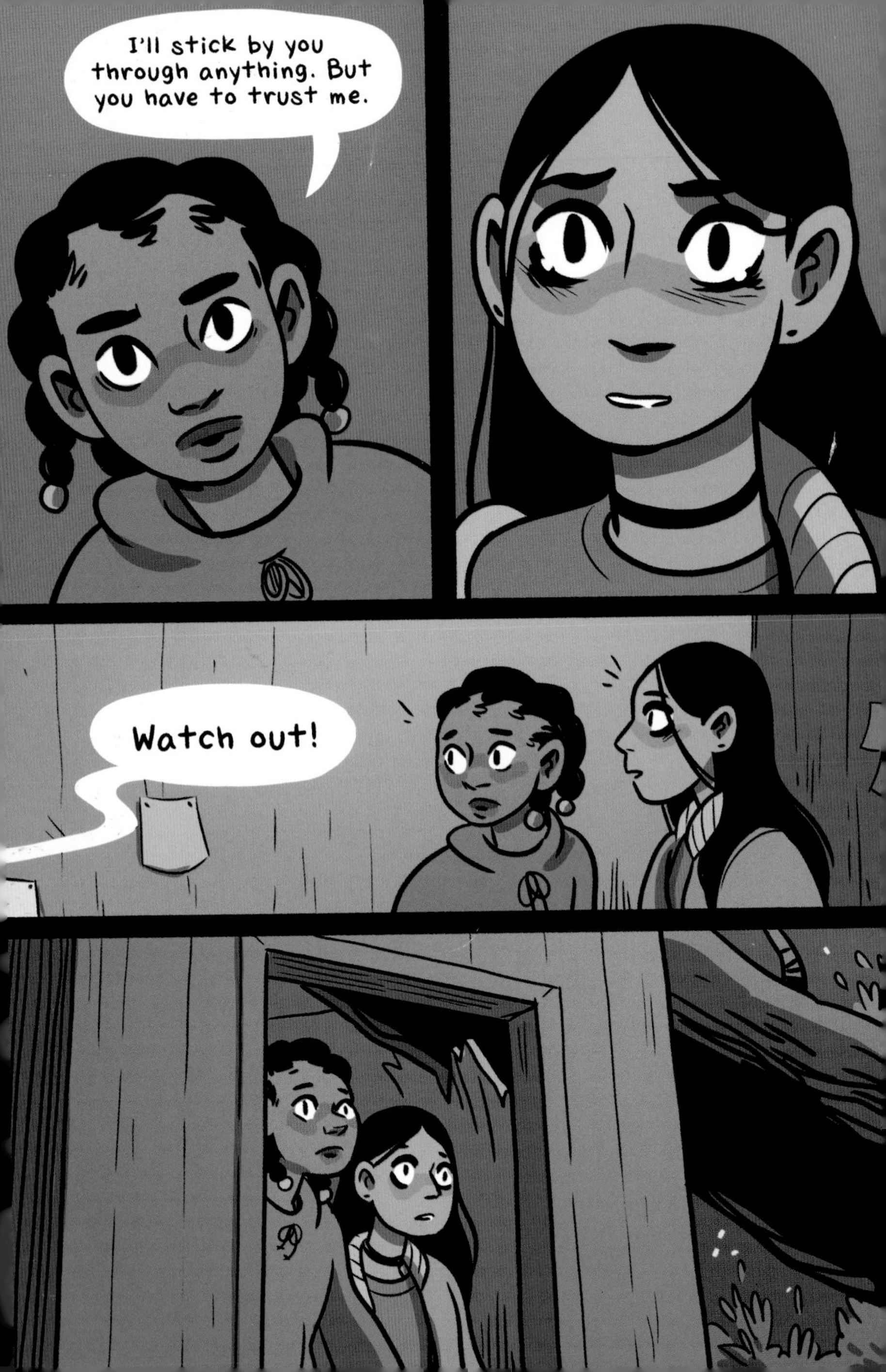
I'll stick by you through anything. But you have to trust me.
Watch out!

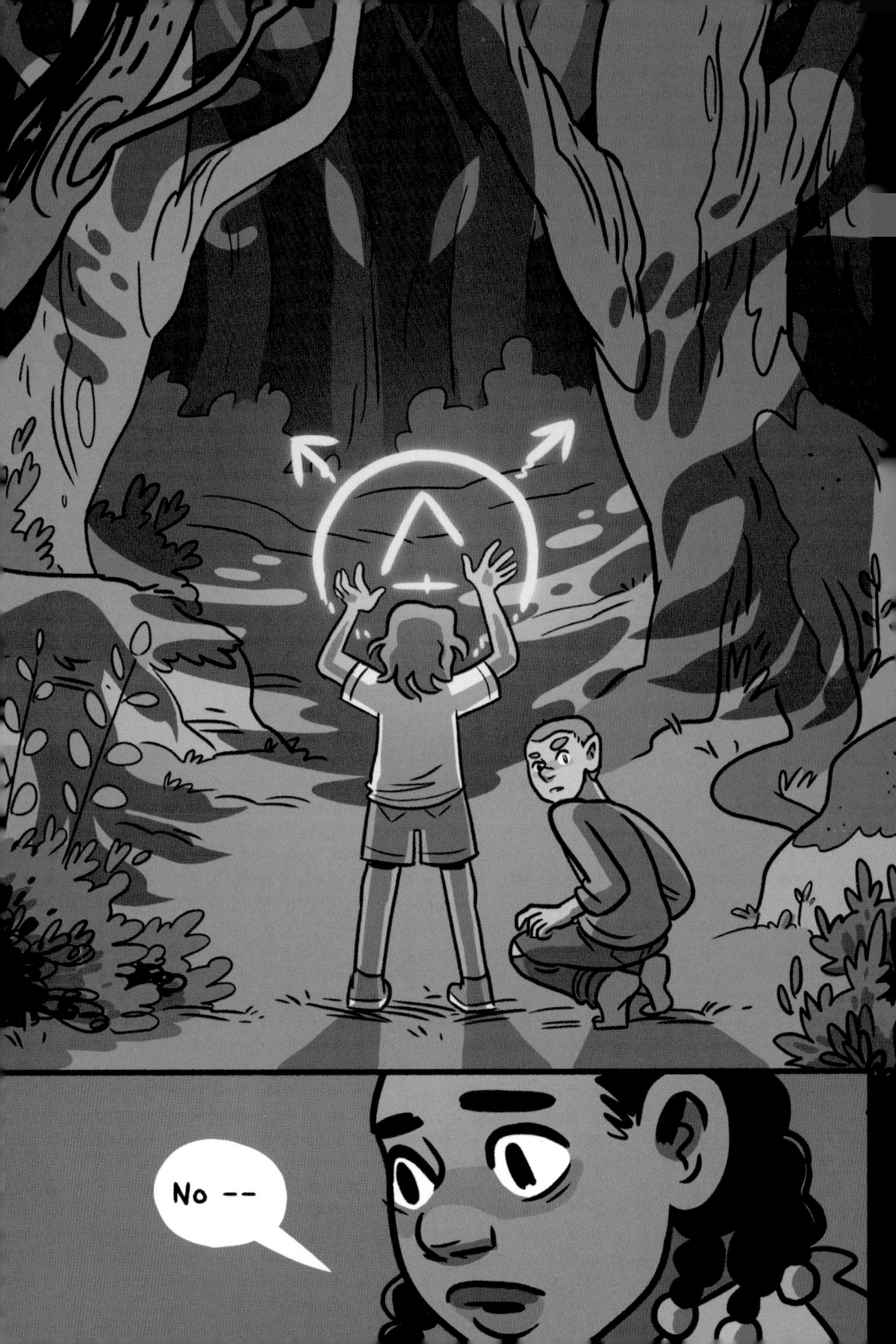
No --

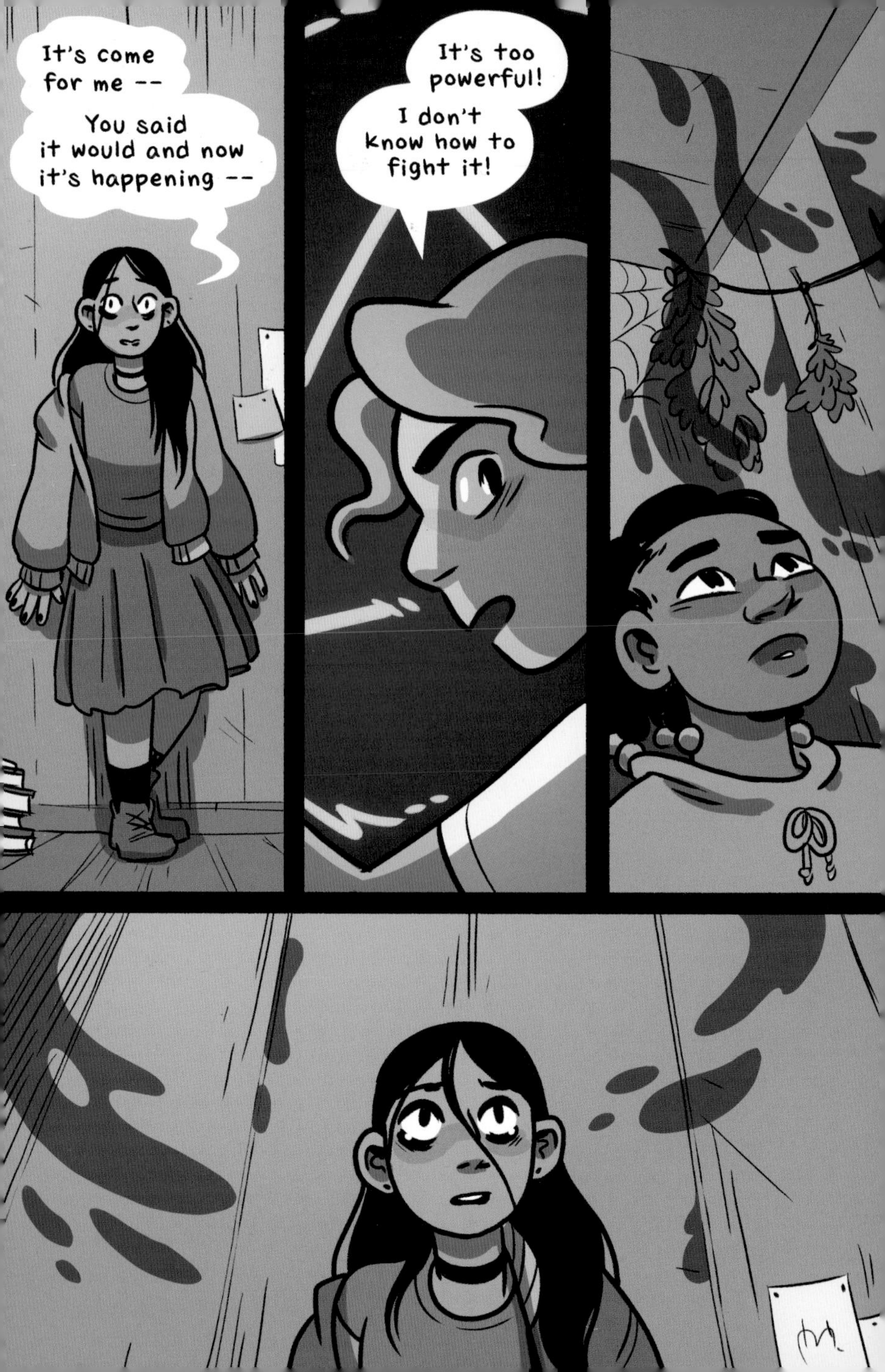
It's come for me --
You said it would and now it's happening --
It's too powerful!
I don't know how to fight it!

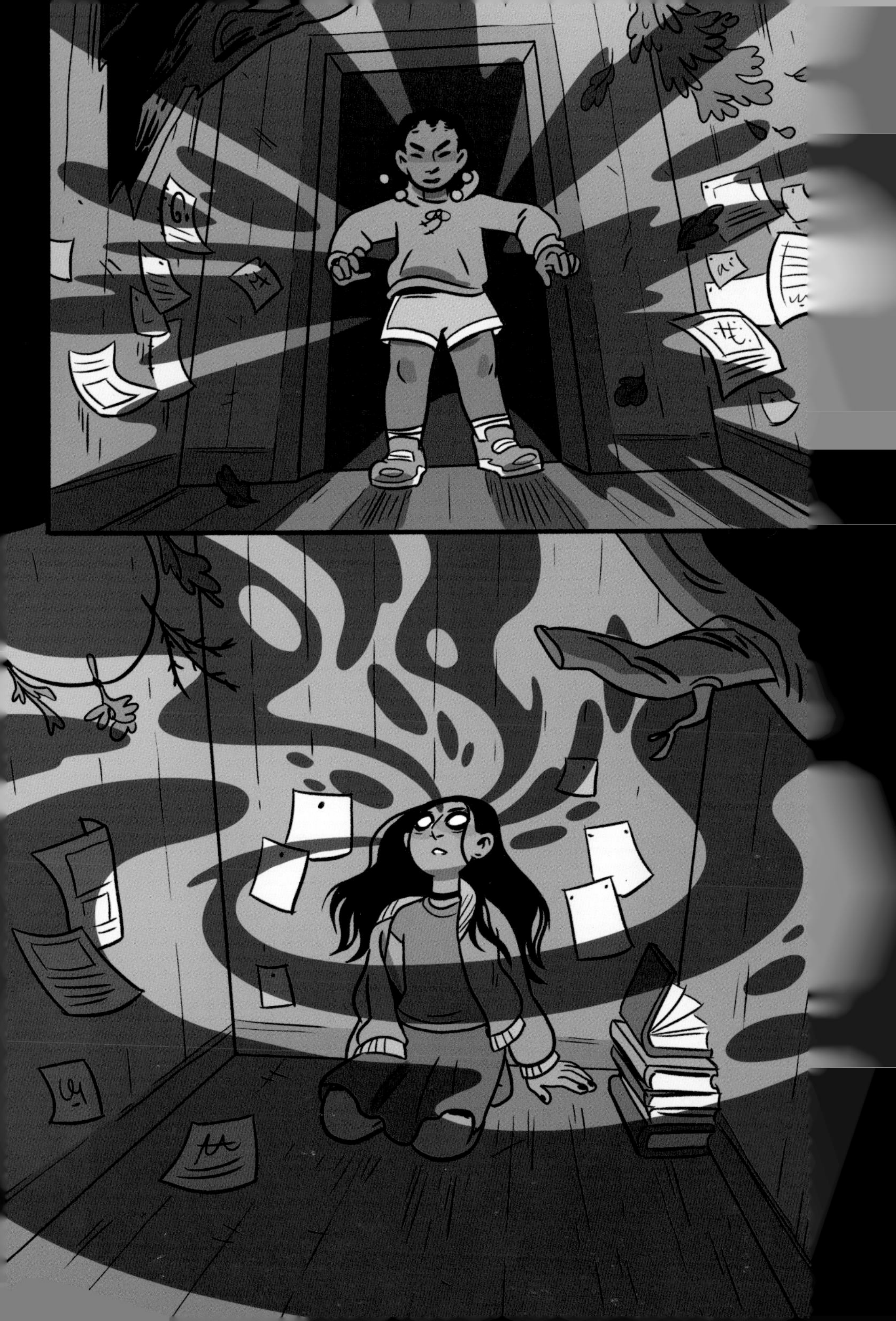

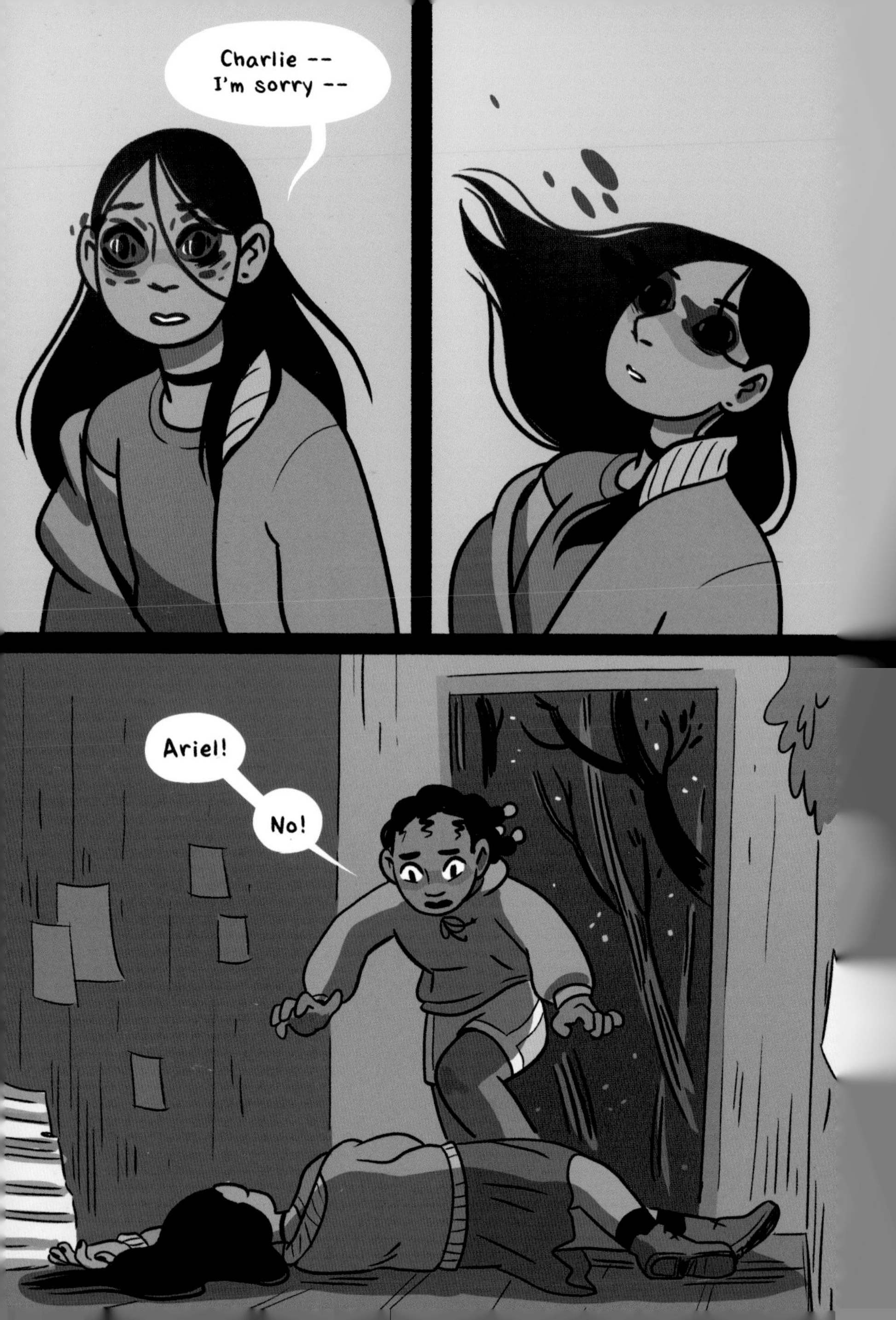
Charlie --
I'm sorry --
Ariel!
No!

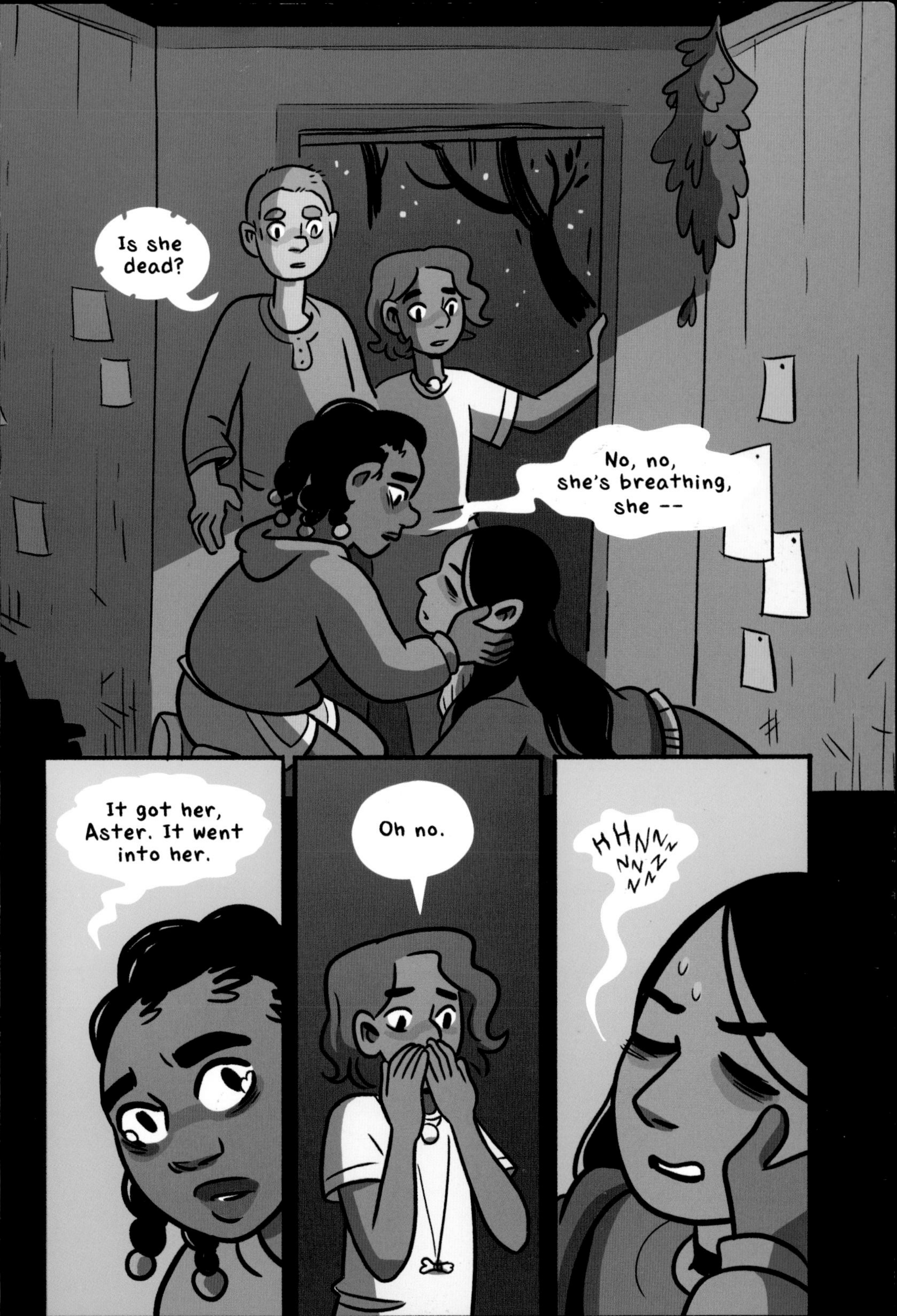
Is she dead?
No, no, she's breathing, she --
It got her, Aster. It went into her.
Oh no.
HHNNNNNNNNN

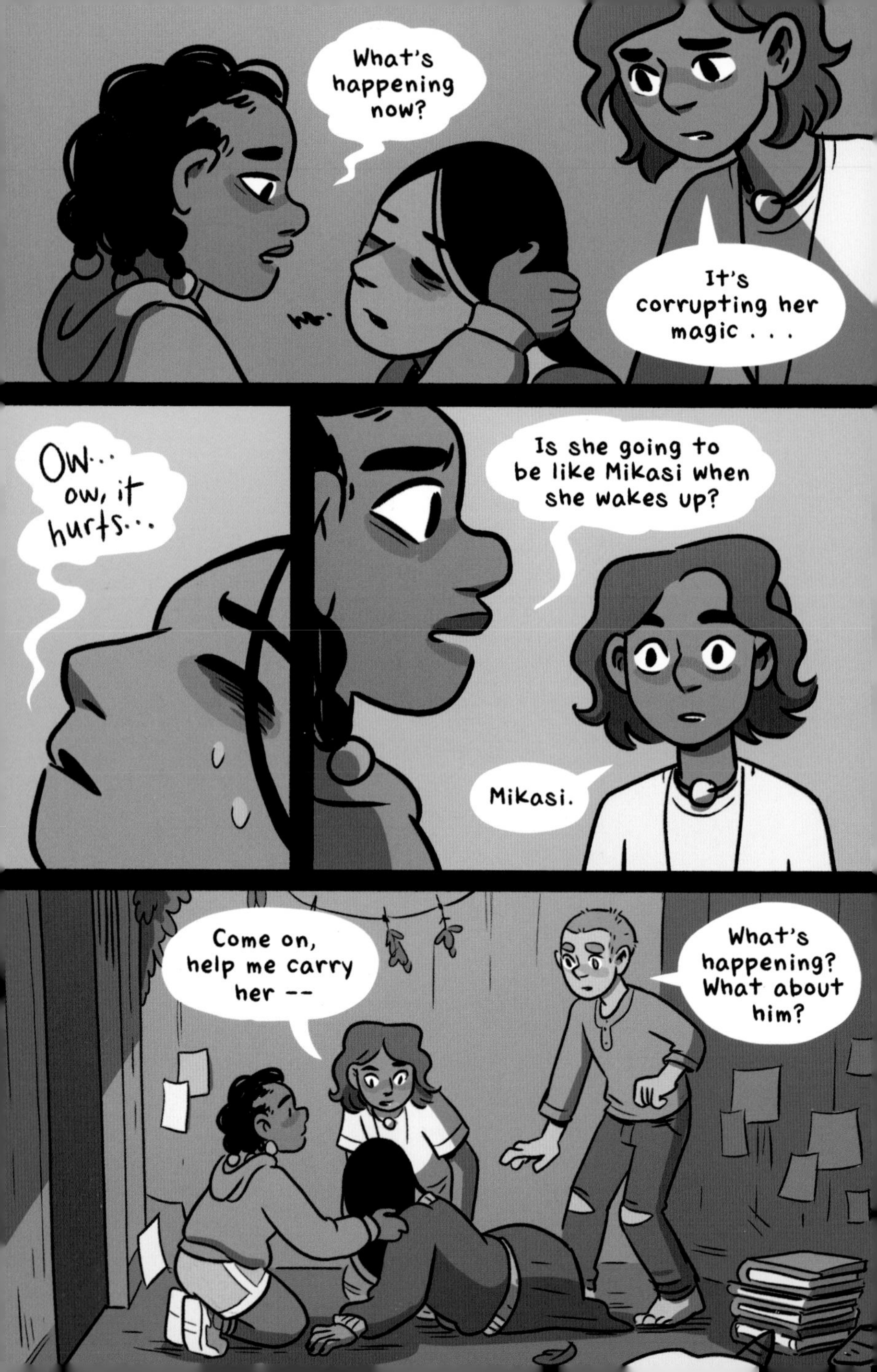
What's happening now?
It's corrupting her magic . . .
Ow... ow, it hurts...
Is she going to be like Mikasi when she wakes up?
Mikasi.
Come on, help me carry her --
What's happening? What about him?

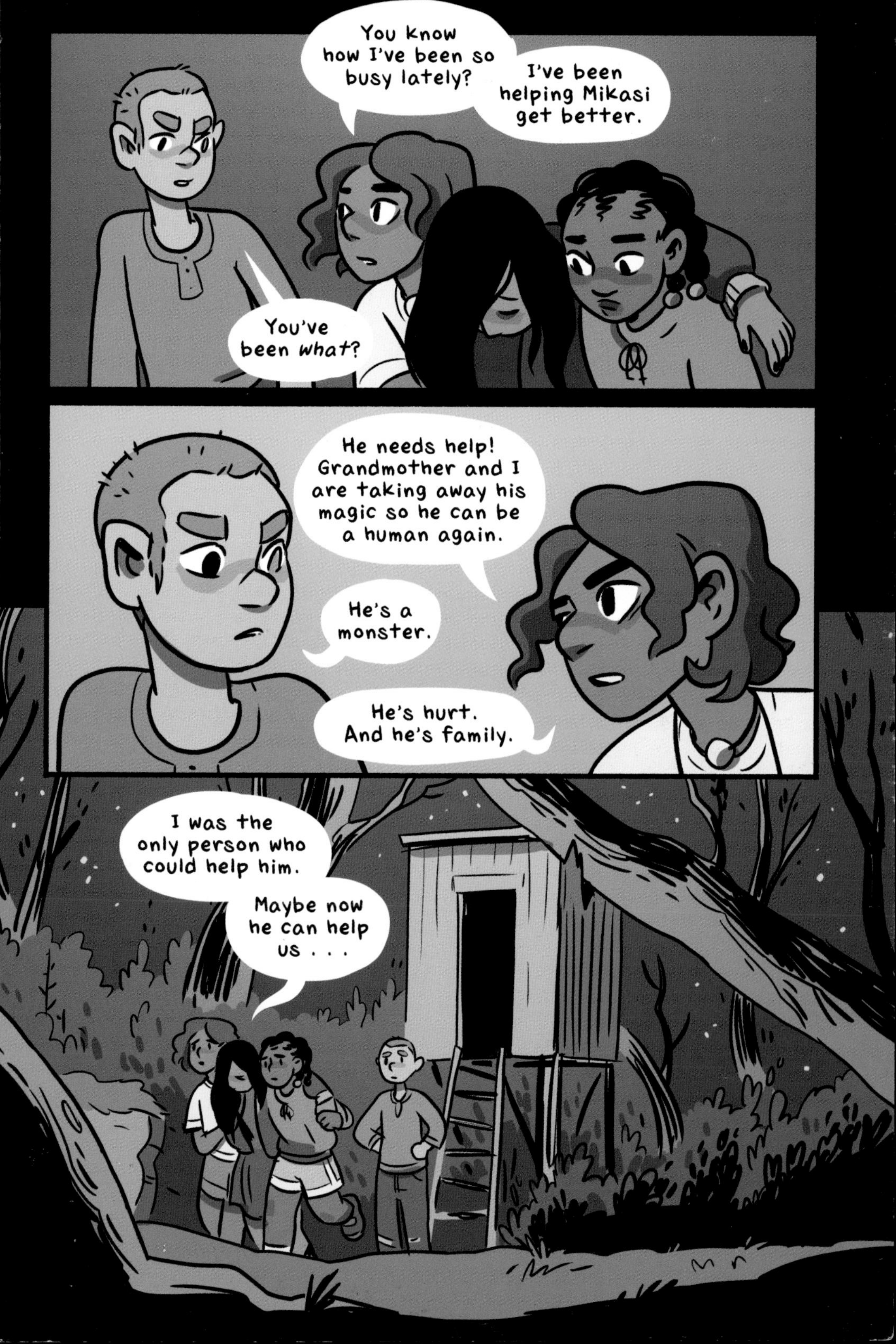
You know how I've been so busy lately?
I've been helping Mikasi get better.
You've been *what*?
He needs help! Grandmother and I are taking away his magic so he can be a human again.
He's a monster.
He's hurt. And he's family.
I was the only person who could help him.
Maybe now he can help us . . .

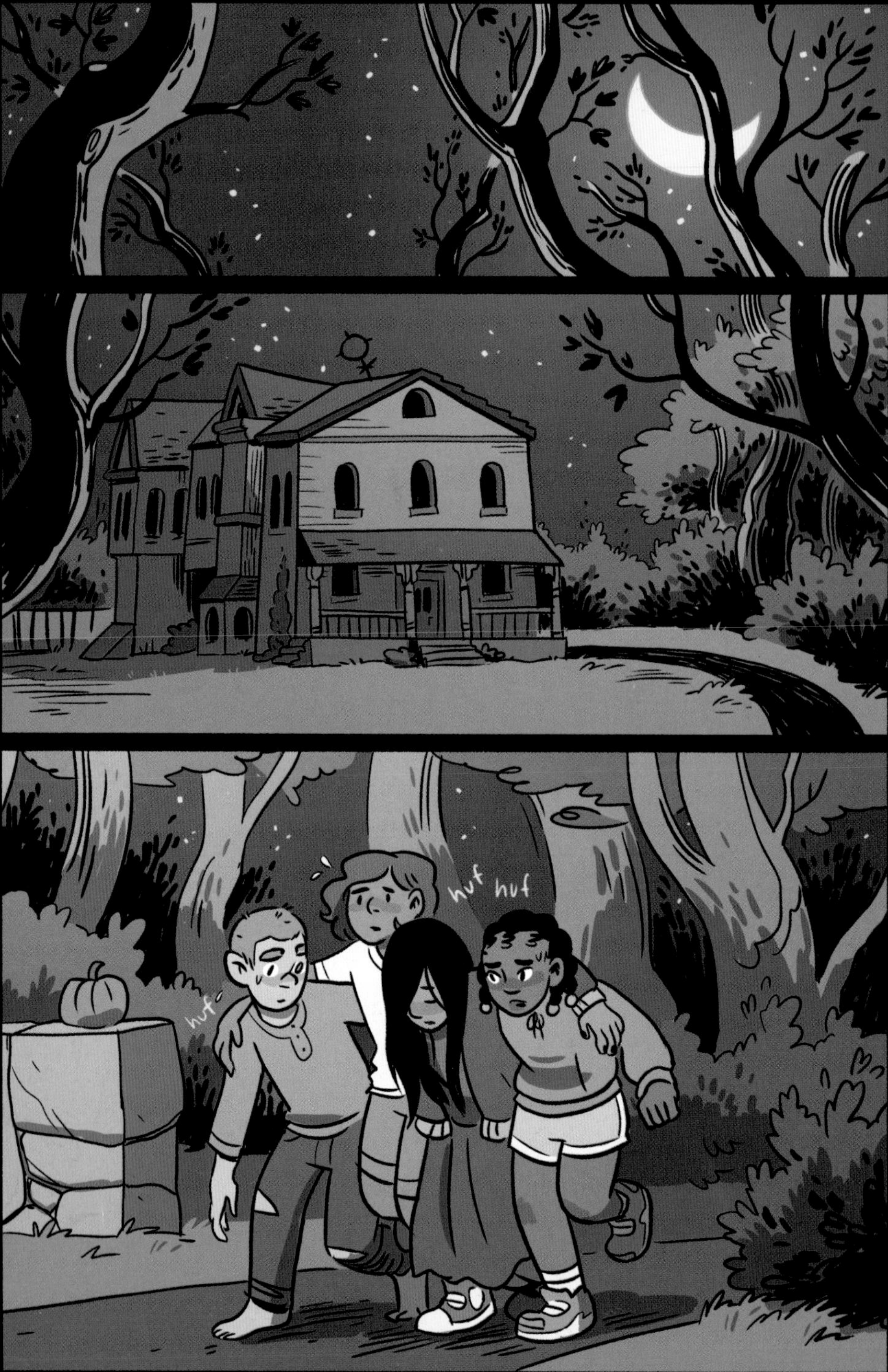
huf huf
huf

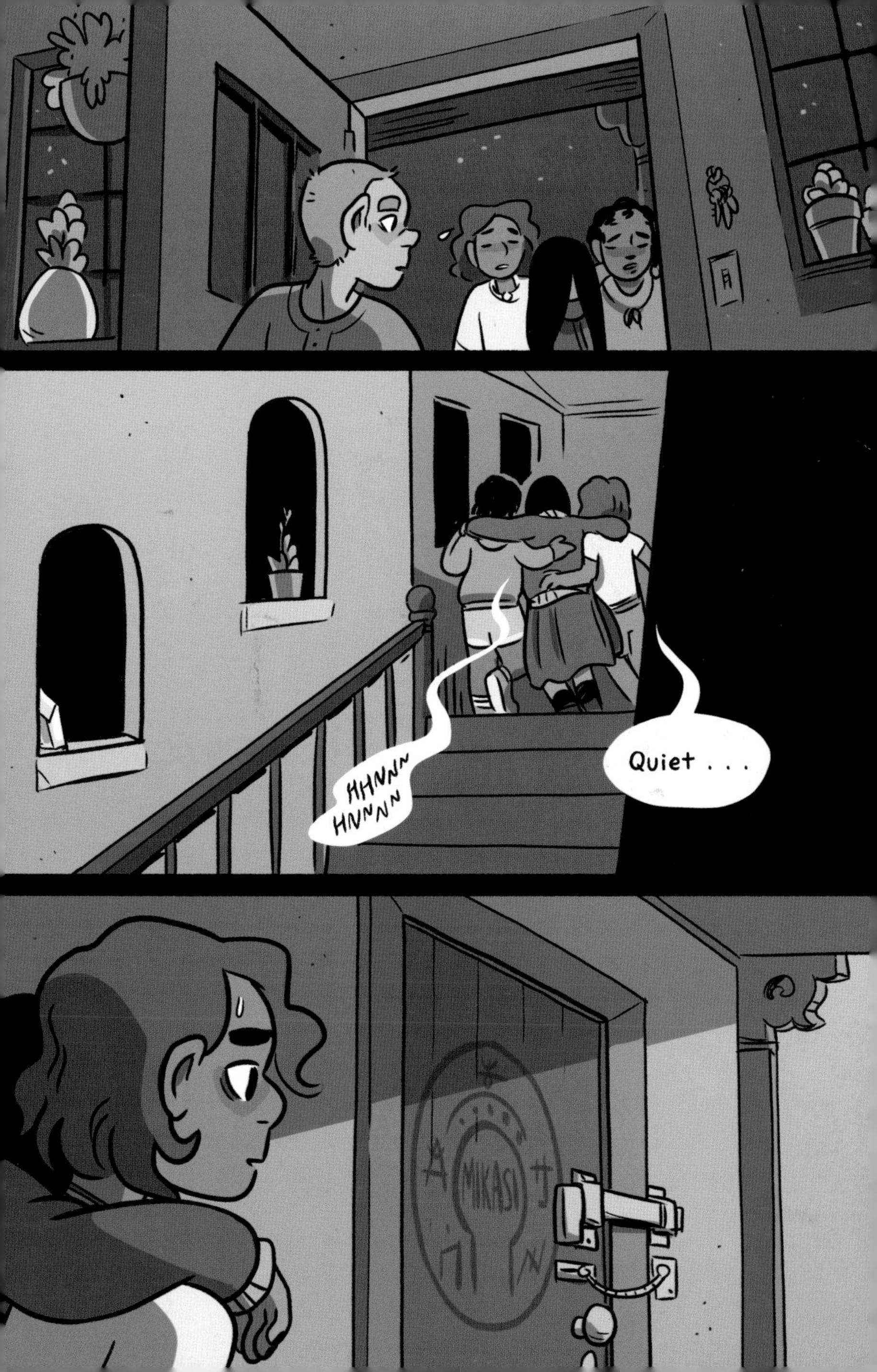
HHNNN HNNNN
Quiet . . .
MIKASI

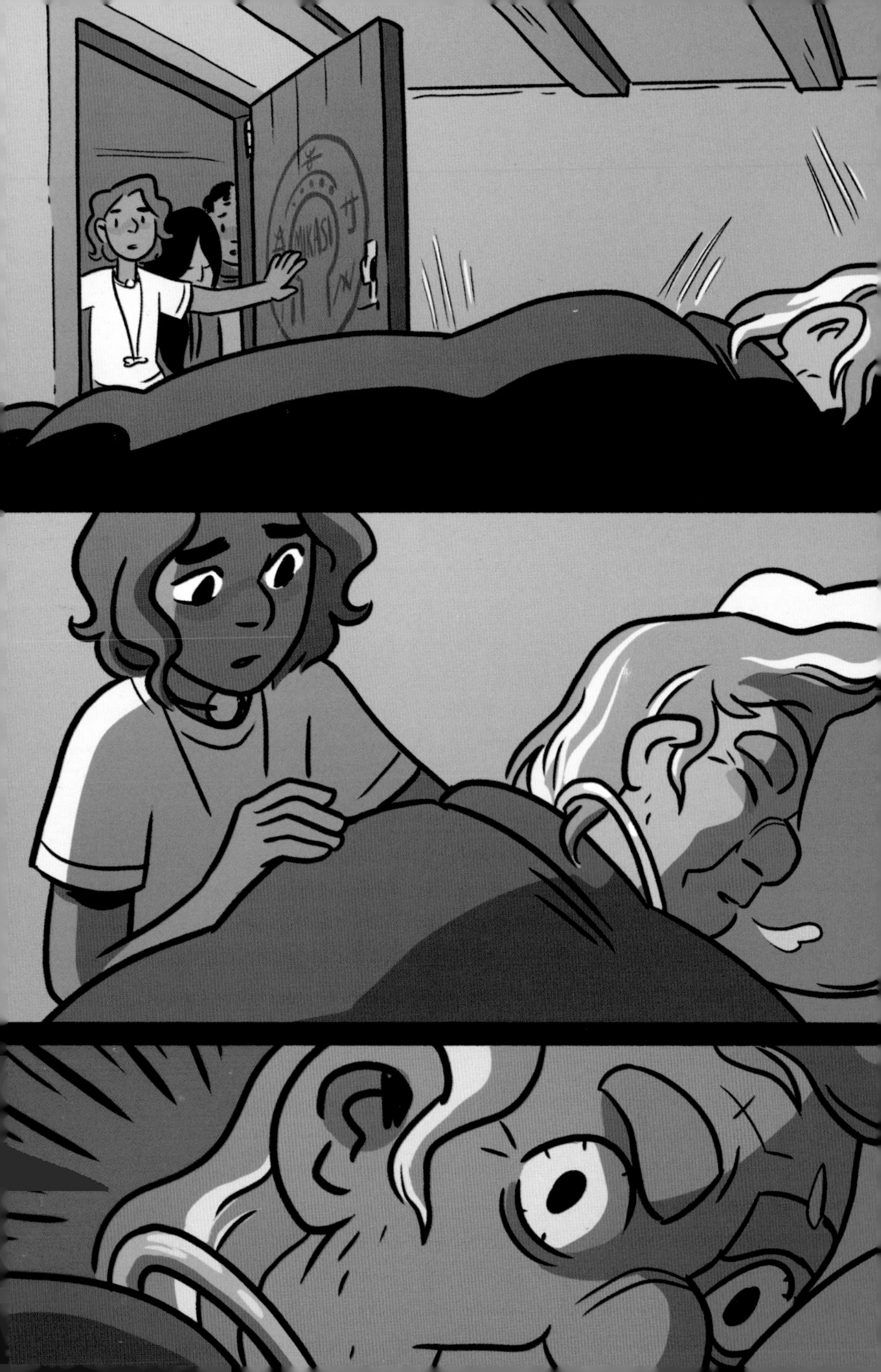
MIKASI

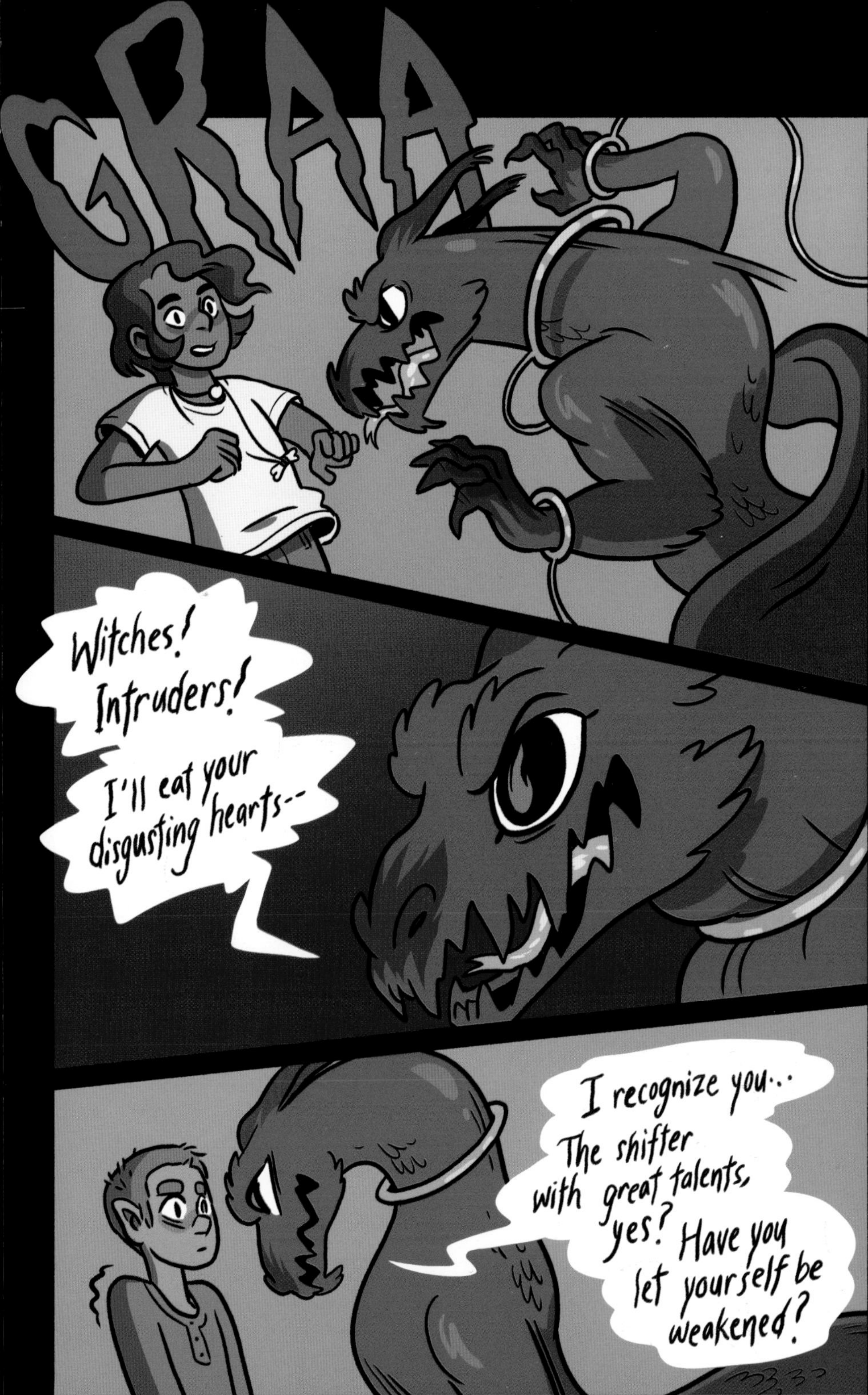
GRAA
Witches! Intruders!
I'll eat your disgusting hearts--
I recognize you...
The shifter with great talents, yes?
Have you let yourself be weakened?

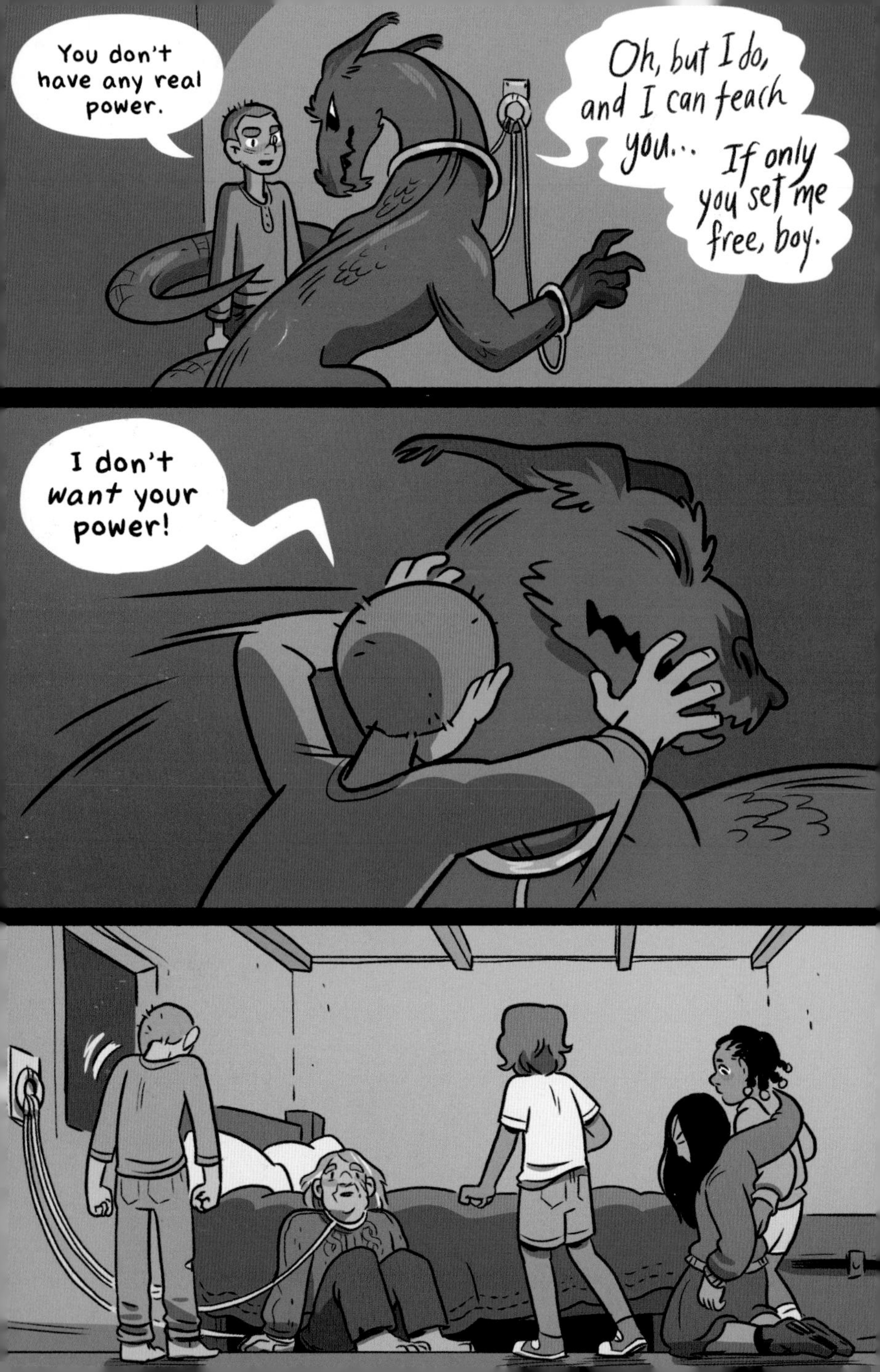
You don't have any real power.
Oh, but I do, and I can teach you... If only you set me free, boy.
I don't want your power!

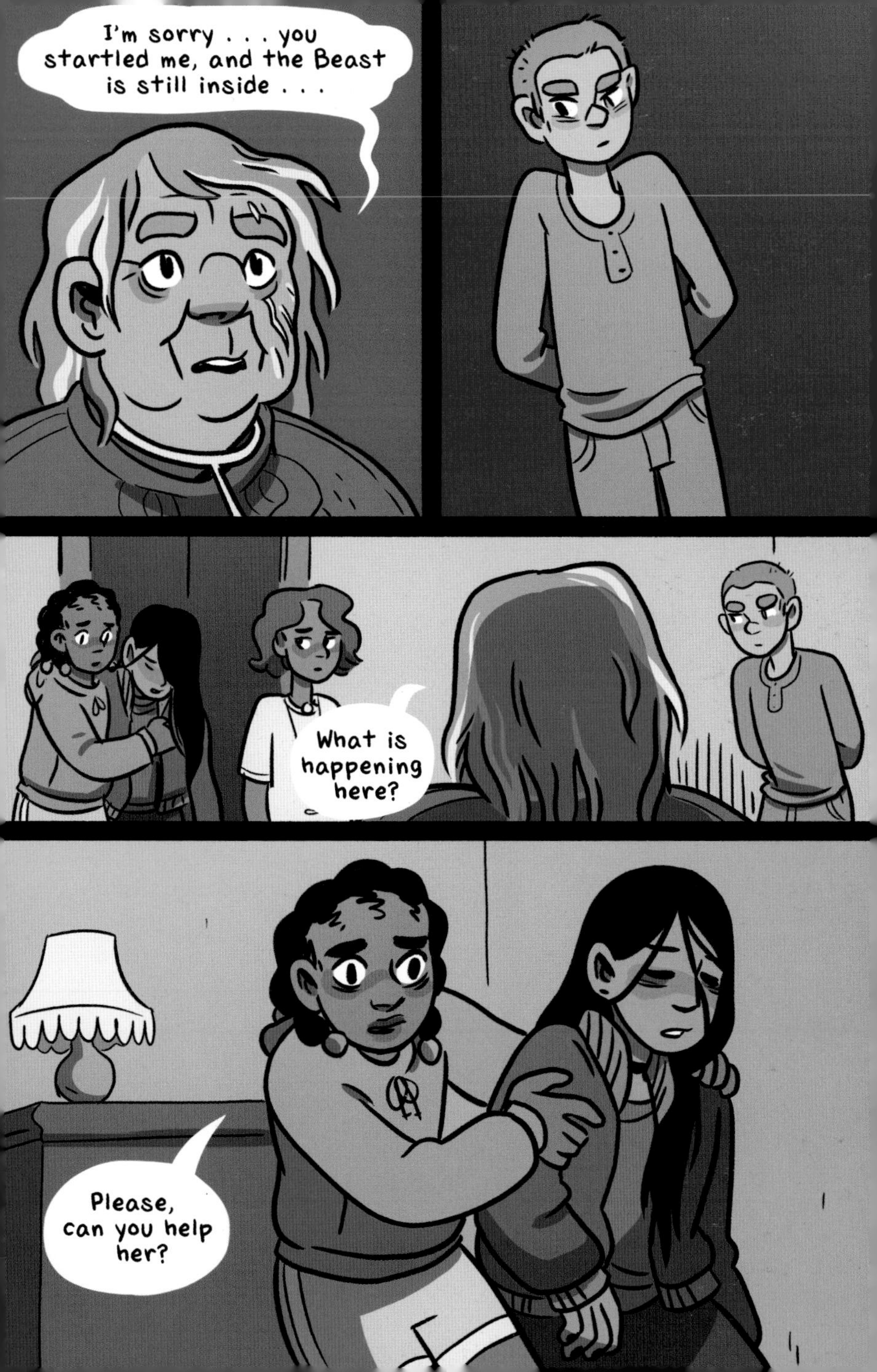
I'm sorry . . . you startled me, and the Beast is still inside . . .
What is happening here?
Please, can you help her?

She is very young to have brought such a curse upon herself.

She didn't know how bad it would get.

She . . . she's different, and she's been bullied a lot, and she gets angry.

People can be so mean, sometimes without even realizing it.

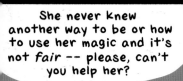

She never knew another way to be or how to use her magic and it's not *fair* -- please, can't you help her?

You care about her.

A lot.

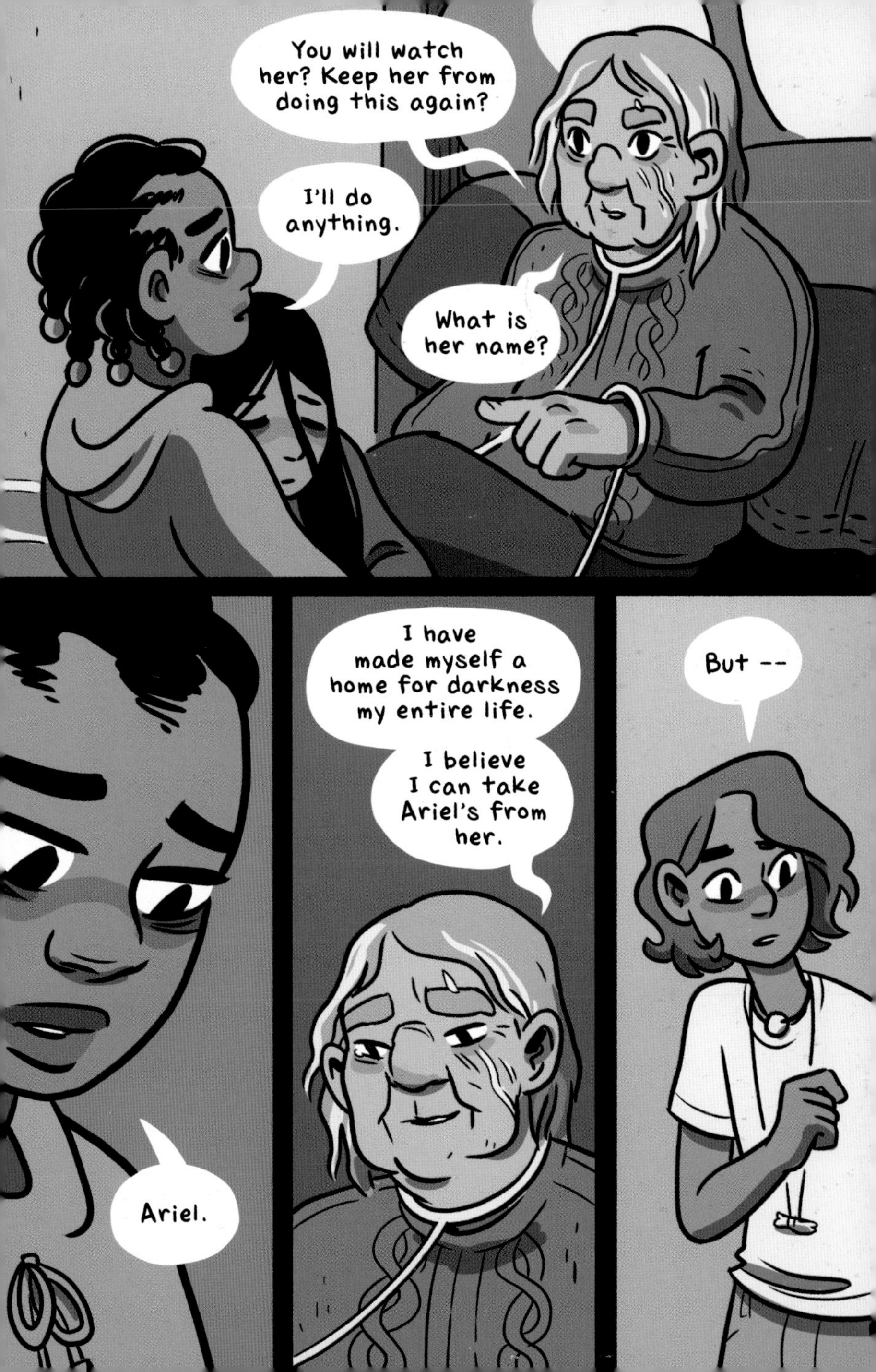
You will watch her? Keep her from doing this again?
I'll do anything.
What is her name?
Ariel.
I have made myself a home for darkness my entire life.
I believe I can take Ariel's from her.
But --

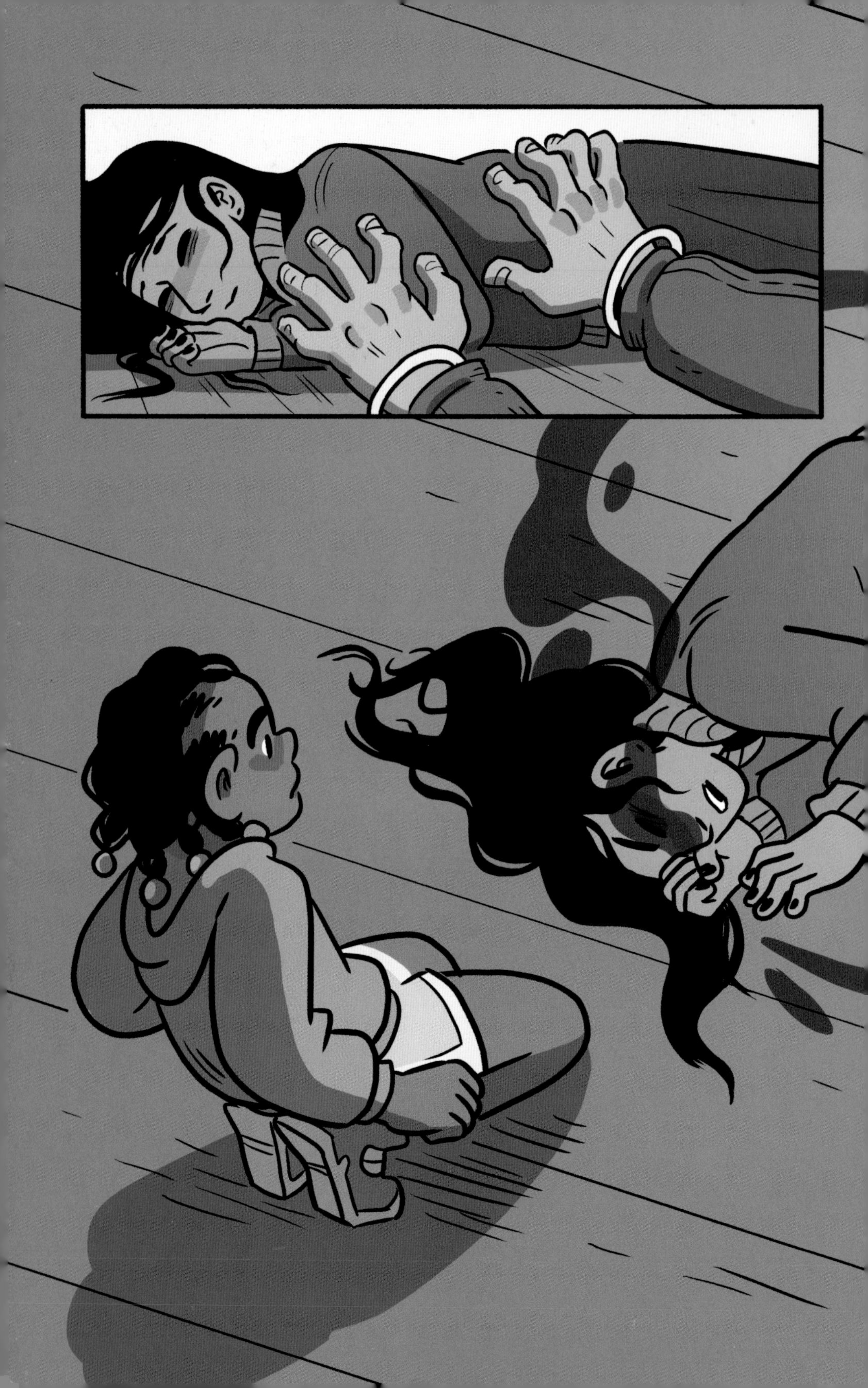

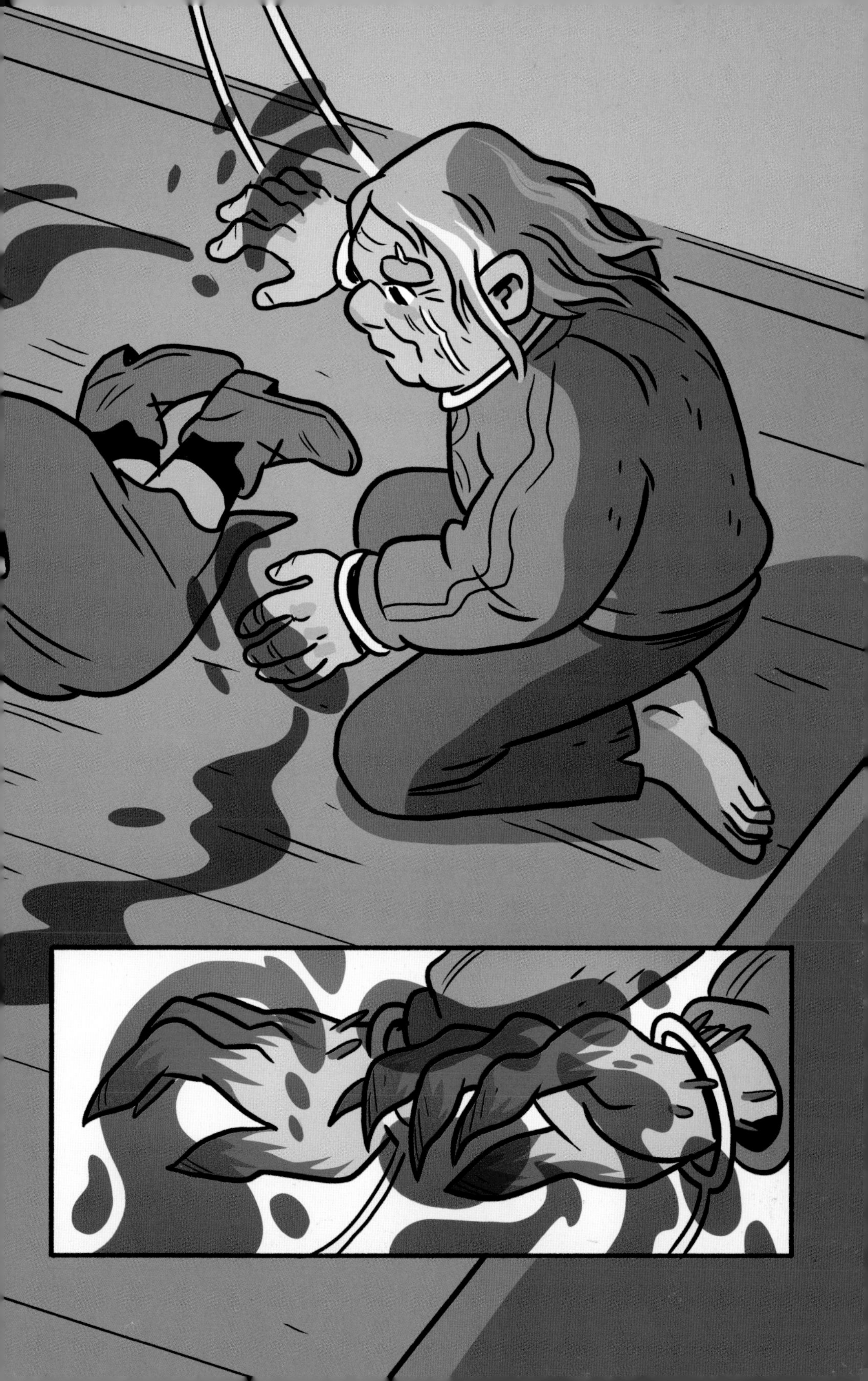

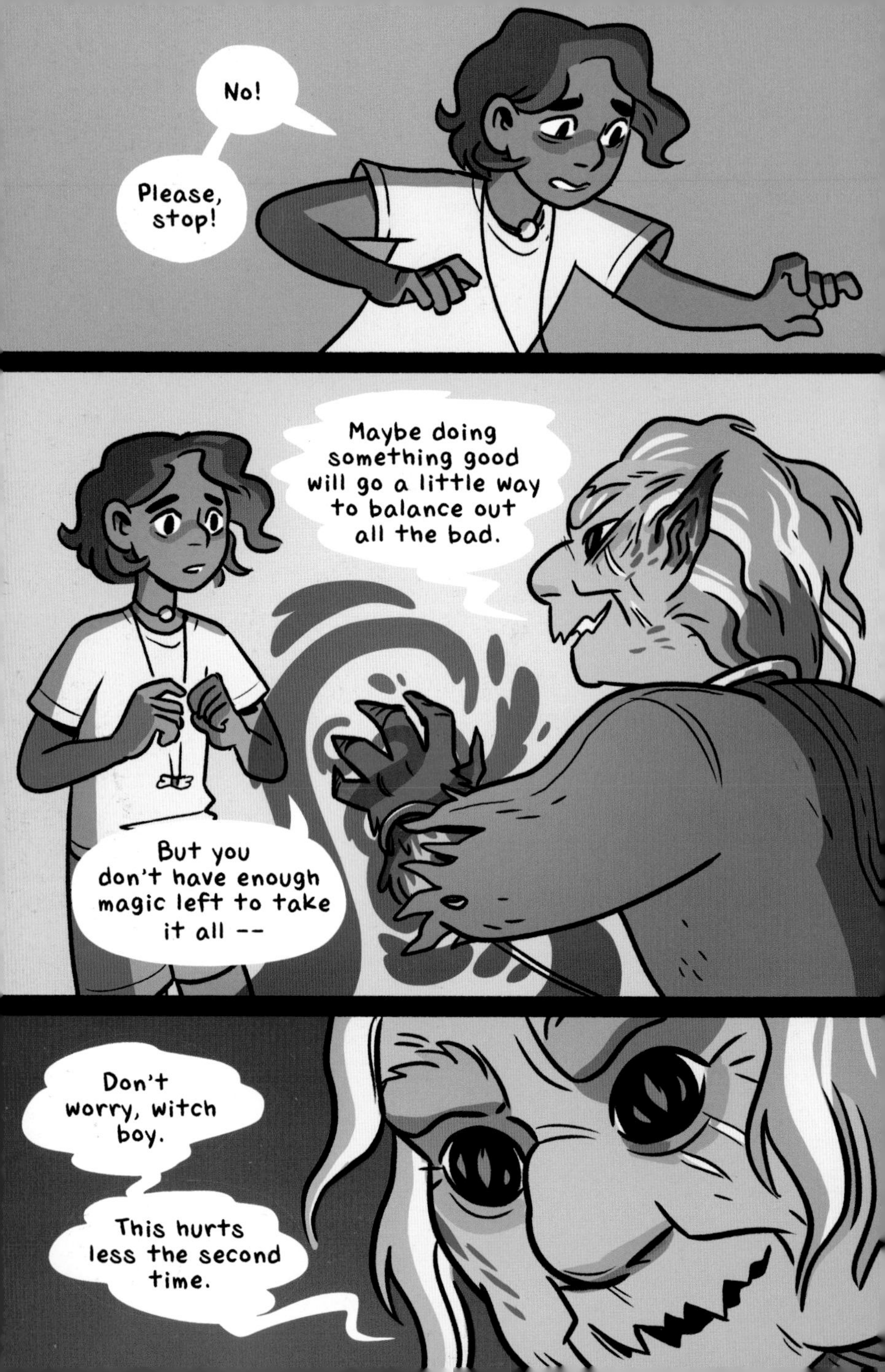
No!
Please, stop!
Maybe doing something good will go a little way to balance out all the bad.
But you don't have enough magic left to take it all --
Don't worry, witch boy.
This hurts less the second time.

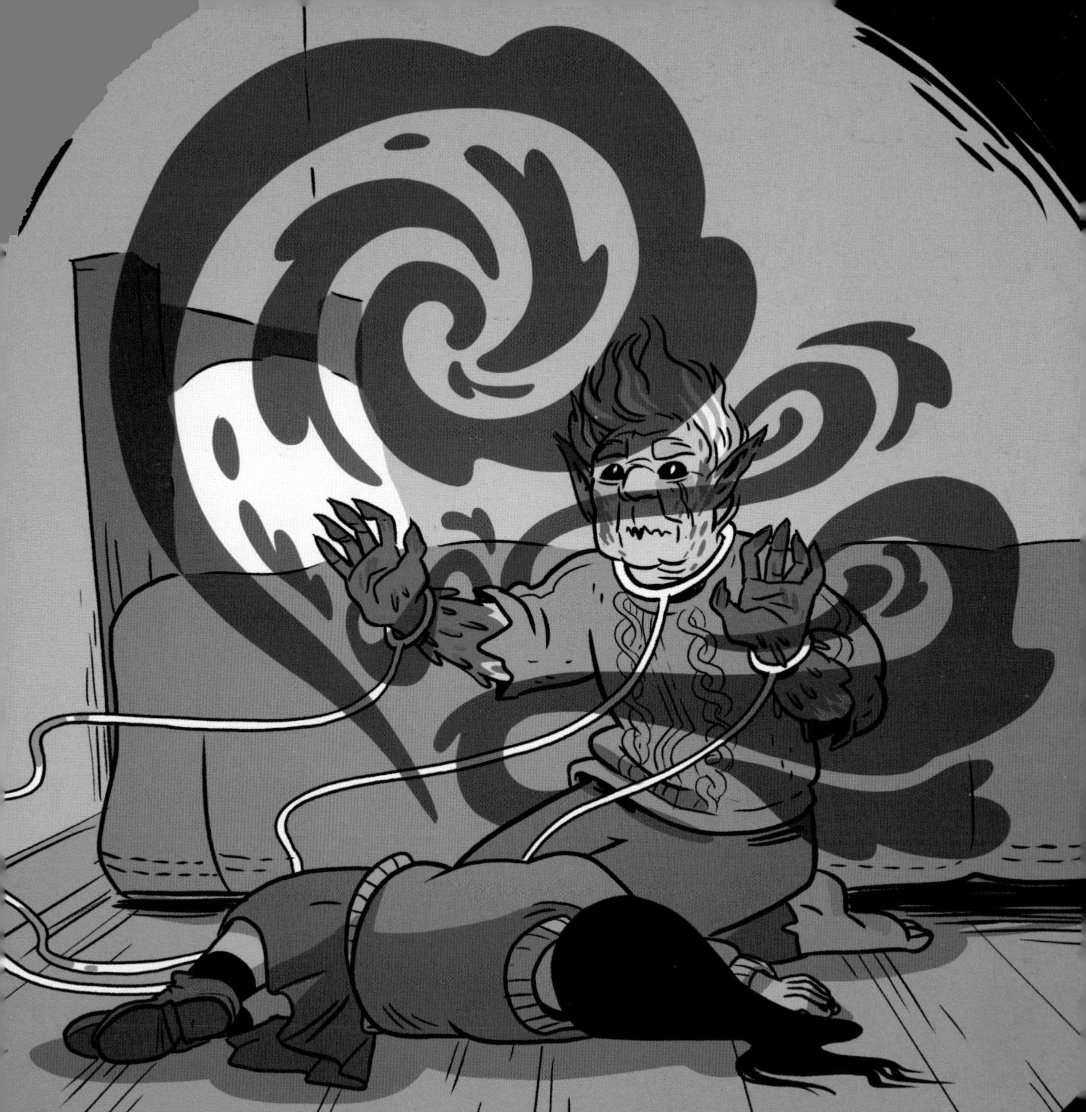
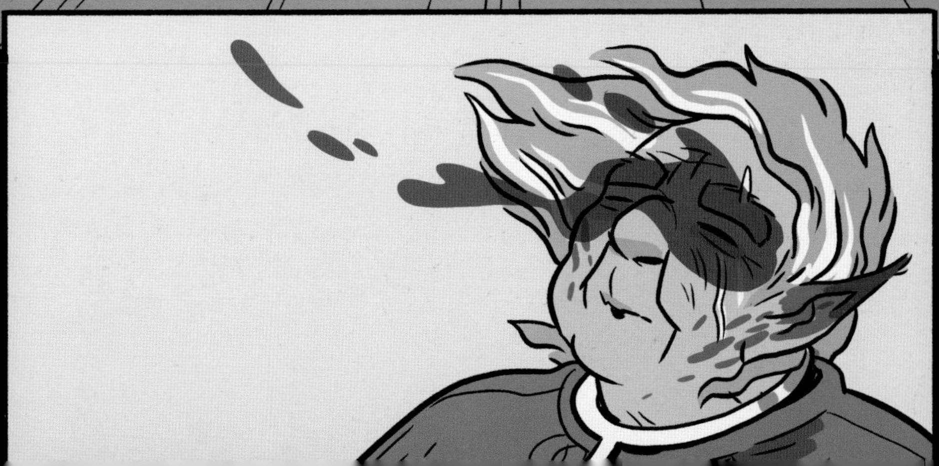

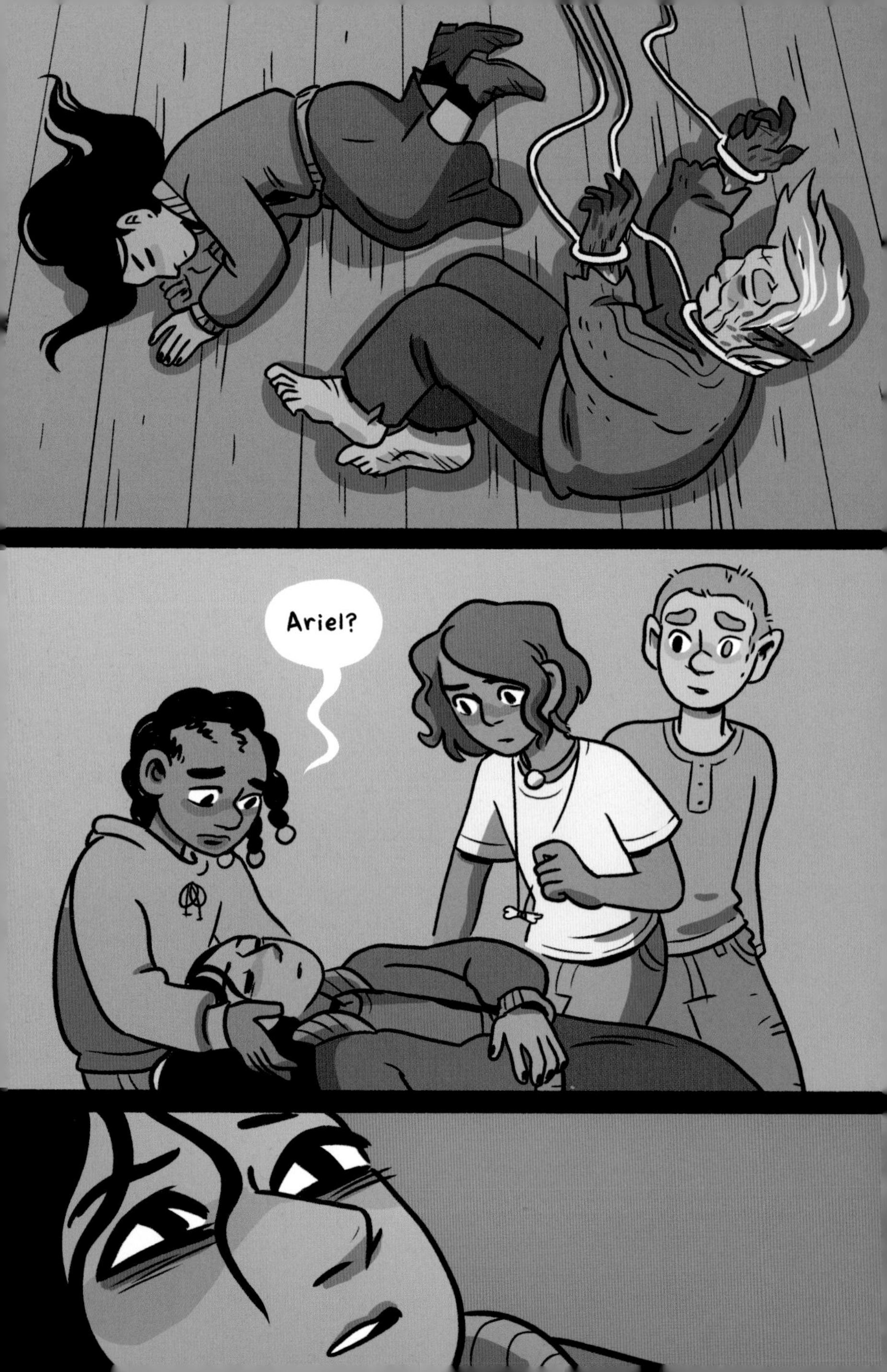
Ariel?

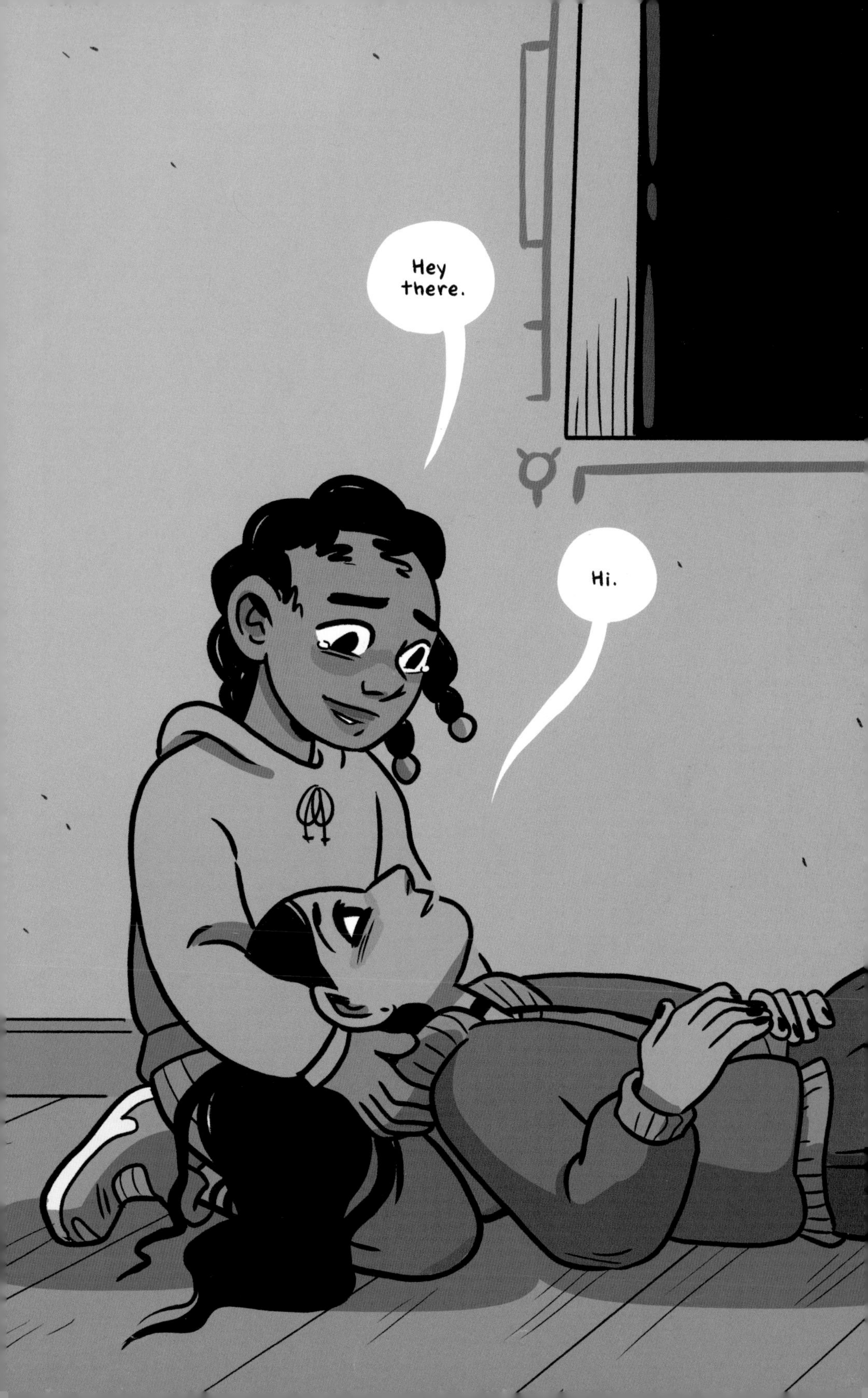
Hey there.
Hi.

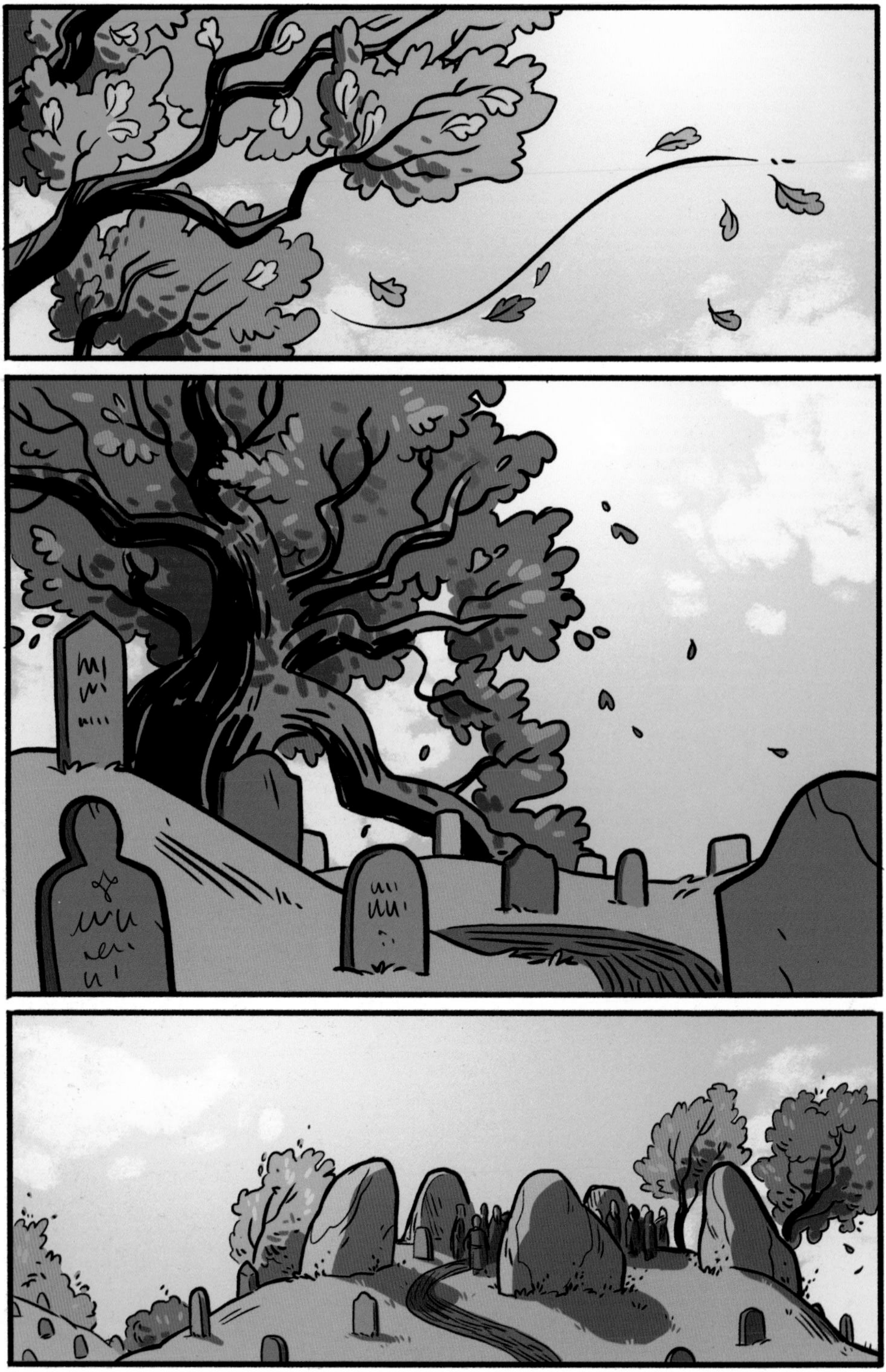

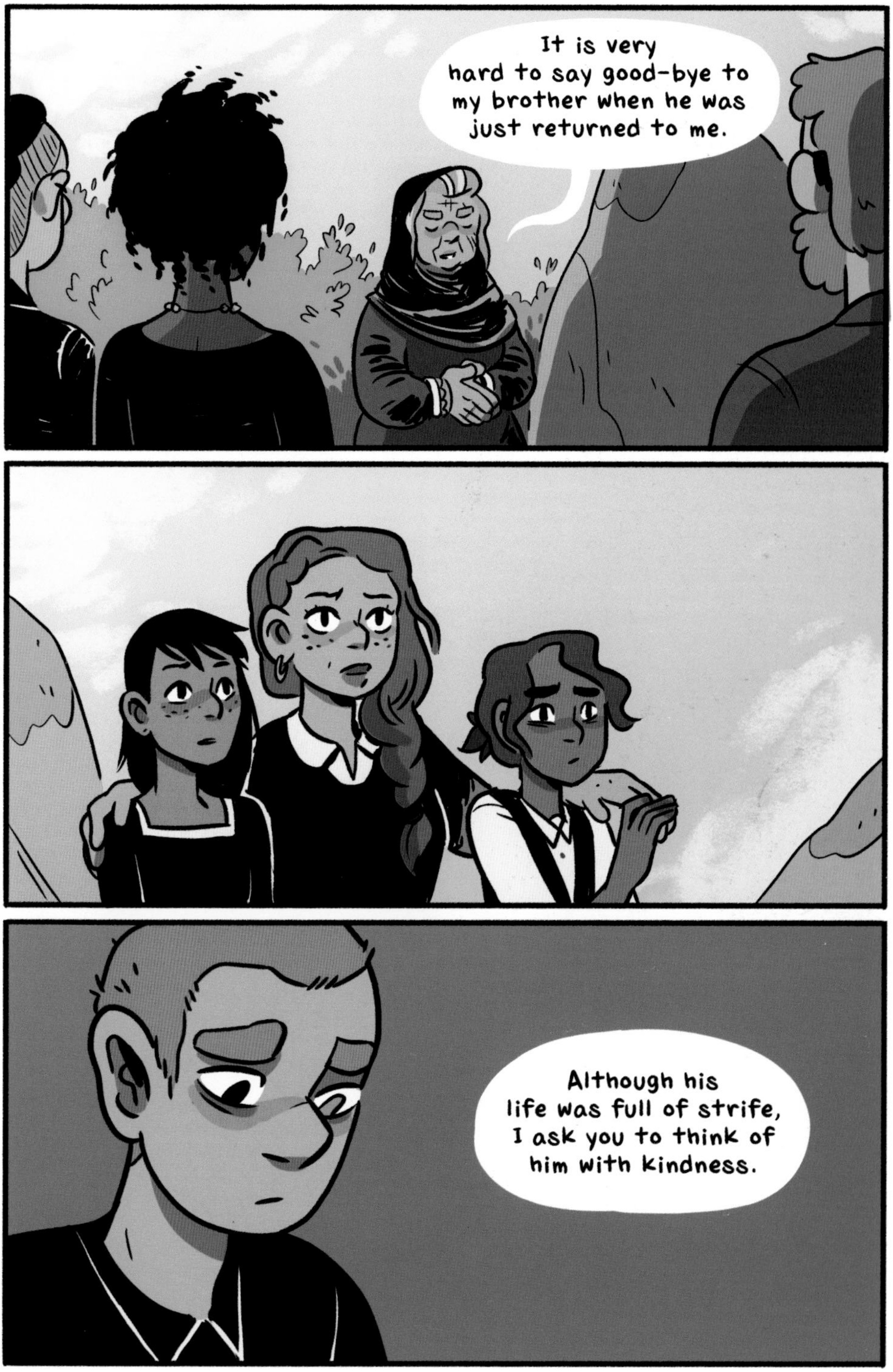
It is very hard to say good-bye to my brother when he was just returned to me.
Although his life was full of strife, I ask you to think of him with kindness.

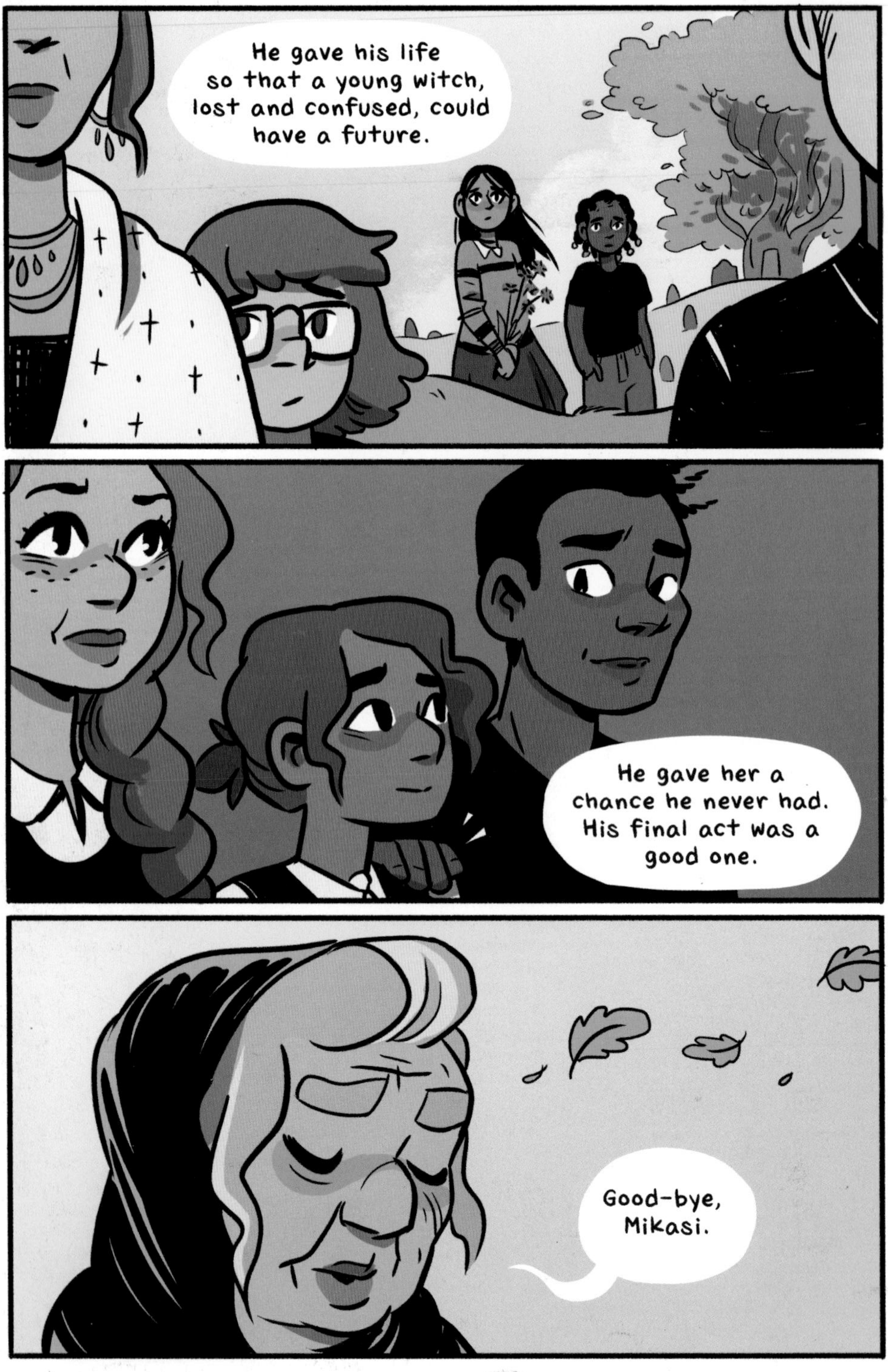
He gave his life so that a young witch, lost and confused, could have a future.
He gave her a chance he never had. His final act was a good one.
Good-bye, Mikasi.

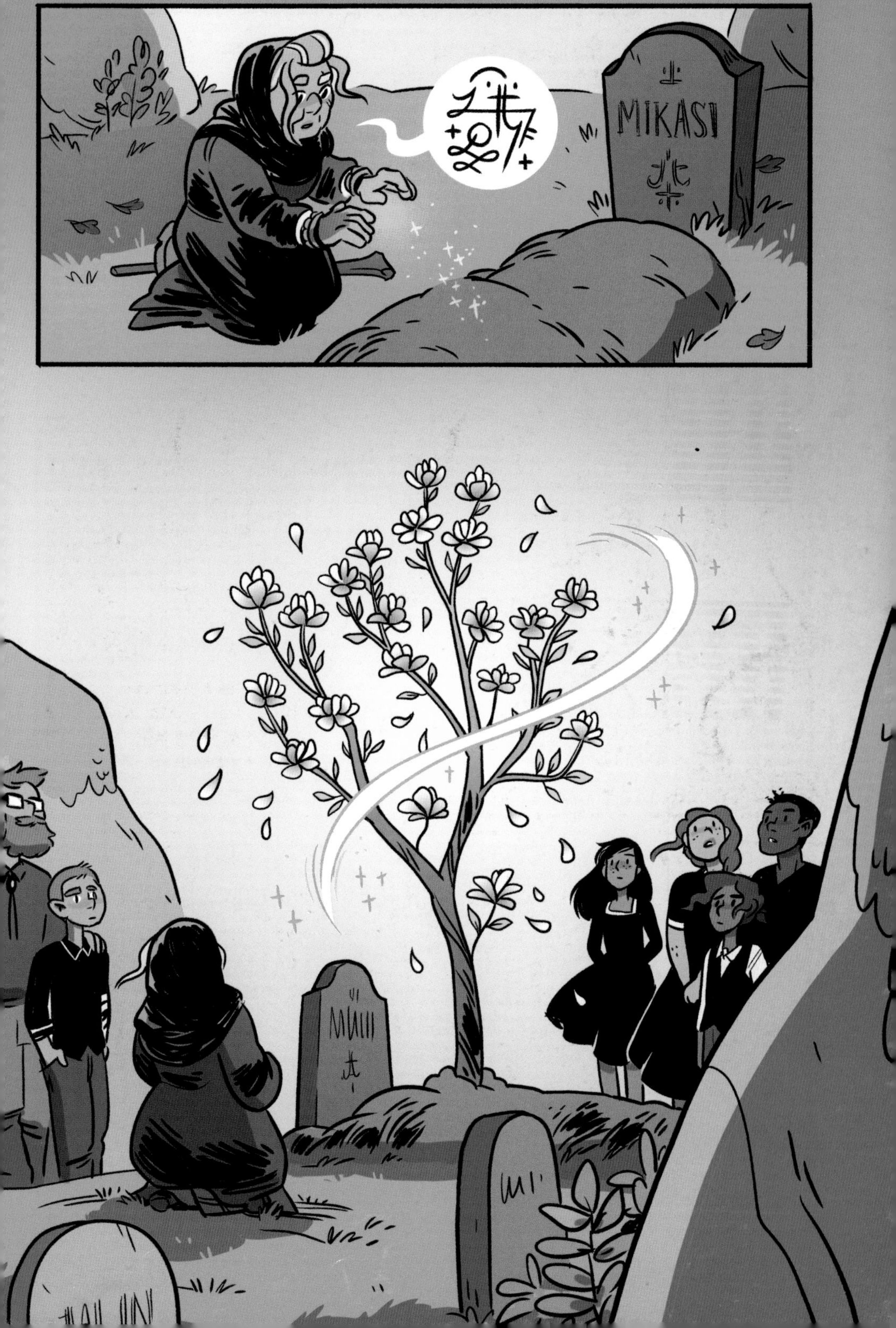
MIKASI

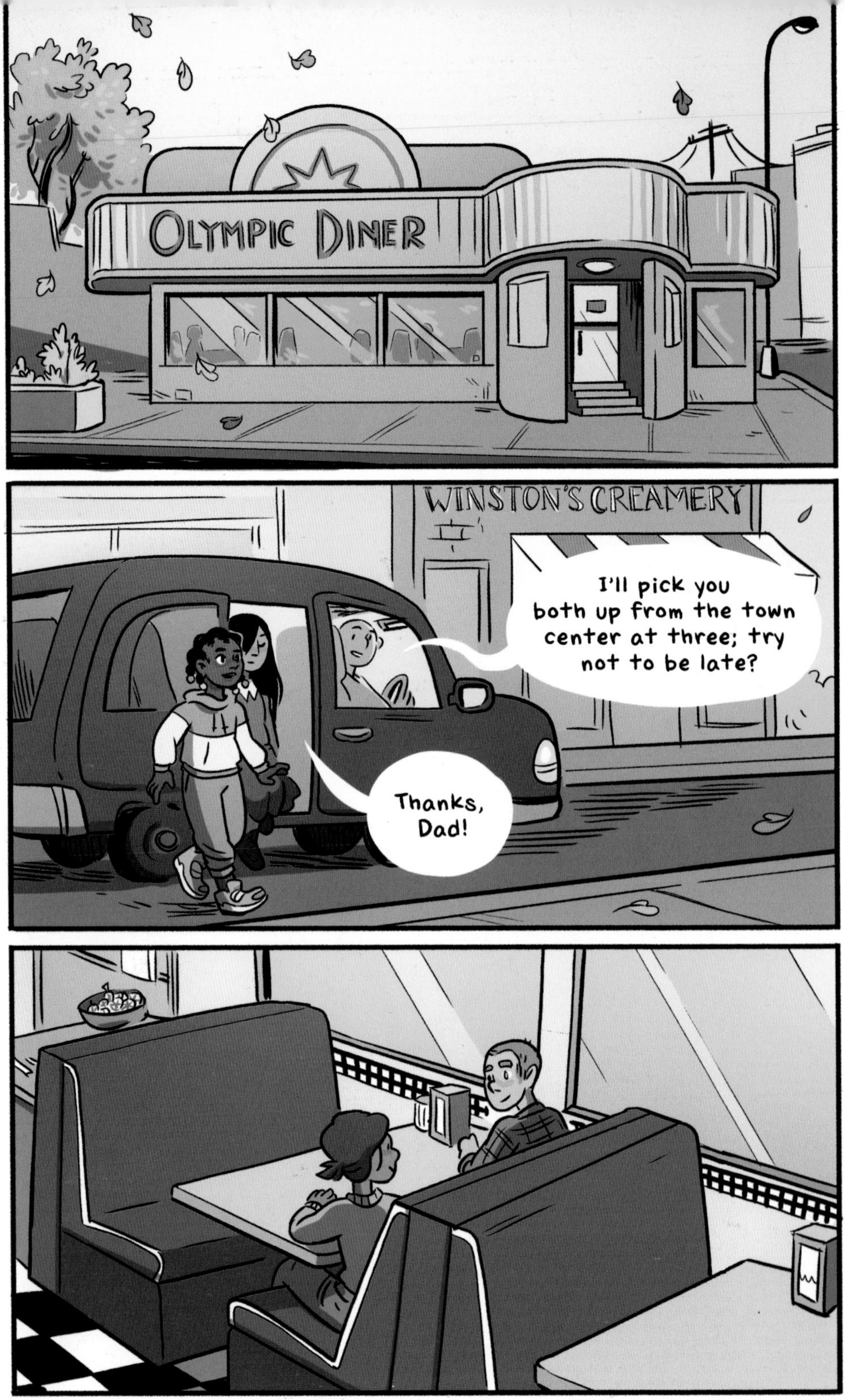
OLYMPIC DINER
WINSTON'S CREAMERY
I'll pick you both up from the town center at three; try not to be late?
Thanks, Dad!

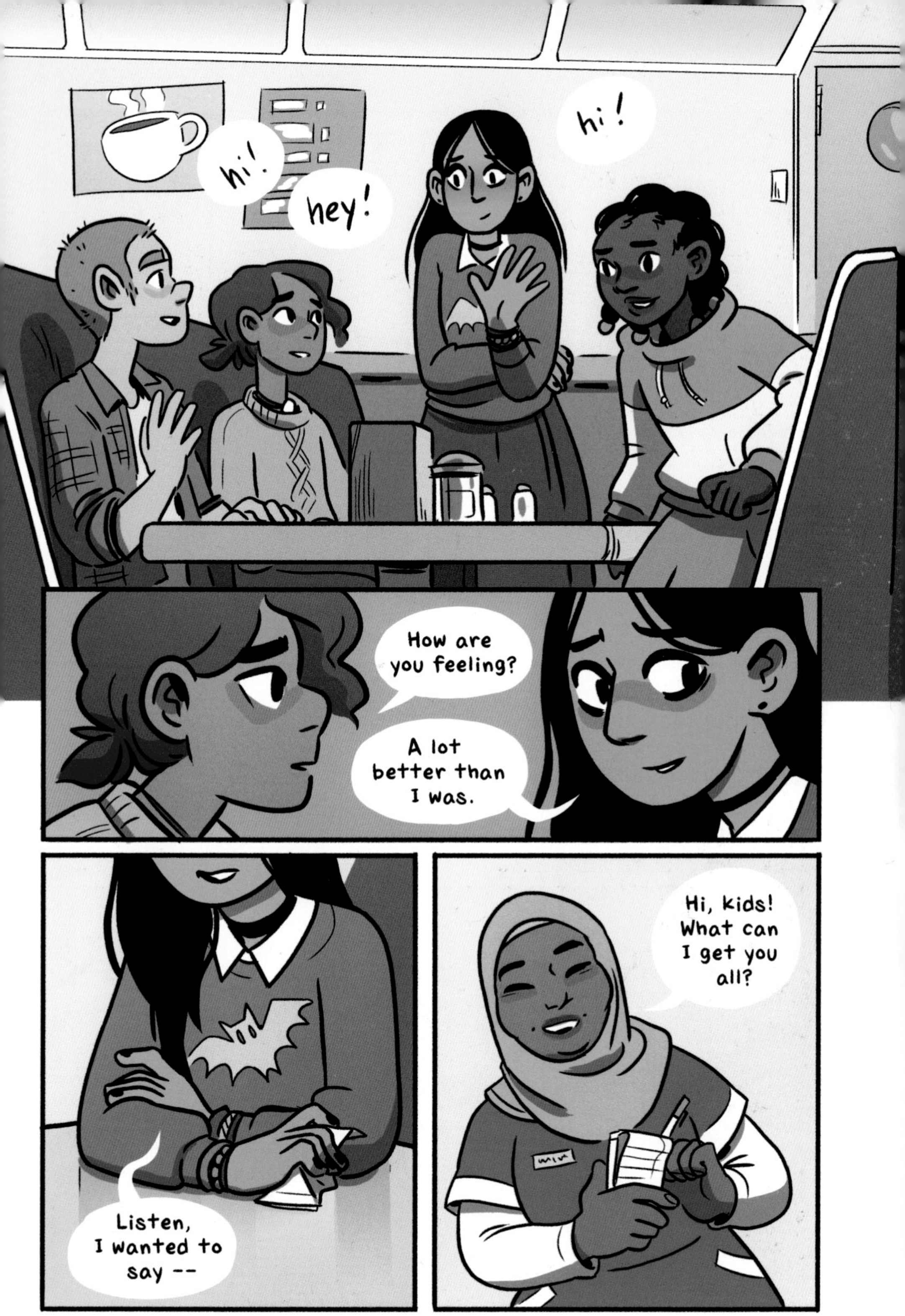
hi!
hey!
hi!
How are you feeling?
A lot better than I was.
Listen, I wanted to say --
Hi, kids! What can I get you all?

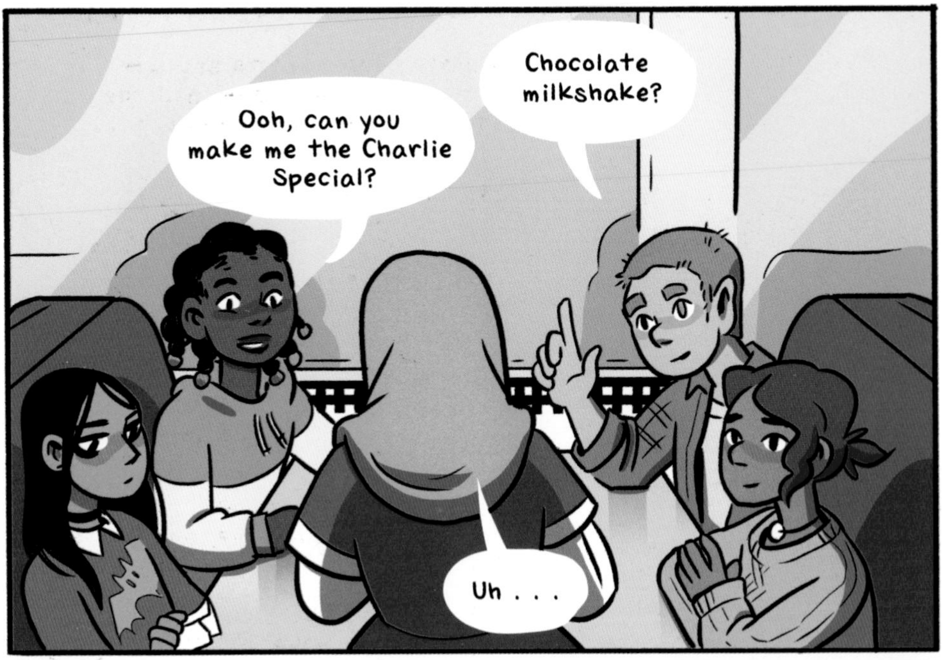
Ooh, can you make me the Charlie Special?
Chocolate milkshake?
Uh . . .

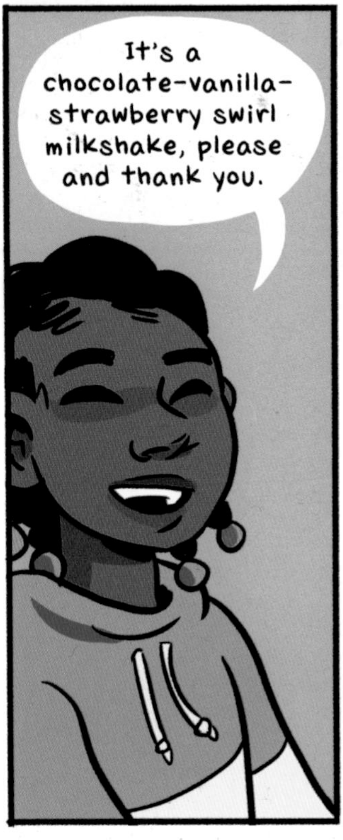
It's a chocolate-vanilla-strawberry swirl milkshake, please and thank you.

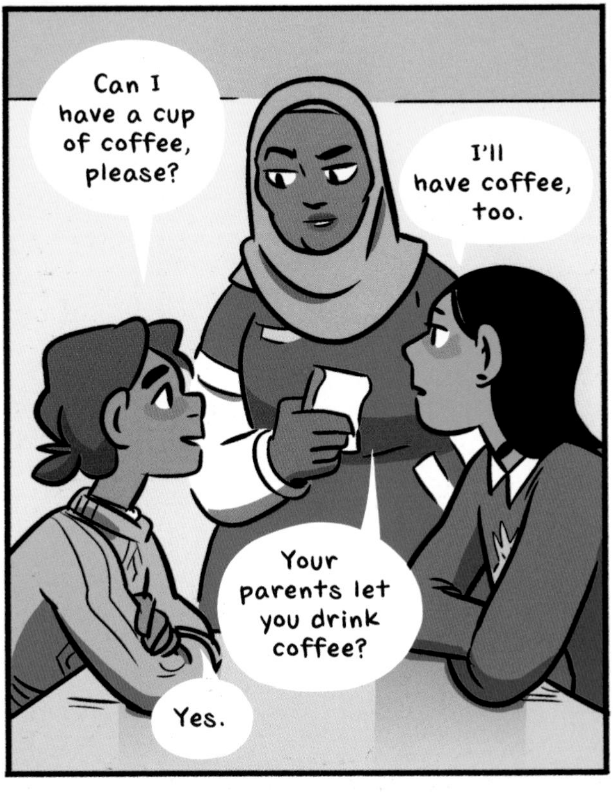
Can I have a cup of coffee, please?
I'll have coffee, too.
Your parents let you drink coffee?
Yes.

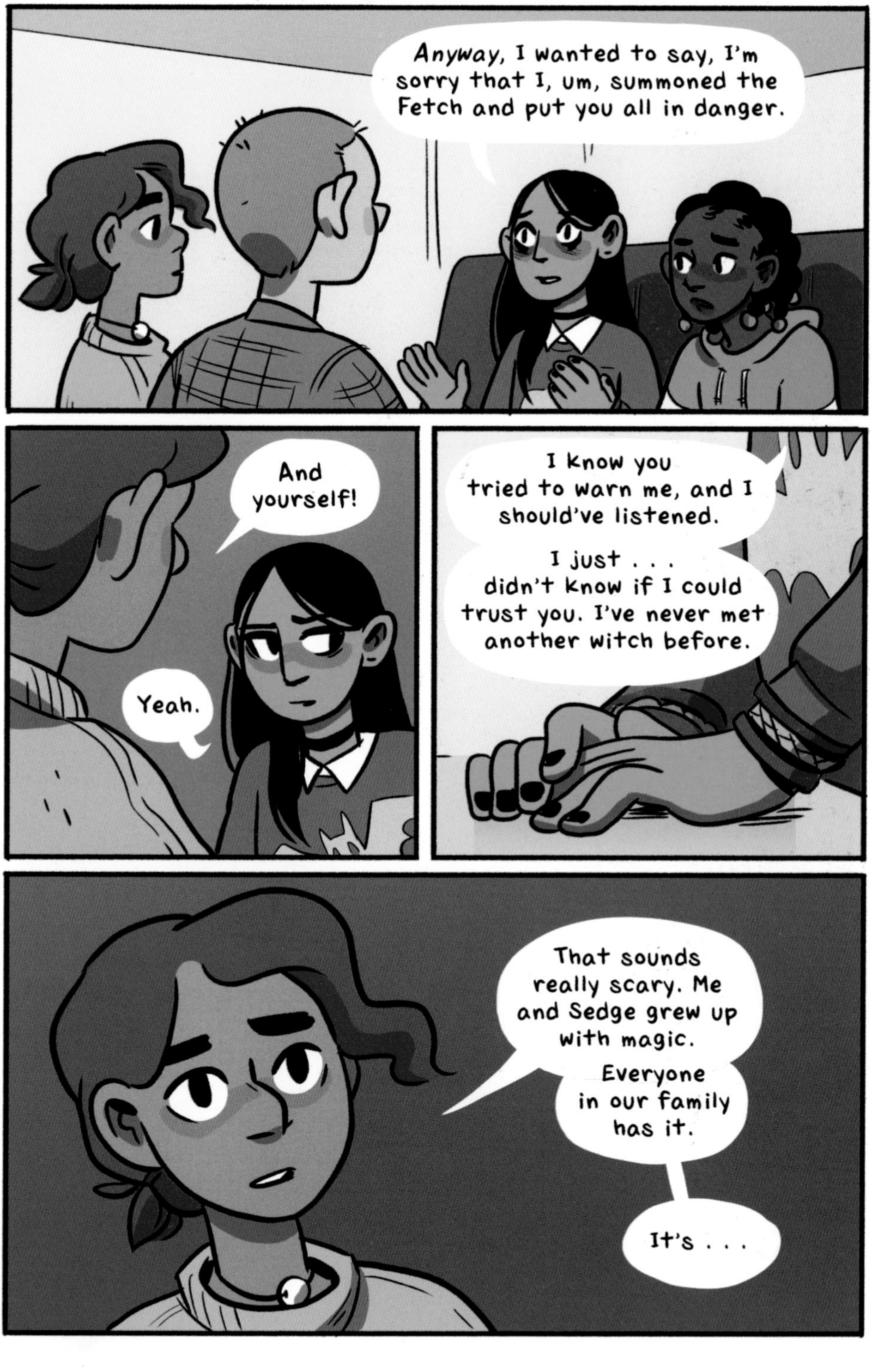
Anyway, I wanted to say, I'm sorry that I, um, summoned the Fetch and put you all in danger.
And yourself!
Yeah.
I know you tried to warn me, and I should've listened.
I just . . . didn't know if I could trust you. I've never met another witch before.
That sounds really scary. Me and Sedge grew up with magic.
Everyone in our family has it.
It's . . .

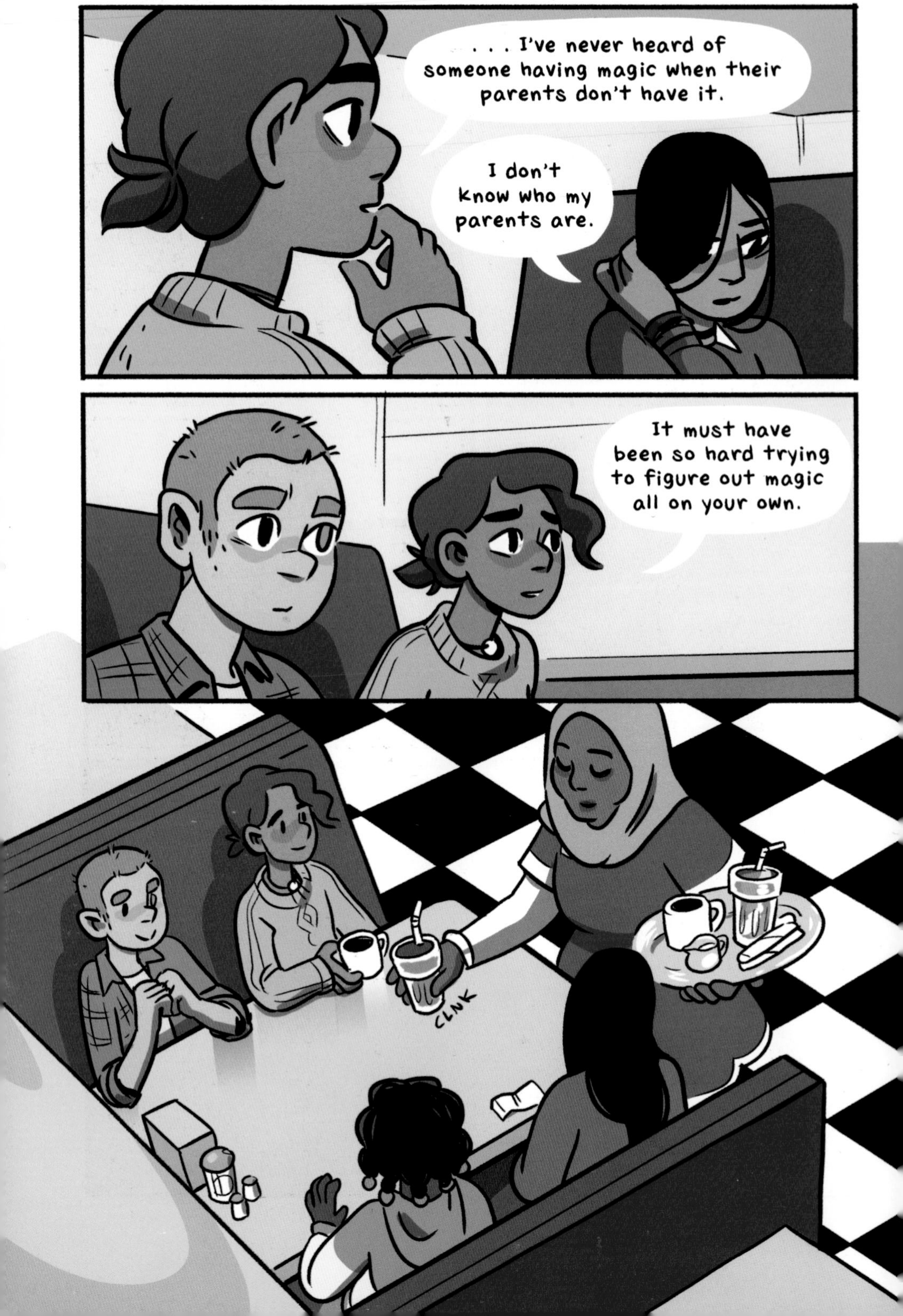
. . . I've never heard of someone having magic when their parents don't have it.
I don't know who my parents are.
It must have been so hard trying to figure out magic all on your own.
CLNK

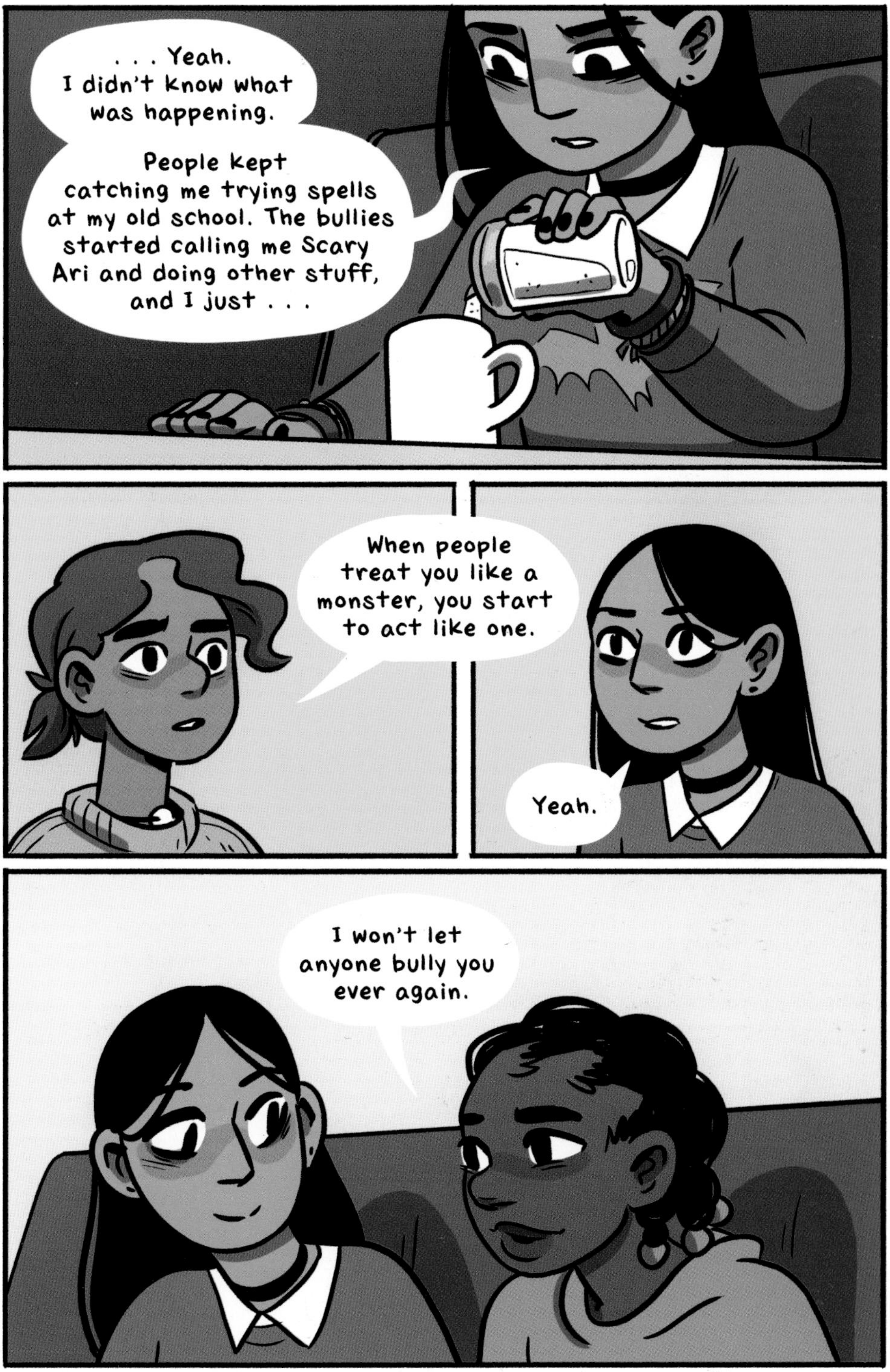
. . . Yeah. I didn't know what was happening.
People kept catching me trying spells at my old school. The bullies started calling me Scary Ari and doing other stuff, and I just . . .
When people treat you like a monster, you start to act like one.
Yeah.
I won't let anyone bully you ever again.

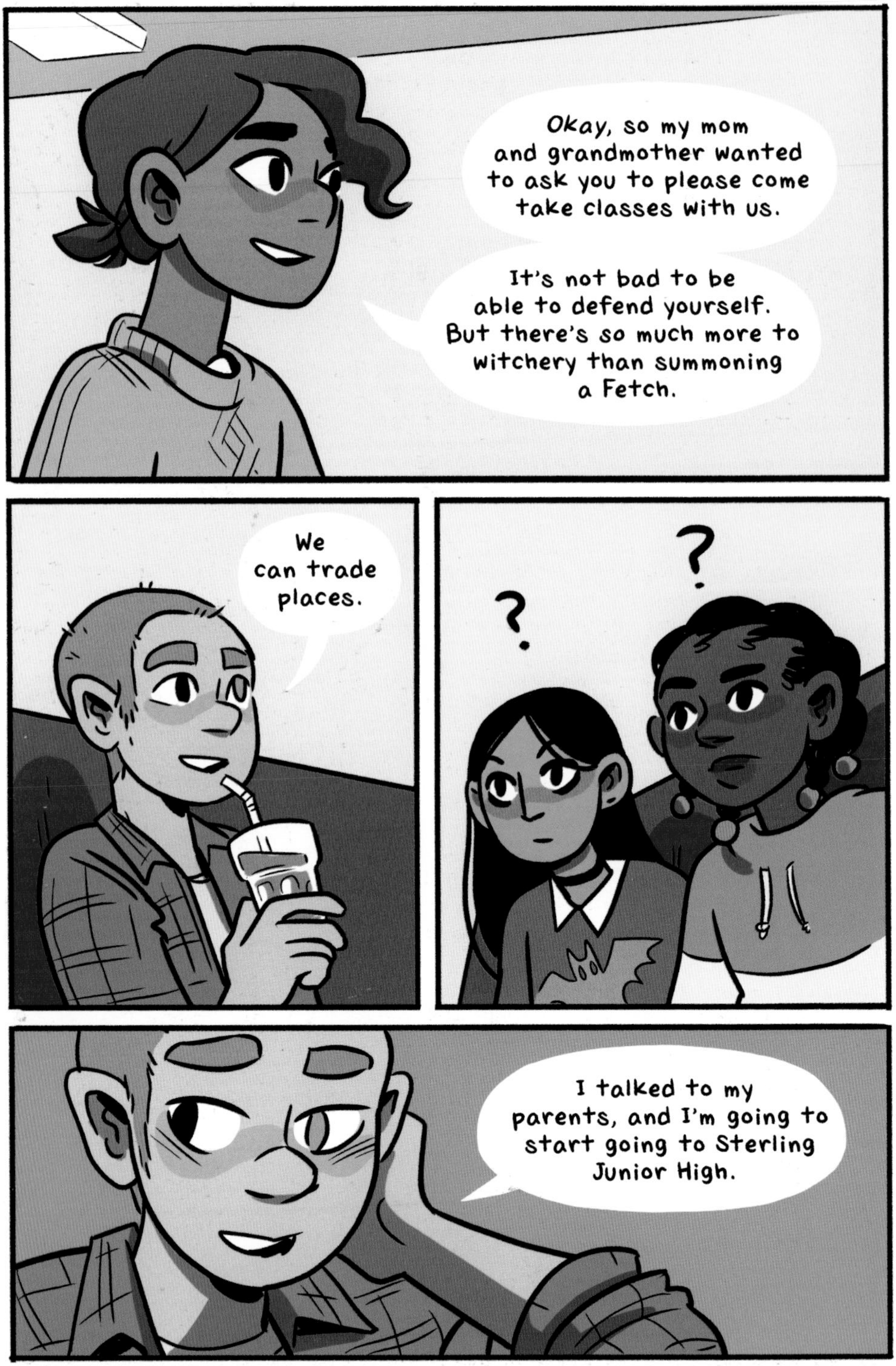
Okay, so my mom and grandmother wanted to ask you to please come take classes with us.
It's not bad to be able to defend yourself. But there's so much more to witchery than summoning a Fetch.
We can trade places.
?
?
I talked to my parents, and I'm going to start going to Sterling Junior High.

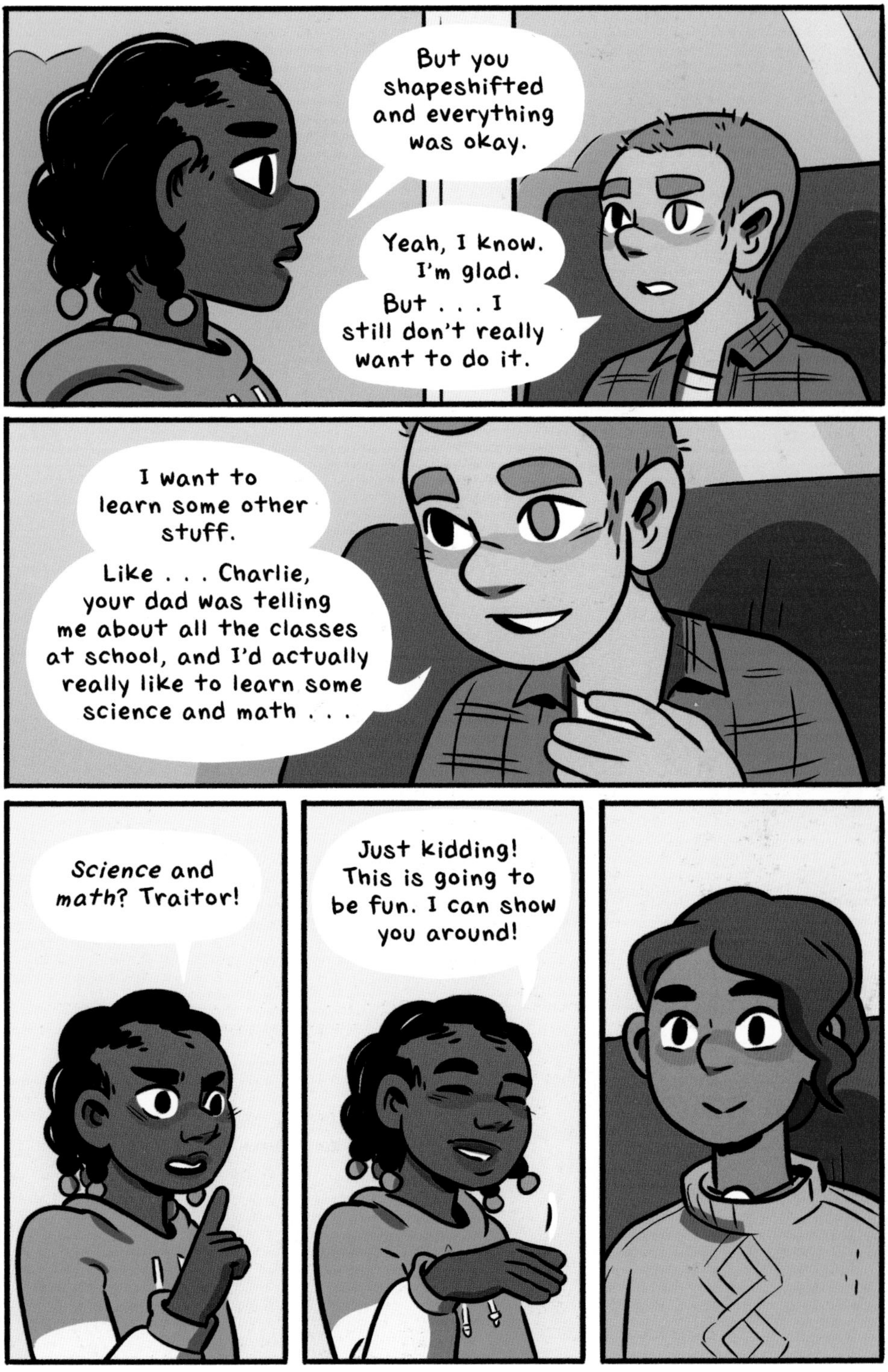
But you shapeshifted and everything was okay.
Yeah, I know. I'm glad.
But . . . I still don't really want to do it.
I want to learn some other stuff.
Like . . . Charlie, your dad was telling me about all the classes at school, and I'd actually really like to learn some science and math . . .
Science and *math*? Traitor!
Just kidding! This is going to be fun. I can show you around!

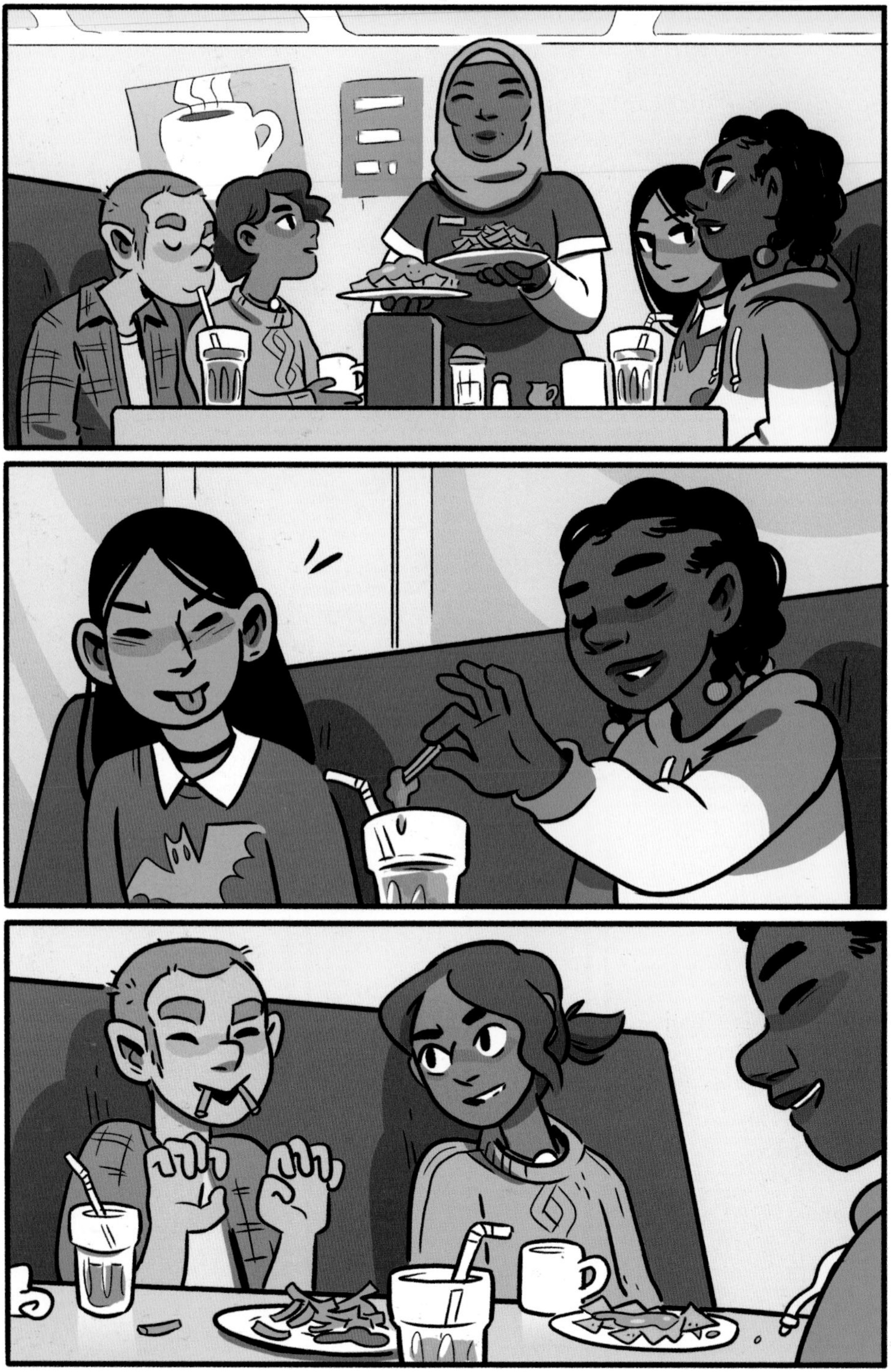

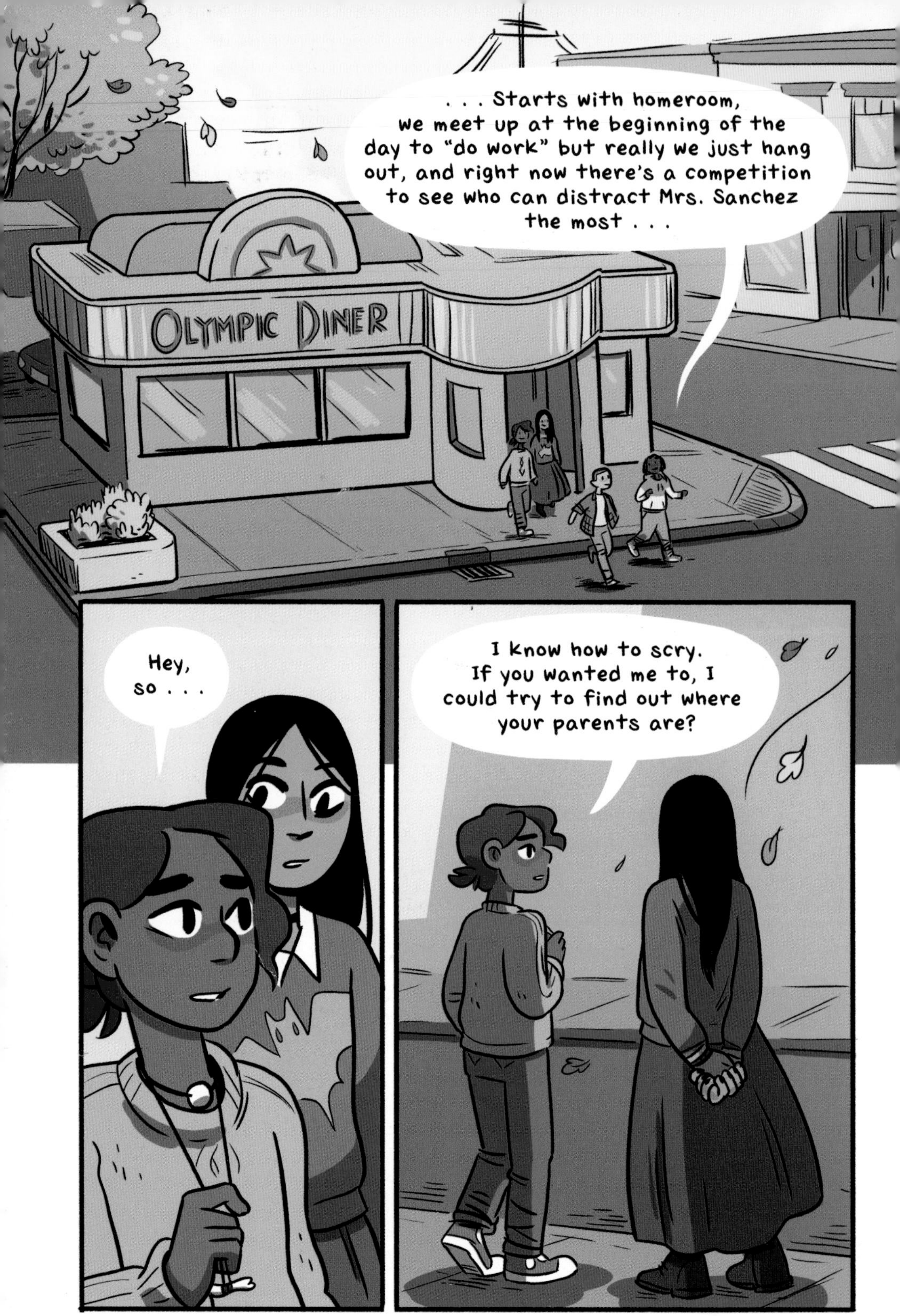
. . . Starts with homeroom, we meet up at the beginning of the day to "do work" but really we just hang out, and right now there's a competition to see who can distract Mrs. Sanchez the most . . .
OLYMPIC DINER
Hey, so . . .
I know how to scry. If you wanted me to, I could try to find out where your parents are?

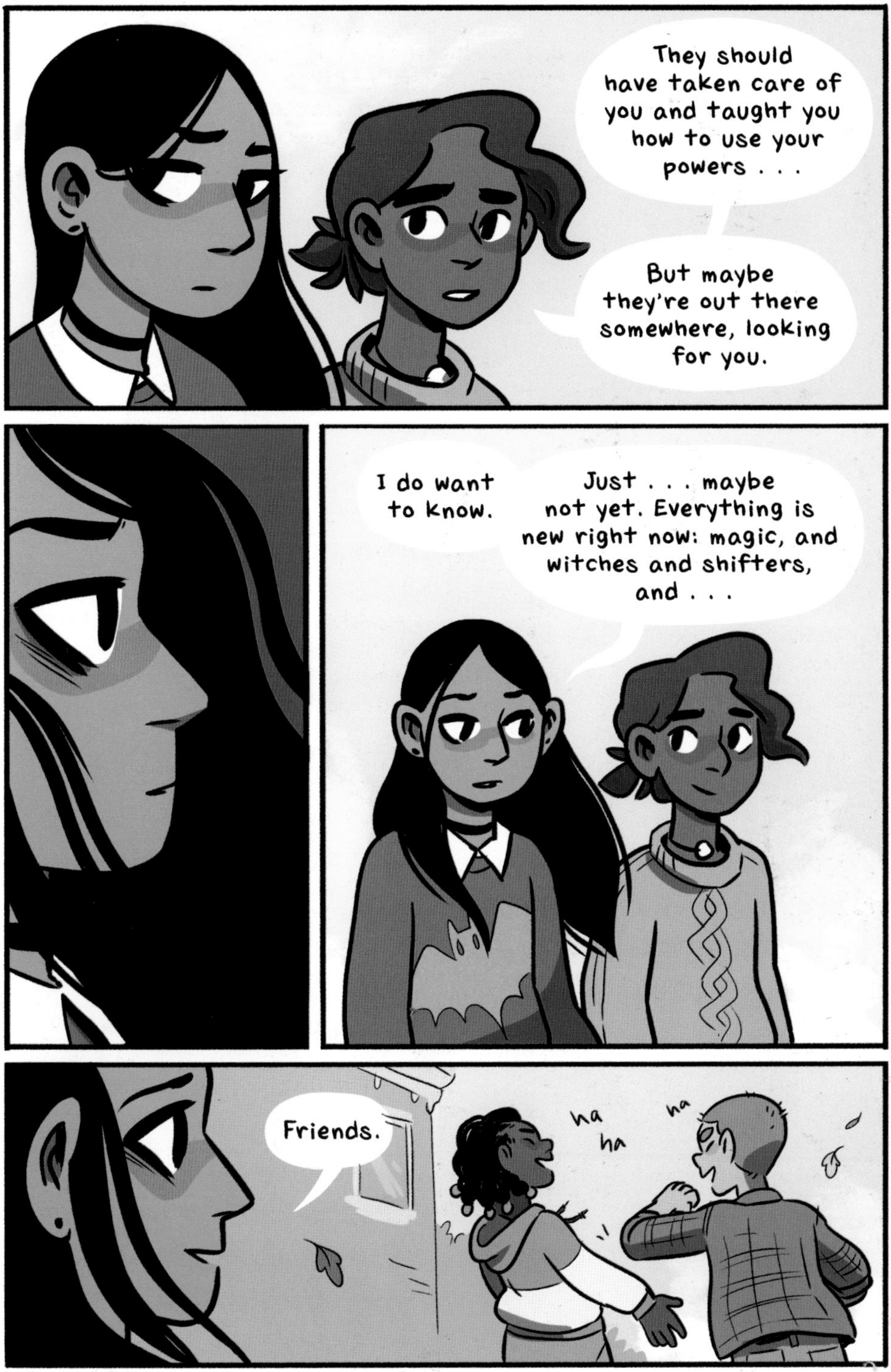
They should have taken care of you and taught you how to use your powers . . .
But maybe they're out there somewhere, looking for you.
I do want to know.
Just . . . maybe not yet. Everything is new right now: magic, and witches and shifters, and . . .
Friends.
ha
ha
ha

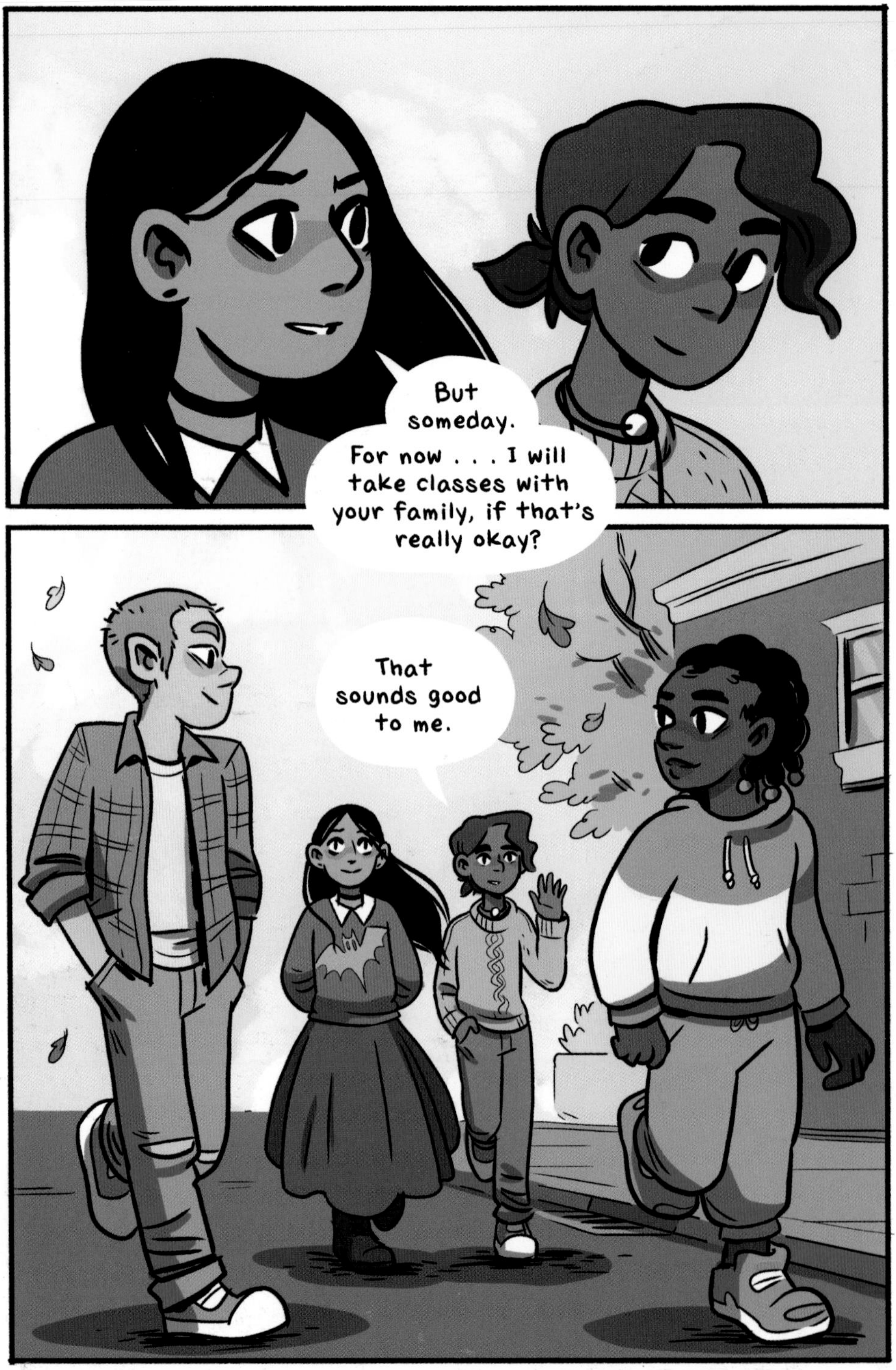
But someday.
For now . . . I will take classes with your family, if that's really okay?
That sounds good to me.

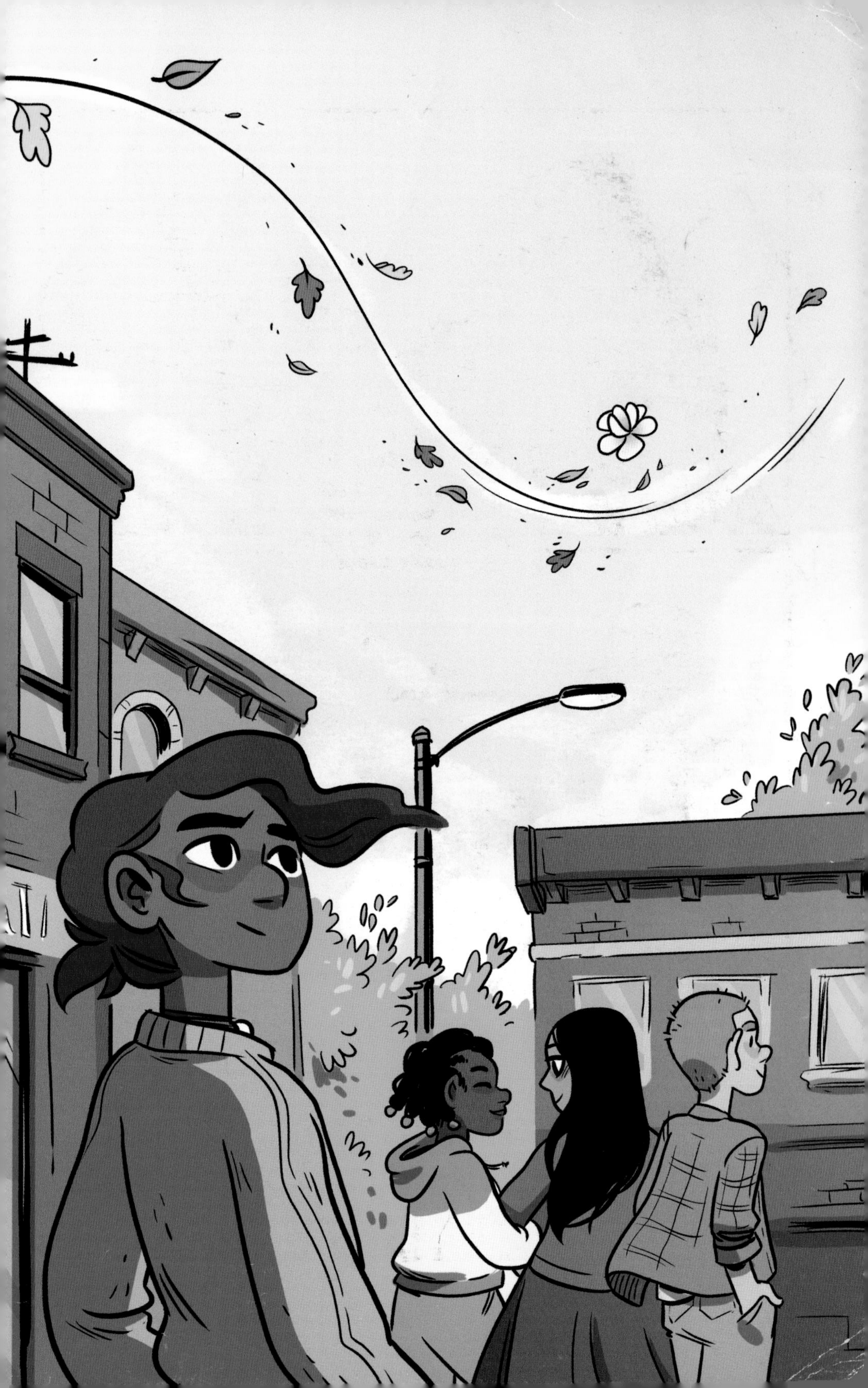

ACKNOWLEDGMENTS

Is the second one always easier, or did I just get lucky? This was one of those graphic novels that flowed so naturally from my first book, *The Witch Boy*, that the process of writing and drawing it was a joy.

I'd like to thank the kind and dedicated people who helped me make it. Jen Linnan, my agent, always responds to my rambling emails and tells me when she has dreams about my cats. Amanda Maciel, my editor, loves these characters at least as much as I do, and always makes time in our discussions to go off track and talk about our shared love of true crime. Phil Falco makes the book look beautiful with his wit and wisdom, and Niki Smith is an amazing artist who helped make the process of coloring this a breeze.

I drew this book with my evenings and weekends while working on the excellent animated show *Star vs. the Forces of Evil*. I really appreciate my coworkers at Disney for many, many coffee trips and our chats about art and comics and storytelling.

The support for *The Witch Boy* from teachers, parents, librarians, independent bookstores, and — most importantly — young readers has meant the world to me. I hope I can keep making books that you enjoy reading!

MOLLY KNOX OSTERTAG is the author and illustrator of the acclaimed graphic novel *The Witch Boy* and the illustrator of several projects for older readers, including the webcomic *Strong Female Protagonist* and *Shattered Warrior* by Sharon Shinn. She grew up in the forests of upstate New York and graduated in 2014 from the School of Visual Arts, where she studied cartooning and illustration. She currently lives in Los Angeles with her girlfriend and several pets. You can find her online at mollyostertag.com.